I KNEW DAISY SMUTEN

Overnight Daisy Smuten becomes the most sought-after woman in the world. Everyone wants her story. Newspapers, magazines, TV companies rush to London to talk to her. No one can find her. She has been spirited away. Who is Daisy Smuten anyway? What is the Big News that has suddenly made her so notorious?

The official announcement says that she is thirty-five, a divorcee born in Liverpool, and was last working as a photographer in London. Nothing else is known. Then seventeen friends from her past come forward. Each has known her intimately at some stage in her life. Each has a story to tell.

I Knew Daisy Smuten is the first edited work of fiction of its type in Britain. Only Hunter Davies, the editor, knows what happened to Daisy. Seventeen leading writers from the *Sunday Times* have each written about the Daisy Smuten they knew. Their stories recreate Daisy Smuten's dramatic life, each throwing new light on her character. Until all is revealed in the denouement. This, above all, explains why everyone, but everyone, wants to know about Daisy Smuten.

Also by Hunter Davies

Here We Go Round The Mulberry Bush
The Other Half
The New London Spy (Editor)
The Beatles
The Rise and Fall of Jake Sullivan

Contributors in alphabetical order

ALAN BRIEN
JILLY COOPER
GEORGE DARBY
LESLEY GARNER
GODFREY HODGSON
PHILLIP KNIGHTLEY
IRMA KURTZ
MAGNUS LINKLATER
DONALD McCORMICK
MICHAEL MOYNIHAN
PHILIP NORMAN
PHILIP OAKES
KENNETH PEARSON
PAULINE PETERS
LUCIA VAN DER POST
PETER WILSHER
FRANCIS WYNDHAM

I Knew Daisy Smuten

edited by

HUNTER DAVIES

Weidenfeld and Nicolson
5 Winsley Street London W1

SBN 297 00084 5

Printed in Great Britain
by Willmer Brothers Limited, Birkenhead

Contents

The Beginning . . . 7

1 Michael's story by Michael Moynihan 13
2 Donald's story by Donald McCormick 24
3 Alan's story by Alan Brien 38
4 Magnus's story by Magnus Linklater 55
5 Philip's story by Philip Norman 70
6 Pauline's story by Pauline Peters 88
7 Irma's story by Irma Kurtz 100
8 Jilly's story by Jilly Cooper 116
9 Phillip's story by Phillip Knightley 137
10 George's story by George Darby 153
11 Philip's story by Philip Oakes 174
12 Lucia's story by Lucia van der Post 193
13 Lesley's story by Lesley Garner 205
14 Godfrey's story by Godfrey Hodgson 222
15 Peter's Story by Peter Wilsher 239
16 Kenneth's story by Kenneth Pearson 256

Letters to Reg by Francis Wyndham and Hunter Davies

The End . . . 273

Notes on Contributors 277

For Tony Godwin
who fancied Daisy right from the beginning

The Beginning . . .

They gave him the news first. They just rang him and said here it is. We'll leave it to you to put it out. It was only what they should have done, of course. After all, he was the bloody specialist, wasn't he. Day after day he dutifully did all the boring bloody stories which they handed out to him, yet every time anything juicy, anything big, anything remotely important came up some other bloke usually got it. It was either passed direct to somebody important, someone far above him whom they'd ring on first names to show off, or perhaps it would be some little diary bloke on big expenses who picked it up in a ten minute chat with some silly girl in some silly club. But no, not this time. They'd played the white man and rung him.

He had been so surprised he hadn't asked all the questions he should have done. All he now had were ten words written in his notebook. The grammalogues were dancing before his eyes. He picked up the phone and dialled FLE 7440. It was engaged. 'Always open,' so the Press Association boasts about its number in the London telephone directory.

He re-dialled, this time to FLE 2366, the direct line to copy. He would have liked to have got through first to the news room and personally savoured some of the effect of his sensational news, but he couldn't wait. The copy taker at the other end, on the fifth floor of the PA building at 85 Fleet Street, was already shouting at him to talk up. He hadn't said anything yet. It was going to be one of those shouting matches when every letter has to be spelt out. He felt his left ear going red and slimy.

'Mark it flash,' he shouted. No, perhaps that was going a bit far. Flash was reserved for events like the end of the world. In all his thirty years with PA he couldn't personally remember an end of the world, nor any other FLASH. This news was far too big for a SNAP, yet not quite up to a FLASH.

'No, make it RUSH. I said RUSH! No, that's not the catchline. I said mark it RUSH, not FLASH. The catchline is, hold on a minute....' And without thinking he said Daisy, the top word on his pad. It shouldn't really have been that.

The copy taker took down the words with no expression. Is that all, he said, several times. He read it back then grudgingly said the news was pretty big, but who was this girl it had happened to, this Daisy Smuten? He checked back the spelling once again, and then hung up.

The ten words about Daisy Smuten were dropped onto the moving belt and the copy taker went for his three o'clocks. The moving belt moved and having moved, the news was soon moved on to be belted out around the world.

At this stage of the Daisy news there were only four copies, a top and three blacks, all in pink. Pink is PA's sign of urgency. Lesser items of news have to make do with the white paper.

The moving belt dropped two copies down a chute where it fluttered to the subs desk, then it moved on to drop the other copies onto the news desk. That was when the fifth floor came to life. The belt moved on. Pink, white or sludge green, it was all the same. Infinite yet un-mysterious, passing round the never-ending news.

The news desk was straight back on the phone to the specialist. Why the hell had he got only ten words? Christ, what was he playing at? And what the hell was he doing sitting at home anyway? There was a stampede, some to the phones and some to the library to get out the cuttings on Daisy Smitten, or was it Smarten, or was it Smuten?

The subs marked up the copy. It took three seconds. Even the slowest sub can't take more than three seconds over ten staccato words. The subbed copy was dropped over a perspex window and was picked up by one of the Creed people. The teleprinter operators are known as Creeds after the make of their machines. The message was marked PA RUSH

DAISY 1. This time it went out simultaneously to one hundred and fifty newspaper offices in Britain.

At the same instant as it reached the Aberdeen Press and Journal in the North of Scotland and the Cork Examiner in Southern Ireland, so it travelled from the fifth floor of 85 Fleet Street all the way to the fourth floor of 85 Fleet Street and the offices of Reuters. PA serves Britain. Reuters is the news agency which sends messages round the world. As the message went round the world, the same question came back – who is Daisy Smuten?

The first message about Daisy Smuten had gone out at 2.50. (That copy taker had gone out ten minutes early, as the chief copy taker had noticed.) The only fact the message contained about Miss Daisy Smuten herself was that she was thirty-five. At 3 o'clock, a PA message marked RUSH DAISY 2, revealed that Daisy Smuten, aged thirty-five, was a divorcee. At 3.30 RUSH DAISY 3 added that she was a magazine photographer. At 3.46, RUSH DAISY 4 announced to a waiting world that she was born in Liverpool and was last known working in London. At 4 o'clock, the first RUSH-FUL on Daisy Smuten repeated the original item of news, including in it all the other facts which had so far been gathered about Miss Daisy Smuten. A thirty-five-year-old Liverpool-born divorcee, last heard of working as a magazine photographer in London. The evening papers sold out on those six slender facts. The papers did get on to the magazines, at once, which is not as easy as it sounds as newspapers and magazines live completely separate lives. Most of the magazines' art editors said they knew of her, but they were surprisingly unhelpful when it came to information. TV and radio were giving special news flashes, all of them practically identical. Someone somewhere must surely know more about Daisy Smuten.

In the Daily Express building opposite PA, an inquisition started on William Hickey. Not only had they been beaten to the best story of 1970, perhaps even the best story of the seventies, they'd been beaten to it by a news agency. Such ignominy. After all the tip-off money they paid out each week. And now when they did have the news, not one of their brilliant contacts knew Daisy Smuten. Schmutten Smuten, said a twenty-two-year-old Left wing ex-President of the Cambridge Union who'd been taken on that morning. At 5 o'clock he got his cards.

At 5.30 in Hamburg, the star feature writer of Der Stern was sitting in a bar in the Reeperbahn, not far from the Eros Centre. He'd been waiting three hours for a Viennese to bring him certain compromising photographs. He didn't know *which* Viennese. They were all Viennese, sitting neatly up at the bar in their camel hair coats with their pekineses on their laps waiting for their girls to come from the draughts and the Japanese businessmen at the Eros Centre. The barman said he was wanted on the phone. At last, it must be the Viennese with the photographs. They told him he was booked on the next plane to London and he had to stay there until he got Daisy Smuten's life story. He said had she got the compromising photographs, then, not the Viennese?

In Tokyo, it was just what Asahi needed. They had had a five hour conference and still not agreed on their next series. Now they could get Daisy Smuten. OK, OK so their London office would get any pick-up photographs, said the Managing Editor (Personnel). There ain't no pictures, said the Managing Editor (News). We want our men there now, ready and waiting.

Practically half the New York feature staff of Time magazine were at the Algonquin. It was a farewell party for an old-time literary hack who felt he must soak up the Algonquin's Round Table literary ambiance for his last soak up. It probably gave them a half-hour advantage over Newsweek. Because so many were there in one place, it meant that half of the feature staff were on their way to Kennedy within five minutes of the news flash coming through.

Within twelve hours of the first PA flash, every major newspaper, magazine and TV company in the world had either screamed non-stop instructions down the phone to their London staff or had new men waiting to land over London Airport, all on the trail of Daisy Smuten, thirty-five, Liverpool, divorcee, photographer. Well, perhaps not every major news organisation. Tass, further up Fleet Street from PA, had done a good efficient job, but as they still hadn't had a word from Moscow asking for more, they'd all gone home to Highgate. In the Chancery Lane office of the People's Daily and Chinese News Agency no one had come in or gone out of the office all day. They were above such reactionary bourgeois stories.

El Vinos next day had no visiting Russian or Chinese firemen, but it was neck to neck with Americans, French, Germans, Japanese, Australian, Italian and Scandinavian journalists, all trying to pick up information from each other, knowing nobody knew anything but determined not to miss anything about nothing.

An Australian in a polo neck was asked by a stiff collared lackey to leave at once. This was El Vinos. Ties must be worn. Even an Australian must know that. The Australian shouted and swore then stormed out, shortly followed by three Germans, two Scandinavians and a Lithuanian, all convinced the Australian must be on to something good about Mees Dezy Smooten.

It was a junior reporter on the Ham & High, the Hampstead and Highgate Express in North London, who managed to dig up the first new tit-bit about Daisy Smuten. He discovered that her last known address was above a butcher's shop in Flask Walk, N.W.3, though she'd only been there a month. He followed up his own lead immediately and got there first, selling the story exclusively to the Daily Express. They paid him five hundred pounds. Had he sold it all round, it could have made ten times as much.

But he did have the sense to sell the picture rights on Daisy's flat to all the other papers. He was so busy counting his money, that he missed the next clue to the life of Daisy Smuten. This was picked up by a Sun photographer, picking up anything he could lay his hands on to photograph, the way photographers do.

It was just a scrap of paper stuck behind a drawer. The drawers had been cleaned but this had been overlooked. It didn't say much, but in twenty-four hours of fruitless searching, almost anything could be spread in forty-two point Tempo heavy across a front page.

There had been another 'official announcement' about Daisy Smuten, but all this said was that further details and information would be given at the weekend, probably even a photograph. As there were three days still to go, every other newspaper lifted the details from the Sun's splash story.

The scrap of paper had consisted solely of a list of seventeen names. Seventeen friends of Daisy's? Seventeen enemies? Were these people with whom she had been intimate? Had she been about to invite them to a party? Or a warning letter? Or was it just a doodle and the names signified nothing?

The seventeen names went round the world. These were the names everyone now wanted to contact. They must hold the secrets to the life of Daisy Smuten. Or perhaps it was just that she held the secrets to their lives?

Nevertheless, for a brief moment in newspaper time, which as time goes is briefer than any other, everyone, but everyone wanted a Daisy Smuten story from each of the seventeen names: Michael, Donald, Alan, Magnus, Philip, Pauline, Irma, Jilly, Phillip, George, Philip, Lucia, Lesley, Godfrey, Peter, Kenneth and Reg.

1

Michael's story

'Charlie's down there!' A little girl had wriggled her way to the front of the crowd of people and her body jerked with excitement.

They had already tunnelled into the caved-in basement and brought up a woman, her face grey with dust and pain. Her son was still silently buried, unconscious or dead.

The faces around me wore that chilling expression I was coming to recognize at bomb incidents, the mask-like faces you might see at a horror film waiting for the bit when the children are told not to look.

I had come from an assignment at the docks but now had my camera concealed under my raincoat. Though there had been sporadic raids on Merseyside for some months and last night's had been the heaviest yet, bombs on this working-class Liverpool district were still enough of a rarity in 1941 to be strictly private affairs. I was an outsider.

A sudden avalanche of dislodged bricks sent up a cloud of dust and the little girl in front of me stepped out of the crowd to peer closer down. A rescue man who had jumped clear of the fall glared up at her and motioned her angrily back. She retreated, pouting, and then noticed me.

'Charlie Bishop's in there,' she said.

'He's a friend of yours, is he?' I asked softly.

'Not my friend. He just plays in our street. He's nine. He – '

She stopped. Her eyes were taking in the bulge under my raincoat and the fractional glint of a lens behind a lapel.

'You taking pictures then?' The question came startlingly loud and clear, her interest totally switched from Charlie. I could sense an immediate stiffening in the crowd, heads turning. I felt cornered.

'What d'you mean?' I said.

'You've got a camera, haven't you?'

I began to edge my way back through the crowd. They gave way grudgingly. I could almost feel the wave of hostility. 'Bloody photographer!' a man snarled.

I got clear of the crowd and walked on, as casually as I could. There was a patter of steps behind and the girl was at my side. 'Aren't you really going to take pictures?' she asked, as if nothing had happened.

'No,' I said.

'D'you take pictures for the papers?' she persisted.

I kept walking but she followed.

'Do you?'

I glared down at her. 'You don't seem very worried about Charlie Bishop.'

'He's not my friend,' she said. 'He pinches me.'

She turned with me into another street of drab, terrace houses.

'I don't like it when people get hurt, do you? I'd rather be killed than get hurt. Wouldn't you?' I glanced at her again, a neat little figure in a grey coat, bare legs and sandals. Her voice was very precise for a child, with hardly a trace of a Liverpool accent.

'How old are you?' I asked, slowing my stride.

'More than six. My birthday's January the thirteenth. My Dad says thirteen's lucky. He's coming home in a week. He always buys me presents, even if it isn't my birthday. Or Christmas.'

'Is he in the Army?'

'Not the Army.' Her voice was scornful. 'He's in the merchant ships. He's a second officer, nearly a captain. My Dad's got a camera,' she went on, smiling up at me as if to suggest that now she knew she'd got me for a friend. 'He took a picture of a ship that was sinking. You could see the heads of the people that had been thrown in the water. He took it to the Liverpool Post but they said they weren't allowed to use it. Are they allowed to use your pictures?'

'Some pictures they can't use,' I said, wondering how far

her knowledge extended. 'It might help the Germans, or it might make people think we weren't winning the war.'

'Are we winning the war? My Dad says we will because we won the last war and we always win wars. Why aren't you fighting in the war?'

It was a hard question, coming from her. 'The doctors said I couldn't. I'm in the Home Guard.'

'Why wouldn't the doctors let you?'

I laughed. 'Are you a spy or something?'

She pouted at being laughed at and came into the attack again. 'Why wouldn't you take a picture when they get Charlie? Wouldn't they allow it in the papers?'

'No,' I said. 'Are you going back to Charlie or where are you going? Home?'

'I only live round that corner. Arundel Street. I 'spect my Mum'll be waiting.'

Two women were standing at the open door of Number 15. The younger shouted immediately: 'There you are, where've you been, as if I didn't know.'

'My Mum,' said Daisy under her breath, enlisting me on her side. 'He's a photographer.'

'Is he then!' Daisy's mother had a hard, assured smile. 'We'll be having our Daisy in the papers next.' She glanced at the neighbour, who sniggered. 'Over at the Bishops' place, was you? Got them out, have they?'

Daisy stood silent, sucking her thumb. I told her mother what was going on and how I had just happened to be passing by. As I walked away I could hear her voice drop from that provocative drawl to harsh attack and Daisy's clear voice retaliating: 'He's a photographer on the Liverpool Post!'

In fact I was a free-lance. I had my foot in the door of a number of Northern editions of the nationals, a modicum amount of hack work, like weddings, and a fluctuating belief in my destiny. I had a tiny office and dark room but, being out more than in, had an arrangement for messages to be taken at the Press Club.

From near Arundel Street I took a tram to Exchange Station to put on the Manchester train the commissioned film I had taken that morning – the Chief Engineer of a tanker who had been awarded the MBE for heroism during a convoy attack and who had growled at me: 'What do I want with an MBE? I'd rather a crate of rum.'

Then I made for the Press Club in Lime Street. It was after two but there was still a group at the bar, going over the last two nights' raids. Bert the barman greeted me dramatically. 'I've been trying to get you. Call from London. Picture Post. They want you to ring them urgent. Picture Editor. Didn't give a name.'

My only dealings with Picture Post had been some months back when I had hopefully sent them a sequence of pictures I had taken at the Seamen's Home of survivors of a torpedoed merchantman who had spent five days on a raft. I tried to sound nonchalant when I got through to the Picture Editor from the booth outside the bar. 'We're thinking of running a feature on children in the blitz. Nothing obvious. Sharp, human stuff. Close-ups when there's something dramatic going on. Or could be a shelter scene. It's up to you. Like your seamen, nothing posed. It seems as though things are warming up your way.'

The radio was blaring dance music in 15 Arundel Street. I had to knock hard before it was turned down. Ever since I had come from the phone box, dizzy with the challenge, I had been seeing Daisy's face wide-eyed against smashed homes, against leaping flames, against the burrowings in rubble or the firemen's cascading hoses. Especially against flames.

Mrs Smuten opened the door, looked at me blankly for a moment and then switched on that smile. 'The Liverpool Post! Are you going to take my picture!'

It was hard to convince her that I was genuine. It was even harder – until I dropped a hint of a fee – that my only interest was in Daisy, who was now 'out somewhere'. By the time I left I had Mrs Smuten's agreement to 'borrow Daisy' if the occasion arose. She was working evenings as a barmaid and whenever the sirens went Daisy spent the night in the communal shelter with a family in the next street, the Hiscocks. 'Some people are easily scared,' said Mrs Smuten, tossing her head. 'You won't find me in any stinking shelter.'

I was obsessed with a determination to make my mark on the most popular and influential magazine of the day. In the Press Club that night I waited for the sirens with an eagerness that now seems unpardonable.

When the banshee wail of the sirens washed chillingly over Merseyside, I made for the door, down the three flights of stairs, out into the dark, expectant night.

I had parked the hired car in a nearby side-street. I had memorized the route to the communal shelter a quarter of a mile from Arundel Street and was there in under ten minutes. Daisy was already at the entrance, the Hiscocks and their two young children grouped around her.

'Sure she'll be alright?' said Mrs Hiscock. 'I don't think it's proper, really I don't. Even if Mrs Smuten says so. She's safe in here along of us.'

'She'll be safe with me,' I said. 'I promise. Ready, Daisy?'

Daisy gave a little, regal, backward wave as we left. She was silent most of the way in the car, swallowing her excitement. As we climbed the hill into Lime Street we could see the distant play of searchlights and hear the far-off bark of ack-ack guns. When we got out of the car in the side-street we could hear them: that deep, remote, ominous shudder and throb.

In the basement of the Press Club building Mrs Jenkins, the caretaker's wife, was already seated in the little room they had sparsely equipped as a shelter. I had told Tom Jenkins, slipping him a note, that I had Daisy's mother's permission to shelter her there so that I could take pictures as soon as the All Clear sounded. I needed to be in the Press Club to know what was going on.

''E's upstairs, watching outa the winders,' said Mrs Jenkins. 'Idjut. 'Ello, dear.'

The lights were out on the second landing and shadowy figures stood at the windows, criss-crossed with sticky-tape to hold shattered glass. Beyond the roofs of the fish and vegetable markets at the rear of the building the sky was alive with the lightning-flicker of the guns and the sweeping beams of searchlights. The tips of three of them suddenly fused and stayed rigid. There was a tiny shape in that cold pool of light, like a silver bird.

Snug behind the heavy black-out curtains in the bar, the regulars were at a stage of hilarious bravado. The Naval Commander, tankard in hand, was reciting one of his bawdier ballads. The alderman's voice boomed loudest.

Bert's jowls quivered as he served me a pint at the far end of the bar, away from the conviviality. 'The bar oughta be closed. I asked the President but he's like the rest of them.' I felt dry and tensed up and gulped at the beer. It would be a long time to the All Clear.

Up here the nearest guns reverberated like thunder-claps, rattling the panes. The whine and detonation of bombs grew more frequent. After another pint I went down to the second landing. Against the black silhouettes of roofs and chimneys pink clouds were mushrooming from out of the city. The group at the window were arguing about their possible locations. 'That big 'un?' I heard Tom Jenkins' gruff voice. 'That's not Exchange Street, more like around the India Building.' And then came the clattering down the roof above us.

'Christ, incendiaries!' someone exclaimed. A flame spurted from the fish market roof below. 'Open that winder!' shouted Jenkins. He flashed his torch down the passage to a wall-cupboard and staggered back with a stirrup pump and bucket of water. 'There's another there an' a couple of buckets. Quick about it.'

He had the nozzle out of the window. The flame wavered below as the jet hit it but already other flames were spurting. 'Keep them buckets going. Tap in your bar.'

An acrid smell of burning wafted through the open window and a crackling sound underscored the shattering gunfire. The whole sky was suffused now with a red flush.

'Jesus, will you look at that!' It was the Commander's thick voice. And then the alderman's, on a sharper note: 'What on earth are you doing here, child?'

Rosy in the glow from outside, Daisy stood wide-eyed and composed as faces gazed down at her. 'I'm with him,' she said, pointing at me.

I grabbed her hand. 'I told you not to move from that basement. Come on.'

On the first landing she pulled back. 'But I want to see. You promised it would be exciting. I don't want just to sit with that old woman. Anyway she went asleep.'

'I'll stay with you. It'll soon be over. Now come on.'

'I won't.' She gave a sudden tug and was bounding down the stairs, across the dim-lit hall and through the swing doors.

As I came out she ran a little way along Lime Street, then, as I caught up, retreated slowly backwards, grinning. 'You forgot your camera!'

'Are you coming back or will I have to carry you?'

'I'll scream.'

I made a grab at her but she was off again.

I stood, breathing hard. 'Close-ups when there's something dramatic going on.' The Picture Editor's voice came back to me.

'Wait in this doorway. Right inside. Don't move till I get back.'

Coming out of the Press Club building with my camera, I almost collided with Victor Slack, the Press Association correspondent. He was panting. 'It's bloody murder. Fires all over. Lewis's. Bloody bonfire. Post Office. Blackler's. . . .' He stared at me. 'You'll need a bloody tin-lid, mate. Shit flying all over the place.'

'Haven't got one. I'll be alright.'

'How long'll you be?'

'Not long.'

'Have mine. I'm sticking to the bloody telephone from now, I can tell you.'

I put on the helmet and hurried along the street. Daisy gazed up at me from the doorway with shining eyes. 'Can't I have one, too?'

'It's for you,' I said, taking it off and placing it on her head. It was many sizes too large and made her look like a kid taking part in a school play or a charade.

We followed the hose-pipes coiling along roadway and pavement towards Lewis's. When it came into sight Daisy gasped. For once even that chatterbox could find nothing to say. That huge landmark, solid as the Rock of Gibraltar, was a raging, roaring inferno. Through the caved-in roof sheets of flame leaped through billowing smoke at the sky. In the lower stories tentative tongues of flame licked around window-frames, darted through cracks. Above the roar and crackle and the sudden explosions that erupted in cascades of sparks, one could just hear the hiss and splash of the firemen's jets.

Daisy's rapt gaze was held by a fireman poised minutely at the top of a hundred-foot fire-escape, the jet from his hose seeming to feed rather than devour the rampaging flames on which it played.

I shot her first just as she stood, gazing up at the fireman, but could get less than a profile, and even that shadowed by the tin hat. I took it off. 'Just look a little away from the fireman. A bit more. That's it.'

Daisy came out of a trance. 'You're taking my picture! Can you take me on a fire-engine?'

A passing fireman, his moist face blackened by smoke, stopped and stared. 'What the 'ell d'you think this is? A bleedin' circus? You oughta be shot.' He looked at Daisy.

She slipped a hand into mine as we left and turned down Chapel Street. 'If it was Christmas would Santa Claus 've got burned?'

'Santa Claus?'

'In Lewis's. He gave me a jig-saw for Christmas.'

It was the first really childish remark I had heard her make. I squeezed her hand. 'Of course not!' I said. 'He'd be hiding up a chimney!'

For over an hour we went from fire to fire. I felt easier now that the guns had stopped and there seemed no danger from bombs or shell-fragments. Numbers of shelterers were now venturing into the open, bunching in awed groups near the more spectacular fires, exclaiming as a shattering explosion sent a whole floor crashing or firemen leaped clear of an avalanche of blazing timbers and masonry. One man, unsteady on his feet, turned slowly round, blinking at the flamescapes that seemed to stretch in all directions. 'Bastards!' he suddenly shouted. 'The fucking bastards!'

I must have taken a good fifty pictures, ignoring the occasional abusive remarks as Daisy ignored them.

The All Clear had already shrilled over the battered, blazing city when we got back to the Press Club building. Daisy was too tired to eat so I tucked a blanket round her on the camp bed and she was almost instantly asleep.

Next morning there was a barrier across the end of Arundel Street and a group of women and children standing in the roadway half way down.

We walked round the barrier. Where Numbers 17, 15 and 13 had stood there was little more than a great mound of rubble. Daisy stood, expressionless, staring.

I could find nothing to say. I took her to the Hiscocks. Mrs Hiscock answered the door. Her face crumpled as she saw Daisy who ran forward and buried her face in her lap.

Mrs Hiscock cupped her hands over Daisy's head. 'I think you'd best go,' she said.

All that week the blitz raged. Liverpool was a city in chaos. Water supplies were so dislocated that hosepipes trailed through the streets all the way from the Mersey. Fire engines had been brought in from as far as London. The Army, busy dynamiting dangerously ruined buildings, rigged up their own telephone wires. Transport was mostly by lorry. Long before dark the trek to the shelters and underground stations began.

I worked hard, not only for the Manchester papers but on the Picture Post assignment, taking pictures of other children at other scenes of death and destruction. But every day I called to see Daisy.

The first three days she was mostly silent, shut away in her own thoughts. Mrs Hiscock said she had not cried at all since that first time. If only she would, instead of bottling it all up.

But on the fourth day, as I came in, I could hear her voice from the back parlour, clear and lively as ever playing 'school' with the two young Hiscocks. They were supposed to be very naughty children.

'She's been on about her Dad now,' said Mrs Hiscock. 'But what's to happen when he's back at sea? We can't keep her long. I'm expecting. Mr Smuten's got parents and there's an aunt at Shrewsbury. I suppose it'll have to be one or t'other.'

Unbelievably there was no raid on the Sunday night. I

had hired a car again and took Daisy and Mrs Hiscock to one of the few city restaurants still serving hot lunches. The convoy was coming in on the morning tide and the seamen would probably get to the Seamen's Home by three. At Daisy's insistence we got there at 1.30. It was a gloomy comfortless Victorian building. There had been a newspaper article about it, slating the authorities for providing nothing better as a headquarters for the gallant but unsung heroes of the Merchant Navy. But to Daisy it was a place as magical as Lewis's grotto.

We sat on a bench in the chill, echoing entrance hall, watching the comings and goings of seamen and the waiting wives and mothers. It seemed an age before a rowdy jostling through the entrance-door heralded the first crew. Daisy was on her feet.

'What's your Dad's ship called, Daisy?'

'The Steadfast.' The way she said it it might have been the only ship on the high seas.

I crossed the hall to a seaman who had just dumped his sea-bag and was knocking out his pipe. 'Excuse me, what ship are you from?'

'Unicorn,' he said.

'We're waiting for the Steadfast.'

He glinted down into the bowl of his pipe. 'Steadfast?' He gave a sudden upward jerk with both hands. 'Torpedoed. Along with two others.'

I stared at him. 'What about the crew?'

'Survivors got taken on the Ocean Queen. Not far out from Ireland it was.'

Daisy had moved away from the bench to be nearer the entrance. I told Mrs Hiscock. 'Oh God!' she said. 'Oh pray to God – '

I saw that Daisy had started to stop men every now and again as they came in. As she named the Steadfast they blankly shook their heads and glanced back as they moved on. I sat there feeling numb and helpless.

It was another fifteen minutes before a fresh batch arrived and I guessed that it might be the crew of the Ocean Queen.

Daisy was already among them and had found that some were Steadfast survivors. I lost her for a moment as she darted in and out. Twice I imagined I saw her father coming, open arms towards her, ready to sweep her up, but each time he walked past her, still with his arms open to be greeted by another family.

Slowly, the seamen dragged themselves out, some unwelcomed and some besieged. Daisy had been rushing round all excited, running into bodies, falling over bundles, picking herself up and laughing. Now she began staring around. She'd met every Steadfast survivor. There were no others. But for several minutes her face remained bright and eager as she looked at the sad straggles of families who'd already subsided into themselves, now that their expectations were dead. Daisy had propelled herself on too far. She'd been caught still laughing while the joke was long over. She suddenly looked frightened.

She hunched her shoulders and stared round. I caught her eye but she stared through me. It wasn't my face she was wanting. Who was I anyway. She'd forgotten I was with her, or why she was here, or what she'd been waiting for. She was completely on her own for the first time and she knew it. Lost and alone, a child yet enough of an adult to try to fight the tears. I have the sequence of pictures in my hand now. They are pictures which bring tears because there are no tears. Picture Post described them as photographs to tear the heart strings, I am ashamed to say.

2

Donald's story

In the summer of 1944 all the sitting around and waiting was ended. I was serving in an LCT, which in the queer back-to-front phraseology of the Services means a Landing Craft, Tanks. Just before the first watch began, I finished the washing-up and made myself a cuppa. I planned to take it down to the well-deck where, by a smart bit of cunning, I had hidden my day's tot of rum. Tea and rum and a spot of day-dreaming: that was my idea of a modest luxury of a summer's evening aboard ship. Hidden away in a vantage point in the well-deck, out of sight, armed with a pair of binoculars to scan the coastline. Somewhere over there, I would tell myself, people were drinking in pubs, or smoking a pipe in their gardens, girls in pretty frocks were dancing in the Services' Club and maybe one or two choice girls (parties we used to call them in the Andrew) were walking along the beach looking out at us. This particular part of the English coast on the borders of Hampshire and Sussex was about as flat and unexciting as a pier at a Welsh seaside resort on a winter's Sunday afternoon.

All I could see was a boring bit of beach. At one end, near the hard, was a long line of Army vehicles waiting to be loaded on to the landing-craft. The other end were a few cottages with neat, trim gardens, full of flowers and with lawns looking as though they'd been manicured. All the same, I was kidding myself that some lush piece of goods would come out of one of the cottages, wave at me and smile.

Bloody silly, of course. All that was likely to come out of one of those cottages was some old bag of a cook, fat and fiftyish, with cigarette ash an inch long curling from her lip, and hair-curlers crowning her greying mop. It made me think of a bawdy rhyme:

> 'The King was in his counting house,
> Counting out his wealth,
> The Queen was in the parlour,
> Playing with herself.
> The cook was in the kitchen,
> Explaining to the groom
> That the vagina, not the rectum
> Was the entrance to the womb.'

That's me all right, I thought sadly. So plumb stupid when it came to the point I wouldn't know the one from t'other. Clumsy at work and clumsy on the job.

The next thing I heard was Jimmy the One bawling down at me.

'Yessir,' said I, stumbling up and knocking over my empty tea-cup.

'What the hell are you doing down in the well-deck?'

'Having a cuppa, sir.'

'Well, you're duty watch, aren't you?'

'Yessir.'

'Then I want you to get out the ship's boat and row over to the Blue Posts and get some beer. The wardroom's almost dry.'

Thirty yards from the shore, drifting with the tide parallel to it, I noticed one cottage away from the others. It had white-washed walls and some bushes in front of it. And there, sitting on the beach, in front of one of the bushes, I saw her.

She must have seen me first, for she was waving. Blimey! I said aloud. This is my dream coming true. Then I sobered up. She was only a kid. But I waved back all the same.

'Hi,' she called.

'Hi, there,' I replied.

'Are you running away?'

'No,' I said, somewhat lamely, as the boat crunched into the shingle. 'I've come ashore to get some beer.'

'I'll show you where the Blue Posts is, if you like.'

'Thanks. What's a little girl like you doing out at this hour?'

She tossed her tangled curls. 'I'm not a little girl. I'm nine. How old are you?'

'Never you mind.'

I got the beer and when I returned I found her squatted athwartships my boat, tailor-fashion.

'Take me for a row.'

'I can't. I'd get shot.'

She pulled a face. 'Not really, would you?'

'Well, I'd be in the rattle anyway.'

'What's that?'

'It's sailor language for being in trouble. And I'd get a Mark One Bottle from the CO.'

'What's that?'

'It means I'd get a proper bollocking.'

'That's very rude,' she said. 'Isn't it?'

'Ticking off then, if you like.'

'My name's Daisy Smuten. What's yours?'

'Donald,' I said.

'I like Donald. Where do you come from? I'm from Liverpool. I'm a Scouse. I'm also an orphan.'

'I'm sorry,' I said. 'I must hop it now. Maybe I'll see you tomorrow.'

'Okay,' she smiled.

The coxswain usually had the pick of the girls when we went ashore. After him came the leading-stoker. He reckoned he had sampled women of every race except the Krauts and the Ruskies. We used to go ashore in threes. If we were lucky enough to find a threesome then the girl who came my way was always so dull, or plain, or both, that I preferred to dream about them instead. The girls in my dreams were always so much classier.

Daisy was different. There was no doubt she had the makings of a good-looker, when she had put on a few years. She may have been too young to snog with, but she was a damn sight more interesting to talk to than most of the older parties. As I prepared the mid-day meal next forenoon my fingers may have been rolling the pastry for the tiddy-oggies, but my mind was full of the kid.

It seemed like a week to wait for the liberty boat at 16.30

hours. Slowly I realized I was more excited about meeting Daisy than I had been about any other girl. She was nearer to the girl of my dreams than any I had seen. She was matey and cosy and comfortable. She was everyone's ideal of a little kid sister, needing protection, yet at the same time she was intriguing.

'What you doing ashore today, then?' asked Hartburn, the leading-stoker.

'Oh, not much,' I replied non-committally.

'Come off it, cookie. Don't be such a bleedin' dark horse. Bunting tosser tells me you've dated up some party.'

I bit my lip. I regretted it at once, but realized I had told the signalman about my meeting with Daisy.

'Not me. He's pulling your leg. I only met a kid.'

'You dirty old man, cookie. Chasin' kids now, eh? You'll get pulled in one of these days.'

I had so much ragging from the rest of the watch going on shore leave that I nearly made up my mind not to see Daisy. I was used to it, of course. I'd had nothing else all my time in the Navy, but somehow when they brought Daisy's name into it I really began to hate their ragging.

By the time the liberty boat glided alongside the hard I knew that, come what may, I wanted to see Daisy. I pretended to go off to the NAAFI and then, when the other sailors were out of sight, retraced my steps to the cottage where I had first seen Daisy.

There was no sign of her. Oh, well, I thought, that's that. She's forgotten all about it. I'd wait five minutes, then I'd push off. If any of the crew came this way and found out I'd been stood up by a nine-year-old kid, I'd never hear the last of it.

I turned my back to the cottage and looked across the water to where my LCT was anchored. Then biff, something hit the back of my head. I swung round and saw a stick land at my feet. Then I heard a tinkling, childish laugh. From behind the hedge of the cottage up popped Daisy.

'Thought I'd surprise you,' she said.

I grinned feebly. Was she making fun of me like the rest? Or was this just her idea of a caper?

'I thought you'd forgotten.'

'When's your ship coming in?' she demanded.

'Heh, watch it, now. That's top secret. Too secret for little girls.'

She came from the cottage garden and slapped my arm. 'Stop calling me a little girl. If you do that again, I'll run away.'

'Okay, Miss Daisy.'

'That's better. What are we going to do?'

That shook me. For the truth was I hadn't a clue what I was going to do when I met Daisy. After all, what does one do with a nine-year-old kid?

I must have blushed, for she added tauntingly: 'Are you afraid to be seen with me?'

'Don't be daft. Right, then. What do you want to do?'

'I want to see your ship when it comes to the hard. There's nothing secret about that. Everyone here knows you take the soldiers and the tanks and guns to Normandy.'

She was right.

'But why do you want to see my ship? There's nothing much to see.'

'I just love ships. All ships. My Dad was a sailor. Not like you. He was Merchant Navy.'

'What happened to him?'

'Well, everyone says he must be dead. His ship was torpedoed a few years ago and he hasn't been seen since. I think maybe he's still alive. When I'm in bed at night I like to pretend he got washed up on a desert island and made himself a little hut and lived on coconuts and pineapples. Do you pretend? It's my favourite game.'

'Sometimes.'

'I also pretend I'm a ballerina and I dance in front of the mirror and bow to the audience.'

'How come you never had any definite news of your Dad?'

'Well, just when he was reported missing, Mum was killed in the blitz at Liverpool. I was taken in by foster-parents. First I lived in Hereford, then my foster-mum's husband was called up and we came down here to live with her sister.'

'Do you like it here?'

'S'all right. No, it's awful. No, it's not too bad now the ships are here. But it's a bit of a dump. No excitement at all.'

We had walked quite a way along the beach, Daisy occasionally skipping along the sand and then pirouetting on her toes in a silly pose.

'Do you dance at school?'

'A bit. But it's not proper dancing. Just kids' stuff.'

Presently we came to a waterside café and we went in.

'Well,' she said, breathlessly, gulping down tea and cakes, 'you haven't answered my question. When are you going to show me your ship?'

'We'll be loading tomorrow morning. Come along to the hard then.'

At that moment Hartburn the leading-stoker and two other sailors came in to the café. They guffawed when they saw Daisy and me sitting together.

'You crafty bastard, cookie,' said Hartburn. 'Kidding us you were going to the NAAFI.'

'Now then, Stokes,' I replied, 'lay off the bad language in front of Daisy.'

'Oh, don't mind me,' said Daisy without a blush. 'I bet I know as many bad words as you all do. Do you want to hear them?'

'No thanks,' I said.

'Blimey! Hark at cookie. Quite the little girl's protector, ain't he?'

'I don't mind bad language,' said Daisy, turning round to them, 'but I do hate being called a little girl.'

That silenced Stokes. Soon they were all sitting down drinking tea with Daisy and me, as meek as lambs and very taken with Daisy's quick-witted conversation. She had them all entranced. It was a revelation just to sit and watch Daisy, listen to her chatter and soak up her all-embracing smile.

I don't think Daisy had a favourite among us. She teased the leading-stoker just as much as she did me. She burst out laughing when the others told her I was the ship's cook. She wanted to know who I was married to and if I had kids. She asked if we had girl-friends and what the officers were like. And why did our ship have a number and not a name? A ship without a name was no good at all.

'Some of the landing-craft have names,' she said. 'I've seen them. There's one called Coralie and another called Jean. Why not yours?'

'They're called after the captains' girl-friends, or their wives,' I replied.

'I wish someone would name a ship after me,' she said with a sigh. 'HMS Daisy. I like that.'

'It's an idea,' said Stokes.

When we came to the hard next day to load tanks and a couple of supply lorries Daisy was there to greet us. This time she had dressed herself up quite a bit. Clean white socks and a blue jumper with rolled-up sleeves that showed the dimples on her arms.

When I thought no officers were looking I brought Daisy aboard and showed her my tiny galley and its pots and pans.

'What about showing her the golden rivet?' said Stokes with his lewd belly laugh.

'Cut that out, Stokes,' I said. 'I've told you before, she's only a kid.'

'I've known some wog kids younger than her who knew what it was all about. I remember once in Port Said there was a dusky little seven-year-old who used to say "Me very clean. Me give plenty pleasure." '

'Well, Daisy's no wog and she's not going to be treated like one.'

I was just showing Daisy the wheel-house when in came Jimmy the One. He wanted to know what the hell I was doing. Before I could reply Daisy smiled sweetly and said: 'Oh, mister, it's all my fault. I came aboard myself and asked to see the ship. You see, my Dad's a sailor. He always said I could see his ship, but I didn't. Now he's gone. . . .'

That left Jimmy the One with very few options. He tacked hard and trimmed his sails. Glaring at me suspiciously out of one eye, he asked Daisy what else she would like to see.

'Could I go up on the bridge?' she asked.

That let me off the hook and I scrammed. Number One grunted and took her up to the bridge, showed her the magnetic compass in its binnacle and the Oerlikon guns and answered all her questions. She watched the tanks being driven across the ramp into the well-deck and saw them shackled down to the deck. By the time the LCT was loaded, everyone on the ship had met Daisy. Even the CO had spoken to her.

'You know,' Daisy told him. 'This ship needs a name, not just a number. I'd love to have a ship named after me.'

'Hum,' replied the CO. 'We must think about it.'

We left in convoy that night, heading past the Isle of Wight and into the windswept Channel which was marked out with dimly-lit dan buoys at regular intervals. I had the middle watch and about 1 o'clock in the morning I went below to make tea. As I returned to the bridge with a cuppa for the CO he said to me, 'About that girl you brought aboard?'

'Sir?'

Had Number One lodged a complaint against me?

'I've been thinking. Maybe she had something when she said the ship should have a name.'

'Yessir.'

'Is it true her father was lost at sea?'

'Well, sir, he's reported missing.'

'I see. I believe she has almost become the ship's mascot. Might be a nice gesture if we named the ship after her. Let me know what the crew think. What about you?'

'Why, yes sir, I think it's a good idea.'

The crew received the suggestion with varying degrees of enthusiasm, but the majority were solidly in favour. The leading-stoker, who always suspected the darker side of everyone's nature, hinted that the CO must have 'taken a fancy to Daisy' and that he was 'a dirty old man'. He also added that Daisy was all right for the name of a bob-an-hour trip-round-the-harbour sort of boat, but not for onc of HM ships. He was shouted down by the coxswain and the chief petty officer motor mechanic. They settled the argument by promising there and then to carve and paint a ship's badge with the name Daisy on it. So it was that our LCT became Daisy.

The trip across to Normandy was uneventful except for a brief air-raid warning as we entered the Gooseberry, the artificial inshore protection for small craft which had been created to enable ships to beach with relative ease even in stormy weather. We beached, disembarked the tanks and lorries and then pulled off and returned to our anchorage near Hayling Island.

We were at anchor for the next two days during which the chief petty officer motor mechanic finished off his ship's badge. It was a wooden shield on which were carved the anchor, tommy-gun and wings which formed the badge of Combined Operations (the command to which we belonged) and underneath these the words 'LCT Daisy'. The whole was painted in red lettering on a yellow background.

I went ashore on the second day, but failed to find Daisy anywhere. I thought about calling at the cottage where she lived, then dropped the idea as I remembered that Daisy had said that her foster-mother was 'a real Tartar'.

Like a nutcase I walked up and down along the beach outside those cottages just hanging around for a nine-year-old kid. I walked back to the hard and the NAAFI, looking in the shop doors, then wandered back to the cottages again. What a daft way to spend a brief leave ashore.

I met some of the crew and they persuaded me to join them in a game of darts at the Blue Posts. But my mind never kept on the game. It was ages before I got a double-top. In between games we drank mild-and-bitter and played the pin-tables. I hardly ever joined in the conversation. I was stunned by the sudden revelation in my own mind that I was smitten by Daisy.

I knew at once that it was crazy. If the crew knew that I was 'gone' on a mere kid, they would roll across the bar with laughter, or put me down as a raving sex maniac. But I knew my feelings for Daisy were neither mad, nor sexual. I wasn't in love with her. At least I don't think I was.

I hadn't returned aboard that evening more than two minutes when Jimmy the One sent for me. 'Did the CO miss the liberty boat?'

'He wasn't aboard, sir, if that's what you mean.'

'Take out the ship's boat and wait for him on the beach. I can't spare any of the duty watch, so it will have to be you.'

I didn't mind taking the boat out this time. It gave me another chance to be alone and to think about Daisy, even, perhaps, to see her. I rowed towards the hard and saw the CO waiting for me.

'I'm not ready to return aboard yet. Come back in an hour's time.'

Normally I would have cursed my fate. This time I welcomed the delay. Instead of returning to the LCT I rowed alongside the shore towards the cottages. And there, sitting on the beach, legs crossed and hands propping up her chin, was Daisy.

'Hello Donald,' she said softly.

It was the first time she had called me Donald.

'Hello, Daisy.'

'I wondered if you might take the boat out tonight.'

I pushed the boat up on the shingle and sat down beside her.

'I came to look for you earlier.'

'My foster-mum sent me on an errand. Then I had to do the washing-up.'

'Would she be cross if she saw me here?'

'Probably. She's an old misery guts. She's probably out with some man now, but if she saw me talking to a boy she'd chase me away and say I was a hussy. She says everyone's a hussy.'

'I've got a surprise for you, Daisy.'

She clapped her hands: 'What?'

'We've made a special ship's badge. It's got your name on it and the chief motor mechanic rawlplugged it, and it's just been put up on the side of the bridge today.'

'Now it really is *my* ship.'

'You know, I've never known a girl so daft about ships as you.'

'My Dad started me off. He used to bring me pictures of the ships he'd been in. I pasted them in an album. Then I started to collect cap ribbons. I begged them from sailors. I've got ribbons for the Victorious, the Valiant, Repulse, Wishart, Pembroke. . . .'

'Pembroke's not a ship, you daft thing. It's just the name of Chatham Barracks.'

She looked crestfallen. I fished out of my pocket a small piece of wood. I hadn't mentioned it to anybody and in fact I'd intended to keep it to myself. But I was so delighted at seeing Daisy again that I made up my mind to give it to her.

It was a miniature replica of the ship's badge which I had carved out and painted myself when I was alone in the galley.

'Daisy,' I said. 'A souvenir for you. I made it myself.'

'Oh, Donald!'

She bent forward and gave me a kiss.

If Greta Garbo herself had appeared and given me the most passionate kiss in the world, I couldn't have felt more thrilled or flattered. I took Daisy by her warm and sticky little hand and we walked together and looked out to sea. There was barely a ripple on the waters of the creek. The only sound was the crunch of our feet on the pebbles.

I wanted to break the silence and be together talking with her, but I could only think of silly things.

'Daisy,' I said. 'That kiss, you know. It was just like a sort of kiss like a butterfly.'

'Like a butterfly? That wasn't a butterfly kiss, silly.'

'No? Then what is a butterfly kiss?'

'You mean you don't know? Honest? You're not kidding? Not trying to get fresh?'

I assured her I wasn't. It was true I didn't know what a butterfly kiss was. As I said, I hadn't had a lot to do with girls, not even after three and a half years in the Navy.

Daisy wrinkled her nose in a grin and said: 'Then if you're good and promise not to get fresh, I'll show you.' Her hussy of a foster-mother must have warned her about blokes getting fresh.

She withdrew her hand from mine and turned round to face me. 'Bend your head down,' she commanded.

Stiffly in my bell-bottom trousers, feet together, I bent my head down towards hers. She then took hold of my shoulders with an arm on each, rose on tip-toes and nestled her face against mine. With her eyelashes she beat a fluttering tattoo on my lips. Then she pulled my head down so that our eyes met, and flickered her lashes against mine.

'There,' she said, darting away. 'You can do a butterfly kiss two ways. Eyes to lips, or eyes to eyes. Which do you like best?'

'Oh, both are nice, Daisy. But – '

'But what? Eye to eye is more difficult because two must play at that. You're supposed to flicker your eyelashes, not just let me do all the work.'

'I'll try again, if you like, Daisy.'

'No, no. No more tonight.'

'How did you learn to do that, Daisy?'

'Shan't tell. It's a secret.'

'Oh, go on, you can tell me.'

'No.'

'Do you kiss other – er – boys?'

'No. At least not often. I only kiss people I like. And you are the first sailor I've ever kissed. I didn't mean to do it.'

'Promise me something, Daisy. Don't kiss any other sailors. They might get the wrong idea.'

'I know. But I can take care of myself. I'd slosh anyone who got fresh. And scratch their face.'

'Won't you tell me how you learned to kiss like a butterfly?'

'Nosey, aren't you?'

'Please tell me. I won't breathe a word to a soul.'

'Well it was at a Hallowe'en Party last year. The room was in darkness and you had to guess what things were supposed to be. A boy came up to me and fluttered his eyelashes on my lips and said: "Guess what?" And I said "A moth", and he said "Don't be silly. That's a butterfly." '

At that moment I caught sight of the CO walking along the beach in my direction.

'Sorry Daisy, trouble's ahead. I'll have to dash.'

'See you soon.'

'O.K. Same time, same place.'

I pushed the boat into the water and shoved off. A minute later I was alongside the CO.

'That kid you were talking to. Wasn't that Daisy?'

'Yessir.'

'Thought I recognized her. Bit young for you, Musgrove. Are you cradle-snatching?'

'I just happened to see her on the beach while I was lying off for you, sir.'

'Well, watch your step with these youngsters. One little slip-up on your part and you could find yourself in dire trouble.'

'Oh, Daisy's not like that, sir. She's just a happy, lively kid.'

'Well, keep it that way.'

The summer passed quickly. We continued to ferry troops, equipment and vehicles to France, sometimes to Gold Beach, sometimes to Juno and Sword beaches. And as the weeks went by and the build-up on the beach-head grew, so each trip became more and more of a pleasure cruise, except for the monotony of it all. The miniature barrage balloon we carried from a winch on the stern became a joke for there were no dive-bombers to contend with. We just beached, waited for the tide to recede so that the tanks could drive off without getting wet, and waited for the tide to come in again before leaving. That interval gave us the chance to bathe and sometimes go ashore and explore a little of the mainland of France.

In between trips we all saw something of Daisy. I can't pretend that I often had Daisy entirely to myself. When I did I had to say I was somewhere else because I didn't want the crew to make up stories about us. You could divide the ship's company into those who had dirty minds like Hartburn, with whom I once had a hell of a row because he would compare Daisy's arse to the 'very ripest little peach I ever saw and the juiciest, I reckon', and those who were plain suspicious, like the CO. But one and all liked Daisy and we almost unconsciously adopted her as the ship's mascot. Soon snapshots of Daisy began to appear on the bulkheads in the mess-deck. Other ships in the flotilla would send us saucy signals such as 'Daisy, your slip's showing' when some idiot had left a ship's fender lying over the side. Our signalman once failed to respond to an Aldis lamp message quickly enough and his opposite number on another ship flashed out 'Daisy, Daisy, give me your answer do.'

On one of our trips across to Normandy I heard that a merchant seaman on one of the blockships that formed the breakwater was named Smuten. Foolishly I mentioned this to Daisy. I might have guessed her reaction. She immediately asked me if I couldn't smuggle her aboard so that she could find out for herself if it was her father.

'I wouldn't be in the way,' she pleaded. 'I could hide away somewhere. Anyhow, we would only be gone two days.'

At first I refused, saying it just wasn't possible. Women were not allowed aboard HM ships and the CO wouldn't stand for it. If we attempted any such crazy plan, everybody, including Daisy, would land in a packet of trouble.

'But I'm not a woman. I'm a little girl. What harm could there be? And anyhow in Nelson's time they allowed girls aboard naval ships. Stokes told me, so I know. That's how you got the phrase "Show a leg". The bosun's mate calls out "Show a leg" when he calls you each morning and that's all because in Nelson's time all a girl had to do was to stick her leg out of the hammock and she would be left to rest. I bet you didn't know that.'

'For the last time, Daisy – No.'

Then Daisy tried a new tack. 'I dare you to let me come aboard. You're just scared.'

I must have been mad. I'm all for a quiet life. But before I knew what I was saying I'd promised to take Daisy with us the following night. She ran off screaming with delight. Back on ship, I told myself I was being stupid and of course I wouldn't do it. Yet I found myself making up a blanket bed in the well-deck and working out how I could smuggle her on board in an Army lorry. Perhaps I could get away with it. She'd love me for ever if I did. It was the end of the war. I hadn't all that much to lose if we got caught. Why be scaredy all my life?

I waited for five hours in the rain on that boring bit of coast line in front of those manicured cottage lawns. Then I fell asleep, soaked through and exhausted in the bottom of the ship's boat. She never turned up yet. I don't know whether it was all a joke and she had no intention of coming with me, or if her foster-mother had packed her off suddenly in the middle of the night. All I know is I never saw her again.

3

Alan's story

Dear Sir: I cannot imagine why you should think that I have anything interesting to tell you about Daisy Smuten. How did you get my name? You do not say in what way she has become, or is about to become, so important to the world that even a few fragments of anecdote about our very tentative acquaintanceship should be worth my time, and your money, after twenty-three years.

Daisy, I do remember you, even though we only met six times on six consecutive Sundays. Your name *was* 'Sunday Times' as we decided when we played those boring games of anagrams you enjoyed so much. You were so clever with letters and so ignorant of words. You didn't even know that the Sunday Times was a newspaper.

Sometimes you seemed backward, even for twelve, mentally deficient almost, when you used to ask me, a very self-conscious highbrow of twenty-two, to tell you fairy stories. I used to muddle up all the plots, so when I had told one I had told them all, but you never seemed to mind. In the middle, you'd go into a sort of trance, and then suddenly awake at the end to ask some naive awkward question, or make some clever, ignorant joke which left me speechless. I told you about the girl who kissed the frog who turned into a prince, and you jeered – 'What a stupid girl, think of how many horrible frogs she must have kissed before she found a magic one. I'm going to begin with the princes. When I'm thirty and old, then the frogs can have their turn.' You would look almost ugly then, and I would notice the spots bracketing your mouth so that those silly lush lips were like a swearword in parenthesis, that scab on your left knee glossy and purple as a joke-shop ink blot, the nails of your left hand bitten so that the fingers seemed circumcised, the hair faintly sheened with grease rising into a corona like an Egyptian head-dress. Then I would say to myself – 'Are you mad? Who would believe you spend twelve hours every Sunday with so plain and witless a child unless for some perverted reason?' – and I would decide this would be our last meeting.

It may be that she has now become a great beauty, or a great artist, but I'm afraid she was very normal and ordinary in those days. If, in her recollection, our relationship was anything other than a couple of chance encounters, then it must be that she is unconsciously magnifying her childhood as so many of us tend to do.

What have you told them, Daisy? For it must be you who gave my name, unless it was Lucy. What was there to tell? Nothing happened. To you. Something must have happened to me. But how would you have noticed? I never met anyone who noticed the world less. Who was more incapable of finishing anything she began.

You left everything half open – your mouth (with its agile, flicking tongue like a humming bird's), the buttons on your blouse (schoolgirl cotton buckling to reveal oddly grown-up silk underwear), your handbag (that dark grey, blistered pouch the shape of a kidney bean I called the elephant's scrotum, always containing at least two tubes of ointment which had lost their labels), even the lavatory door. The only time I took you back to my digs, you dashed into it and then sat, cheerfully squirting, while I hummed with embarrassment in my bedroom across the corridor unable to keep my eyes away from the scuffed brogues, and concertina'd socks, draped with a pair of loose-legged glossy pants, which were left in full view. You always broke everything off in the middle. You would agitate to leave the cinema in the middle of the big picture, jump off the bus between stops, wash one hand and forget the other, ask a second question before you had heard the answer to the first. You left behind you a trail of clues as if for some Father Brown to follow: a sequence of hairpins, buttons, gnawed choc bars, apple cores, pencil stubs, diary pages scrawled with numbers, cuttings from women's magazines, tiny bottles of cheap scent, even slivered scimitars of painted nail, smelling of pear drops (right-hand only).

It is very kind of you to suggest that I am some kind of prose-laureate of nostalgia and that even a few paragraphs of fine-spun filigree nonsense (my word, but I suspect, your meaning) in remembrance of things past would be invaluable to your project. Proust at least had his madeleine cake. I have not even the crumbs of a Mars bar. Already, at forty-five, I have written many (far too many, my agent says) thousands of words of autobiography. If Daisy Smuten had even a crowd-role in my scenario, she would have long ago been embalmed in warm storage among my uncollected works.

Daisy, of course you are there already if those idiots only knew where to look. I have forgotten very little, perhaps because I had very little to forget. If we had spent the last twenty-five years together, those six summer Sundays in Oxford would now have shrunk to a couple of minutes. But you broke me off in the middle, no, at the tip, threw me away untasted after a hasty lick, so I can still switch on my mental projector, to screen, uncut, the seventy-two hours we shared, at the drop of a bottle cap.

Oxford, 1947, the first Sunday of the summer term. It is eight in the morning. The sun, a congealed fried egg among cold gravy clouds, telegraphed a faint, residual warmth to our empty-hearted planet. (Stay with me, Daisy. I wrote like this in my school exercise books even before I discovered The True Life of Sebastian Knight in 1943. The style is the man. Would the man had been the style, my Tamara, my Lolita, my Ada.)

But I am already falsifying my feelings in retrospect. Until then, and since then, I have never been attracted to little girls. As I grow older, the age limit rises. You captured me (if an open city, which admits invaders as if they were tourists, can be said to capture a pirate raider) by the very fact that you had no sex appeal. You were almost the only kind of female under the age of forty-five, in those randy, fantasy days, I did *not* fancy in bed.

Oxford, 1947, the first Sunday of the summer term. I had been awake in college all night. Doing what? Playing the gramophone, telling lies about war and women, reading out favourite passages from Herzen, Nabokov, Donne and both the Lawrences, drinking a thick, slick, hick mixture of gin and welfare orange juice which glugged into the veins like plasma. I left Jesus (a strange locution I never noticed until I said to you one Sunday in the Turl, 'Good God, they're giving Jesus a wash!' and you replied: 'Why not? You never know where he's been.') as soon as the gates opened in the morning. It was too early to arouse my landlady, so I walked down through Alfred Street and the House into Christ Church Meadow.

The sun was just beginning to stir the riverside mists, shreds of chiffon scarf caught in the slippery green branches of the elms. Oxford was being unpacked like an expensive birthday present. I stopped and wrote in my notebook – 'A dirty hand covered with jewels. Or a dirty jewel covered with hands.' Undergraduates are bad writers, worse critics. The phrase, reversible as a glove (skinside inside or stoutside outside?) pleased me. Already, it seemed worth the wasted night and the champagne bubbles of condensation which covered my dark charcoal grey trousers, sweater and raincoat like silvery chain-mail. Only the white silk muffler, as worn by Sunderland pitmen on Saturday night and thought by my new Southern friends 'rather common', gleamed dry and bright in the pearly-barley air.

I walked under dripping boughs to the Botanical Gardens, opposite Magdalen, and back, imagining myself a new Auden, another Isherwood, already overtaking Spender. Then, on the bench I had just passed five minutes before, exactly on the stroke of eight, for I remember counting the golden rings of sound falling like fair-ground hoops from the high Cathedral and wondering had I invented the image or had I stolen it from Conrad Aitken, I saw you, Daisy.

I saw your legs first, lemon-yellow as always (Did you paint them? Was it a kind of jaundice? An inherited characteristic?) like a pair of brass nut-crackers – thighs branching apart, knees knocked together, calves and feet splayed wide. I know you were wearing a skirt, but at my distance you seemed half a golden girl left there by the gods to refresh the wandering Odysseus on his travels, a young hero's dream of home. As I drew nearer, I saw you had a top half too – the careless hunch of a schoolgirl in a mossy green blazer, citrus-fruit breasts like Cranach's Eve just keeping the unbuttoned lapels open, dark hair falling in panels over the ears, while lighter wings soared from each temple, like a Norseman's helmet. Sixteen, fifteen, fourteen, thirteen, twelve, Christ, you looked barely eleven as I slowed down to see whether I had the nerve to stop. My heart sank – you were too young. My heart rose – you were no challenge. I sat next to you, but three feet away, just for the practice.

Did you make it easy for me? I begin to wonder now. Then, I just breathed plumes of steam like a jousting horse until I heard you reading. You moved your lips when you read (even when you read the advertisements on the slides at the cinema – 'Taj Mahal, for that special evening out. Our curries curry favour.' 'Elliston and Cavells. A London store at Oxford prices.'). You read, in barely a whisper:

'And I thought well as well him as another and then I asked him with my eyes to ask again yes and then he asked me would I yes to say yes my mountain flower and first I put my arms around him yes and drew him down to me so that he could feel my breast all perfume yes and his heart going like mad and yes I said yes I will Yes.'

'Molly Bloom,' I said. 'Yes?' I said.

'No,' you said. 'Daisy Smuten.'

But you laughed, or rather half-laughed, using up too much breath too quickly, and your lips gaped, and your tongue licked in and out, and your knees tremored apart and snapped shut with a bony click, and your hair shook and showered dew drops, and you tucked the book deep down between your unclosable inside thighs as if about to return it to some secret drawer, and your eyes turned up as your blue-veined lids dropped like shutters for a full five seconds. I can remember every thing about you except your eyes.

Half the time I was with you, thirty-six hours of you, the shutters were down, even when you were talking. (What was the message? There must have been a message for, like Cressid, your body always spoke though your tongue was silent. Wanton spirits looked out at every joint and motive of your body. Or is this middle-aged lubricity? – you were, or said you were, only twelve years of age.) I do remember under your eyes, each Sunday morning, a faintly puckered smudge as if a pair of large male thumbs had pressed there to keep you watching. (What did you do on Saturday nights that gave you that luxurious air of tired satisfaction, stirring under your school uniform as if in a warm bath? Could those Scrabble sessions with your father – sometimes he was a step-father – have been so onerous and so enjoyable?) But that first meeting, even up to the dawning of our sixth meeting, I no more lusted after you than I did after the fawns in Magdalen deer park, so innocently pushy, so daintily greedy.

'No,' you said. 'Daisy Smuten.' And you half-laughed, opening your eyes after that pause to look me up and down with an oddly expert yet dispassionate scrutiny like a member of the Royal Family making sure that an equerry is wearing all his medals in the right order. 'What do you think of Gerty MacDowell?' I asked you.

You rubbed your skirt up and down your thighs a couple of times, as though polishing them, then handed me the warm book. The final chapter was much thumbed and marked. The rest might never have been opened.

'Oh, I've only read the one story,' you said. 'They were passing it round the class at school. Why do you believe in God?'

'Why do you believe in Zeus?' I asked. It was what I always asked when somebody mentioned God. It was a diversionary feint to allow the heavy artillery to fire over open sights. But it was based on the assumption that the enemy would keep still.

Only you stood up, sending another spray of droplets steaming up like incense, stretching those sunlit legs like a colt, pulling out the seat of your skirt where it had damply moulded itself into twin melons, as unselfconsciously as if you were alone in front of a mirror. Then you smiled at me through closed eyes, minuscule pulses jumping in your lids, your neck swelling then elongating as if you had just swallowed – 'Father brings me in for church then I can spend the whole day just mooching about. Will you carry my book?'

So I carried your book (I still have it – with another girl's name on the fly leaf) and I held your hand as we walked around an Oxford where the cherry trees were bursting and overflowing their trunks like cones of pink ice cream, where the yellow Cotswold stone crumbled in the heat like old Cheshire cheese, and I felt happier than I had since I too was twelve.

My certain information about Miss Smuten is very meagre. She was a boarder at some school within a bus ride of Oxford. There cannot be very many of these or more than one Smuten. She had a friend in her class (I do not know why I have retained the name) called M. Forster. I never met her father (step-father?) or any other member of her family.

I took you to the Cadena for breakfast – soupy coffee, warm and sweet; giant size slices of toast, hard as brick around the crust, soft and springy inside, you called them 'double beds'. I read the Observer, you looked at the photographs in the Sunday Pictorial and kept on quoting the captions aloud in a voice that often seemed to pick up comic North-Country overtones, presumably to tease me. (Who are you mimicking now? 'Beware of imitations' was one of your catchphrases whenever I took seriously some tall story you began to invent and then abandoned. Another was 'It's going *awfully* well', which you muttered as an aside to an invisible girl-friend if ever I criticized your behaviour.)

That first Sunday, and every Sunday I think until the last, you waited outside the Welsh Pony, like a neglected daughter, while I loaded up a greaseproof bag of Scotch eggs, sausages, meat pasties, French bread and cheese, cream buns, a bottle of Tizer for you and a quart of light ale for me. Then we caught a bus to some outlying village and picnicked in a field. You were far more fussy and demanding than any girl undergraduate I ever took out.

You always had to sit on my jacket, never on the grass. You made me carry your bag, your macintosh, even uncomfortable, heavy parcels addressed to your father (Colonel D. Smuten) which you picked up at a variety of Porters' Lodges, as well as the food and drink. You objected to any walk above a quarter mile. '*Outer* Mongolia!' you would moan. Any monologue by me – and most of our conversations were one-sided – which strayed from frivolous whimsy into serious education would provoke you to roll into a ball, pillow your head on my chest, and fall asleep murmuring – 'Goodbye, Mr Chips.'

I never made a pass at you, even on that last Sunday, you must admit. But what was a man, especially a young man, to do, stretched out, closely hugged by a sizeable nymphet (if only we'd known the word) with a waist that would worry a wasp, restlessly scissoring legs, and fingers which hooked into every buttonhole, hidden from the world in a black, spidery wood, like an armpit, between two swelling ploughed fields, all of a sweltering afternoon. Occasionally, perhaps, my hand might close comfortably around some snug protuberance, my lips might slide down some upper slope. Invariably, one eye would open impossibly wide and you would drawl – 'She's only a *cheeyild.*'

And so you were, Daisy. You were more like a dog I sometimes thought – a cuddly nuisance, a loving drag, a simple-minded responsibility.

If you ever said anything interesting and original to me, it was probably by accident. Every now and then, I thought I detected a note of irony in your remarks but whenever I asked you to explain yourself you relapsed into high-grade nursery language. Do you remember the last conversation we had? You wrote the dialogue and I followed your lead. It embarrasses me that I should still have it by heart.

'Knock, knock,' you said.

'Who's there?'

'Banana.'

'Banana who?'

'Knock, knock.'

'Who's there?'

'Banana.'

'Banana who?'
'Knock, knock.'
'Who's there?'
'Orange.'
'Orange who?'
'Orange you glad I didn't say "banana" again?'
And you went giggling and prancing out of the door of my bedroom, drunk with laughter, in your ridiculous, adult, glossy underwear, carrying your school uniform over your arm, leaving me on the bed. And I never saw or heard of you again, until I got the letter from this prying fool who makes such a mystery of why you are suddenly famous.

I think it possible her father, or guardian, may have been a military man though for reasons which I now forget I did look him up in the Army List without success. Only one other source occurs to me and that is a common acquaintance of Miss Smuten's and mine – a Miss Lucy Church. She was an Anglo-Peruvian and so far as I know she returned to Peru and is still there. But she knew her probably even less well than I did.

Why I never told Lucy about you, or you about Lucy, until too late, I am only now beginning to understand. You never showed any interest in my weekday life. I do not recall you asking about where I came from, who my parents were, what I was doing in Oxford when you were not present. It was as if you accepted me as an uncle who had no choice but to entertain you whenever you appeared. You obviously never asked yourself what I would get out of the arrangement.
I was on the point of explaining our friendship to Lucy a score of times, but I could not quite find the words to fit. It all sounded so improbable and peculiar. Lucy *was* concerned about me, to a degree which might have driven any other man nuts. It was like having an affair with a police dog. She would sniff me when we met, holding me at arms length, asking: 'Whose perfume is that? When did you smoke Turkish cigarettes? Where did you eat onions?' She would examine my clothes, even my underpants, with embarrassing zeal. I spent a couple of nights a week with

her for a term, climbing back into college with trembling muscles just before dawn. And each time I was obliged to rehearse the events of missing days, against the clock, like the major suspect in a detective story. She was never satisfied with an anecdote, or the précis of an incident, but she would narrow her already elliptical eyes to demand – 'and then?' – She had a devouring appetite for footnotes, appendices, variant readings, scribal errors, in our personal relationship.

I enjoyed her jealousy because I was jealous myself. (Was this her way of anticipating and deflecting the questions I otherwise would have asked? Did she pretend to scrutinize my minutes so that I would overlook her hours?) And it would have been difficult to invent a job more likely to provoke a lover than hers – she was a model in an art school.

Sometimes I would call in on the life class just in order to punish myself. I stood at the back, watching her over a bobbing, ducking frieze of heads, angry when they stared at her nakedness, even angrier when they turned away to stare at the crude images of her on their canvases.

She would have driven a Cubist to suicide for she was all loops and bobbles and circles, buttons and bows. Her skin had a faint, purplish, grape-like bloom which betrayed her Peruvian ancestry, against which her lips and her nipples stood out in shocking pink. It was a painter's figure, opulent rather than elegant, overflowing, overpowering, as if she had been poured into her skin and forgotten to say 'when'. She was my idea of an odalisque. Making love to her was like being buried in a room full of cushions.

If her body was Renoir, her face was Gauguin, rather prettified and pettish. She was the sort of girl that men always touched – fingered is perhaps the word I'm not looking for – five minutes after they met her. And she never seemed to mind. She behaved as if her flesh were a new dress and it was only natural that those who admired it should want to feel the material. I shall never forget the evening you met Lucy. It was Sunday, supposedly my working day, when my friends imagined me barricaded in my rooms behind battlements of books. Instead you and I had gone to the Scala to see a John Ford Western. You didn't want to go because the star was Henry Fonda and you said – 'He's such a drip. He always gets killed in the end.' But I liked you almost best in the cinema. You looked ten years older in the silvery light reflected off the screen, a pearly goddess with dark moist lips, warm and squashy in the flickering dark. It had been raining. Your cheek was faintly wet against mine, and a delicious smell of steaming girl spiralled upwards like Bisto. In my dark glasses (a film-going accessory I had copied from Gavin Lambert) and my wide-brimmed, already period, demob trilby, I should have remained anonymously enfolding you within a fraternal arm until 'The End', if you had not begun giggling at the supporting feature, *The Cabinet of Dr. Caligari.*

I had already seen this three or four times so I watched you instead, thinking how your face resembled an over-exposed photograph of some film star when all the childish quirks and crinkles were erased. I must have floated off into a half-doze because the next I knew your forced, mechanical, fourth-form laughter was loud in one ear, while the other picked up several priggish, censorious voices saying things like 'Can't you keep that child quiet?' and 'Some of us came here to see the film'. I really believe you thought it was meant to be funny in an exaggerated old-fashioned way like the Keystone Cops. But all I thought was – I'll never become President of the Film Society if I'm recognized – so I bundled you into the aisle like a drunk, hoping to sober you down on a sticky, chemical, orange drink. Lucy held open the door to the foyer for us. So unthinkable had it been that such a confrontation would ever occur, that I had no cover story to fit the occasion. When Lucy said, in her theatrical, foreigner's English, 'So this is the homework you college boys do in the night times,' all I could say was 'She had a fit of hiccups. She was frightened.' You gave a kind of whoop and tried to slide across the foyer in the pools of rainwater. Lucy gave you her policewoman's quick up-and-down, whistled aloud, and rolled her eyes to the ceiling. 'My Jesus,' she said. 'This is cradle-snatching with a revenge. It is positively an infant.'

One of the many drawbacks to going around with a twelve-year-old girl is that after 6 p.m. there is nowhere to take her. Even wearing a hat with feathers and a veil (which you tried on one embarrassing occasion) landlords spotted you instantly for a minor. The only cafe which remained open, near the bus station, was full of sniggering louts who offered you bubble-gum and waitresses who referred to you as 'the little girl'. When I could afford it, I took you to dinner but even at The Stowaway we couldn't sit over omelette and chips for much longer than two hours.

College landladies were also as alert to possible deviations among their lodgers as Krafft-Ebbing. One friend of mine was asked to keep his sitting-room door ajar in future after being found kissing his mother goodbye. Later he gave me a useful tip – 'Always take two girls back with you. That's beyond even their dirty minds.' I didn't have two girls. Until that night. 'Let's all go to your place,' I begged Lucy. 'You can't stand Henry Fonda either.'

There should be a dissolve, or a new chapter, at this point. But in Oxford, in 1947, there wasn't even a taxi. We queued in the rain for a bus. Lucy mounted an elaborate examination of you. You lied. And I stared at my soaked shoes and hoped the other people around weren't listening.

It was an appalling evening. I had told Lucy, with only an occasional dab of false colour, that I was a working-class genius from Sunderland, an heroic sergeant airgunner in the RAF, and the man who loved her and her alone. I had to sit there while you explained that I had been a subaltern in the regiment commanded by your father, Colonel Smuten; that I had gone to Haileybury (why didn't you make it Eton?) with your cousin, Peregrine; and that I took you out every Sunday because I knew so few girls of my own age.

Lucy refused to talk to me for two days after that. I had to follow her round the Ashmolean Museum, whispering eloquently, just to get her to have a coffee at the Randolph. I don't suppose you ever knew what ghastly, bitchy things she said about you. I might have known she'd be compiling a dossier.

'Your infant, she is some sort of monster, I think,' Lucy

enunciated, doing her Carmen Miranda bit. 'I have seen her, and her friends. You are so easy-minded. Do you know she picked you up that morning only because she thought you were a clergyman? A joke. She has more friendly men than you have hot suppers. They write to her, give her their telephone numbers, leave all around for her marvellous presents. Do you think they do that for nothing? Pshaw!' (She pronounced it – 'P. Shaw' – and I always wanted to add 'Esquire'.)

'Do you know, the one thing she asked me? What did I do about the venereal diseases? How about that for a baby monster?'

The poor creature. She must have loved me after all. But I couldn't stand such viciousness at that moment.

'You will regret saying those things, Lucy,' I told her bluntly. 'Daisy is *twelve*, for God's sake. Two years younger than you were when you were seduced by your headmistress's brother. I don't want to speak to you until you are in your right mind again.'

On the Friday, outside the Radcliffe Camera, Lucy was waiting for me. Beside all those washed-out English blondes, and sallow English brunettes, she was a Technicolor insert in a black-and-white Ealing comedy.

She moaned, and clutched me. 'You are right. My imagination is awful. That little girl is a sweet-pie. She and I are friends. You and I are whatever you want. She is coming to tea at your diggings on Sunday. See you soon.' And she hipped away, rubbing all her limbs together, watched by every eye in the square.

The next morning, my landlady, who had long ago seen through me and classified me as an outsider, a provincial, a phoney-gentleman, a sex-maniac and poor with it, was suspiciously polite. 'That Miss Church called,' she said. 'Your niece is coming to tea and I've arranged a lovely blow-out for the little thing. If I'd known you'd been walking the streets with the child, of course I'd have done it ages ago. I'm only human, you know.'

That afternoon, you came for the first time to my digs, Daisy. You looked like Hollywood's idea of Alice in Wonderland – so clean, so satin-smooth, curry-combed and rubbed-down, I hardly recognized you. Knees and elbows akimbo, for once I thought your schoolgirl costume was a disguise.

Never before had you brought me a present. But here was a bottle of whisky hidden inside your satchel, and I began to drink it quickly and boastfully. What happened next, I have not been able to remember. Perhaps I have suppressed the details.

I only know that I played a passive role in whatever occurred, I think. If we talked, then it was without listening to each other. If we embraced, it was without feeling. Somehow, we were lying on my prickly single bed, like a bespoke hair-shirt, while I was naked except for a sweat-shirt, and you wore your grown-up ladies underwear. I threw away the bottle when it was empty, when you began to writhe and wriggle and bite and chew. I imagined myself entirely devoid of free will.

The room became dark in the day time, as if a great crow had flown between us and the sun, so that past and future, good and evil, masculine and feminine, no longer made any sense.

Then, suddenly, I was sticky and chilly, guilty and self-conscious, sober enough to know I must be drunk. I couldn't bear to ask myself why I felt so drained. I only hold for ever the picture of you giggling and prancing out of the door, your school uniform over your arm, as you chanted: 'Orange you glad I didn't say "banana"?'

I never saw you again. Lucy ceased to answer my telephone calls and my postcards. The next time I saw her, she was tarted up in frills and lace, a nipped waist and a plunging neckline, like a French maid in a farce. Her companion, crew-cut, tight-trousered, heavy boots and brass-buckle belt, would have passed for a man anywhere – except in a Turkish bath.

Lucy was the only person I knew who had ever met you. I tried to ask about you, but her friend was too attentive and proprietorial. The nearest we managed was a swift interchange when she slipped out for a cheroot during the interval at the Playhouse.

'What have you done with Daisy?' I asked.

'The littler said about her the better, you pervert,' Lucy hissed. 'You do not know how near you came to being policed.'

And that was all.

It does occur to me, finally, that Miss Smuten may have attracted your attention because she is in some kind of trouble. If this is so, I would be grateful if you could pass on to her my name and address, and the assurance that I would be proud to provide her with any assistance in my power.

Yours faithfully,
Alan Brien.

Daisy, Daisy. Just as I finished this dull and discouraging letter, I watched the TV news. Now I know why you are about to become famous. Now I see you at the age of thirty-five. In a way, I think it is the best thing that ever happened to you. In another way, I think it will be the worst thing that happened to the rest.

(Extract from Picturegoer magazine, June 1950.)

'Bachelor, 26, seeks Pen Pal, preferably of female sex and under 17. Interests: Margaret O'Brien, Farley Granger, modern ballet, travel, physical culture. Write c/o Picturegoer, Box 334F.'

Banbury Road
Oxford
June, 1950

DEAR MR WHATEVER-YOUR-NAME-IS,

I saw your ad in Picturegoer and am writing this letter to say I would like to be your Pen Pal. I am fifteen years old and I am very lonely because I do not know many people of my own age and I do not know anybody with the same interests as me so I have practically nobody to talk to or write to. I am quite tall for my age and very well-developed, my hair is strawberry blonde like Rita Hayworth and my eyes are a peculiar shade of green and I have a tip-tilted *retroussé* nose. I am very interested in Farley Granger and have been for years and years and years. I don't think I could respect a person who did not love and adore Farley Granger. I wrote to him in Hollywood and got a divine photo back, it took ages to get here, he wrote on it 'Best of luck – Farley Granger.' I like older men much better than younger men, in my opinion the latter are inclined to be soppy. So I would like to be your Pen Pal please and trust you will reply to this letter at above address at your earliest convenience.

I remain,
Yours sincerely,
DAISY SMUTEN (MISS)

Banbury Road
Oxford
July, 1950

DEAR REG,

Many thanks for your most welcome letter received this morning, what a weird coincidence that we live in the same country, I thought you must be living somewhere miles and miles away like Australia or somewhere. As a matter of fact I don't think I shall be staying here much longer, it isn't really my home you see. I am soon going away far away to have an exciting job.

It is very sweet of you to say that you are interested in my life and that you want to know everything that happens to me and everything I think and do and feel. I absolutely take a solemn vow and promise that what I tell you about myself will always be the sacred truth, like going to confession or something. And I quite understand when you say that you think it better for us never to meet, even though we could quite easily, because if I never see you then I will never be tempted to lie about myself, even if I am ashamed of what I have done. Wouldn't it be funny if we saw each other on a bus or something and didn't know we were us? Went to 'Samson and Dalila' last night. I do think Hedy Lamarr must be the *most* beautiful woman in the *world.* Hope you don't mind me calling you 'Reg' at the beginning of this letter, 'Mr' sounds so formal somehow and I do think 'Reg' is a very nice name, when I was little I had a cat called that who I worshipped, he was a neutered tom and he got run over by a lorry. So please answer this letter *at once* and when you do just call me

DAISY

PS: What do you do? Don't tell me if you don't want to – then I can imagine that you're something very glamorous like a spy or a burglar or an actor or a football player or something.
PPS: Perhaps you *are* !!!

4

Magnus's story

It was still half-dark when I clocked in at the factory on the day I met Daisy Smuten. Wrestling with the green-stained overalls we all wore, I rammed my card into the slot and pulled the lever: 6.09 am, one minute inside the time-limit (ten minutes late and they docked an hour's pay).

I don't suppose Daisy would remember the place now, but I thought it was fairly impressive – hot, wet, noisy, smelly, dirty, but big. The first thing you saw was the pea-drying plant. Six giant chutes, piled high with soggy, new-boiled peas, sloping away into the distance, shaking and clattering, spouting jets of steam as the dampness evaporated. As you walked to the other end the smell became gradually less suffocating, the slurp-slurp changed to a distinct rattle, and finally there was the end-product, a steady stream of dry, shrivelled pellets, bouncing into a hopper. Some people used to chew them like gum, but they weren't very good for the teeth.

I worked in the other half – the fancy end, where the peas were canned, labelled and packed. It was cleaner there, and the noise was less intense. It was also the place where every red-blooded male worker wanted to end up: the machinery was manned by fifty-two people. And forty-nine of them were girls.

It was also supervised by Michael Flynn O'Neill, otherwise Mick the chargehand, whose main asset was his command of the English language.

'Move your arsehole, four-eyes,' he shouted at me that morning as I did up the last fly-button and pulled on my greasy white cap (the factory posters were most insistent about caps. 'Keep those germs under your hat' they urged). 'You're in a sodding factory now, not an arty-tarty school,' Mick added.

I was well aware of it. Eton was only six weeks behind me, and for half that time I had been working at Lemgard's pea-factory, twelve hours a day, seven days a week. It had been a fairly savage experience, one way and another, but at least it hadn't done my overdraft any harm. Twenty-two pounds ten a week, including overtime: I couldn't really believe that three years at Cambridge would help me to earn more than that for a long time to come.

I touched my cap in apology to Mick, and picked up my first box of the day. He stood over me as I opened it up, slipped it over the frame and pulled the long handle which started the mechanism. Eight metal fingers prodded eight cans of Lemgard's Garden Delicious Fresh-Picked peas into the box. Another pull and eight more cans were rammed in on top. I rolled back nonchalantly on my heels as the box slid into the pit of my stomach, then swung it onto the moving chute beside me, and reached again for the handle.

It was at that point that I saw Doreen and Lorrayne moving past behind me.

' 'E's so good-looking it makes me ache to look at 'im,' said Lorrayne into my ear.

' 'Oo was the lucky girl last night, then?' said Doreen. 'Bet yer didn't 'alf give 'er a rough time.'

They both giggled and walked on, swinging their hips. I blushed and grabbed too hard on the handle. The prods shot forward, caught one of the cans lop-sided and pinioned it against the edge of the frame. I watched, horrified, as the next eight cans piled up, then churned over in the relentless machinery. Too late I reached for the cut-out button. There was a sharp crack and a jet of boiling, pea-green liquid spurted up to the ceiling. I punched the button and the noise died away, as a pile of bent and broken cans settled into a sad heap at my feet.

'Christ Jesus, you clumsy bastard!' roared Mick. 'What in God's name have you done now?' He leapt at his beloved machine and began nursing it back to sanity as I scrabbled on the floor in an attempt to salvage the few cans that hadn't suffered too badly. Doreen and Lorrayne, the cause of it all, came back to help me.

'That's the trouble with you upper-class gentlemen,' said Lorrayne kindly. 'Can't do a man's work.'

'Oh, I'm not so sure about that,' said Doreen, giving me a wink. She knelt down beside me, flashing a generous cleavage, and picked out three undamaged cans with one hand, while with the other she tickled the back of my neck.

One of the many inadequacies of a public-school education is its failure to equip a chap for life on a sexually-integrated factory floor. I never knew how to react to Doreen. A pinch on the bottom? A nudge in the ribs? A saucy 'Give us a kiss?' It was always too late, and this time was no exception. Both girls had disappeared by the time I got over the shock.

Not that Doreen and Lorrayne were any better than the other forty-seven girls. They all seemed to be under twenty-one, and without exception wore engagement rings – 'for protection' they said (but against what?). They used heavy make-up, with emphasis on green for eyes and orange for lips. Their stockings were cheap and well-laddered and shoes smart but impractical. The factory insisted on uniform head-gear (white dust-scarves tied at the front), but had no say in the way the top-coats were worn, with the result that they were barely thigh-length and usually unbuttoned down to the belt. Because of the heat few of the girls wore anything more than a lacy bra and skimpy pants underneath.

Sex, in fact, dwelt heavily in the atmosphere. The language was coarse and the jokes were terrible: 'Know what my boy-friend said last night? "What 'appens when yer die?" 'e said. "Dunno," I said. "Yer go stiff, don' yer?" 'e said. "O.K." I said, "so wot?" "Well," 'e says, "put yer 'and in me trouser pocket. I think I'm going ter die".' None of my dirty jokes, when I ventured to tell them, were in the same league.

Which meant that I usually spent a silent dinner-break. Not that I minded. The dinner-break was sacred – forty minutes of heavy, satisfying food. You grew to understand fervently why a man would go on strike and shut down an entire factory rather than lose five minutes of tea and Individual Fruit Pie.

I was half-way through the Daily Mirror cartoons when somebody tapped me on the shoulder and told me the manager wanted to see me. Immediately I reckoned it must be the sack, for my performance that morning. But I was not a semi-skilled man – and temporary member of the Union – for nothing. The manager couldn't sack me, could he?

I walked down the corridor, summoning up irritation against the bosses. You saw them sometimes on the floor dressed in white coats and bush hats, carrying little sticks. It gave the whole thing a distinctly colonial look: the overseers and the natives.

By the time I reached his office I was feeling belligerent. I pushed open the door, and met Daisy.

She had her high heels off and was sitting at a desk in the outer office reading a copy of Vogue. She was wearing a little blue dress which buttoned up to the neck but the top button was missing. Her hair was brown, streaked with blond, and hung loosely down the back of her neck, narrowly by-passing two wiry earrings. She looked about seventeen and had no make-up on. Suddenly I was fed up with sexy factory-girls.

'Yes?' she said, not putting down the magazine. I saw that it had tea stains all over it and was three months out of date.

I took off my cap, which, in the circumstances, was a mistake, and demanded: 'Where's the boss? I'm in a hurry.'

'Mr Macdonald's busy. I think you probably want the Personnel Manager. Third door down on the right.' And she began reading again. An irritating gesture.

I rapped on her desk. 'Look, Miss, your Mr Macdonald has just sent for me. It might be worth your while to tell him I'm here.'

Mr Macdonald himself saved the argument by opening the door and walking in.

'Ah – Linklater, isn't it?' he said. 'Awfully grateful you could pop along. I wanted to ask you about a couple of things. Promise I won't keep you more than a few minutes.'

He took me by the arm and steered me towards his office.

'We've been doing a bit of work on conditions here at the factory, and I thought it would be interesting to talk to one of you public school chaps. Find out what the other half thinks and all that sort of thing. By the way, I believe I know your father – Miss Smuten, no calls please, while Mr Linklater and I are talking if you don't mind.'

I had a quick glance at Daisy before the door shut. She was looking at me through half-closed eyes. I couldn't tell whether she was angry or interested.

I don't suppose I would have got anywhere with Daisy if it hadn't been for Johnny, the Nigerian box-sticker who worked next to me, pasting up the cardboard boxes I passed him. He was the only person who retained any sense of fun in the long, weary afternoon when the girls had gone home and the machines were beginning to give trouble (I never found out if there was any connection, but it always happened).

Johnny was enlarging on his favourite theme.

'Some people have class,' he was saying, 'and some ain't. Now, I got it, and maybe you've got it, but those,' and he gestured at the girls behind us, 'they've got none of it.' He laughed and shook his head. 'Just none.'

'So where do you find these classy birds you're always talking about?' I asked.

'Here and there, you know, but mostly at this joint where the young society girls of Manchester congregate.' He laughed again, missing two boxes which drifted past him lids flapping open. 'And mostly they congregate round me. Because they ain't seen nothing like me before. And because class goes with class, that's what I say.'

'Where's this place?' I said, casually.

'It's in town. In Manchester. Why don't you come along? I'll show you some action.'

'OK,' I said. 'I'll give you a lift in.'

Johnny's club was called, originally enough, The Discotheque. For Manchester it was quite a breakaway from the plush leatherette of places with names like El Paradiso or The Casbah. There was loud music, a frenetic disc-jockey and a roving green light which settled on each table in turn for about three minutes (at ten o'clock the green light turned to red – doubtless an elaborate joke on the part of the management).

Johnny selected his 'bit of class' without hesitation. A rather stout red-headed girl with glasses who appeared to be considerably shaken at having scored so early in the evening.

Encouraged, I began looking around for myself. Almost immediately I spotted Daisy, sitting in a corner, alone at a table.

I could have done with a bit more time to work out an approach. After all our last meeting had not been entirely satisfactory, and I had the impression that Daisy was distinctly unpredictable. But as I hesitated the relentless green light settled on Daisy's table. I could hardly have asked for a clearer sign than that. I walked over and sat down in front of her.

For a moment neither of us said anything. Daisy betrayed no hint of surprise, simply surveying me through those same half-closed eyelashes. Perhaps she was short-sighted, I thought. Then the light moved, mercifully, away from our table, and Daisy said:

'You look better in green.'

'Thank you,' I replied. 'Are you expecting anyone?'

'Yes.'

'Can I buy you something to drink?'

'Do,' said Daisy. 'I'll have an Americano.'

I think Americanos were about ten years out of fashion even then. Perhaps Daisy was not quite as cool as she made out.

'I'm working through the list,' she said, pointing at a card on the table in front of her, which bore the names of about a dozen appalling cocktails from Absinthe to White Lady. 'I'll have a Bloody Mary next if you can afford it.'

'Of course I can afford it,' I said, nettled.

'Oh yes, I expect you have private means. You don't have to work at the factory do you?'

'As a matter of fact I do. Just because I'm, well – '

'An Old Etonian?' said Daisy casually.

'How the hell did you know that?'

'I looked you up, of course.' She smiled. 'We've got a file on you. Did you know?'

I pretended to look annoyed, though I was flattered that Daisy should have taken such an interest. It was a bit like studying form. I regained some advantage by ordering an Americano, a Bloody Mary and something called a Discotheque Special all at once. The waiter set them solemnly in a row in front of Daisy.

Just then we were interrupted by a tall, bent young man, hair well smeared down and glinting in the light, chin clustered with pimples. I recognized him as one of the trainee managers from the factory – Mr String. We called him Stringy.

'Excuse me, Miss Smuten,' he said, looking at me. 'I think we arranged to meet.'

Daisy raised a devastating eyebrow. 'Did we really, Mr String? I seem to have forgotten all about it. Very silly of me. I *am* sorry.'

'You mean you're staying with 'im?' Stringy's accent was slipping.

'Well, you see, we're very old friends, aren't we?' She smiled at me, and stroked my hand.

'Of course,' I said.

'Makes yer sick,' said Stringy and retreated.

'I can't stand greasy hair,' Daisy murmured, withdrawing her hand. I did a surreptitious check on mine. Dry as a bone.

Daisy could do three things well when I knew her. (Apart from making you feel uncomfortable.) She could talk, drink and dance. The first two she did well, the third brilliantly. We were still jiving in those days in Manchester, and the clever boys were swinging their wretched girls all over the place, even across their shoulders, while they themselves moved as little as possible. I thought I knew roughly how to dance before I met her, but Daisy managed somehow to make me forget everything I had ever learned and then teach me exactly how to move – without my realizing what was happening. Then when the music changed to something slower she slipped in closer and left the guiding to me, as if I had been doing it the whole time. Very skilful it was. I wonder if she kept it up?

In between (it was always Daisy who led the way back to our table) she probed delicately and relentlessly into every aspect of my life, my work, my background; my friends, foibles and future. She didn't shoot questions or demand answers, she simply nudged me forward every now and then, or gently prevented me from pursuing the odd red herring. I remember waxing eloquent and effusive and loving every minute of it.

She had progressed down her list as far as a Screwdriver without appearing to feel any effect, when finally she leaned back in her chair and smiled. Rather like a surgeon who has performed a difficult operation with complete success.

'I like you,' she said. 'Did you know that?'

'Well – no, I don't think I did.'

'That's nice. Do you like me?'

'I think you're great.'

'Why?' asked Daisy.

I couldn't really think of anything in particular, so rather weakly I said, 'Because you're different, I suppose.'

Daisy smiled again. 'I'm not really,' she said. 'I would say that you're more different than I am. I'm just a very ordinary girl doing her best to get somewhere. The thing about me is I don't need any help from anyone, really. But there are some people who are useful, don't you think? That's why I took the job at the factory. I thought I could get Macdonald to give me a sort of running course on business if I picked up enough hints. Actually all I do is take down a few letters and fend him off when he tries to seduce me – which he does occasionally. I suppose I'll have to stop being a virgin soon. It doesn't seem to be doing much good. But sex is so boring, don't you think? People talk about it the whole time as if it was the only important thing there is. I could do without it altogether. Well I have done so far, but then I'm only seventeen. I feel far older – about twenty-five I should think. What would you say?'

'Seventeen,' I said rashly.

'What on earth do you mean? I'm far more able to take care of myself than any of the girls I meet. Specially the ones with clinging boy-friends and one problem after another.'

'I think that's what you need.'

'Rubbish.'

'Have another drink.'

'No,' said Daisy unsteadily. 'I think I'm going to be sick. Let's go.'

Daisy wasn't sick, but she did fall asleep in my car as I drove back to my flat. There was obviously no question of our sharing a bed, and I couldn't find out where she lived. So when we got back I slept on my sofa, Daisy passed out in my bed. I lay awake for a long time, feeling immensely protective towards her, and sketching out a grand and complicated plan which entailed me arriving in Cambridge with her and demanding suitable accommodation. 'Our love is bigger than your petty bourgeois traditions. I don't care if Henry VIII was the last man to take a woman into Trinity Hall after midnight, there are times when the cobwebs have to be ripped down. Stand aside I tell you. . . .'

Privacy is not one of the hallmarks of factory life. Especially if you happen to arrive two hours late for work with a smudged and tangled girl beside you. Daisy and I had woken disastrously late, tumbled into the car and driven at top speed out to Lemgard's. We were too flustered to think of walking in separately, and appearances didn't suggest that we had spent the night apart and asleep.

Mick was in towering form.

'Jesus God, you motherless arsehole!' he shouted at me. 'How in heaven's name is a man supposed to run a decent Christian canning-line when he's surrounded by drunken whoring sons of the devil who don't know an honest day's work when they see one, and wouldn't know what to do with it if they did. I'm docking half a day's pay, Mister, from your God-forsaken packet.'

For once I was not impressed.

'You can stuff it up your arse for all I care,' I said calmly as I reached for the handle.

Johnny told me later that Mick went chalk-white and for once couldn't find words to fit the situation. I wasn't looking. I was packing those cans with an ease and grace I had never achieved before. Open – push – pull – push – pull – rock back – twist – drop – open – push – pull . . . it was a new sort of dance, a rich and satisfying ritual. I was happy.

On Doreen and Lorrayne the double-effect of me arriving at the factory with a girl who not only turned out to be real, but who had clearly had 'a rough time', was sensational.

There was a new respect – almost awe – in their voices as they taxed me during the first tea-break.

'What happened, then?' said Doreen. 'Did you make the first move, or was it her?'

'I bet she was asking for it,' said Lorrayne enviously.

But the roles were reversed now. I tapped the front of Lorrayne's coat. 'She 'ad a couple on her that makes you look like a walking matchstick,' I said, 'but, of course – ' and I squeezed Doren's sizeable bosom, 'you can't 'ave too much of a good thing.'

They flounced off with pained looks.

Vulgar behaviour, but satisfactory at the time. Looking back I realize I could never have talked like that if it hadn't been for Daisy. All my thoughts were revolving around her, and the marvellous things we were going to do together. Everything else I did was absent-minded and unreal, a by-product of my new obsession with Daisy.

Which doesn't explain why I tumbled Doreen in the box-room.

Twice a day I ran out of cardboard boxes. I used to time it carefully, so that I came to the end of the pile exactly half-way between two tea-breaks thus giving myself a reasonably idle period just when I needed it most. I would amble past the canning machine and the cooling-vats towards the box-room which lay off a corridor at the back of the factory. It was a good fifteen-minute trip there and back, and for some reason no one had noticed that it seemed to have an adverse effect on productivity.

That day I ran out at five past three. I pressed the stop-button and began my leisurely trek, collecting a trolley on the way. The box-room was a tall, dusty place, stacked high with cardboard and virgin tin-cans. There were usually one or two skiving workers playing cards in a corner, but that afternoon it was empty, and I began piling the boxes onto my trolley, without pausing, as I usually did, for a comfortable cigarette. Then, behind me the door creaked open.

'Well, look 'oo we've got to ourselves today,' said Lorrayne, standing, grinning, in the doorway.

'Mr Casanova 'imself.' Doreen was right behind her.

There was something distinctly predatory about them (two

she-lions temporarily without a mate) as they slunk into the room, shutting the door behind them. But I was still riding high on my new-found confidence.

'All words, no action, that's the trouble with you two,' I replied, continuing to pile the boxes with a nonchalance that might, I admit, have been artificial.

'Wouldn't mind a bit of action with you, pet.' Doreen's generous breasts brushed my left ear.

'Keep 'em buttoned up, you'll over-balance,' I said.

' 'E's got a tongue in 'im 'asn't 'e?' said Lorrayne. 'Wonder wot else 'e's kept 'idden away from us.'

'Nothing that would interest you,' I was beginning to get a prickly feeling up my back.

'Ooh, don't be modest,' giggled Doreen. 'We'll be the judge of that.'

She was standing in front of me by now, one hand on a jutting hip, overalls loosely tied, and I made my big mistake. Trying to regain the advantage I leant forward cunningly and tugged her belt. It came away in my hand. Doreen gave a little scream, stepped back and tripped over a pile of cans. As she fell her white coat flapped wide open revealing the regulation black lace bra and pants to match. Nothing else, unless you count the shoes. I took in the rest at a glance as Doreen disappeared into a pile of brown paper, pulling a neat stack of cardboard and about a gross of cans with her. Two long white legs waved in the air.

Things might still have been all right if Lorrayne hadn't joined in. Laughing helplessly she shoved me hard in the small of the back. 'Don't keep a lady waiting, will yer,' she said. I pitched forward, spreadeagled, on top of Doreen. A rich smell of scent mingled with the dust as I reached out for support. 'This way, pet,' whispered Doreen, and grabbed my hand, pulling it firmly round behind her back. She rolled over on top of me, dislodging a pile of labels in mint condition, and began undoing buttons – there are sixteen of them on the standard overalls – with a speed which dazed me.

'Just a min – ' I began, but Doreen's lips smothered the words, and her left hand snaked down between my legs. 'Just relax, pet,' she breathed, tucking a thumb into the crutch of my trousers and tearing them off down to the knee. 'Why

E

don't you 'old on 'ere,' and my hand was round a cold white buttock as her own pants disappeared down her legs. My mouth met a nipple, and somehow (somehow?) latched on. Fingernails dug into my shoulder-blade. Slowly the movements became rhythmic, rather than flurried, purposeful, not haphazard. The solid weight of her hips pressed into mine and the cardboard shifted gently beneath us.

'This is rape,' I murmured.

At what stage did Daisy come into the room?

She may have been there from the beginning, for all I know, watching the whole grotesque performance. She may only have seen the last heavings and sighings. What she cannot have failed to see was me, splayed out amidst tin cans and brown paper, pinioned by the firm shoulders and thighs of Doreen. I know, because I saw her as I peered over the horizon of Doreen's left arm. She was standing in the doorway, looking at the scene through half-closed eyes. As I tried to scramble out, she turned and disappeared down the corridor.

'Excuse me a minute,' I said, heaving Doreen aside.

' 'Ere, give a girl a chance,' she shouted, and grabbed me by the ankle. 'Daisy – ' I cried as I fell forward, catching my chin a nasty crack on an empty can of Garden Delicious.

'Better get yer trousers on,' said Lorrayne, who had watched the whole scene, flushed with excitement. I scrabbled feverishly round my feet, got one leg into a trouser-leg and made for the door. But Daisy had gone. I sat down, exhausted and prayed for the floor to open up and swallow me in a bottomless chasm.

Doreen was trying to trap an errant breast and squeeze it into her bra. 'Sod,' she said. 'Missed me bloody climax.'

The whole thing seemed to have lasted a few seconds. In fact it had taken twenty-nine minutes and thirty seconds as Mick informed me savagely when I got back. He handed me my cards and told me to pick up the rest of my pay in the cash-room.

I calculated that Daisy would be leaving in half an hour, and posted myself outside the gates. But it was only five minutes later that she appeared, swinging her handbag.

'What's happened?' I said. 'Are you leaving the job?'

She walked on. It was almost dark so I couldn't make out her expression.

'You're not going because of me,' I pleaded, catching up with her.

'Good heavens no,' said Daisy coldly. 'Why on earth should I do that?'

'Look, I must try and explain what happened.'

'Why?'

'Well, because it must have been an awful shock for you.'

'Not at all,' said Daisy. 'It was rather funny, actually. She must have been quite a weight.'

'What are you going to do now?' I was desperately trying to delay her.

'I haven't thought about it yet. What do you suggest?'

'Well,' I said, trying to keep my voice steady. 'You could come with me. I thought I'd go down to Cambridge tonight.'

She stopped and looked at me. Once again her eyes were narrowed. 'I'm afraid that's not really possible. You see I've got rather more important things to do.'

She turned and crossed the road.

On the other side was a beige Hillman car, one of the lumpy 1950 models. A man was standing beside it. As Daisy approached he opened the door for her and the car-light glinted on a greasy head of hair. It was Mr String – pimples, prospects and all. He saw me, grinned triumphantly and got into the car.

Daisy was looking straight ahead. She didn't suit a Hillman, somehow.

YWCA
Euston
January, 1955

DEAREST REG,

Well here I am in London my dear. I'm still working as a secretary which needless to say I hate loathe despise and detest. I think my fingers must be abnormally sensitive and delicate or something, anyway I have great trouble in pressing down the keys of the typewriter hard enough to make the bloody thing write and I'm covered in blisters which is *agony*. They tried me on an electric one but I didn't seem to be able to manage that either, it just ran away with me, too terrifying. And I can never read my own shorthand back which is frightfully embarrassing, obviously I'm not cut out for this type of work. Just discovered Scott Fitzgerald – isn't *The Great Gatsby* the most moving thing you've ever read? The girl in it is called Daisy like me and she's *really glamorous*.

Write, write, WRITE!
LOVE DAISY

PS I'm going to give up working, everything, and just be me. To think I once thought of being married to a pea canning executive in Manchester. Reg, on no account ever tell anyone that. Perhaps I won't be me I'll be a waitress first.

Highbury
May, 1955

DEAREST REG,

Nothing much has been happening. I went to the Gargoyle last night but somehow the magic had gone. Things have been rather ups and downsy since I moved in with Jenny but now have finally resolved themselves into a pretty monotonous even keel. Jenny's new lover arrived romantically sunburnt from Spain with masses of bullfight posters and a large bottle of Anis (of which they kindly gave us two drinks each and then kept the bottle in their bedroom) but after only one night they were asked to leave by Tony who suddenly realized he MINDED. Really! And so they've gone to live on somebody's barge and Jenny is *ever* so pleased and Tony is sulking and I'm on my own and you know what I'm like on my own. It means I'll have to go out and find another job. I've just finished *Goodbye to Berlin,* don't you adore Sally Bowles? God, how that man understands women!

All my love, Reg, do write and cheer me up,

DAISY

XXOOXX

Highbury
September, 1955

DEAREST REG,

I'm tremendously in love with somebody – at least I think I am but it may only be because he lived in Paris for so long and he has a lovely flat by the river with lots of marvellous Billie Holliday records and bottles of drink and is called Alistair and is rather romantic looking and so on – anyway it will come to nothing because nothing ever seems to anyway – really it's depressing I'm always doing it, falling in love with people who aren't with me – then they are and by that time I hate them rather – *also* I can never fall in love with somebody if they are in love with me first – is this psychopathic??? It never leads anywhere. I always seem to attract such wet men. But *also* I hate not being in love with someone, just anybody. When I'm not I go around searching madly for my one big great and true romance – then it all starts all over again. I suppose it's just LIFE but it isn't because look at Jenny who's madly happy adoring Jim and vice versa – oh such a dilemma. I had a letter from Tony today and in it was a present, a cheque for ten quid, I felt so awful, I mean a bitch you know, and then immediately wondered if I could add another nought on without anyone noticing. I woke up with pink-eye yesterday but it disappeared after lunch. If you don't write soon (I don't care what about) I'll throw in the sponge. I'm in the middle of *Down and Out in London and Paris* – Orwell. Have you heard of him?

Love and kisses,

DAISY

XXOOXX

5

Philip's story

I slept four or five times a week, when I was at Charrington's, with a relentlessly clean girl. What moved me about her most was that she had *two* flannels. It became unthinkable to hurt her because I was so used to watching as she got ready for bed in a frame of light. My room in Abingdon Road had mock Tudor panelling all round it, and one panel opened to reveal the wash-basin.

She patted her face and ears dry. After that she picked the second flannel up to wash between her legs – looking totally unattractive from behind with her shoulders drooped and the knobs sticking out in her back. Late at night, when I saw her feel under herself like that, and heard the flannel's slouching noise in her hairs, something always hurt and shifted inexplicably in my heart. I'm practically in tears thinking about it now. In my mind she's always brushed ready for bed, waiting to be kissed. No sweet picture like that remains of the other dreadful sow, Daisy.

When I think of *her* I blush and feel insulted. I can remember the awful, physical weight of her apathy towards me. I keep thinking she might have become radiant about me instead, which was what I longed for, if I hadn't worn woolly gauntlets and a waistcoat. Did I love her? Even now I have to look away from the kind of Daisy girl one sees sometimes from a car. Yet it's still far easier to banish thoughts of Daisy Smuten than of that first sweet, clean girl's second flannel.

No one's perfect: the Second Flannel was an expert in dry-sob hysterics, and always ill. She wanted to get engaged. I did not. 'You are *foul,*' she repeated, pronouncing it 'fawl', 'you 'eally are.' She had difficulty with her Rs. 'You don't want any 'esponsibilities at all, do you? You 'eally don't.' She came from a lah-di-dah family in Bexhill and her best friend was the daughter of a highly-placed executive in British Railways Catering.

For about the first week after it ended, when her mother and father and aunt and uncle and sister took her back home in that Austin Princess, I had a powerfully good time. In particular it was a treat to be able to go to sleep without cleaning my teeth; straight to sleep without hands slippery with Oil of Ulay grabbing me directly the light in the wash-basin panel clicked out.

I was interested, rather than upset, by the plum-dark coloured flush that steals over one after a regular partner's removal; when one goes, in theory, back to wanking. It was wonderful to feel free to spend all my salary and dividend cheques in accumulating, if I chose, a richness of non-iron shirts. I cried a little, of course: at the recollection of her washing between her legs, even at the one of a late-night fart she had accidentally produced, lying in bed by herself while I sat up listening to the Jack Jackson Show. It seemed to have a touching and innocent quality – the little fart I mean. However, that was nothing to the liberation of waking up by myself in my own bed, flinging my legs out to cool places that had always been occupied before, getting up to find that the bed scarcely needed making.

But I hadn't realized how much two years with the Second Flannel had altered me. It was only when I was trying on the first of my new non-iron shirts that I saw how fat she had made me. A clamorous but fastidious eater she either demanded to be taken out, or else she cooked me suppers at her bedsitter: these as a rule consisted of plates of rice and mince, absurdly overloaded, the rice dotting everywhere, accompanied by the dry, racking sobs that always seemed to occur around seven fifteen, during Radio Newsreel, when my disdain for any responsibility came to a greatness.

The thing I chiefly remember at the moment of first seeing Daisy Smuten is the coal-grit and wildly fashionable taste of black coffee. To lose more weight I was living on it almost entirely: small, transparent cuplets which seemed the more romantic and acceptable as they cost up to two shillings each in an espresso bar. There were three around Kensington High Street – La Fiesta, the CariBou and another which had clearly given trouble and disagreement to some Neapolitan committee as it was called Très Etoiles. In the evenings I sat in one or other of them, reading War paperbacks, hoping to be mistaken for a student with a secret sorrow; and finally I went only to the CariBou. One reason was that it sold the least food of the three, just a thing called a Cheese Toasty which I felt I could eat sometimes and not violate my diet.

The fascination that these coffee-bars held for people like me was based mainly on a rumour that, although owned by the fat and the foreign, they were actually staffed by the daughters of the rich and titled, and that was the other reason for going to the CariBou exclusively. The serving there, within reason, was done by a girl who looked about my age – twenty-three. She had a way of cocking her head so that one end of hair touched her mouth and the other hung free. I must have stared at her for hours, for weeks, as she palmed and leaned on and drew down those machine-handles. At first, before I fell in love with her, I rather disliked her. She seemed lazy and exaggeratedly long suffering. Once, when several people including myself were waiting to be served, she just lounged at the back of the imitation pine counter eating a pear; holding it the wrong way up to eat it.

I nicknamed her, and remember her as Dandini (some words and phrases I cannot bring myself to say, like Fullers' Candy Kisses and Daisy Smuten). Suddenly in the CariBou I found myself following her every movement, wondering what the soft parts of her legs felt like and if she had any brothers or sisters, quivering about her so much that all vestiges of desire for food, even a Cheese Toasty, vanished. I drank more and more coffee for her, watching her through the brown fogs of the see-through cup as I finished the dregs. I wanted to take her out and dazzle her with a knowledge of the theatre: at the same time it was impossible to speak to her now that we had gone so long without speaking more than the terse formality of a Cheese Toasty. And I couldn't ask her in the evening because the CariBou was always full. It was full of hoofbeats as much as anything. She liked Frankie Laine's record 'Gunfight at OK Corral' and played it endlessly thanks to some key-concession she had on the jukebox.

One day I pretended to be ill. I rolled about in bed all morning biting a hangnail; then I got washed and shaved at four thirty in the afternoon and walked round to the CariBou breathless with adoration, an execution-day feeling, and lack of proper food. The jukebox was dark: the only customers were two old and practically bald women in pastel blue Pakamacs, holding on their knees tall drycleaning bags. Their work-worn fingers played endlessly with the folded rims of the bags; their cigarette cork tips, with elongations of ash, were all that remained in their mouths.

Dandini was dressed all in one colour, blue, with the buttons of her woolly down the back, a round-necked woolly that suited the rather sulky fulness of her face, the short ends of hair touching her cheeks. As I got ready my question through waxy lips, all I could see were the women's tongues cough-hanging over the tops of their drycleaning bags. She had her back to me already. The smell of my Cheese Toasty seemed to tear at my heart and lungs.

'Exc . . . um . . . USE me, would you like to er go out with me . . . er some . . . ?' I began to cough as well.

The Second Flannel wasn't just clean, she was *crisp*. In fact I think I was put off her finally by the spotlessly white bunchings of underslip that always crowded between her knees when she sat down. Another thing about her that touched me was her way of folding everything up carefully before she washed: the great expanse, the glacier of stiff petticoat laid on the chair and everything else resting on it, stockings laid down it so that their feet touched the floor. When I took her in my arms, fully dressed, there was always a sound like tearing newspapers.

The quality about Dandini (Daisy) that first attracted me I can only describe in a phrase I read in one of the Second Flannel's Georgette Heyer books – 'uncorseted grace'. Not that she was in any general way graceful. She managed – especially when signifying irritation with a customer at the CariBou – to take enormous strides yet shuffle her feet at the same time. But there was a limpness about her, a sort of agile referee quality accentuated by her blue clothes and the buttons down her back. In my arms she seemed to yield, bend – a welcome change from the Second Flannel's crackling corselette – and she had a generous mouth, I decided. In fact the first time I kissed her, it opened so abruptly and widely that I thought I had put my whole head in it.

The foregoing evening hadn't been memorable. Because she worked in a coffee-bar, this for some reason had to make her a connoisseuse of coffee-bars. When I called at the Cari-Bou for her she said, 'Oh let's go to the Two I's,' and made a game of leading me off there by my scarf; a performance which led me to suspect that she was younger than I had thought. She must have been just twenty.

We went in my car (about which she offered no comment at all) to a place that seemed constructed of boards, like a sale of work stall. Whereas the CariBou's walls were decorated with silhouettes of guitars and sombreros, this famed cockpit was done out in silhouettes of guitars and treble and bass clefs and of girls with ponytails free-falling in skirts as full as the Second Flannel's used to be. Dandini wore the same blue woolly, back to front, and jeans and a short white duffle coat which she refused to take off. She sat ignoring me, and jigged around, sending warm glances towards a guitarist in the Worried Men Skiffle Group who were appearing. It was impossible in that noise to talk to her. I felt for the first time, but not the last, that my conversation, my autobiographical details and any funny little stories I knew were all corked up inside me. Even if she could hear, she wouldn't be interested.

I was also anxious to be told I looked smart. I had had a shampoo and second shave for her, and put on my new bronze lovat jacket and Royal Artillery tie, hoping she would ask me what it stood for, and also Grandfather Wizard's heavy gold watch and chain. All that happened was that I got hot, smelling my own BO and shave lotion in the coffee-bar; all she said was: 'Do you always go to Burton's?'

'It was from Weaver-to-Wearer.'

Then, in the hallway of a house in a yellow-lamp street in Highbury (I think) I found my head in her mouth. I felt somewhat embarrassed at having missed the decent preliminaries, the first intertwining of fingers and that sort of thing. I searched in my memory for the correct thing to do next and realized it was to ask to be invited upstairs for coffee. I suspect I blenched. Coffee! I had done nothing for weeks but drink coffee; with coffee I had made a coal-hole of my throat. So instead of asking to be given coffee I put my head in her mouth again and she received it, opening her jaws in a routine manner, her eyes remaining open, as if I was the dentist and knew best.

One soon tires of that sort of thing. I gave up secret-sighing and moving myself against her uncorseted grace. As I had scarcely spoken a word to her, there was then an awkward silence. I got the impression she was looking above my head, so I put it in her mouth. She continued to allow this. From time to time she appeared to come to life and nipped painfully the end of my tongue and the soft, gumboil areas; and when this hurt particularly, I got annoyed and pressed hard against her, and was amazed to feel her index finger touch my fly. 'Ssshhh,' she said. In the end I felt hot, hungry and ashamed. I could also feel my autobiography pressing to get out and the new white collar burning my neck. Suddenly she bit my cheek, just below one eye and it shocked me so much I almost clouted her.

I almost clouted her again as she sat eating mushrooms on toast another night in the Très Etoiles. I like women who eat shyly, stealing a glance at you over the tops of their wine-glasses. Dandini went at the hard, black parts of the toast using her knife and fork as if driving a team. She chewed with her mouth open. Spars of toast went with her conversation. She sipped coffee with her mouth full. If my autobiography was corked securely, hers wasn't. She gave shrill cackles at her own escapades, and showed off plenty more toast. She told me amusing things about boarding school (which I now believe must have been lies) and about a week she had spent misguidedly training at Helena Rubinstein's to be a beautician.

'I was tribe leader at school. When you left, the amount of good you'd contributed to the school was reckoned in the amount of clapping you got. I had to bribe my friends to clap.

"Aha Dezi," Header used to say, the old bag, "Vous êtes bêtise. Bêt-*eez*."'

My autobiography still unused, I wondered why she'd ever agreed to go out with me at all. It was peculiar to think of the alacrity with which she accepted – 'Oh, I'd *love* to,' with a hoarse intonation on 'love' as if she was recovering from crying. 'Where should we go?' We toured coffee-bars.

'You see they always said to offer a client an eye-bath after the facial and dewhiskering. When I offered it to this silly old cow she said "Oh thank you very much dear" and drank the bloody Optrex straight off.'

'This great dobble of burning wax, *right* in her hair. Anyway I knew she was going to stay asleep for at least another half an hour, the old bag, so I tried to undo her hair but it was all in – ugh – coils and coils and . . .'

I sat and felt like a great hulking, blushing dolt and ploughboy. I was receiving the rebuff that should have come in the CariBou that afternoon in front of the two old dry cleaning bags, but which had been delayed. Dandini sat with her elbows on the pink formica, cupping her face in her hands, her jaws moving her wrists as she talked and talked. I put my chin in my hands as well, to be equally soulful, so that our forearms touched as in a Sicilian feat of strength. I then tried to hook one of my little fingers in one of hers: she slid her hand away. As she did so a tomato sauce dispenser in the shape of a tomato fell over.

'I'm sorry.'

'That's okay,' she said, and picked up the blackest crust in her fingers, to gnaw.

'I didn't mean to offend. . . .'

'Oh don't get all worried, just because I won't hold little fingers.'

'I'm not. I just mean. . . .'

'I'm just rather unconventional,' she said; and I suddenly realized the independent 'I's' that began each set of our remarks, never 'you'.

By the time we got back to Highbury I was even looking forward slightly to going away by myself and, by supreme willpower, getting over her. When she said crisply, 'Well, don't stand down in the cold Mr Man,' I seriously considered striding off into the yellow night light. I had still told her nothing about myself. She had still not asked me anything about myself. I thought I would prefer to sit up in my own bed, read Forester or Henty and eat chocolate.

At the top of the first flight of stairs she turned round and I put my head in her mouth: she went into the old routine of nipping my tongue and gums but at the same time she seemed to want to make herself small in my arms, a gesture that recalled, very strongly, the Second Flannel. I also realized that I had misjudged the landlord of the house in thinking that his hallway smelled of corned beef and sauce: it was her hair.

We climbed a long way to a low landing with a skylight. She opened a door which had an oval pane of glass set in it like the entrance to a good class suburban home. On the inside of this she walked away and round a sharp bend in the dim, cream-painted hall. Having expected to put my head in her mouth again, I was furious and walked thunderously into the nearest room, which was bathed in the yellow light from the street. I knelt, for no accountable reason, to examine a record player of a sort so cheap and tiny that an LP overhangs it as a pancake does a saucer. Then I found a standard lamp, switched it on and looked into a bedroom off the lounge. In the roof-shape of light I glimpsed a plunder of dresses, coats, handbags and shoes hanging on and off a divan: there was the vague sour smell of a female's summer bodice, nicely matured as this was October.

I walked round the same bend that she had, not able to find the light, and found myself looking through a kitchenette, through the window at the night-spangling and interlaced lights of a power-station, and then at a closed door I took to be Dandini's. I retired round the corner, waited a moment, then looked again. Finally when nerves and a faint thudding of pipes in other flats had made me desperately urgent to pee, I knocked on the door that must have been hers.

It was a tiny room, bathed in a fierce circle of light from a one-bar electric fire of a kind I associate with headmasters' studies or the War. The firelight showed up her clothes on the floor. She was sitting up in a small bed, holding her knees, her hair falling sideways as it always did, and she was wearing something with generously cut sleeves. 'I'm sorry,' she said, formally, 'I just *had* to come and get into my basket.'

Uncertain really of what to say, feeling only the heat of the fire and the weight of the pee and my autobiography, I sat close to her on the bed and put my head in her mouth a few times. As she appeared not to expect me to leave I finally said, 'I'm going to come in next to you': she, for a reason I've never discovered, replied 'bloody hypocrite'.

I believe I've mentioned already how smartly, after a regular partner's removal, one reverts to the basest kind of uncoordinated adolescence; my behaviour over the tomato sauce dispenser in the Très Etoiles, the pressure of my unspoken autobiographical details both prove this, so does the fact that I was now as nervous (in the words of the Second Flannel's Georgette Heyer again) as a boy with his first whore. I posted myself into that ferociously tightly-tucked bed having taken off only my Royal Artillery tie, jacket, waistcoat and shoes.

She closed readily enough with me; she already felt boiling hot. I also happened to be wearing cavalry twill trousers as thick as cylinders. When she threw one heat-damp leg across mine, they were at once so warm that I could scarcely feel them: I fought my head and shoulders out of the bedclothes to find air, and it was singed by the smell of the electric fire. Engulfed by all this misery, burnt and close-fitting, I realized my hand had settled on her behind, moulding it through a thick, ribbed garment. If only there had been time to marvel: at its size, its elevation, its lovely proportion, its probable capacity, when she was on her feet, to balance a tea-tray. But my mind, my nostrils, were full of sweating legs, the smell of corned beef and sauce from her hair, of burnt oxygen, old blanket material and rubber: all I could feel were the sides of the bed that wouldn't come untucked and a shameful, overweighted tiny whistle deep down in my pants needing, as much as every other portion of my distressed frame did – air.

I sat on the bed on the cold side of the bull terrier electric fire, my head in my hands. It was not altogether a theatrical gesture. I had just finished reading Colin Wilson's

Encyclopedia of Murder in which he said that the murderer John Reginald Halliday Christie had in his youth been nicknamed Reggie No Dick and that was what turned him. I could, therefore, sense the beginnings in me of a mass murderer, helped by the spreading patches under my arms and along my underpant rims and by her refusal even to get out of bed. She leaned and switched on a bedside light, a bulb so enormously strong that it had sucked holes in the shade's plastic woven material, and then she pulled a folder of snapshots onto the bedspread in front of her, and looked fondly at them, leaning on one elbow, one end of hair touching her mouth, the other hanging loose.

There was also, on her bedside table, a plate and eggcup with an old shell in it.

I looked through my fingers at her jeans on the floor: my head was now in my hands with such intensity that I could feel a species of arthritic cramp in my wrists. Then her voice, rich and toneless, said: 'It's all right.'

The heat *was* receding a little.

'It's easy to say . . .'

'Come on,' she said in a lacrosse teacher's encouraging voice.

'What?'

'I said, come on. Don't sit there all worried.'

'I get *so*. . . .'

'Come *on*.'

'But can't . . .'

'Come on.'

She kept looking at her snapshots and saying 'come on'.

'Look, it's easy for you to get. . . .'

'Come on.'

I wrenched the bedroom door open, scarcely noticing that its handle was all sticky (and, I later discovered, sweet to the taste). I glared at her, then looked appealingly at her, then looked forlornly at her: she went on examining her snapshots, her wrists made graceful by the wide-cut sleeves of the blue garment she wore.

Eventually she looked up.

'*Come* on.'

I pulled the string of the bathroom light much too violently, keeping my eyes half closed to avoid seeing myself in a mirror. Then I fully opened them. If my description of that bathroom appears too much rehearsed, too full of military metaphor, that is because I've often got a laugh in company with the details, and because G. A. Henty and Forester are my favourite authors (as I had been waiting to tell her).

It was painted cream, with black and white checked lino, but over-all lay a fine dust that any abrupt movement, even the pulling of the light-string too hard, seemed to stir into the air; a dust compounded as much of talcum powder as of neglect, and therefore suggesting in its odour nothing so much as a dead baby. It lay around the rim of the bath, on the top of the Baghdad-shaped laundry basket, in dunes on the glass shelf above the washbasin and in the crevices of the piece of wooden trellis that someone, in an effort to make the bathroom resemble that of a hacienda, had placed unsteadily between the basin and the bath.

On this trellis, also covered in dead baby dust, hung a pair of black knickers. I believe they were not Dandini's own; they were too large and copious with lace; possibly they belonged to a tenant before her. They gave the impression of having a *right* to the trellis. They hung there like the black flag of the Mahdi above Khartoum.

In the dust, everywhere – on the bath-edge, on the basin above a pack ice of soaking underclothes – were little petrified blades of soap, little chips so cracked and hard white that they seemed meant to exercise your budgie's beak: they were dust dry and the striped flannel that lay on the edge of the bath under the Ascot had the texture of a successful omelette. Next to the flannel lay a Gillette razor, with elegant whiskers caught in it, and next to that stood a jar of Crosse and Blackwell pickled walnuts.

The bath itself had a brown and grey flaking ring round it. Now, I'm perfectly human. I myself dislike cleaning out baths. I think that one day Walt Disney will make a film called Ring Around the Bath. What I was totally unprepared to see, much lower than the ring of dirt, was a big, crispy, frilly wet balloon mass, lying in a few centimetres of cold water; in fact it astonished me so much that I, forgetting my role as a mortally wounded strong man, called out: 'What on earth's this thing in the bath?'

'That's my charley,' she called back through the thin wall. '*Charley*. My petticoat. I soak it in sugar and water to stiffen it.'

I thought gloomily that I could do with some sugar and water, and crossed to the pedestal, my eyes half shut again, because the naked bulb in the bathroom was as severe as in her bedside lamp. I kept my eye fixed on my own fountain; it seemed to be the only thing I could be sure of, but I was wrong. I looked away and had to look back again. *It* was down below. I pulled the lever, the water swelled and *It* remained. I pulled the lever and *It* rode back still on half a tide, there it was again. There, with no water left in the tank, *It* was, riding gently at anchor. A long way down, locked in its secret fjord, a stately and immaculate pocket battleship, pure white but for the stain of recent action; the Bismarck run to earth by my seaplane at last.

I didn't walk out never to return. I went back at about half-past eight three evenings later: the door was ajar to the flat but Dandini wasn't there.

She had had a party the night before, or possibly the night before that. Circular basketwork chairs were over-turned to support the piles of mixed rubbish that rose from the fluffy living room rug at the precise angle of coal-slides: bent cork-tips huddled inside Crown bottle tops and on one of the arms of the sofa a banana skin lay in the shape of a fast-moving squid. The hall smelled of a badly maintained corridor to a pub Gents': old wood and beer and urine together, and cigarettes stubbed into orange peel. In the kitchen with the view of the power-station, the fridge door stood open, dripping on the blackened green-fleck linoleum with the tears in it: the fridge itself was stacked with old newspapers, magazines and pattern books.

Even after all this I still thought I might leave a note for her – enigmatic, perfectly-phrased, sorrowing manfully – and so I went into her bedroom, not surprised to find the bed a pulled tangle of old blue-stitched and Utility marked blankets. But as a conjurer of dirty objects she had quite surpassed herself. Another plate, eggcup and old shell stood by the first on the bedside table. When I knelt to try to retrieve a stub of pencil I'd seen behind the headboard, there was another complete eggshell set under the bed, with dark woolly lumps all over it.

Nola Churchill, to whom I laid siege next, was beefy and wore pink jumpers and matching cardigans (but grey pleated skirts) and a crucifix and was, moreover, full of moral phrases like 'my bucket's got a handle to it' if I ever neglected to address her by her Christian name: but I'm grateful to Nola Churchill for letting me pour my life story out to her.

She was, however, cagey of the flesh. We had this sort of conversation. ' 'Lo.' 'Nola.' 'Yes.' 'Nola dear, would you like to come and see *Yeild to the Night* tomorrow?' What as?' 'What *as*?' 'I mean, do you mean as a *friend*?' It wasn't surprising that after a little of Nola Churchill's company, 'uncorseted grace' seemed a wisp of a dream of a vanished wonder and even the accumulation of eggshells a pardonable and girlish eccentricity.

Dandini had gone from the CariBou: an icy-creamy voice, raised above Gunfight at OK Corral, told me she had taken a job in the kitchens of an important hotel – the only one I'd ever been to, as it happened: there was a sales conference there. This was why I could put on a show when I walked into its onyx vestibule and made what I see now was the appalling gaffe of asking for Dandini – asking for Miss Smuten – at the main reception desk. It seemed to take all the bottle-green men there by surprise, however, and one of them was detailed to take me through the kitchens, which one entered through a disordered banqueting room and around a screen.

Smelling hot, sour gravies, browning batter and poultry skin on enamel trays, I was guided past endless open metal levels over which tall hats bent to examine stock bones jumping and mangling about in cauldrons, or else they struggled along holding, with their stomachs thrust against them to steady, trays of purple-coloured small fowls or pieces of ham, tightly rolled and arranged with the symmetry of cars in a park. There was a low aluminium roof in which the tall hats were perfectly reflected, upside down: blinded for a moment by a scalding of steam, then clear again, tall hats balancing other attentive tall hats on their crowns, and then all mugged over again by the hot gasps of the cooking.

Then we walked into a high ceilinged room, much quieter but still smelling of chicken skin and enamel. It was occupied by one tall hat only, a man who even from that distance smelt like a ferret's cage. He had flaky hands, and moved them about among glass dishes of trifle and cream and hundreds and thousands. He was shaping a brown lump the colour of house pebbledashing and shooting glances as he did so at a tray of little balls of meringue. As I passed he looked up, smiled and said obligingly, 'profiteroles'.

Finally we got to a tiny room off a corridor hung with dishtowels over radiators, where the green porter left me. All that the room contained was a black sink from which the pipes ascended past a window through which you could see people's feet. Dandini was here, talking to a black-haired youth of whom I was at once insanely, unspeakably jealous. 'Dino,' she said, pronouncing it 'Din-ew', 'Go on and do it for Gawd's sake. You know they only check coats, carriers and duffle bags.' With that she impatiently grabbed something, whipped off his hat – half a tall hat – placed a piece of meat on his head and put the hat back: he darted gratefully out of the room.

'It's up to us to nick the odd thing,' she said. 'It's expected.'

Then she started to laugh. But it was in a different way to the chortles through toast crusts at her own exploits; it was now a ripple of wet and gleeful laughter, quite calculated, obviously about me. She tried to stop herself. 'I'm sorry – really. Don't take any notice.' Then she produced another ripple. 'I'm sorry . . . it's just that. . . .'

'*What!*'

'We're all down here wrapped up in dirty teatowels, right in the bowels of the earth, especially when Dino de Felice lets off, and then you come in, *you* come in. . . .'

My ears were boiling over.

She spat on the visible air with laughter as she said, 'Young Conservative' and then she started to laugh *and* cough. She came up to me and put the uncorseted grace against me in the usual way, still trying not to laugh: I nevertheless put my head in her mouth, into a cathedral of gummy laughter at my own expense.

'I left there because I couldn't stand Aldo and his little remarks,' she said. I'd asked her an earnest question about the CariBou to try to make her be serious.

'Well, in that case, can I . . .'

'I don't mind,' she interrupted. To stop herself rippling again she turned round to the ancient sink and began to struggle to wash something, the ends of her hair moving as she worked on the crusty object in the black water. I asked her another earnest question.

'I know it's foul here,' she said.

'Why have a job here then?'

'Well, money is of no importance is it, as Orwell said.'

'Look, is there a film on you'd like to . . .'

I had reached the usual stage of wishing to be home in my own bed, eating chocolate instead of down in that steam. But now she turned round again, in a patient way.

'Listen, don't bother with me because I'll only make you fed up. There's a painter working down here, making profiteroles. You know, little meringues. I took the job to be near him.'

'You're going out with . . . ?'

'I don't "go out" with him. He doesn't "go out". I should think not. He either makes profiteroles or does his art. He's a master of both.'

'And you're engaged. . . .' I began carefully.

'No I'm not,' she said. 'He says I'm a bourgeois cunt. He hardly knows I exist, except to stick it in me. I'm all mixed up about what he paints. I want him to tell me about painting. I'd rather do that than talk about your best suit or hold white little girly fingers.'

'But you went *out* with me all the same.'

'Yes well, he doesn't mind that. He doesn't mind anything. Neither do I. I went out with you because you were quite sweet and I had nothing else to do while I was working at Aldo's. *He* was just round the corner in the Kensington Close.'

I waited until she had quite finished all her supplementary bits of information before uttering 'Oh God' in a voice that was a mixture of the regimental and of the wounded simple-hearted boy. At this she turned round again from the sink, wiping one end of hair away from her face with a wet fist.

'Do you just want to stick it in me, is that it?'

'I mean. . . .'

'Is that what you want?'

She undraped that filthy overall to reveal the same blue clothes, the buttons down her back. Picking up her duffle coat with unusual care, she walked out; I followed; down the corridor that was hung with teatowels and up to a white slab of a wall with a huge refrigerator handle. The handle was stiff but she insisted on dealing with it. We got up a high step and I put my head in her mouth, surrounded by the big, scrubbed-looking and faintly mauve sides of meat. I expected to feel cold but instead felt cool: she caught hold of my fly again with such vehemence that for an instant I felt I knew what it was like to hang in a deep-freeze room.

For the first time I felt moisture in her mouth instead of finding it as wide and empty as the North Sea. I was a little worried about my suit, but my mouth had gone dry, suddenly, with a pressure that for weeks since the Second Flannel left, had outweighed even that of my autobiography.

'Will anyone come? You're *not* going to do it here, right on top of the dry ice? Everything's shutting up.'

She put her hands behind her back to undo the buttons, which made me sigh in my trousers and put my bowels on a tightrope. I tried to remember that I was experienced, merely somewhat out of practice. To act naturally I picked up her duffle coat by the hem to try to arrange it into some sort of cushion: and suddenly she yelled 'Christ, watch *out!*' her voice raised in passion for the very first time in my hearing, echoing among the beef. 'Put the coat down for Christ's sake.'

From the pockets of the duffle coat a number of hearty-sized, wonderfully green frozen brussel sprouts dropped and bounced and bonged on the thin dust of ice. She must have stolen them to take home. They bounced in all directions around the tall pillars of meat, and ran and rolled everywhere, sparkling with masks of cold. And somehow my moment with her passed.

The opposite to love, I read somewhere, is apathy. I had overcame her apathy: taken (as G. A. Henty might have put it) her citadel of non-feeling. But she lost her apathy to yell with uncontrollable laughter at the sprouts, and that's not quite the same thing, is it?

I Knew Daisy Smuten

HM Prison, Holloway
January, 1956

DEAREST REG,

Just my luck to get nabbed for hoisting in a *really* crummy Oxford Street store – honestly, I bet they've never *had* a hoister before, they ought to be flattered. I can't think why I wandered in there, wouldn't be caught dead there normally, and of course I didn't mean to take anything, at least I don't think I did – the whole thing's a bit of a blank in my mind now. I saw this girl looking at me but it never dawned on me she was the fuzz – when I got out into the street they found some hair-spray and a *very* common nightie in my bag, and no money so I couldn't very well say I'd been trying to pay for them. I had no bread for bail and couldn't think who to phone so I spent the night at the station and the next morning came up before three lay magistrates (the woman was rather sweet but the two men were shits) and they remanded me pending a medical report so I'm in the hospital here which funnily enough isn't too bad. It must have been the hash which my painter gave me.

It's quite interesting, the girl in the next bed murdered her baby and she's a very sweet and intelligent person. All the screws are dykes of course and *very* attentive to me! (Bet that bit never got past the censor!) I don't know what the medical report will say – but they *can't* fine me or send me to prison, surely, I mean for a bottle of hair-spray, wouldn't you say? The Probation lady explained this wasn't really a punishment. They wanted the medical report in order to find out why this happened and to see that it wouldn't happen again. She said very often when people do what I did it isn't because they're dishonest or anything, she said it's more in the nature of a cry for help.

With love from
DAISY

PS Have you ever had a letter from a jailbird before? Today's my birthday – what a place to have it in! Please cut out *all* the horoscopes and keep them for me. Sometimes I think all my troubles are due to being a Capricorn with Gemini rising. You see, I'm two people really – perhaps even three.

YWCA
February, 1956

DEAREST REG,

This is where I came in. Back at the old YW. I only got six months probation so that's OK as no one will ever find out, except you Reg. I can trust you. At least I have no parents to have to tell, unless the Steadfast is still going strong somewhere. I suppose *not* having parents caused it. Least that's what the Probation woman says. She says it's not me, all these silly jobs and silly down and outs. She knows I expect better of myself. I take the mickey out of her all the time, but she's right, isn't she. I'm going to reform. I'm not reading any more books. I'm going to get on. All by myself.

Your friend,
DAISY

6

Pauline's story

In normal circumstances, I must make it plain, I would never have got to know a girl like Daisy quite as well as I did. But there it was, I'd agreed to let them have one of my nice flats and I had to keep an eye on things.

Ah how sweet they looked the night they came to view. She was wearing a bowler hat, a red one, they were all the thing at the time. He looked outrageously young to be smoking a pipe. She let him do all the talking though she said enough to let me know she wasn't quite – well, out of the top drawer. He said they'd been married six months and now they were expecting some good news. He blushed. So unusual for a young man to be so delicate. They inspired me with a lovely vision of youth. I wrote a poem about them that was actually read out at our literary circle. It didn't make the magazine but that was the time Miss Baxter was the editor of it and I'm afraid we were having problems with the green-eyed monster.

Although I realized one or two things about Daisy straight away, I thought that here was a young person I could help and encourage. I live for helping people.

They moved in here on Saturday in such lovely weather. Daisy looked the picture of an efficient young housewife straight out of a magazine all in gingham, new rather than clean if you know what I mean and her hair tied back in a long ribbon.

Daisy had apparently decided to stop work. She'd worked in an office she said, but was very vague about it. I've never done a day's work in my life, but then I always say, I wouldn't have the time I have so many interests. Whenever I went across she'd have the mop out or a tin of polish open. You could see she was anxious to do well but she was so unmethodical. First she'd hoover then she'd dust, so she had to hoover all over again. Hopeless! I told her time and again that ever since I got married I have always done my housework in an hour and a half first thing in the morning and that's that and I have time for my other interests, my writing, my college work, my pottery classes, all my creative things.

Gerald was an accountant, chartered of course. My brother, he has a half share in the flats, said to me once that he couldn't understand what Daisy saw in Gerald. Good heavens! What I could never understand was what he saw in her. I don't think she had any real feelings for Gerald but he was a very good catch as a husband. Most young women of her position would have been grateful for the support of such a sound young man.

The first weekend they were here his mother came to lunch. A very nice woman, blue hair and if she'd have been a man you'd have said gout. I went over while she was there just to make sure they'd got enough milk and they pressed me to have coffee with them. Poor Mrs Eliot. She'd married again and was widowed again, so unfortunate, as I know, it's quite bad enough to be widowed once. Now she was a woman who could have been my bosom friend. She did say something about bridge the last time we met but it never came to anything. Of course I could see we were in sympathy about Daisy. She was sulking. Apparently Mrs Eliot had proffered some advice about cooking, and now Daisy was sprawled over an armchair, her legs in the air, most ungainly, reading a comic and leaving Gerald to do everything, even boiling the milk for the coffee. I said how commendable of him and Mrs Eliot glanced at Daisy and we looked at each other. She was related by her second marriage to a peer, you know. Such a charming woman. She said how pleasant it would be if these young people could make some local friends. It's so easy for young people to get bored in the suburbs, she said. I knew what she meant as quick as a flash and because I really did want to help, I said I'd been on the brink of asking

Daisy to go with me to a sherry morning. To tell you the truth that wasn't quite the case. I'd half had it in my mind to take her to a coffee morning in one of the new houses. I thought she wasn't ready for a sherry morning. But I was carried away.

On the day of the sherry party I called over for her in good time just in case there was any advice I could give on what she ought to wear. But I will say this for Daisy, I must be fair, she did sometimes have a sense of how she ought to look. That day I remember she wore a navy blue maternity smock with a white peter pan collar, so suitable and some pearls which I expect she got from Woolworths because, dear me the minute we stepped inside Mrs Piper Robinson's drawing room the string snapped and there were these cheap pearl beads flying simply everywhere. Mrs Piper Robinson said 'You must send them to my jeweller's for re-stringing. I'm taking my hair brushes for re-silvering.' Of course, I should have realized, dear Daisy was bound to go and drink too much sherry. Downing it like lemonade only it was Harvey's Bristol Cream. Mrs Piper Robinson always has the best. Soon it was obvious she ought to be taken home, that was all there was for it. But hints were useless! In the end, dear robust Miss Mortimer said 'Come along. You take one elbow and I'll take the other.' Daisy just grinned. Her face was flushed and her hair was all over the place. I kept saying, 'I'm so sorry Mrs Piper Robinson, I'm so sorry.' Miss Mortimer drove us off in her little Banger as she calls it. Daisy fell slump asleep. Miss Mortimer said she'd had plenty of experience of this sort of thing in the ATS. She simply parked the car in the drive of the flats and left Daisy to sleep it off.

One day I took Daisy a jar of my home-made tomato pickle. Young people like tomato pickle. I asked Daisy if she would like to accompany me to The Beeches. It's a home where I go to give help every other Wednesday morning, a very special place for retired gentlefolk, nice people, admirals or Indian Civil Service, that sort of class. I take a trolley round full of knitted egg cosies and pin cushions and other useful and delightfully decorative things made specially by the sewing circle I hold once a month in my front room with some of my friends for the purpose.

Mrs Eliot, her mother-in-law, was at the flat that morning when I invited Daisy to The Beeches. She'd dropped in for tea on the way back from a very grand funeral. When I made my suggestion, Daisy didn't say anything but Mrs Eliot said very firmly 'How splendid. Just what you need my girl. A bit of charity work will do you the power of good.' Daisy looked as if she was about to be rude but I got in first with one of my cheerful remarks.

It was a mistake, of course, taking her to The Beeches. She was in such a sarcastic mood. Of course they wanted my egg cosies. And of course they weren't the worst off people in the world. I have always felt that here was a place where I personally could make a very special contribution.

By this time she was eight months pregnant, getting to be quite a size and very grumpy. I said to her, 'When I was your age I had an eighteen inch waist.' She burst into tears, if you please. Well I said to her, nobody could have an eighteen inch waist if they were eight months pregnant. Then I said, just to cheer her up, 'Show me your layette. Let's look at it together.' Do you know with that baby four weeks off being born she hadn't got a stitch, not a stitch for the mite to wear. Well it so happened that my ladies sewing circle was coming that very afternoon so I said to Daisy I will bring the ladies over here for I can see you might be embarrassed at coming over to my cottage and you can tell us what you need and we will see what we can do.

My ladies rose to the occasion splendidly. Somebody said she knew her daughter-in-law was trying to get rid of her cot and somebody else said she knew about a pram and everybody else said they'd got lots of baby patterns they could fish out. Four of us went over, we were really very excited about it. Daisy wouldn't let us in. I knew she was there. There's a little window in the living room of that flat that you can just see through if you perch on the cover I had built for the dustbins. She was lying on the sofa, her feet up, drinking sherry and eating a bag of doughnuts. 'It's no good, ladies,' I said. 'We have a very real problem case here.' If it wasn't for that poor baby we would all have gladly washed our hands of her.

As it was we said we would help the baby in spite of Daisy and as it turned out it's as well we didn't waste any time about it.

Anyone could tell you that sherry and doughnuts are not fitting food for a woman who is eight months pregnant no matter how young and healthy she is. And sure enough that very night Gerald came over, banging at my door looking absolutely desperate. I said as soon as I saw him, 'You want to telephone for the ambulance.' Gerald went with her and I expect he paced up and down with his pipe for they didn't let fathers in at that time. Four hours later I heard their gate go. I rushed to my bedroom window and saw Gerald actually dancing round and round the path of the flats. Oh he was a nice boy. I opened my window and called out to him and he shouted back, 'It's a girl. It's a girl.' I've never seen anybody so happy as that young man that night. He inspired me. I sat down there and then at my dressing table and wrote 'Joy' one of my best sonnets. But ah, short lived was our joy.

The next day I went to the hospital, a nice place, a cottage hospital you'd call it, I've done a lot of Red Cross work there so I knew the staff. Mrs Eliot was there and I think she was glad of a kindred spirit, she looked so pleased to see me. 'But where's the baby?' I said. 'Where's our little princess?' If you please Daisy had left the baby in the crèche because she couldn't stand the crying. Now if I'd been Sister I'd have had no truck with that. The funny thing was Daisy was a marvellous breast feeder. Three ounces every four hours on the dot from the third day, a splendid achievement, Sister Benson said.

When she got home Gerald was at his wits end. I didn't know it at the time but Mrs Eliot told me later that Daisy absolutely refused to get up in the night. Gerald had to make a bottle and get up and feed her, never mind that he had to go to work next morning and Daisy's own milk was just let go to waste. One day I actually caught him washing nappies. He put on a brave face, pretended he was just doing it the once, 'Got to find out what it's all about,' he said.

I said to her one day, 'Daisy we all have to go through it. I remember when my daughter was a baby I slaved away, washing and hardly had any sleep at all in the night. In the afternoons I went out for a walk and there's baby all nice and clean lying against a lovely white pillow slip with starched frills.' But the minute Gerald walked in through the door Daisy always wanted to be off to the pictures, on her own.

I was over there one evening and he said, 'Daisy's such a lively girl.' He was trying to excuse her. I was irritated by his forever referring to Daisy as a girl. She had a woman's responsibilities. I said to him a woman knows in her heart that when she has a baby her place is with the baby. Daisy yawned, right out loud in my face.

I made a last attempt at helping. I said to her one afternoon, 'Now Daisy isn't it time this child went to the clinic.' She just looked at me blankly so I said come along now. I'll come with you. I chivvied her into putting the baby a clean nappy on. Do you know at five weeks of age that baby was given a clean nappy only once a day. The steam that came off that baby's bottom! Between us we got the baby ready and then I said to Daisy, 'Now why don't you put one of your nice dresses on for a change.' Since she returned home with the baby, she'd let her appearance go, drooping about in her old maternity things still, probably to make herself look pathetic. Anyway I went to the wardrobe and I fished out a nice yellow dress. I was getting quite interested in organizing her in spite of myself. I told her to get washed and then I brushed her hair, such pretty curls, and I saw a scarf on the dressing table. I tied it round her neck and she looked very presentable indeed. It cheered her up. She actually smiled. I hadn't realized until then that I hadn't seen her smiling for months.

As we neared the clinic the line of prams grew thicker and Daisy grew more and more quiet. In the clinic there were two rows of chairs back to back with a bucket in front of each chair. You had to undress baby, put the clothes in the bucket and queue up for weighing with the baby bundled up in a shawl to keep warm. After that you could discuss her little characteristics with the lady doctor. There were a lot of toys at one end for the bigger children to play with. It was very warm and you could smell Johnson's Baby Powder everywhere.

I thought Daisy was being very dozy, just standing there rooted to the floor. I'd carried baby in from her pram. I said to Daisy shall we have a red bucket or a green bucket, something like that and then I caught sight of her hands, clenched together so tight that her nails were digging into her flesh. I said Daisy what's the matter. 'They're shrimps,' she said. 'Shrimps swarming everywhere,' and then she rushed outside. I followed her to find that she was at the door being sick, so there was a to-do about that. Too many doughnuts I expect. I said. 'Come along Daisy I expect you'll feel better now, let's get ourselves organized.'

She pulled out a handkerchief that I recognized as mine. That was another thing about her: she had this habit of helping herself to things. I must confess that I would like to say that she was a common little thief because in the end I really disliked her. I am convinced that despite all her tales, she had been brought up with no background, nor a proper home, so she felt entitled to anything of anybody else's. I don't think she saw it as stealing. Whenever she took anything of mine, an ashtray, a handkerchief or something, she was convinced that I could spare it because I had so much more than she had. In many ways that girl was ahead of her time. You look around Piccadilly and you see Daisy everywhere, scruffy self-centred girls behaving as if they owned the world. Fifteen years ago I have no doubt if you asked any young girl who she would like to be, she'd answer, that lovely girl who became the Countess of Dalkeith. The women's magazines were full of her, clean and nice in powder blue twin sets and pearls. You don't hear of powder blue any more.

Gerald was a saint. I think he must have decided that for the sake of the child he would have to pander to Daisy's every whim. Quite the worst thing he could have done if you ask me. I often heard him say, quite seriously, 'What do you want me to do now, Daisy?' She would reply, 'Make me some toast,' or 'Very well you can take the baby for a walk.' Very grand. You certainly wouldn't address a modern servant in that tone.

One particular morning, it was a Thursday, there was a gang of gypsies in the street. I thought Ah, my bonnies, I'll keep an eye on you, let's see what you're up to. So I thought I'd clean my windows, that's much better than gardening for keeping an eye on what's happening. You can see more. They knocked on my door and I could see one had a basket of clothes pegs and another was going to ask if he could cut my lawn but I said very sharp, 'Be off with you or I'll call the police.' That's the only language gypsies understand. They said, 'Very good lady, we'll go straight away lady, we're very sorry lady.' It makes you squirm a bit when they act so humble but I know from experience that you have to harden your heart to them or they'll be round burgling you the next thing.

I watched them go over to the flats. I knew it was my Miss Bowden's day for physiotherapy, she was beginning to get arthritis, and my nice couple in the top flat were both out at work which left Daisy in on her own. Well I saw three gypsies go in and I saw two gypsies come out. I've no need to tell you that the one who stayed was a young chap with his shirt all undone. I thought this is it. She's cooked her goose now. This is evidence. I wasn't sure what I should do, whether to ring up Gerald at his office or Mrs Eliot. I thought perhaps I'd better make absolutely sure of my facts. It's as well I did. I went over to go round the back meaning to have a look in through the little window. I was absolutely rooted to the spot.

I think I must have cried out, I was so horrified. This young thug of a gypsy was actually taking a saw to my magnificent yew hedge – hacking it down. It was twenty feet high if it was an inch, my grandfather planted it. It was the best yew for miles around, people were always remarking on it. He'd got at least a fifteen foot stretch of it sawn down to white jagged stumps. He was killing it. Daisy was shouting at him, her face glowing, 'More, more,' she yelled. 'More, more.' He was laughing out loud as he chopped. A huge section came down in one fell blow as I watched. I was shouting at him, 'Stop it, stop it,' but he just carried on laughing and chopping. It was a terrible sight, all our privacy going – the sheerest vandalism. I pulled myself together though I was on the edge of tears. I mustered some authority and I said very firmly, 'Young man stop that immediately. This is my hedge not hers.' I wanted to stick all the sawn off branches back again, ridiculous, you know that feeling when your hair's been cut too short. I remember how I felt as a girl when I'd been shingled. It was the same sort of pain with the hedge. I felt exposed and bereft.

Daisy actually paid the man. In fairness to her I suppose I must have been wrong about what I had previously suspected was going on between her and the gypsy. She gave him a pound. She didn't say a thing to me and I most certainly couldn't address her. I was far too upset. I said to the gypsy, what about all these clippings. We can't plant any of them back and we certainly don't want them here. You'll have to move them. Every single one or I'll call the police.

I went back to my cottage. There are some little things that are very consoling when you're truly upset. I dosed myself with a tablespoon or two of brandy and made a nice strong pot of tea and took the tray into my front parlour which I never really use except for visitors. It's full of my mother's things, things I grew up with as a girl and in moments of distress it offers me a lot of comfort. I had a little cry. I had to talk about it but I could no more have faced my immediate neighbours than fly so I went out visiting further afield. It just happened that I was near the station when Gerald was due home so I went to wait for him. He looked surprised when I told him but of course he didn't take it in until he'd actually seen it. He was even more upset than I expected. He kept shaking his head and repeating he couldn't see the point. I left him to go in and have it out with Daisy.

We were in summer then. I remember thinking what a long time until dark and I can draw the curtains and blot it all out. But worse was to come. At about nine o'clock there was a knock at my door. It was Mr McNiel my old friend from the Preservation Society. He was as kind as I could expect in the circumstances. You see it wasn't my hedge after all. Although my grandfather had planted it, he had for some reason of his own planted it on the other side of our railings. That meant that it was considered common land and so was included in a preservation order that I myself had helped to fight for. The humiliation of it. It was the talk of the neighbourhood. You see what that wretched gypsy did was to dump it branch by branch in every house he passed. That's the kind of thing that makes people furious, especially if they're proud of their gardens. You really find out your friends at a time like that. I didn't know what he'd done with it until I woke up next morning and found my little garden crammed with these huge branches of yew. I could hardly get out of the house. Mr Ferguson, nice man, burnt what was dumped in his garden, so did Mrs Appleyard and young Mrs Fig. The rest of them must have had many a joke at my expense bringing it over in the night. Of course it was sheer malice that made them put it in my garden. There's a lot of jealousy about you know for an artistic woman who has property. I seriously thought of leaving and going to Scotland or somewhere and if I'd thought I'd make a profit on my property I would have.

I went over to the flats first thing. I wanted to make sure both Gerald and Daisy knew whose responsibility all that yew was.

The baby was crying, inevitably. So was Gerald. The door was wide open. He had his head on the table, sobbing. She'd gone. And before she left she'd smashed his pipe rack and all his pipes including some very nice Meerschaums. She'd taken a pair of scissors to his best suit and slashed it and there was a horrible note. It said, 'Silly Gerald. I'm off. I'll never see you or it again, thank God.' It, I suppose, referred to the baby. You can tell how immature she was, to write a childish thing like that. I'd have thought Gerald would have been glad to get rid of her.

I said, 'Gerald. Have you told your mother? Have you told your mother?' But I got no sense out of him at all. So I went back to my cottage and rang her. She arrived within the hour. 'I've made up my mind,' she said. 'I'll take the baby with me. There's an old nanny living in our village who's dying to get back into harness again. You Gerald,' she said to him, 'can stay here and finish things off and then you can come and join us and make your home with us for as long as you wish.' What a splendid woman she was. 'Yes mother,' said Gerald finding his tongue at last. I was asked to look after the baby until Mrs Eliot could return with the nanny.

Mrs Eliot made it plain to Gerald that he was well rid of Daisy and that it was his responsibility to get rid of the yew. He burnt it, bit by bit in the dustbin. We'd had some rain so he had to use paraffin and the first time he put a match to it all his eyebrows got burnt off and the front of his hair was actually a-flame. He looked a terrible sight after that. You don't notice a man's eyebrows until they're not there.

I was reprimanded by the Preservation Society even though they knew it wasn't my fault. It was very hard to bear. I resigned of course. That old cat Miss Baxter was trying to egg them on to sue me. We've got privet growing there now. It sticks out like a sore thumb. We'll always know that Daisy was here.

Maternity Ward
December, 1956

DEAREST REG,

Thank you so much for your telegram. I didn't know you read the Times. Sorry I haven't written for so long. I think I must be in the dreariest ward with the dreariest two women in the world so it was nice to get some sign from the outside real world. It seems utterly remote. They are two tiny officers' wives from an army camp with tremendously genteel ways and voices and they heard me swearing blue murder while I was having the baby and wouldn't speak to me when I was moved back into the ward! I suppose she's quite a nice baby with lots of hair down the back of her neck and she's got finger-nails and everything but she always has awful wind which makes her fart and cry until about two o'clock in the morning which is an awful bore. I feel terribly well and sort of new which is nice. No more for now.

My best love,
DAISY

PS My husband is called Gerald. Can't think of anything else to tell you about him.

7

Irma's story

Over the chromium counter next to the round table where I was arranging, disarranging and arranging again the same six paper doilies, and through the mirror writing which told people on the legible side that Schrafft's was a popular, hygienic place to eat, I was watching the sun sinking below the other side of Park Avenue. Europe, my dream, was there beyond the smells from our kitchen, beyond the pink neon lights just coming on in our windows, it was there beyond the streets where melting tar gripped the heels of every shoe, and it was there five days beyond the edge of our sweltering, summer island.

'Oh Christ,' she said. 'Another boring bloody sunset watcher.' That was my first introduction to Daisy Smuten.

I hadn't seen Daisy come in through the manic, spiteful revolving door or even noticed her at all until I heard her voice. It was deep and metallic, not really pleasant, but to me then it was beautiful because it was foreign. She was about my own height and, like me, at the beginning of her twenties; slim, her hair was tangled, blowing around high, hard cheekbones, a shiny forehead, a small, tense nose; it was a controlled face that only at its very bottom carried, like oversights, a child's full mouth and the shadow of a double chin. Certainly, she was a good-looking girl, but it wasn't Daisy's beauty that struck me at first so much as her intensity. Inside the smudged frame of an exotic make-up, her eyes were a keen blue, grey, green, every colour but the sentimental brown that Manhattan's daughters inherit. They were genuine, five-dollar, sparkling windows to a clever soul. She looked exciting and theatrical. She could have been an actress between starring roles. Smuten, the very name was redolent of a Dickensian character.

Anyone unblinkered by devotion to Schrafft's could tell that Daisy, like me, didn't intend to be a waitress for long. Every time she swung the heavy tray, creased a linen napkin, or smoked a Chesterfield openly in the kitchen, her negligent gestures announced that Daisy was only passing through. Even the customers, a faceless and clamouring mass, rarely got from Daisy the kind of service that Schrafft's advertised. 'Look here, sir,' I overheard her tell a portly businessman once, 'you're making a mistake ordering three starches; you want a nice green salad and a bit of grilled steak.'

He had the steak too, and left her a dollar hidden, as paper tips always were, under the saucer. Daisy told me that first evening, as we waited for the cook to dish up our orders, that she was working her way around my continent just as I was working my way towards her own.

'I thought it was time America saw me. And besides, distance can be a very convenient remedy.'

Within a few days of arriving in New York with barely a hundred dollars in a crocodile wallet, Daisy had seen one of our genteel 'Help Wanted' notices. A few hours later she was secure in one of the few jobs where not much attention was paid to immigration formalities. Not many healthy natural-born Americans accept waitressing as part of their heritage. Daisy and I were profoundly different from our weary colleagues, most of them middle-aged women abandoned by alcoholic husbands, some of them older spinsters with ailing parents to support.

'In the end we all get exactly what we deserve,' Daisy said to me one evening as we dressed side by side. She threw her uniform carelessly into the locker. It was a severe rig which suited the vivid drama of her face better than the little-girl walking-out clothes she liked to wear in those days.

'Why should I feel sorry for them because they've given in?' The dingy straps of her lingerie were held together with safety-pins. 'The whole world has always been there for them too, hasn't it? Well, hasn't it?'

She slipped her arms into a frilly nylon blouse.

'It's their own silly faults if they've been too gutless to break out and take what they want.'

Our friendship grew from the very first evening. Although I knew that I wanted deeply to be Daisy's friend, I could never understand what I had to offer her beyond sharing her aloneness. My family had moved West right after my graduation from university and my former classmates were all busy distributing judicious favours among potential husbands. Alight as I was with my dream of Europe, I was naturally drawn to Daisy, the European; Daisy, who had a dream too.

'I want everything,' she told me. 'I want it all.'

The North American sky was clear and full of falling stars in late September, the breeze carried the sharpness of red maple leaves from the Jersey shore; and even now, after living more than ten years in Daisy's homeland, I ache for that autumn in America. To walk through the crisp evenings with my new friend after a day of steaming work, was the first plunge into the sea at the end of a long, hot trip down the mountain.

'Isn't it marvellous!' Daisy said, as we stood on the corner of Park Avenue, looking down the steep, blue canyons where I had grown up. 'It's so man-made. So tough. It's what I call human achievement. Nothing dictated the way they built it, nothing at all made them have it any way but exactly the way they wanted to have it.'

Golden lights coming on up high behind the curtains of fabulous penthouses, brilliant shop windows, huge cars painted in boudoir colours. It all hurt the pit of my stomach, like vertigo or too many green apples.

'Someday I'm going to come back here,' Daisy used to say, as if she weren't altogether there already.

'And I'm never coming back again,' I told her as we stopped in front of the Plaza Hotel to watch a man in evening dress scrabble for pearls as if he was in a silent film while his wife stood laughing and holding her broken necklace.

'This place could turn me into a thief,' Daisy said, and she turned her head towards an older man, a celebrity, who was slipping past his chauffeur into a waiting car. 'Except that I'm one already.'

It was a good joke. I wished I'd thought of it.

On Yom Kippur, the Jewish day of fasting and atonement, a day when whatever He may be elsewhere, in the area between the Bronx and the Battery there is a good chance He is Jewish, Schrafft's was so quiet that the eternal background waltzes were actually audible.

We were hidden behind the lunch counter, kneeling on the damp, slatted floor-boards, sneaking ice-cream sundaes.

'You're not a Jew, are you?' Daisy asked me.

I was embarrassed, as I always have been by a bald declaration of religion, bank-balance or a lover's surname.

'I don't think I've ever met a Jew before,' Daisy said.

We stared at each other over the melting chocolate. I was sure I'd never met anyone who had never met a Jew before.

'I'm not a very good one,' I said, dipping in my sinful spoon.

'Tell me something, Lovely.' Daisy had started to call me by that pet name. It puzzled me, for next to her own beauty my only attraction was youth which did little to disguise numerous structural flaws. 'Tell me, do you feel full of atonement today?'

If I worked hard at it, and to hold Daisy's attention I was always willing to work very hard, I could rouse sorrow; a softer version of the feeling I'd had during the war when the letters with bright, delicate postage stamps from my unknown relatives in east Europe had stopped coming forever.

'I feel sad,' I said.

'Not bitterly guilty in other words.' She sounded disappointed. 'Just apologetic, is that it? You do let me down, Lovely. Anyway, it's a funny idea if you think about it, to set aside one day every year for mass atonement.'

'What about you then?' I spoke out of irritation with myself for having failed Daisy in some way. 'Have you a real sin? Something terrible to atone for?'

'Only one.' Her voice was plummy with ice-cream. 'My daughter.'

My pride in Daisy's attention to me grew even heavier from then on. While I still thrashed about in cloudy romances, she had been getting all the hard business of life put aside. Not only had her soft, girlish body been enjoyed by a man, a man I could barely imagine, but it had functioned already in its essential way. Daisy invited me one Sunday to visit her at her rented rooms in Greenwich Village, on a street with a real name and not one of the numbered rectangles we lived in uptown. I took the invitation as a thrilling sign of an approval which I longed to have and only feared I couldn't earn.

Daisy's room was stale with the hangovers, remorse and homesickness of a parade of previous tenants. A landlady's suspicion peeped out from the cupboard where the bones of a kitchen were devoured by cockroaches. Her contempt for her boarders who, she knew, were all junkies and Communists, was caught in every bilious twist of the flowered wallpaper. Her clean-living, American hatred for strays from the bosom of the family was caught in the overhead light bowl along with cobwebs and dead flies. As Daisy rinsed two glasses at a sink piled high with dirty dishes, I decided to lift a large, grey, toy cat and free the single, stable chair.

'That's Sherman,' Daisy said, as she poured the noxious Gallo Wine out of the same two-gallon bottle I remembered from clandestine parties at school.

'Sherman travels with me. He's my slave and my little brother.'

She whisked a yellow pullover off a box of Ritz crackers and brought the box with the full glasses to a little table between my chair and the bed. The top of the table was littered with hairpins, tablets of some kind, a dirty cup with spots of blue mould at its bottom, five or six pennies, a tattered copy of *Extraordinary Women*, and a diaphragm case which was full of cigarette ash. A similar case was hidden in the bottom of a dresser-drawer at my own tidy room uptown, unopened, unused. During an intense study of the romantic poets at school it became important for me to exercise caution about a half-dozen times in the arms of a French exchange student.

'Sherman is great company,' Daisy said, throwing herself back on the jungle of unmade bed. 'Much better than my husband was; more intelligent. Lighter on his feet.'

'You're divorced, Daisy?'

'Dee-vorced. Bloody dee-vorced!' she said. 'You haven't been married, have you?'

I was so flattered by the question that I could barely stammer my reply.

'Very wise too. Marriage is folly. As a matter of cold fact, marriage is nothing but a criminal excuse for half the human race, the male half, to suppress the other half. It's like signing a contract to give up living. Believe me, there is nothing in that shabby contract for women but drudgery, boredom and the instant coffee of whatever half-wit lives next door. And then of course there's the long suffering hubby; we mustn't forget that. "Look how nice I am. I bring home twenty five pounds a week and I've got steady prospects; haven't I? So love me, feed me, honour me, and where's a clean shirt?" No. Thank you very much! I've bought all the yards of loo paper I ever mean to buy. From now on I get along without any husband hanging around for attention. Women have to stick together.' Her incomparable audience, so wide eyed, so ready, was admiring every extravagance.

'After all, Lovely, we've got interests in common. Real interests. If only women realized their own solidarity. If only they understood they can have deep and lasting relationships with each other. Most relationships between women are treated as temporary, waiting until some man comes along and then the real loving can begin. I'd choose friendship with a woman any day in the year over the demands of one of those pathetic, crawling, sniffling creatures. And they're so simple-minded! Do you know how simple-minded men really are, despite all their so-called logic? Do you know that there is an infallible way to get any man in the world that you want?'

Obviously, I didn't.

'Just remember one thing, just one, Lovely, and you can catch any pair of trousers that you have the misfortune to want. Remember that there isn't a man alive whose mother loved him the way he really wanted her to. Bear that in mind and you can start out with the upper hand. Should you ever be stupid enough to want to.'

She poured us both more wine, and then sat back, watching me over the top of her glass, waiting to be entertained in her turn. I felt the machinery inside me grinding my short history to bits, trying to sift out something that was worthy of her time. I talked about my family, my school and the place where we both worked, in cynical, unloving terms which came hard to me. Each time I saw Daisy's eyes fade and begin to wander, I searched for a new, amusing insult to myself, my beliefs, my life, until finally there was nothing left to say short of blasphemy.

'Haven't you ever had a lover?' she asked me.

I had to tell her then about my French student. It sounded thin stuff in front of Daisy.

'Is that all? Christ.'

She got up, poured more wine and sat back again while I watched her like a patient awaiting diagnosis.

'You're a virgin. What a useless thing to be. You can't even become a nun, can you if you're Jewish?'

'Except for Jean-Pierre I was never really interested. I thought that in Europe . . . I mean, American men are so inept aren't they?' I floundered in mysterious currents.

'All men are inept,' she said. 'You've really fallen for the crap they ladle out in women's magazines, haven't you? All those "whirlpool kisses" that lead you to unspeakable pleasure, all that bright purple brainwash. If I were you, Lovely, I'd stop this purity lark immediately; it's bad for your sense of perspective, you'll begin to overrate the whole business. Sex is a game for men, not for us, but we've got to learn to play it just so we know how trivial it is. Truthfully, I've never really liked sex much, except to talk about. As a topic of conversation it has everything: plot, passion, horror. And it's a hell of a good joke.'

'Without love,' I asked her, for with the help of the poets I had been convinced that I loved Jean-Pierre, 'what's it like?'

'Under the best of circumstances,' she said, 'I've always found it messy.'

Daisy drank a lot of red wine in the next few hours as she paced from her bed to the single, small window, with her glass in her hand, telling me about her lonely childhood, her misty parentage, her unsuccessful unions, and all the terrible things that had happened to her and would never happen again.

'Oh, Lovely, the worst was that I was so unspeakably bored, bored, bored!'

I said very little; I just watched her with what I hoped looked like wisdom, although my reeling head was only full of bliss that I was being granted her confidence. Any friends I'd had before in Daisy's shadow became childhood friends who knew nothing of marriage or childbirth or the dreadful persecution to which our sex was subjected. At one point, she put a record on the rickety portable gramophone, a throaty woman singing those rhymes that tell New Yorkers what love should be, all the tunes that slithered out of dry martinis and long, dark bars. With unusual grace, Daisy danced a turn around the room, pausing in front of me to echo my own moist thoughts: we would always be friends, we would never forget each other, we were each other's only hope in this big, man's world.

Suddenly, she turned to the window with its minuscule view over metropolitan trees, already surrendering their leaves to the first winter wind. She rammed both fists into the small of her back.

'It's these goddamned ovaries! It's this blasted physical disability! Who needs it? Not me!'

She danced around the room and stopped on her bed.

'My trouble has always been too much indiscriminate kindness. I've been too bloody kind to the wrong people, to people who didn't deserve it. When I think of it! All those people I helped, all those people behind me now, finished! I will not be eaten alive ever again, and I will not be kind to anyone but you, Lovely. Oh, Lovely, what a generous fool I've been.'

I, who had no more been able to imagine tears in her eyes than pearls or coal-dust, sat frozen, horrified, watching her cry with her face in her hands. Finally, I touched her shoulder and tried to tell those sharp, fragile bones that I was Daisy's friend and that I would never hurt her or let her down. She fell back on the bed after a while and seemed, abruptly, to fall asleep. I managed to put myself in order for the journey home. From the door, as I turned to switch off the light, I saw Daisy stir, she reached out for Sherman, lifted him high above her head, and began choking into his shoe-button eyes. For a second it seemed she was laughing, but I turned away, despising myself for even thinking that Daisy would laugh at such a time. Or was she?

We never discussed that evening in Daisy's room, but we started meeting every Sunday and soon we began to communicate in the shorthand of real intimates. Any man who followed us in Central Park during our weekend stroll, was erased, eradicated, annihilated by a look that we knew how to exchange with each other. Bound up in woolly scarves and ear-muffs, we presented a welded front to the world; behind that front, we laughed, impervious, and self-contained as the children tracing concentrated circles on the ice-skating rink. Sometimes we went to the cinema where Daisy entered into a coma-like ecstasy.

'I love movies,' she said to me once as we came out of a cinema and found New York muffled in fresh snow. 'They're so much easier to remember than dreams.'

Because we were both saving money, we often went to a Village coffee bar in the evening and tended two cooling cups until Daisy's fair hair and clear, mocking laugh drew a man who would buy us each another coffee and invite us, perhaps, to a local party. Daisy received these invitations the way a cat might receive the courtesy of a mouse, and usually she accepted them with an elaborate gratitude which underlined her contempt. She said that she hated parties. Perhaps that was why she was so very good at getting to the centre of them while I, who still hoped a hero might emerge from the throng, was too shy to take much part in them. It almost always happened at a party that Daisy ended up in the middle of a circle of men arguing about something basic like sex-roles or politics with me standing by, her silent auxiliary.

'Don't tell me,' she said once to a bearded painter who was our host, 'that down deep you don't cherish a sense of your superiority over women.'

'Step into the other room, baby,' he said, 'and I'll show you my sense of superiority.'

'You see, Lovely,' Daisy turned to me, 'it's the beastly nature of the beast.'

Daisy's rage was always articulate and devastating when any man had the temerity to offend her.

My twenty-first birthday was the third week in April. To my annual disappointment it dawned, and grew, and began to pass just like any other day. Every April I mean to keep the agonizing day a secret, and every April I tell someone. That year, of course, it was Daisy I told. She had a date that night, she said, and my yeasty self-pity doubled. But she would break it for me and we would have a birthday celebration together. Daisy had been having more and more dates in the evening recently, but we still shared our Sundays in the park when she made fun of the men she had met during the week.

'Men are so absurd, Lovely. So terribly absurd,' she said, as we strolled through the zoo.

I listened to her attentively, trying to suppress an unworthy desire to know more of male absurdity first-hand.

'They don't understand anything about us women. I mean about our kind of fidelity, our gentleness, our intelligence. We're so much better off without them.'

She squeezed my arm, while the seals lowered their demure lashes and slipped into the water.

Daisy chose a big, Italian restaurant for my birthday celebration. It had a dance floor and one of those sad orchestras whose rhythm is set by the cash-register. It was not the cosy place I would have liked, but we sat in a corner booth, and the high-backed benches, the thick, reddish light gave an illusion of intimacy. The waiter, a stooped Italian with none of the dazzle I expected from his homeland, brought us each a dry martini with the reluctance that women alone are always served alcohol in America. It was Daisy who noticed the stranger watching us from the bar, and it was Daisy who agreed when he asked, politely, if he could join us. He was tall, as handsome as an unmarked football player. His name was Peter, he told us, as he slid into the booth next to me, and he had just come down from New England to take a job in a big advertising agency.

'I like to think of it as communications,' he said. 'I guess it helps to save my pride. God knows when I was studying English Literature I never thought it would come to this.'

'Above all, save your pride!' Daisy was using her belligerent, public voice. 'But I hope you have something more valuable to communicate to us than the heavenly properties of any one brand of soap-powder.'

Peter shrugged. 'Somebody has to sell soap.'

'Don't you see what you're really doing? Are you too blind to notice that you're not really selling soap at all, that you're really selling slavery to half the human race? You make it all look so bloody jolly. The dear unsoiled baby! The shining gadgets in the kitchen that's always clean! Doesn't it ever enter your mind what a hypocritical, egocentric, male business you're in?'

I had seen a number of Daisy's Village opponents rise to this bait and to her flashing eye, but Peter wasn't stung at all.

'That's a very interesting concept,' he said mildly.

'You're the worst sort of male fink!' Daisy's knowledge of American had swelled in the past months. 'You're the kind who says "it isn't my fault if I'm enslaving millions of women. I'm just carrying out orders!" Well, we all know where we've heard that before.'

'It's interesting what you're saying. But nobody is dumb enough to be a slave these days unless he – or she – chooses to be one.'

'When your ego has been pulverized like a smashed egg-shell, you damn well don't see anything else to be but a slave, and women are raised with egg-shell egos.'

Peter looked around desperately.

'It's all very, very interesting,' he said. His look found me. 'You're awfully quiet. Don't you agree with your friend?'

'It's my birthday,' I told him.

Peter was a champion. Over a swift round of champagne cocktails he toasted me and my birthday until everyone turned around to look. Even the orchestra gave us a corporate smile and played Happy Birthday as if it were the wittiest composition ever to come into their long, night-time life. Somehow, when the excitement had subsided, Peter started to talk to me about Europe.

'Wait until you see how wonderful it is over there! Everything falls into place for you. All that history and art, all those dull classes we went to, suddenly come alive and you find out that they were about real people, real emotions. When you stand in the Place des Vosges, and wait until you see the Place des Vosges! You know that Victor Hugo wasn't just the creation of some college lecturer with nothing else to talk about. He was real, he lived in a real time, a real place; a beautiful place. And the history! Our history is so phoney because they're always building on top of it, destroying all the marks of it, and then asking us to believe the pages of boring books without any proof to our eye or our imagination that any of it really happened at all. It's just not like that in Europe. Europe is haunted, because they've had the good taste to leave all their ghosts a place to come back to. Wait until you see it! Lord, I really wish I were coming with you.'

He touched my arm with his hand and a breeze ruffled the back of my neck. For a moment we looked at each other, two brown-eyed people, and we both laughed.

'Isn't enthusiasm a beautiful thing?' I said to Peter. 'There's so little of it around; it's becoming unfashionable. Pretty soon people are going to be ashamed when they really care about something.'

'I'm hungry,' Daisy said in a loud voice. 'Come on, Peter, order us something to eat.'

Then Peter made a mistake. He suggested to Daisy that he ring up a friend of his and ask him to join us for dinner.

'I'm sure you'd like him. He's awfully nice. He is. Intelligent. Really.'

Peter's suggestion slid away into the dark pool of Daisy's scorn.

'You're all the same, aren't you? One man, one woman; it's the only equation you understand, isn't it? Are you planning to do anything naughty under the table? Or do you just feel insecure when you're outnumbered? Lovely is my best friend. She likes you. You can get on with me, if you try. So why do we need another man? For Christ's sake, stretch your imagination a little bit and think of us as human beings, not just as ornamental sex objects. If you bring any man to join us, I promise you, I'll leave. On principle.'

Of course, Daisy's principles were mine too; nevertheless, I was irrationally disappointed when Peter was persuaded.

'I think it's extraordinary of you,' Peter said to me, after ordering our meal. 'Working so hard for something you *really* want, knowing what you *really* want. It makes me wonder if I'm doing the right thing, living the way everybody's always told me I should live. Maybe that isn't the way I want to live at all. Do you know what I mean? Maybe I don't just want to be an audience for everything I love, a sort of high-powered fan, maybe I want to be part of it. You know what I mean, don't you?'

I knew exactly what he meant.

Daisy jumped up. 'Come on, Peter,' she said, throwing her arms wide. 'Let's dance your troubles away.'

They danced twice. I saw them now and then moving among the other couples on the floor, Daisy's fair hair blowing under his chin, her arm negligently behind his neck. 'To hell with the bloke,' I remember she had told me once at a party, 'I dance for myself.'

By the time they returned the waiter had brought dinner. Peter and I tucked in with a good appetite. Daisy just played with a few strands of spaghetti, twisting them round her fork and studying them as if she saw in them all the tangled threads of her own life.

'What's wrong, Daisy dear, aren't you hungry?'

'Oh!' She looked at me, startled out of her reverie. 'It's alright, Lovely.' Her smile was infinitely, beatifically sweet. 'Please, you two go right on eating. Don't worry about me. After all, Lovely, it is your birthday, isn't it? Perhaps I shouldn't have come with you tonight. I'm not very cheerful company.'

'Daisy, of course you should have come. What sort of birthday could I have without you? I only wish you felt more yourself.'

'Dear little Lovely! Look!' she lifted the fork with an immense effort to her mouth. 'I'm eating. See?'

'Heartburn,' Peter said. 'It's the garlic. You need some bicarbonate.'

Daisy laughed, just a little.

'No,' she said. 'It's not heartburn. Not the way you mean it, you prosaic darling. It's just . . . oh, what is it? An awareness. A loneliness. A feeling I've been here before. Nothing, really, I'll be fine. Please don't fuss.'

Peter filled her glass with chianti, the only cure, he promised her, for all known ills. He pushed away his empty plate and he turned towards me to ask me to dance, I knew.

For the first time, I was eager to dance and be close with a man.

'Listen!' Daisy said. She clapped her hands together. 'They're playing "For All We Know", my favourite song. It makes me so sick for home, for Europe in April. Come on, Peter, one more dance.'

This time when they had tripped away, I decided that I too would ask Peter for a dance. I waited impatiently for them to come back. They returned slowly to the table, lingering on the floor after the other couples had left it. Daisy was talking to him quickly, her eyes bright in her pale face, and before they reached me, she put her hand on his arm so he stopped moving; lifting on tiptoe, she pressed against him and whispered into his ear.

'Gosh,' Peter was saying to her when they slid into their places. 'That's terrible. Really rough. You just a kid too, and with a war on! You know,' he said, turning to me. 'We Americans have had it too easy; we don't know anything about human suffering.'

'What were you telling Peter, Daisy?'

I thought she must have recited one of her memories, stories I knew better than my own, something she had told me and could refer to in shorthand: 'Merseyside' or 'Gerald' or 'Oxford'.

'Nothing, dear, nothing at all. Just something I was telling Peter.'

The atmosphere had shifted and I could not bring it back. A weight of fierce animation had slipped to Daisy's side of the table where, for the next half hour or so, it was her evening as she talked about anything that came into her head, only pausing to pour Peter's coffee and add the required two lumps of sugar. Peter was troubled, playing with his glass, twirling it by its stem between two fingers of his long, handsome hand, then lifting it to his mouth with brusque gestures as if he felt duty-bound to wash away all the grief of her war-torn world. My birthday misery was back and worse. The pleasure had died inside me as each of my tentative opening sentences died between Peter and me.

The next time Daisy stood up, Peter didn't have to be asked; he rose immediately.

'Lead on, Milady, I will follow you anywhere.'

With pain, I recognized the jocular tone that people always use when they mean a cliché and while they danced, I sat trying to conquer something ugly.

The music stopped playing, all the couples drifted back to their tables, the dance floor was empty, and I didn't know a soul in the room. Our waiter stood over the table and then leaned towards me solicitously. I knew that if he said anything kind to me, or even offered to get my coat, I would begin to cry.

'You know,' he said, 'the tip isn't included.'

Peter had paid the bill before being whisked away into the night. He had to be forgiven for forgetting, in his heat, to leave a tip. But for Daisy, a waitress, the oversight was unforgivable.

The next day, Daisy and I were not alone together until our lunch-break when she slid into the bridge chair next to mine at the staff-room table.

'Hi, Lovely,' she said.

'Hello, Daisy,' I said, but I couldn't look at her and stared down at my peas and meat loaf. I was trembling with dread of the apology which I knew was coming.

'Oh Lord!' She dropped her fork on the metal table-top. A few of the older waitresses glanced over at the noise with hostile, maternal eyes. 'I feel so awful! So awful! I feel filthy!'

'I won't hear it, Daisy.' My voice shook with what I trusted was love, and I knew that I was going to forgive her, that I was not going to make her suffer, or ask her to atone in the tradition of my race. 'There's no need to feel awful,' I said. 'Honestly, I perfectly understand that these things happen.'

'Understand? No, you don't understand. How can you understand?' she said. 'You're not a mother.'

I looked at her. The smell of meat loaf was sickening.

'I have a child. Even separated from her, I have a responsibility to her. How can I, how can I just go off into the night with any good-looking bloke who crooks his finger? Oh Lovely, please, Lovely, tell me it's alright. Tell me I didn't do anything wrong! Tell me, please, that I'm not immoral.'

'You're not immoral, Daisy.' I listened to that little coward in my heart speak aloud. 'You're not immoral.'

Greenwich Village
N.Y.

DEAR REG,

I've told you about this schmuck Irma I sometimes drag myself around with. I've got a brilliant idea to fix her up with a soul schmuck – Gerald. They'd make a perfect pair. Perhaps I'll send him a telegram telling him to come, leaving Irma to meet him. He'd fall for her and they'd settle down into a schmucklike shell. That would be great. I'm getting the hell out of this joint and I couldn't bear to think of Gerald being in the same country when I get back.

See you,

DAISY

PS I don't sound hard do I? Reg, I'm trusting you to tell me. All I want to do in life is have fun and not hurt anyone. Does that sound awful?

8

Jilly's story

Dear me, how time flies, it must be twelve years now: 1958 – a marvellous summer, not as good as 1959 but marvellous all the same. I seemed to spend the whole time making jam, or picking great armfuls of roses from the garden. It was the year one of the labradors came second at Crufts and Boy bought that pony for the children which they never rode.

Little Daisy – fancy hearing about her after all this time. She certainly disturbed our rather uneventful existence like a rock tossed into the washing machine.

We'd only been living in Darrow-in-Wharfedale a few years at the time. Darrow is one of those sleepy little towns nestling in a fold of the Yorkshire moors. Most of our friends were in the wool trade and had more money and less to do than was good for them. Life revolved round the bridge table and the tennis club.

Boy was Vice President of the Club that year, which caused a certain amount of ribaldry among our friends. I remember how unhappy I was because I knew he was having one of his 'things' with Sue Manners, a bridge friend of mine. Every evening if it were fine, he used to play down at the Club with her before dinner.

One Friday in July, however, he was particularly late home, and as the pork chops shrivelled in the oven, I grew more and more depressed, imagining him and Sue downing gins and tonics together in the fading twilight. Usually when he was late home, he picked a quarrel because he was feeling guilty, but that Friday when he eventually turned up, he was in excellent spirits and didn't even grumble about dinner being overdone.

A heatwave had just started and we ate out on the loggia. Stars crowded the sky, and the air was heavy with the scent of tobacco plants.

Boy helped himself to runner beans:

'I've been having a drink up at the Manners' house,' he said.

Usually Boy avoided Sue's husband, who was grey and defeated in spite of being almost a millionaire.

'They've got this girl called Daisy staying from London,' he went on in that offhand way, which always means he's interested.

'What's she like? Pretty?' I asked.

'Pretty extraordinary – never stops talking. Sue met her in town at a party and said 'come and stay' in the way one does but never expects people to take you up on it. And suddenly she strolls up with no cases and three carrier bags crammed with dirty washing. I must say poor old Sue does get landed with some lame ducks.'

'Nonsense,' I said briskly, 'Sue's the sort of person who takes a perfectly good duck, breaks both its legs and sends it out into the world. Look at poor Peter.'

Boy guffawed: usually he wouldn't hear a word against Sue.

'Well, I think she's met her match in Daisy,' he said. 'Funny little thing, bit naive really, must say I wouldn't mind teaching her a thing or three.'

He couldn't resist talking about her all evening and as we were going upstairs, he put his hand up my skirt and patted my bottom.

'Go and get kitted up, old girl,' he said – for the first time in weeks.

With a sinking heart, I went off to the bathroom. Boy only made love to me when he was revved up over someone else.

Later after he had fallen asleep in his own bed, I lay awake for hours. My body, taut with misery and unsatisfied desire, took a long time to quieten down. I knew that as he had grunted his way to his climax, he had been thinking of Daisy.

During the night I decided to drive over to Sue's house

next morning and size up this new threat to my existence. Boy was working a half day. As soon as I'd packed him off, I picked a marrow and some raspberries, and set out.

A few industrious souls were cleaning their cars before the heat became too fierce. Mowing machines sung behind neat laurel hedges. A white Jaguar stood on the gravel outside the Manners' large and ugly house. Flower beds made bright banners of colour round the smooth green lawns. I parked the car, the bumpers knocked beads of dew from the scarlet petals of a row of begonias.

After the sunshine, the Manners' Oak panelled hall seemed dark and forbidding. No one was about, but suddenly I smelled burning, and rushed into the kitchen to find a girl sitting on the table. She was only wearing tasselled, flesh-coloured knickers and a very grimy white bra, welded together with safety pins.

'Hi,' she said, 'I'm Daisy Smuten.'

'I thought the house was on fire,' I said stupidly.

'I'm trying to defuzz my legs with this stuff I found in Sue's bedroom, doesn't it stink? Not all the perfumes of Arabia can sweeten this little limb.' She waved a long leg in the air.

'I've got to play tennis this afternoon,' she went on. 'I'm so pale I thought I'd try some of Sue's instant tan, but I'd better get the hairs off my legs first. Isn't it hellish, the battle one has, not to become sordid?'

'Where's Sue?' I asked.

'Out – they're both out.'

There was a pause.

'Once there lived a little white bull,' sang Daisy Smuten.

I felt an idiot standing there clutching a huge marrow. I put it down on the dresser.

'I brought it for Sue,' I said.

Daisy giggled: 'I should think the old thing needs it, I don't imagine she gets much from Peter.'

I felt myself blushing and quickly added: 'I've brought some raspberries too.'

'Oh how fabulous,' she said, getting off the table and helping herself.

I didn't think she was very pretty – not half as smart as

Sue, and very pale with shadows under her eyes and a spot glowing on her cheek. Her dyed red-blonde hair was going dark at the roots, and stuck out like Strewel Peter from so much back combing. She had good eyes though, the colour of faded denim, but slightly bloodshot as though she'd been swimming underwater too long.

'Once there lived a little white bull,' she sang.

'How long are you staying here?' I asked.

'As long as they'll have me. I'm so bloody broke.'

'Don't you have a job or anything to go back to.'

'No,' she put on a phoney American accent. 'Let's say I'm resting, darling.'

Having finished the raspberries, she went over to the sink and wiped the white paste and black hairs off her legs with a dishcloth, which she left unrinsed on the draining board. She looked around for her cigarette, found it burning a large hole in the table, took a few frenzied puffs and then stubbed it out in a pat of butter.

'Let's have some coffee,' she said, putting the kettle on.

I watched her as she started reading the instructions on the instant tan bottle. Her very large pointed breasts seemed out of proportion to the rest of her body.

'Once there lived a little white bull . . . honestly I hate men, pounce, pounce, leap, leap, all the time. I thought it was only New York and London, but it's just as bad here.

'Peter crept up on me in the passage this morning. Ugh – he'd cut himself shaving and put a bit of cottonwool on it. He looked diabolical. Then I met this man last night. "Boy" somebody. We're all playing tennis this afternoon. Do you know him? I mean he's quite sexy, but I bet he picks up little bits of fluff like a hoover.'

I felt myself go hot: 'I'm Boy's wife, Jennifer Lester,' I said.

'Oh Christ,' she put her hand over her mouth, 'I do put my bloody feet in it. I didn't imagine you'd be like this. From the way Sue was going on, I thought you'd be all Hoo-ray with an undivided bust and Aertex shirts.'

She started to put the instant tan on her legs.

'Boy says you've got some darling little labrador puppies. I'd love to have one.'

'They're pedigree and cost well over fifty pounds each,' I said stiffly.

The telephone went: 'Oh that'll be my call to America. Make the coffee there's a love, I'll be back in a minute.'

At lunch I told Boy I'd met Daisy.

'Bit of a nutcase, isn't she?' he said, cutting himself a large piece of pork pie. 'Super tits though.'

'She's been ringing America on Sue's phone.'

Boy laughed: 'Are you coming down to the Club this afternoon?'

'I've got far too much to do,' I said. 'I must do out the boys' rooms, and catch the raspberries before they pass their prime. And the dogs haven't had their walk yet.'

I sensed his relief and felt desolation creeping like a chill wind through my stomach. I'd been unhappy over Sue, but at least I knew she liked money too much ever to consider leaving Peter. But what about this scatty immoral Daisy, who seemed to have no ties?

After he'd gone, I couldn't settle down to anything. An hour later, against my will, I found myself wandering across the fields towards the club. The heat had laid a silvery haze over the countryside and down by the river the air was musty with meadow sweet. Fat king cups glistened gold at the water's edge and the dogs charged in up to their stomachs, lapping frenziedly, their pink tongues lolling out.

I halted at a row of poplars flanking the club. All the courts were occupied, the figures brilliant against the green. I edged round until I stood behind the court where Daisy and Boy were playing Sue and Peter Manners.

I watched Peter, lanky and bespectacled, serving to Daisy who hit the ball nervously into the net. She was wearing one of Sue's old tennis dresses which was far too tight across the bust, gold gypsy earrings and white tennis shoes without any socks. When she ran her feet turned out like Donald Duck. The instant tan hadn't worked either, striping her legs and stopping in a hard line three inches below the bottom of her skirt. I thought how absurd she looked.

Boy on the other hand, although he was nearly forty then, looked superb on the court. He has the kind of sallow skin that has only to look at the sun to go brown, and he had kept his figure. But was it necessary, I wondered, for him to wear his shorts quite so tight or so short. I watched him crouch down to receive Peter's service, frowning with concentration as the ball came like a cannonball at waist level. Boy took it with a powerful backhand drive to Peter's forehand. Taken by surprise, Peter lobbed his return and the ball sailed over Boy's head to Daisy on the baseline. She gave a squawk of horror and prodded it gently into the net. Boy grinned at her sympathetically.

Then it was her turn to service. After two double faults she managed just to get the ball in, Sue whipped it back, and everyone came up to net in a confusion of white. Boy and Daisy clashed racquets as they both tried to hit it. They stood giggling hysterically. I could see the whiteness of their teeth, the darkness of their throats. Boy put his arm round Daisy's shoulders, his hands digging into her flesh. As she bent forward beating the court with her racquet, Boy leaned over and peered down her dress. I wasn't even comforted by the expression of hatred that cracked the enamel perfection of Sue's features as she stared at them.

Later Boy brought them all back for a drink. I felt very much at a disadvantage, wearing an old tee shirt shrunk in the wash and my face scarlet from jam making. Daisy looked much prettier than she had that morning. She was wearing a black cardigan, tight red matador pants and masses of clanking jewellery. She'd covered the spot with make-up. Boy seemed pixilated, his eyes running over her like little black beetles, pressing her hand or shoulder on every possible occasion. Sue Manners looked so sour you could have made yoghurt out of her.

'What's your poison?' Boy asked Daisy.

'Oh gin and platonic,' she collapsed on the sofa curling her legs under her. As Boy turned away to pour out her drink, I saw her hastily undo the top four buttons of her cardigan, then she caught me looking at her, blushed and pretended she'd been only fanning herself from the heat.

'What a lovely home, you've got here,' she said. 'Oh look, forget-me-nots,' she added, pointing to a bunch of delphiniums.

Boy handed her a drink and a plate of crisps.

She shook her head: 'I mustn't get fat.'

'You should follow my diet,' said Boy.

'What's that,' said Daisy, looking at him sideways under messy black lashes.

'Hard liquor and soft flesh,' said Boy with a leer.

Daisy giggled and I turned away to talk to Peter. Sometimes Boy makes me feel sick with shame. I tried not to listen to Daisy's chatter but it was difficult.

'I've been reading *Lady C*,' she told Boy and Sue. 'Think of festooning a man's cock with forget-me-nots. I think it's rude.'

Sue went brick red with rage and Jester, our wire-haired terrier, the only dog allowed in the house, overcome no doubt by the tenor of the conversation, suddenly mounted Daisy's leg and started copulating briskly.

'Jester,' shouted Boy, giving him a kick so he yelped and flounced off.

There was an embarrassed pause.

'Tie me Kangeroo down, boys, tie me Kangeroo down,' sang Daisy.

'Oh Daisy, must you sing that awful thing,' snapped Sue.

'It was Little White Bull you were grumbling about this morning.'

'We must go,' said Sue getting up.

'Oh stay and have something to eat,' said Boy staring hard at Daisy.

'No there are too many of us. Poor Jennifer has *quite* enough to cope with as it is . . .' said Sue.

'Well at least have one for the road.'

'Once there lived a little white bull,' sang Daisy.

The heatwave showed no signs of abating. Blazing day followed blazing day. The moors burnt beneath a hot white sky, the river dried up to a trickle, and insects hummed in the purple heather. As Daisy's relations with Sue Manners worsened, she began to haunt our house. She would arrive in the morning, lie out in the garden stretching her skinny white limbs to the sun. When she grew too hot she would wander in, have a bath and follow me round while I did my housework, chattering incessantly, spilling ash everywhere. To this day, the parquet bears the scars of her broken stiletto heels.

'Books do make a room, don't they,' she said to me one day, taking one out of the shelf and flipping idly through it. 'I love books. I want to spend my life with artists and writers.'

'Do you know any?' I asked.

'What?'

She seemed very moody, one moment on top of the world boasting about her travels and her endless successes with men, the next moment in floods of tears over some tune on the wireless that reminded her of a former lover. But she would never let me turn the wireless off.

'It does people good to suffer,' she would say. The next moment she would be grumbling about how badly the world had treated her and she'd never had a chance in life.

At other times, she raged about Sue Manners.

'Silly, silly bitch,' she would storm. 'All that money and she's so mean. She went mad yesterday because I gave the dog some meat we were supposed to be having for supper. Poor thing, it's half starved.'

'Whippets are meant to be thin,' I said.

'Trust her to buy a thin dog. Peter made a pass at me last night. I don't fancy him a bit, do you?'

'Not awfully.'

'I bet he's pale grey all over from the top of his scurfy head to his ten corns.'

Although she did make me laugh, I did all I could to get rid of her, but she stuck like a limpet. I assumed she was feeling guilty about Boy as he played tennis at the club with her every night. We ate a lot of dried up suppers that week.

As she got brown, she took to sunbathing in the nude.

'Sue won't let me, because of the gardeners, silly cow.'

'I can see her point, I'm sure the people next door can see you now.'

'Well, what if they do. Come and talk to me.'

I sat gingerly on the edge of the rockery, but could find no comfortable place to put my eyes.

'Do you know what they call you round here?' she said.

'What?'

'The fair Miss Frigidaire.'

I winced.

'Oh they'd all like to have a go at you, but they don't believe you're interested in sex.'

'It's very kind of you to discuss me,' I said in a tight voice.

'Not at all. I think you'd be very attractive if you grew your hair.'

'I like it short. It's cool in hot weather,' I said.

She shrugged her shoulders: 'Or wore bright colours occasionally. I can't think why you stay with Boy, he's such a bastard.'

'Boy and I have been married nearly fifteen years,' I snapped. 'We've built up a lot of things together: the boys, the house and garden and the dogs.'

She rolled over on her front. I could see now that her breasts were smaller and very round, entirely different to the impression given by that stiff pointed bra.

'Don't be cross,' she said coaxingly. 'I've got your interests at heart. I just think you must be a very frustrated old thing. But I think you're nice. Leave your horrid jam and come and sunbathe.'

She took my hand and nearly pulled me off the rock.

Hastily I leapt to my feet: 'I think I've left something on the stove,' I said.

The Marshalls are a very rich couple, who give the sort of parties that always end in tears, outraged husbands, necking on the verandah, flushing loos, and people being sick. The sort of party that's heaven to Boy, purgatory for me.

I went out that afternoon and bought a new orange dress.

'Do you like it,' I said to Boy, as we drove to the party.

'Hm, yes, not sure about the colour though, got to be a bit careful when you get to your age, old girl.'

The Marshalls' house is large and set back from the road. Lights blazed from every window.

'Boy, how lovely to see you,' said Deborah Marshall, flinging fat braceleted arms round Boy's neck. 'We've got lots of pretty girls for you, darling.'

Boy grinned wolfishly: 'Don't bother to wrap them up, I'll

eat them now,' he said.

Guests were beginning to swarm through the large rooms. People grouped and re-grouped making desultory conversation. In another room the radiogram was belting out an Adam Faith record. Through the door, I could see a few couples self-consciously moving round the floor. Boy's face was already a mosaic of red lipstick where all his girl-friends had kissed him. I knew it was only a matter of time before he abandoned me. He got us drinks and we started to talk to a couple of wool magnates, sweating profusely in their own products.

Then he stiffened like a pointer: 'There's Daisy, be back in a minute,' and he made a bee-line towards her. I felt every semblance of party spirit oozing out of me.

Daisy looked gorgeous and very brown in a scarlet dress with a tight waist and full skirt. She said something to Boy and looked in my direction. Hastily I turned away and went to talk to a couple of women friends. While I tried to concentrate on their chatter about washing machines, I saw Daisy and Boy disappear into the other room to dance.

Half an hour later, Boy walked past me and returned a minute later carrying two full glasses.

'How's it going,' he called to me, but didn't bother to stop.

My smile felt as brittle as a dried chicken bone.

'Shall we go and watch the dancing? I love seeing young people enjoy themselves,' said one of the women.

'No,' I said with such intensity that they looked at me amazed.

Sue Manners came over and drew me aside. She was wearing far too much make-up and a dress with a white collar which was too young for her.

'I don't know why you put up with it,' she said, her eyes sharp, her voice sibilant.

'There's not much I can do.'

'The little slut. You should see the mess she makes of the bathroom, powder all over the floor, make-up on the towels, and she pinches all my things without even asking. Then to walk off with Boy right under your nose, it's disgusting.'

Deborah Marshall swayed towards us: 'Break it up girls, grub's next door.'

I had found myself a plate of food and a corner of a sofa, when Daisy came over and flopped down beside me: 'Hullo, I haven't had a chance to talk to you all night.' She kicked off her scarlet shoes: 'Mustn't forget where I put them.'

I realized she was already drunk. Boy came over with two plates of paella and sat between us. They were both over-excited, chattering away and not listening to what each other was saying. Daisy was picking out the prawns and mushrooms and leaving the rice.

'Chocolate mousse will be arriving in a minute,' said Deborah Marshall, bustling through.

'I hope it's been invited,' said Daisy and giggled.

Boy had taken off his jacket and tie, and a mat of black hair showed at the open neck of his shirt.

'Go and get us more drink,' Daisy told him and as soon as he'd gone she turned to me.

'What's the matter, I don't understand you, you're like one of those buildings surrounded by huge walls with bits of glass on top to keep everyone out.'

'And you're the sort of person,' I said shrilly, 'who eats the prawns out of the paella and leaves the rest! Take, take the best and leave all the dross to everyone else.'

She looked at me appalled: 'What's got into you?'

'I've had about as much as I can take,' I said, and went off to talk to someone else. Later I saw her dancing, going from man to man, her wild hair tangled, her eyes glittering, bare footed now, her red skirt and stiff petticoats flouncing round her legs.

I watched Boy move in as the music slowed down, and put his cheek against hers. Jealousy overcoming all discretion, I went into the garden, and sat on a wooden bench. I must have drunk more than I realized. My head was becoming muzzy and the overpowering scent of the honeysuckle, swarming over the warm red brick, was beginning to make me feel sick. I heard Boy's voice, sounding almost as though he were drugged:

'Oh Daisy, Daisy, Daisy, please, please, you promised.'

'I didn't.'

'You did, you said so yesterday.'

'What I said yesterday, has absolutely nothing to do with

what I said today. Anyway you're married.'

'So what, doesn't Mr Right always have a wife and two children. Jenny doesn't care. She's only interested in dogs and compost and asparagus beds. She'd rather make,' he paused, casting round for an example, 'make marmalade, than love.'

I stumbled upstairs and locked myself in the lavatory. The seat was discreetly covered in a riot of mauve chintz. I lifted it and sat down, shaking with misery, close to tears. Oh why did Boy have to humiliate me like this?

For ages I sat gazing at a horrible picture on the wall of a curly headed child in a white nightie with a bare bottom. Underneath was written 'Peek-a-boo.'

Someone rattled the door. I couldn't stay here for ever. I gave a vicious tug at the lavatory paper, which suddenly started to play the Skater's Waltz.

'I'm going mad,' I groaned, 'I can't take any more of this.'

As I came out into the passage, steeling myself to face the party again, I heard a sob. I went into a nearby bedroom. Faint spirals of smoke curled towards the ceiling. On the bedside table, a glass was overturned in its own puddle of wine.

Daisy's dress, a splash of scarlet on the yellow counterpane was rucked up round her thighs, showing long brown legs. She lay face down, one brown hand clenching and unclenching the pillow. Her hair covered her face in a gaudy tangle.

'Get out,' she screamed. 'Get out you bastard.'

'It's only me,' I said.

She raised her face which was blotchy with crying. 'I'm sorry,' she muttered.

'Are you all right?'

'*I'm* all right. There's only one thing the matter. Other people. Life's lousy. It isn't beautiful at all, it's randy sods and chemist shops.'

'Where's Boy,' I said.

'Somewhere, I don't know. Poor old Boy. He picked a wrong 'un with you. He ought to be married to some hot-arsed bit like Sue."

She broke into hysterical laughter and then started to cry. I sat there patting her awkwardly on the shoulder.

'You're the only nice person in this dump,' she moaned.

'And you hate me.'

'I don't, I don't,' I said stroking her hair, letting my hand trail down over her grubby neck. She was as warm as an oven against me.

And suddenly I knew I hadn't wanted anything so much since I was a child. It was in the war and sweets were rationed and my mother was saving a great slab of chocolate for my sister's birthday party. I came home from school, starving hungry and went into the larder and there was the chocolate. Even though it was going to be the most wicked thing I'd ever done, I knew I was going to eat it.

I felt like that now about Daisy lying there with her smudged face and golden body. Trembling with repressed desire, my fingers crept down inside that hideous padded bra. She didn't move. At first I thought it was compliance, then I realized she had fallen asleep.

I escaped through the front door into a cool, still world laced with moonlight, and I ran stumbling past trees, gardens, empty streets finally into open country.

When I got home to an empty house, the memory of the heat in Boy's eyes, the drink, the music and Daisy lying in my arms had left a great ache of disquiet. The sobs rose huge in my throat. I cried for no reason. When Boy came in much later, I pretended to be asleep.

'Why are you going to the office?' I asked him next morning. 'You worked last Saturday.'

'Briggs is away,' he said, concentrating on the sports page. 'I want to clear up a few things, then I thought I'd have a sandwich and call in at Blubberhouses on the way home and buy some plants. We've run out of pesticide too, and the greenfly are getting out of hand.'

As he was leaving, I saw him surreptitiously slip his toothbrush into his brief case. When he shut the front door behind him, he immediately broke into a run. I knew he'd gone to meet Daisy. In a potting shed, I found a full can of pesticide. I went back into the house. I couldn't stop shaking. Jester came over and wagged his tail. I hugged his solid smelly body for comfort.

Oh God, please help me, I sobbed.

For once, God was listening. There was a crunch on the gravel outside, I looked out of the window and saw Daisy and three carrier bags getting out of a taxi. She turned and waved.

'Have you got any money,' she shouted. 'It's cost more than I thought.'

As I went to look for my purse, I felt as though a great spear had been pulled out of my side.

She left the carrier bags in the hall and came into the drawing room clutching two bottles of wine.

'Old Sue Bad Manners turned nasty and kicked me out. I'm going back to London on the four thirty so I thought I'd come and spend the rest of the day with you.'

She sat down on the sofa. 'I've got an awful hangover. Look,' she stuck out a completely blackened tongue. 'Have you got a cork-screw. I nicked a couple of bottles from Sue, since she's been so bloody.'

I opened a bottle and poured out a couple of glasses.

'You're shaking,' she said, 'What's up?'

'Nothing,' I said. 'Your hemline's coming down.'

'I forgot to transfer the safety pins from my other skirt.'

'What are you going to do when you get back to London?'

'Oh go abroad again probably. I'm not sitting around in that snake-pit any longer, listening to everyone celebrating their neuroses. I'm fed up acting and performing, just as a meal ticket.'

We finished a bottle. I found I had the utmost difficulty concentrating on what she was saying. Oh why didn't she go now, and leave me to the lesser discomfort of missing her.

She slid down to the floor, putting a green cushion behind her head. She seemed to be waiting for something to happen.

'Are you hungry,' I said flustered.

'Only for you.'

'Don't be silly,' I got to my feet. 'I must give Jester his lunch.'

She went on staring at me. I seemed to have lost the will to move. 'I'm not silly,' she said.

Suddenly she kneeled up and shuffled towards me, grabbing me round the thighs. I nearly fell over as she pressed her face convulsively against my stomach.

'You want me,' she whispered triumphantly. 'I know you do.'

I looked down at the gaudy hair and the wide staring eyes: 'I thought you wanted Boy.'

'Boy,' she gave a snort. 'I'd rather climb on a cobra than go to bed with him. Why do you think I've been hanging round you all this time?'

I couldn't stop myself stroking her hair. It felt stiff and tacky. 'I wish you wouldn't smother it with this horrible laquer,' I said.

She turned her head and kissed my hand: 'You sound just like my mother would have done. If I'd had one.'

I was bewildered and afraid, part of me repelled by her kneeling there, clutching me, and yet knowing I wanted her to go on and on and do anything and everything.

'Let's go upstairs,' she said.

On the bed she went very still. The light seemed to fade from her face, a terrible greyness taking its place. I was suddenly sad.

'Don't worry', she whispered.

I dropped onto my knees beside her. I couldn't stop kissing her. I felt her hands on my breasts moving on and on. In turn I moved into her, till we were together.

'You do love me,' she said.

'Yes,' I said reluctantly. I resented having my heart ripped out like this.

The pale blue eyes gazed at me with excitement and anticipation.

Afterwards I was glad she had long hair in which I could bury my face and hide my shyness. I remember how brown she was against the white sheets, and how her nipples grew hard as the rest of her body went soft, and how a blue-bottle crashed against a window-pane.

Afterwards surfacing in a tender strangely new world, we were shy of each other. She looked so touching, all mixed up in the blanket, her eyes huge and curiously gentle.

'I'm glad it was good,' she said.

'Better than anything ever before.'

She snuggled into the crook of my arm: 'I feel as though

I've taken too many Veganin and the pain's all drifting away. I suppose we wouldn't have done it if I hadn't been leaving. It's like one only waves at the handsome stranger on the platform when the train's moving safely out of the station.' She fell asleep when she said that, but I didn't, not for a long time.

I must have dozed at last because the next thing I remember was Boy crashing into the bedroom.

'There you are. Are you ill or something? Some bloody idiot left the gate open. The sheep have got in and eaten all the roses.'

I was frozen with terror, overcome with that convulsive fear you feel just before your car hits somebody else's. Boy drew back the curtains and noticed the shape of Daisy's huddled form under the bedclothes.

'How many times,' he exploded, 'have I told you I won't have the dogs upstairs, particularly in the beds.'

He turned to go out. A muffled giggle came from under the sheet. Boy thought it was me: 'It's not funny either,' he snapped.

Then to my horror, Daisy's tousled head appeared: 'Wow wow, bow wow, bow wow, Grrrr, bow wow, wuff wuff Grrr,' she said, and went off into fits of giggles.

Boy looked like an enraged beetroot.

'What the hell are you doing here,' he roared. 'You were . . .'

'Supposed to be meeting you in Leeds. I found someone more attractive here. So I thought I'd get you out of the way.'

So he *had* been sneaking off to meet Daisy.

'You beast,' I said furiously. 'Get out, get out.'

Boy turned on me: 'You dirty bitch,' he shouted. 'I'll divorce you for this, and I'll cite her as co-respondent. You won't get away with it.' He charged out of the room, stumbling over Daisy's shoes.

We looked at each other and started to giggle nervously.

'I should have asked him to join us,' said Daisy. 'I hope he won't be too awful to you. I supposed I'd better get dressed and catch my train. Can you lend me a fiver for my ticket?'

I insisted on driving her to the station. She was embarrassed when we got there because she had to admit that Peter Manners had already bought her ticket for her. But she didn't suggest returning the fiver.

'Will you come and see me in London?' she said.

'Of course,' I said, knowing I wouldn't.

'I'll write,' she said, knowing she wouldn't.

I never saw her again, but she did send me some awfully good snapshots of Jester, much better than our local photographer took.

Boy and I avoided each other when I got home. I was too numb to think straight. He seemed very subdued. It was as though we were convalescing from a long illness. He went to bed early and I hung around for hours, dawdling over my bath in the hope he might go to sleep, but when I went into the bedroom he was still reading.

'I'm sorry,' I blurted out, 'It must have been horrid coming home like that.'

'That's all right, old girl. But I'm glad she's gone. It might have been a bit tricky with the boys coming home from school next week. Why don't you come into my bed for a minute.'

Oh the coolness of those sheets as he gently took off my nightgown. There was a passionate concentration in his eyes I'd never seen before. He was breathing heavily as he bent over and whispered: 'You looked so beautiful lying there together. Go on, tell me exactly what you did to each other. . . .'

Letters to Reg

c/o American Express
Paris 1
December, 1958

DEAREST REG,

Lots of nasty but also very exciting things have been happening to me. First, I found myself really unhappy with Kenneth. Sort of absolutely dead relationship, no feeling of life or progression in any way at all, and no desire to be with him. Yet he's so clever, being a university don and all that, yet not at all clever. Of course I'm still fond of him and always will be, but I found him impossible to live with on any basis. For the first week after I came back I felt completely dead and lifeless and overpowered with inertia and apathy and a sort of blanketed dull despair. Everything that has happened to me over the last two years has been bad for me. Finding out so quickly that I didn't love Gerald. Then after all that pain and despair, poor R. killing himself, *not* being able to love Felix or Sally, and finally coming back to Maurice and finding him exactly the same and not being able to love him either.

I feel as if I am in a most ghastly void, with no point or direction in life at all. I thought I'd die last week. Anyway then somebody called Boris appeared who's Maurice's oldest and greatest friend and was absolutely wonderful and sweet and cheering and understanding. Took one to lovely nightclubs and luxurious hotels with nice food and drink and was awfully helpful to Maurice who was almost as gloomy as me. I do think he is a more than nice person and as easily as anything could love him so much, but that would be a bad idea as he has all sorts of people in Paris and it's really almost time for me *not* to have another unhappy love affair. We're staying with Boris in a marvellous flat with huge great rooms and high ceilings and silk-hung walls and enormous beds and pretty terra-cotta coloured tiles. My life at the moment ought to be lovely. Waking up in a room full of sun and flowers and breakfast at about half past ten. Not getting up (except to sunbathe on the balcony) till about four. Peacefully drifting into sundown Negronis and Americanos, lovely late slightly drunken dinners of T-bone steaks and champagne, and rather more drunken nights in clubs with jet set people who Boris knows like Aly Khan and ex-King Farouk etc. Going home at dawn in a carriage which Maurice says is vulgar but which Boris and I adore, then bed until it all starts over again. Just the things I like best. But it won't last. I cut my wrist with a razor-blade the other day. The wound was *huge*. I had to be rushed off to a doctor and have stitches and terrible bandages etc. – terribly ashamed of myself now.

Love, love, love,
DAISY

c/o American Express
Rome
January, 1959

DEAREST REG,

I've had a wonderful offer made to me which I think is going to be a sort of answer to all my boring problems, which is to go to Hollywood!!! There's a young American film person here who's a friend of Boris and terribly sweet and funny and who quite rightly thought I was miz. One day I told him just how miz I felt and that I couldn't go on living with Maurice because of it being dead but what could I do because there was no money. He says he'd pay my fare to Hollywood and put me up in his house and buy me some nice clothes and find me little jobs in films and look after me generally till I found out what I *really* wanted to do and who I *really* am. He's a marvellously kind sincere person and I absolutely trust him and I'm sure he'd be all right. This may sound mad to you about me being so unhappy but I tried to explain in my last letter. I'm convinced that going to Hollywood will make me alive again and also give me a direction in life which is entirely absent now. I'm overjoyed but Maurice is utterly miz and against me going. But I feel too strongly for my own self-preservation to give in to him. Do you remember how I used to dream about Hollywood when I was in love with Farley Granger?!!! Darling will you write to me *now* and tell me what you think. I did an *awful* thing by running off with a skirt of Jenny's and now I can't bear to send it back. Also owe four pounds to Wheelers! I want so much to hear from you and get your advice because to tell you the truth it's all getting a bit tricky about Boris.

Molti bacci,
DAISY

PS Don't laugh, Reg. I do want to find myself. I'm fed up being a phoney, living off people, using them, yet for nothing. But what can I do? Don't say go back and be a secretary or I'll scream. I mean what can I do with my life *now*. You know what I've done. I've told you everything. What is the point? There must be one. Is Farley Granger still alive?

In the clouds
September, 1959

DEAREST REG,

I'm writing this in an aeroplane. I got my fare out of Boris' drawer, and that's all the money I've got. I've been awfully confused recently about various things and I felt I just had to get away somewhere, all by myself, to work things out. (Christ, what a lot of cliches in one sentence!) But seriously darling things got *so* involved when we came back to London. I found I just wasn't thinking about anything that happened to me. It was as though I'd forgotten how to think – or perhaps I'd never *known* how. So nothing made any sense. Then suddenly something happened which made me realize that my actions could be destructive. I've always thought of myself as a *victim* for some reason, the person who *gets* hurt, but now I see that all the time *other* people have been getting hurt – and by me! Honestly, Reg, it's an awful feeling – I wonder if you've ever had it? Thank God I've never hurt *you*, at least, and never never will. I've always felt alone in a sense, as you know, but now I feel alone in another way. What I mean is – don't laugh, Reg – I want to find God. Or *something*. It's not that I believe in God exactly, but then again how do I know there isn't one? And if there *is*, one ought to do something about it. I know this must sound drivel (I've just had two *enormous* Scotches which on top of my Kwells have made me feel lovely and high!) but it's just that I can't express what I feel properly. And what I feel isn't drivel. Do you think there's a God, Reg? And if there is, do you think I'll ever find Him?

DAISY

New Delhi
October, 1959

Thought you might like this pc of the Taj Mahal. Noel Coward was wrong – it doesn't look a bit like a biscuit box. I prefer the Hindu temples though, they're really sexy. Having wonderful time. Love, Daisy.

9

Phillip's story

The Swami Krishnan Ashram and All India Centre for Mystic Research lies on a high plateau of the Ghat mountains that rise behind Bombay. It can be reached by taking the Deccan Queen which leaves Bombay Central every day, changing at Guntakal, taking the metre gauge local train and then climbing the last two miles on foot, or by driving from Bombay to Lonavla and walking from there.

Daisy nearly did not get there at all. The Sikh truck driver who had picked her up ten miles out of Lonavla, ashamed at seeing an English girl hitch-hiking in India, behaved immaculately until he got over his surprise. Then as the heavy Mercedes truck thundered around the corners of the narrow mountain roadway he seemed to be able to change gears, wrench the steering around, get his one hand round Daisy's neck and the other halfway up her skirt. As they wrestled back and forth over the cracked leather seat Daisy bitterly regretted changing out of her slacks that very morning.

Daisy's escape came as they roared through a village. A chicken lazier than the rest failed to run fast enough and disappeared under the bonnet in a flurry of squawks and feathers. The Sikh stamped on the brake, stopped the truck and ran back to claim the body, leaving Daisy enough time to grab her rucksack, slip out the passenger's door and seek refuge in the general store. The Sikh saw her as he walked back to the truck and grinned as he waved goodbye. It was getting dark rapidly and she had no idea of how far she still had to go. She turned to the Hindu shopkeeper who had been watching her from behind his sacks since the truck had stopped. 'Do you speak English,' Daisy said.

'Yes.'

'How far is it to the Swami Krishnan Ashram?'

'About four miles. Perhaps four miles four furlongs.'

Daisy was about to ask if there was a bus service and then had a better idea. 'Can I use your telephone, please.'

'Two annas,' the shopkeeper said.

She found the Ashram number in her wallet, written on the back of her permit, that much valued Customs paper which allows foreigners a ration of alcohol in Prohibition India. After a little difficulty she managed to get someone to the telephone who understood her. After a long wait, he returned to the telephone to tell her that the Swami would be sending his assistant to pick her up.

The assistant, who arrived twenty minutes later, turned out to be a large Indianized German christened Heinrich Berninghaus who now called himself Sunder Rao. Rao wore Indian clothes, refused to speak German any more and had the clear piercing eyes of a religious fanatic. Rao hated Daisy before they had even met. His devotion to the Swami had homosexual undertones, and he sensed a rival. He introduced himself curtly and then took Daisy with him into the back seat of the car while the driver put Daisy's rucksack on the seat alongside him.

'You do not have many possessions,' Rao said as they moved off. 'That at least is good. Swamiji considers possessions the shackles of the soul. True liberation lies in the renunciation of, not the worship of, objects. I hope you have not been conditioned by western society to regard the acquisition of objects as the main aim in life, to be achieved whatever the cost. Of course, any society which preaches this ensures its own eventual corruption.'

'Well . . .' Daisy said, but Rao interrupted her.

'I may as well tell you that Swamiji expects great things of you. If you have a true calling you will be able to do for Swamiji as much as Vivekananda did for the great Paramahamsa many years ago. A western disciple can be of great benefit. That is, if you have a true calling. If you are a dilettante then. . . .'

'I'm not a dilettante,' Daisy said. 'I've come all the way from

London and I've paid for my course. I know what I'm doing.'

'I hope so,' Rao said. 'You see, many young women find the lack of purpose in their western civilization frustrating and come to India seeking to enlighten their souls. But corruption has eaten deeper than they have imagined and they seek only superficially. Their resolve weakens and temptation takes them back on the path of decadence from which they had hoped to escape.'

'I know what I'm doing,' Daisy said. 'I know why I've come to India and I know the Swami can help me. I need someone to guide me and I'll be alright. I know I will.'

'We hope so,' Rao said. 'Now, the timetable. We rise at three a.m. Ablutions and prayers. Instruction from five until nine: meditation until eleven. You will be free until three but Swamiji would prefer that you fill this time with spinning and meditation. There will be further instruction from three until seven. Prayers will follow and bed will be at eight.'

'What about meals?' Daisy said.

'Meals?' Rao seemed surprised. 'Oh, there will be some curd and molasses in the morning. You can have some bananas and milk in the middle of the day if you like. Or a little vegetable. And there are curds and molasses available in the evening.'

'Christ,' Daisy said. 'That's not enough for me. I get weak if I don't have a decent breakfast. Is that all the Swami eats?'

'Swamiji is not concerned with the demands of the body,' Rao said. 'He is approaching full Samadhi, the deep sleep state where the mind has dissolved and can no longer perceive the individual.' Rao's eyes took on a far away look. 'There he will know no desire, no virtue or vice will taint him, no fear disturb him. Just as one embraced by his beloved is innocent of all else, so Swamiji will embrace the self and in doing so realize all and be at peace.'

'Isn't that what we are all looking for,' Daisy said. 'Peace, I mean.'

'We are,' Rao said. 'But the path is long and difficult, and only Swamiji can light the way.'

Daisy felt she had been asleep only minutes when there was a soft shaking of her shoulder through the mosquito net and a distant voice saying persistently 'Memsahib, memsahib.'

She made an effort and opened her eyes. It was still dark and although a light in the compound outside her room shone through the curtains it took her some time to make out that the bearer was crouched by her bedside holding a cup of tea towards her. She sat up and shivered. Bombay had been hot but here in the mountains the night had an edge of chill. She reached down and found her dressing-gown, then pulled the mosquito net aside and took the tea.

'Half past two, memsahib,' the bearer said. 'Sunderbai says you can come to Swamiji's washing. When you are ready I'll show you the way.'

Daisy dressed hurriedly. She was uncertain what the bearer meant but she was anxious to meet Swami Krishnan and had been disappointed that he had not appeared after her arrival the previous evening. She had gone to bed tortured by doubt. Had the whole adventure been incredibly foolish? It was one thing to be interested in yoga in London, another to pack up and come to India to look for . . . what? Was yoga a path to some spiritual plateau where all the problems that had crowded her in London would seem insignificant? That had not been her goal when she signed for her first lesson. Then she had considered it just another way of getting out of Boris' flat.

But Mrs Baksh, the yoga teacher, had encouraged her. 'There is a limit to what I can show you,' she had said. 'I myself did not become interested in yoga until I arrived this side. It's an amazing and comforting thing, but I only know the beginnings, that's all. You know, my dear, I have seen in you an unhappy person. I think that you're at a crossroad in your life. Why don't you go to India. In India, under a good guru, you will find the right path.'

The Ashram's main room, a large one, was brilliantly lit. About twenty people, all Indians, stood along the walls, women on the left, men on the right. Facing the door was a large carved armchair raised on a small platform. In it sat the Swami, naked except for his dhoti. He was a much smaller man than Daisy had expected but in most other respects he lived up to what she had imagined a holy man of India should look like. His head was shaved and his skin had a soft glow that was almost luminescent. His eyes, too, shone with health, energy and some inner force that Daisy sensed rather than identified. His body was almost hairless except for his ears where small tufts of black fur sprouted heavenwards giving him an appearance of a faun. He was an unusual and attractive man and Daisy felt instantly drawn to him. Unfortunately she arrived as the Swami was in the last stages of his ritual ablutions and was rinsing his mouth into a stainless steel bowl. His favourite disciples had been admitted to watch this as a privilege just as those who merited special reward were allowed to listen to the Swami on the toilet.

His gargling complete, the Swami composed himself and a group of children began to sing a hymn. The Swami closed his eyes and seemed to drop off to sleep. Daisy waited for the singing which seemed to be repeating itself, to finish, or for the Swami to wake up, but half an hour passed with nothing happening. She gathered her courage and moved across to Sunder Rao and asked: 'When will the Swami wake up?'

Rao turned to her annoyed. 'Wake up?' he said. 'Swamiji is not asleep. He is in Samadhi, a trance state.'

'Oh,' Daisy said. 'How can you tell it from sleep?'

'You can't,' Rao said. 'You just know.'

The next half hour seemed interminable. Then the Swami stirred, stretched, belched and slowly opened his eyes. He looked sleepily around as if not certain where he was, then he waved his hand in dismissal and Rao ushered everyone through the door.

Daisy slept through the morning instruction period but made the afternoon one. It took place in the same room where the Swami had held court in the morning but everyone sat on the floor, some balancing notebooks on their knees. The Swami waited until the rustling and coughing had stopped then suddenly launched into his subject. 'Bondage is caused by attributing reality to objects which arise only in the thoughts. Before the seeing there is no seen and there is no seen after the seeing. Indeed there is no seen even at the time of seeing. Objects do not exist and so a thought cannot have an object. If it cannot have an object then it cannot be called a thought. The objectless thought is the real Self and all experience and knowledge are inside this Self. . . .' Daisy struggled to keep up. Other students were making frantic notes and Rao looked transfigured. Daisy's mind drifted, lulled along with the Swami's monotone until his words ran together in a soothing flow. Daisy felt relaxed and contented. Was this, she wondered idly, the beginning of enlightenment?

On the fourth day Daisy cornered Rao leaving the dining hall after the evening meal. 'I want to know when I am going to meet the Swami,' she said firmly. 'I want to talk to him about my instruction and I want to know when we are going to get on to some yoga. All I've heard in four days has been talk. I paid for personal instruction. When am I going to get it?'

'Typical western impatience,' Rao said. 'If you had remained silent you would not have made yourself appear foolish. I was going to tell you later that tomorrow after prayers your instruction will begin. You will be privileged to watch Swamiji examining a candidate for staff. The Swamiji himself will explain the examination to you. Good-night.'

Daisy joined the Swami's group soon after six a.m. It was a still, cloudless morning but the sun as yet had no heat in it and even the Swami had wrapped a light grey woollen shawl around his shoulders. He stood with five or six disciples in the centre of the compound where the wooden cover of a large cement water tank had been removed. At one side the candidate, a middle aged man of slight but athletic build with bright and fierce eyes squatted on a scrap of matting on the ground, wearing a small loincloth and apparently oblivious to the chill. The Swami greeted Daisy, concentrating his full attention on her. 'Good morning, Miss Smuten,' he said. 'We are about to start. I shall allow Sunderbai to instruct you on the preliminary stages of the examination and I myself will detail the more advanced procedures.' He turned to the candidate and spoke to him in Marathi. The man stood up, dug into his loincloth, and produced what appeared to Daisy to be a roll of surgical gauze. He unrolled about a foot of it, tilted his head back and began to eat it, feeding more of the cloth from the roll as the end vanished down his throat.

'Dhouti,' Sunder Rao said, watching Daisy carefully to see how she would take it. 'He will swallow the full length of the cloth, about seven metres, say twenty-two feet, and then pull it out again. This cleanses the waste matter coating the wall of his stomach and prepares the individual for further stages. No doubt you did this in London?'

'No,' Daisy said, struggling against gagging as the yogi swallowed another six inches.

'Strange. It is an elementary precept that the stomach must be cleansed. I find it odd that all those ladies in London did their yoga with dirty alimentary tracts.'

Daisy did not answer. The yogi had reached the end of the bandage and was steadily hauling it out casting it aside like a fishing line as he did so. When he reached the end he squatted down on the mat again folding his legs under him in the position Daisy had learned so painfully. He then tucked his chin tightly into his neck and after a few rhythmic breaths he sucked his stomach into his spine and held it there.

'I know this part,' Daisy said. 'I've seen it before. One of the Indian girls in London could do it.'

'No doubt,' Sunder said. 'It is called Maha Veda, and it involves locking the air in the body. The folding of the legs under the body is so as to use the pressure of the left heel against the anus. The chin is pressed into the jugular notch to seal the air passages into the throat. The candidate is also using khecari mudra. This is he has lengthened his tongue several inches by cutting the tendon underneath and tugging at it daily. It can reach his eyebrows. Now he has swallowed it and is blocking the holes of his nostrils. Shortly he will expel the locked in air at will.'

As if to punctuate the end of Rao's discourse, the yogi rested both his palms flat on the ground, raised himself slightly and bounced up and down on his buttocks, removing his left heel sufficiently from its resting place so that each bounce expelled a portion of trapped air with a gentle girl-like exclamation.

'You look disgusted, Miss Smuten,' Rao said. 'Surely the significance of the exercises you did in London were explained to you?'

'No,' Daisy said faintly. 'They were not.'

'Good then,' the Swami interrupted. 'The instruction will be all the more beneficial.' He spoke again to the yogi and the man, after a brief glance at Daisy, undid his loincloth and stood naked alongside the water tank. One of the disciples went into the dining hall and came back with a plastic glass. 'The ultimate aim of yoga,' the Swami began, 'is union of atma and mind, a final samadhi in which a stage of deep dreamless sleep is entered into. By an act of will the mind and body dissolve into one and a never-ending ecstatic bliss follows. To achieve this the physical self must be mastered, those bodily functions which in the west are considered voluntary must be brought under the control of the will. I have instructed the candidate to demonstrate the degree to which he has achieved control over an involuntary function and the contempt his will now has for that function.' He gestured to the yogi and the man dipped the plastic cup into the water tank and partially filled it. Holding it with both hands he tilted it and inserted his penis into the water almost to the bottom of the glass.

'Watch closely,' the Swami said, as he sensed Daisy about to turn away. For a few moments nothing appeared to happen. Then, with a sickening feeling of disbelief, Daisy watched the level of the water slowly but steadily fall until only a few drops were left.

'Vajroli mudra,' the Swami said as if nothing unusual had occurred. 'The mastery of the involuntary function of the bladder culminating in the reversal of the excretory process: the sucking up of liquid through channels normally used for the expulsion.' The Swami spoke again to the yogi and the man clambered over the rim of the tank and stood up to his waist in water. 'Once mastery of the involuntary muscles has been reached – and the path began with that first lesson you took in London – then there is no limit to what may be achieved.' The Swami went on, 'liquids may be ingested through all orifices; through the anus the sakti-nada may be removed for a thorough cleaning and . . . Miss Smuten!' He frowned as Daisy burst past the disciples crowding close to the Swami's words and dashed across the compound. In the tank the yogi, oblivious to the disturbance, had taken out his intestines and was busy scrubbing them.

Back in Bombay Daisy settled into the Salvation Army hostel while she tried to decide what to do. If she had had enough money she would have taken the next plane to London but this was out of the question. She could cable Boris asking for a loan or try to make it back overland with what little money was left. She put off a decision hoping that someone would make it for her, spending her days at the cinema or window shopping, eating at the cheaper Indian restaurants at Churchgate.

Phillip Close met her when she was wandering through a handloom silk store fingering the expensive materials. Close, big and bearded, was the art director of one of the Indian advertising agencies. He had seen Daisy at Churchgate once or twice and had wondered who she was. Now he introduced himself by offering to bargain with the shopkeeper on her behalf. They went from the shop to an ice-cream parlour and by the time Daisy was halfway through a milk, ice-cream and fruit concoction she found she had accepted an invitation to Close's party that night. Close told her his parties were the best in Bombay, which was fairly true. He had a knack of mixing a hard-core of Indians and resident Europeans with a floating pool of visitors. There was always enough liquor, mostly the locally distilled stuff which, although foul, had not yet sent anyone blind which was more than could be said for some of the village home-brew that Prohibition had brought into being.

Daisy arrived late because she had trouble ironing her only suitable dress. As the bearer ushered her into Close's flat the first person she saw was Swami Krishnan. The Swami was not usually part of Close's social scene but Close's wife was a concert impresario. She had arranged a private recital by a newly-discovered sitar player all India was talking about and the Swami had not been able to resist a chance of hearing him. Daisy hesitated a moment and then quickly decided she could not face meeting the Swami again and turned to leave. Close caught her by the arm as she reached the door, bustled her into one of the side rooms and got her a drink. 'I've been doing a bit of checking on you,' he said. 'Just out of interest, and I've heard what happened up at the Ashram. You know what I think? I think it serves you bloody well right. You need your head read. You and that whole yoga lot. You go prancing around squatting on your heels and standing on your heads and think you're yogis and all the time none of you have the faintest bloody idea what it's really about.'

Daisy laughed. 'Well, it was a bit of a surprise.'

Close came and sat on the arm of Daisy's chair. He seemed very fatherly. 'Look. All that happened up in the Ghats was that the old Swami put you wise. He did it deliberately. He gets hundreds of girls who think they want to do yoga and he's developed a crash course in showing them what it's really about.'

'All right,' Daisy said. 'Since you seem to know so much. What is it about?'

'Christ,' Close said. 'I thought you knew now. It's about death.'

'Death?'

'Yes. Death. All that stuff they talk about – the never ending deep dreamless sleep, the union of body and soul.'

'The final samadhi?'

'Yes, that's it. Now you tell me another name for eternal sleep.'

'Death?'

'Right. Death. The end product of yoga is death. And all those exercises you and your girlfriends thought you were doing to improve your figures and your souls are really the first steps in a devilish programme designed to make your body connive at its own destruction. You keep practising at it – closing the orifices, reversing the function of organs, suspending the breath – until one day you will the body to do them all at once and wham – you blow up! That's it, you've annihilated yourself.'

Daisy laughed. 'I suppose it'll make a good story back in London. If ever I get back to London.'

'Look, baby,' Close said. 'I've been in India nearly thirty years. I can switch off my European mind and think like an Indian. I know them. And that's what yoga is all about. If you don't believe me read the Swami's book again. Ignore the crap and just concentrate on his description of the final union, the dreamless sleep or whatever he is currently calling it. No matter how you read it, baby, it's death.'

'I wonder if I could have a drink,' Daisy said, and got up. 'I suddenly feel like getting really sloshed.'

'Great,' Close said. 'I'll join you. And don't be too hard on old Swami. We've all got to make a living and he's drawn the holy man bit. Give him a smile when you see him and he'll know all's forgotten. Oh, and about getting back to London. Come round here tomorrow afternoon about five. I might be able to help you.'

'How?' Daisy asked.

'I just might. I'm a bit of a miracle worker myself.'

Afterwards everyone agreed that the party had been one of Close's best. Daisy quickly got involved with two English jockeys who were sitting out the steeplechase season riding in India, and a tall and elegant Indian film star who although at least thirty had brought her mother along as chaperone. Close's living room ran the depth of a block of flats so that one balcony overlooked Colaba Causeway with its dusty and sleepless night while the other faced the sea with its slap of waves against the retaining wall and the dim light of an Arab dhow heading back to the Persian Gulf, making slow progress against the incoming tide. The guests sat on cushions on the marble floor or stood leaning on the balcony rail. The bearers padded in and out of the kitchen carrying drinks, nuts, sweetmeats and snacks. There were half a dozen girls from Close's office as sort of assistant hostesses, astoundingly pretty in bright saris and pale, almost invisible lipstick. An Indian poet from Kashmir, a handsome and intense young man who told Daisy he was an atom physicist, an old man in a dhoti who looked a little like Gandhi, the editor of a weekly newsmagazine who was trying to persuade Close's wife to run away with him, three American students on holiday, the Norwegian consul and dozens of minor characters drifted on and off stage, some performing, others just passing through. Daisy took Close's advice and nodded at the Swami when he passed her. The Swami smiled, waved a drink and continued talking to the actress.

Daisy excused herself from the jockeys and went to stand on the balcony with Close. She was pleasantly intoxicated. The party had an atmosphere quite unlike any she had ever attended in Britain, an underlying air of sensuality, one of those evenings when one felt almost anything could happen. She was about to remark on this to Close when a bearer, obviously agitated, approached Close and said, 'There's a policeman at the door, sahib.'

'Policeman?' Close said, then: 'Christ! It must be a raid. It's a raid, everybody,' he shouted. 'Get rid of the booze.' He flung his glass over the balcony, abandoned Daisy and ran to the kitchen. Daisy stood undecided what she should do. All around her Indians were scuttling to hide the evidence, hindered by among others the old guest in the dhoti who had suddenly announced himself as 'Inspector Bhose, Anti-Corruption Squad' and was trying to snatch glasses before they were emptied. The front door had burst open and uniformed police waving long bamboo canes poured in, headed by a large Anglo-Indian Inspector shouting 'Nobody move!' One of the constables tried to grab a glass from one of the jockeys who promptly punched him, and a struggle broke out. Daisy fought her way through the chaos to the kitchen where Close and one of the servants were frantically pouring bottle after bottle of home distilled spirits down the sink. 'Here, you do this,' Close said. 'I'm going to try to arrange some diplomatic immunity. There must be a bloody diplomat here somewhere.' Daisy grabbed a bottle and up ended it in the sink. It was barely empty when another was thrust at her. 'Faster, Miss Smuten. Tip it right up.' Daisy looked around. The Swami, a bottle in each hand, neatly cracked the necks against the edge of the sink and the liquor gushed away. Close reappeared, stopping to lock the door to the living room behind him. 'No diplomat,' he said. 'I'll have to fetch one. Come on Joseph.' He bundled the servant through the back door. 'Lock it,' he said to Daisy. 'Don't let anyone in. And don't go out. They're checking permits. You'll be alright but they'll put the Swami away for six months. I'll be back as soon as I can.'

Daisy locked the door while the Swami finished emptying the last two bottles.

Someone tried the kitchen door, then knocked, waited, knocked again, and then apparently gave up. The Swami composed himself on the servant's bed and lay back, hands clasped behind his head, staring at the ceiling. Daisy found herself trembling. 'I wish we hadn't poured all of it away,' she said. 'I need a drink.'

The Swami got up. 'I too find my nerves somewhat strained,' he said. He took a small tobacco tin from his pocket. 'Perhaps this will calm us. Would you see if there is any milk in the refrigerator?'

Daisy got the milk and the Swami poured two glasses, pinched a little powder from his tin, and stirred it into the glasses. 'Here, drink this,' he said. 'It will do you good.'

'What is it?'

'Bhang, Miss Smuten. A distillation of cannabis indica. An aid to the liberation of the mind.'

'No thanks,' Daisy said. 'You turn on by yourself. My mind is liberated enough as it is.'

'As you wish,' the Swami said. He drank his own glass and then Daisy's. He returned to the bed, lay down again, closed his eyes and soon appeared to sleep. At first Daisy amused herself examining the contents of the kitchen cupboards but an hour passed and nothing happened. She tentatively tried the door handle but this brought a brief but loud renewal of knocking so she retreated and sat on the foot of the bed. The Swami did not move.

'Hey Swami,' Daisy said. 'Are you asleep?'

The Swami opened his eyes. 'No,' he said. 'I have not been asleep at all. I have been seeking guidance. By allowing my conscious mind to rove at will I hope to allow it to solve for itself a problem which has been presented to me.'

'What's that?' Daisy asked, not really interested.

'It has occurred to me that I have failed you, Miss Smuten. You came to me seeking and I was unable to give. I shocked you. I was brutal to you. Where you sought gentleness I gave only cruelty.'

'Well, it wasn't really as bad as that,' Daisy said.

'No. You are kind, but I see how wrong I was. I wanted to offer you affinity on the spiritual level before we had found that affinity on the physical plane. Perhaps if you had looked to Shiva, if you had allowed Kama to occupy yourself, then in this there would have been comfort for your storm tossed soul. I should have guided you on this path, I should have shown you that desire in itself is not wrong, it is in the recognition of desire that bondage lies. Release your desire, embrace Shiva, and desire no longer exists.'

'Listen, Swami,' Daisy said. 'I'm not sure what you're getting at, but if it's what I think it is, then . . . then it's against all you believe in. Why, in your book. . . .'

'Book learning can be superseded, Miss Smuten. Practical knowledge sometimes takes precedence. I have found, from time to time, that it is necessary for one to recognize desire so as to liberate oneself from bondage.'

The Swami sat up. He was sweating and his eyes seemed glazed and slightly bloodshot. He suddenly reached out for Daisy who hastily stood up.

'What about the vital fluids, Swami? Page eighty-four. "The loss of the bindu is a physical and spiritual impoverishment. It takes forty drops of blood and forty days to make one drop of vital fluid." '

The Swami laughed. 'Vajroli, Miss Smuten. You have forgotten Vajroli. With the aid of the Madhavadasa vacuum technique of which I am master the vital fluid can be withdrawn from the yoni and reabsorbed through the organ which deposited it there.'

The Swami tore aside his dhoti. 'Come, Miss Smuten. Embrace Shiva. Let us find non-existence together.'

'Keep that vacuum cleaner away from me,' Daisy shouted, backing to the door. 'You dirty old sod. I've never heard anything so disgusting. Let me go. I want to get out of here.'

'Miss Smuten,' the Swami begged. 'Shiva awaits you. Let us exchange pranas, let our soul forces meet and mingle until we sink together in a flood of heavenly light.' He made a rush across the room.

'I'm getting out of here,' Daisy said, and unlocked the door. Inspector Bhose of the anti-corruption squad pushed in, his cheap rubber sandals slapping after him. He ignored Daisy and made straight for the Swami, naked and very erect alongside the sink.

'If you have a Customs permit for the consumption of alcohol,' he said, 'then by the authority invested in me under

Section Eighty-Four of the Prohibition Act of 1947 I demand to see it.'

Daisy arrived at Close's flat a few minutes late but according to the bearer Close was still asleep. He showed Daisy into Close's studio, cluttered with partly finished canvasses, the blinds still lowered against the late afternoon sun. Close came in from a side door ten minutes later. He had just showered and was wearing a towelling robe.

'Hi,' he said. 'Enjoy the party?'

'Thank you,' Daisy said. 'I've never been to one quite like it before.'

There was a knock on the door and the bearer came in with a tray holding a bottle of gin, ice and some freshly-squeezed lime juice. Close poured.

'I've got some good news for you,' he said.

Daisy sipped her drink. Over the whirr of the air conditioner she could hear the children playing in the compound eight floors down.

'I've got this deal,' Close said. 'I do some art work for an airline. Instead of paying me in cash they credit me against travel. I've got more credit than I can use, so . . .well. . . .' He dug in the pocket of his dressing-gown and pulled out an airline ticket. 'I thought that since you're so anxious to get back to London, you might like to fly.'

'You're giving me a ticket?'

'It doesn't really cost me anything,' Close said. 'It's all a matter of book entries. But on the other hand . . . let's see how I can put this delicately . . . or perhaps I needn't say it at all?'

Daisy looked at him. He was probably over fifty but India had been kind to him. His face was lined but suntanned and he radiated the energy force of a much younger man. His hair was still wet from his shower, he smelled of baby's prickly heat powder, and he was more and more obviously naked under his dressing-gown. Daisy noted all this while rejecting the alternatives: a humiliating cable to Boris or an uncomfortable hitch-hike overland. And after all, she decided, who would ever know.

Blackpool
January 1st 1960

DEAREST REG,

I hereby make a solemn New Year's resolution so keep this postcard for ever. From this day forward I am going to *stop* drinking, sleeping around, being phoney, and making a mess of my life. I am going to concentrate only on work and make a very great deal of money and become the best photographer in the whole world and before I die I am going to be the most famous person there has ever been. So one day you will be able to boast that you knew Daisy Smuten better than anybody when she was nobody. There's a change in the weather and a change in the sea and from now on I swear to you Reg there'll be a change in me.

DAISY

10

George's story

You won't believe this, but I only took Daisy out once – and all we did was play croquet with a monk. Nobody believed it at the time either, which, in the end, was what changed everything.

It certainly made a difference to the business. Until then, with Wolfe playing very dirty, 1960 had looked like being an all-time lousy year, I can tell you.

Wolfe rang just after the July holidays. He had to see me. It was personal. It was urgent. It was the usual bloody pantomime. But I went straight away, just the same. 'Look after the shop,' I yelled to little old Jessie.

I walked through the buzz of the production floor picking up bits of scrap towelling and chucking them into skips, out of habit. As the rubber swing doors flapped to behind me, I could see my thirty-five machinists through the Perspex windows – all flogging themselves to death trying to make Wolfe's diabolical towels at impossibly high speeds. And all for a measly eight pound-odd a week.

Not that I seemed to be making much more myself. At thirty-two, I was owner of Bydar Ltd, Bank Street, Bolton, and what was I getting out of it? Nothing but worries – worries about machinists' kids keeping them off work, worries about the cost of materials going up, worries about delivering on time to Wolfe.

I stepped out into Bank Street, down past Joe's Umbrellas, turned left at the lights and went in at Number 77. Wolfe's office was on the second landing with Textile W. Green and Co., Exporters on the door. I went in knowing that whatever

Wolfe had to say it would be bad news.

'Georgie, Georgie,' he shouted, as if astonished to see me. He shot to his feet and smoothed back his thick greying hair.

'So ask me how business is,' he said.

'All right. How's business?'

'Don't ask me.' He crumpled into his chair and put his forehead on his desk. He was playing the music hall Jew – and that meant he was being serious. I'd been here before. The act hadn't changed.

'Georgie, my clients just don't want to know at the present price. "Look," I told them, "my maker-up's margin is so small he has to give his bank manager binoculars. He can't do it for any less." So what do they say? "Get someone who can." You know their new price? Thirty-nine and nine.'

'It's bloody well impossible,' I said.

'I know, Georgie, I know,' Wolfe said, getting up and walking to the window to get a better view of the girls in the Co-op. 'That's why I told them I'd probably have to find another manufacturer.'

Ever since my old man decided to work exclusively for Wolfe ('Better to have steady work on a small margin than bigger profits in occasional bursts,' he used to say) Wolfe had been grinding that small margin even smaller.

I picked up Wolfe's desk calendar and turned it to the right date. Wolfe was still looking out of the window.

The old man's problem had been that nobody wanted to know any more about the quality towels he was turning out. The only bit of the market left for the small boys became the cheap and nasty export stuff. And when you'd managed to get an outlet you hung on to him like grim death. You didn't kick him in the teeth even if he was a bastard.

Wolfe turned from the window. 'Remember, Georgie,' he said, 'there's hardly anything in the world that somebody can't make a little worse and a little cheaper.'

'Well I'll have to work it out properly on paper, Wolfe,' was all I said. 'I'll let you know. I dare say it could be done, at a pinch.'

Wolfe had me over a barrel and both of us knew it.

The noise of Workers' Playtime on the loudspeaker hit me

as I went through the swing doors. I pulled a funny face at little Jessie as I crossed to my office which was partitioned off in the far corner of the floor.

'Mr Ronald Glasgow rang while you were out, Mr Darby. I said you'd ring back.'

Ronnie was conductor of the Bolton Chamber Consort in which I played clarinet. He was music master at a local school and a right old fusspot. But he did all the organizing, set out the music, collected the music stands at the end of rehearsals – all those jobs that no-one else wanted to do. I rang him up.

'Want to hear some good news?' he said. Daft beggar – like a schoolgirl.

'You've come to the right place, Ronnie,' I said.

'I've got an oboe player for the Consort – so at least we can do the Brandenburg.'

'Full marks, Ronnie,' I said. Well, credit where credit's due. 'Who is it?'

'Daisy Smuten.'

'Who's she when she's at home?' I remember saying.

'She's a photographer on the Evening News – been with them about a month. Pretty thing. I met her when she came to photograph our end-of-term concert. She rang me yesterday to say she'd suddenly thought, did we need an oboe?'

An oboe was just what we needed. We'd rehearsed Bach's Brandenburg Concerto Number Two the year before. But old Fred Sutcliffe, who played oboe, had been attacked by some yobboes while shutting his shop and he'd never really been what you'd term right, since. So we were without an oboe for the solo part. We were without a F trumpet, too, but I played that part on my clarinet.

'I think I'll drop the Haydn for our concert. It's going none too well,' Ronnie said. 'And do the Bach while we have the opportunity. Apart from Miss Smuten we are all fully rehearsed already, so it should present few difficulties.'

Well that depended on how good Daisy turned out to be, but you couldn't say that to Ronnie, could you? It would have spoiled his school lunch.

The next Tuesday the Consort met for its usual weekly rehearsal at the Welsh Tabernacle in Bark Street. When I arrived, Ronnie was already there, shoving the harmonium to one side of the little hall. A very glam piece was putting music on the stands. 'I like the violas in the centre, like Sir Thomas, Miss Smuten,' Ronnie was saying.

So that was Daisy Smuten. 'Pretty thing' was all Ronnie had called her – which didn't say much for his opinion. He introduced us. Since nobody else had arrived yet we couldn't very well not talk to each other. So I said how glad we were to be able to have a stab at the Brandenburg again. She said she hoped she'd be good enough because it had been a bit since she'd played oboe in the school orchestra.

The rest of the Consort rolled up ten minutes late. They always did – that way they avoided boring tasks like moving chairs and putting up music stands. Most of them were teachers or solicitors and fancied themselves as musicians. They'd read the right books, gone to the best concerts, bought the dearest LPs and they spent all their time talking about whether the allegro non troppo's contrapuntal effectiveness had been marred by a palimpsest on the second Geneva manuscript, and all that rubbish. All right to play with, they were, but chronic to talk to.

Daisy looked a bit smooth and sophisticated, I must say. 'Aye, aye,' I thought, 'another one of Them.' But it soon turned out that she wasn't.

As the soloists, Daisy and me and Edward Grey-Smith on flute were sitting at the front under Ronnie's nose. 'Would you give us an A, Miss Smuten, please,' said Ronnie. (Orchestras always tune up to an A from the oboe for reasons I shan't bore you with.) Daisy played an A and there were the usual frowns from those smart-Alec violinists who'd already tuned up to their own 'perfect ear' and now found they were about a semitone out.

'Near enough for jazz,' Daisy said, smiling at old Ronnie. Ronnie gave an unconvincing little smile back. He wasn't used to flippant little jokes at the Consort.

Daisy leant across to me. 'Oh Christ,' she whispered, 'I hope I haven't put my foot in it before I've even played a note.'

'I shouldn't worry,' I whispered back. 'Ronnie's a bit of an old woman, that's all.'

Anyway, she'd obviously decided that I was on her side.

And that was nice.

To start with, we ploughed through the whole of the concerto non-stop, ignoring all the cock-ups that occurred en route.

'Well, ladies and gentlemen, we finished together at least,' said Ronnie as he put his stick down. It was one of his two jokes.

Apart from a few squeaks, Daisy hadn't played at all badly, considering we'd rehearsed it for months and Ronnie had only given her the oboe part to practise a few days before. The only thing she'd really messed up was her entry in the last movement, which is very prominent because the only other person playing is the trumpet.

We were well ahead with the rest of the programme so we spent the rest of the evening slogging through the Brandenburg. At the end – when the intellectuals amongst us had disappeared, leaving Ronnie to tidy everything up – Daisy was still sitting there, foot tapping, going through that fatal entry.

Suddenly she saw Ronnie, his braces damn near snapping, trying to fold up one of the stands.

'Can we give you a hand, Mr Glasgow?' she said.

'That's very kind of you, Miss Smuten,' said Ronnie, who I reckon fancied her a bit, in spite of everything. So she collected the music into piles and put the chairs back into rows in the hall. Well, it made a change.

I hung around while she put her instrument away, then said goodnight to Ronnie. I held the door open for her, like mother always taught me.

'God,' Daisy said as we stepped into the little cobbled street. 'What on earth's that smell? I'd been thinking it was going to be a lovely evening.'

'Round this neck of the woods, it's never a lovely evening,' I said. 'It's something to do with the sewage works. They call it the Bark Street Stinks.'

We cut down a scruffy alleyway called Velvet Walks, next to the Tabernacle.

'Velvet Walks,' Daisy read. 'It's a lovely name, isn't it? I bet it was beautiful round here on a warm light evening like this a hundred years ago. There must have been fields running down to the River Croal where the lads could bring their girls.'

'That's a bit hard to imagine,' I said.

'There always turns out to have been fields and posh houses in the town centre and farms where the gas works are. I can just see all the people clopping about on horses and lighting themselves to bed with candles. I'd love to have lived two hundred years ago. I'm not all that keen on now.'

Did she want me to ask her about her past? She was obviously trying very hard with her present. But before I could say anything she'd seen a chip shop and dragged me in.

We had a bag each and the bloke put little wooden forks into them. 'What's the idea of these?' I said. 'Bit fancy, aren't they?'

'Mr Darby,' said Daisy, putting on what I recognized immediately as Ronnie's voice. 'It is clearly a not inconsiderable time since you last consumed the delicacy known as chips.'

I had a good laugh at that. It was my sort of joke. We tucked our instruments under our arms. 'I go up Chorley Old Road, which way do you go?' I said.

'Same way. I've got a sort of flat on Mornington Road.'

We set off walking past the fire station. 'I wouldn't mind a flat myself,' I told her. 'I live in my dear departed mum and dad's house – bloody great thing with no mod cons on Harper's Lane.' We walked past the blind school eating up all those crisp bits that get left in the corners of the bags.

'Do you know much about the oboe?' Daisy said eventually.

'I know it's an ill wind that nobody blows good.'

She smiled again, which was very nice of her because it's a very old joke. 'The thing is, I'm having a bit of trouble with the octave key sticking. That's where the strange noises were coming from. I hate making a mess of things – especially when it's your first outing in a strange town and you're hoping people are going to think you're OK. And I want to succeed in everything I have a go at, don't you?'

'You don't want to get into a lather about what most of that lot are thinking,' I said. 'Edward Grey-Smith drones on for hours with intellectual rubbish about how Bach demands disciplined yet romantic playing.'

We were just starting to walk past Musgrave's mill which stretches up Chorley Old Road for half a mile.

'This place scares me. It seems so horribly all-knowing,' Daisy said. 'Those long rows of little windows everywhere. You can just imagine the generations who have pressed their pale faces up against them with nothing to see but a maze of brickwork, like those kiddies' puzzles where you have to find the exit.'

'I see what you mean,' I said, though I didn't. 'Did you know Musgrave's is the biggest spinning complex in the world? Oh, hang on, or is it Swan Lane? I forget now.'

We got to the junction of Chorley Old Road and Mornington Road down which Musgrave's stretches for hundreds of yards more. Over our heads was a sign in luminous letters saying: 'Wanted: Cone Winders, Frame Tenters.'

Daisy tucked her oboe under her other arm. 'I'll have to look at that octave key or else get the shop to. It's not mine, I've hired it from Smallpiece's in Burnley. Then I can put in a bit of practice on my own. I mustn't let you all down.'

'I don't suppose you will for a moment.'

'Nice of you to say so. I'll see you next Tuesday then. 'Bye.'

She obviously didn't want me to see her home. It was only a few yards away, she said. But it was probably not so much a flat, more a crummy bedsitter. I didn't want to embarrass her. I carried on home, opened a bottle of Magee's Crown and watched the TV. I forget now what was on.

By the end of the next morning I was fed up to the back teeth. I'd had a chat with Edwin Kirkpatrick at Rawtenstall who seemed to make a tidy living turning out luxury bathsheets and bedspreads. If anyone could give me the work I wanted, he could. But he was sorry, business was slack and he'd got enough on his plate keeping all his own people busy. Thank you and good morning. At half past twelve I was more than ready for Ye Old Man and Scythe at the top of the road.

Terry Banister, who I knew at school, was already there. He was already there every time I went in.

'I don't know, Terry, you supermarket blokes have an easy

number. I'll have a pint of best and two sausages.'

'Who said I was buying?'

'I did.'

'How's the torrid love life then?' Terry said as he put a quid on the counter.

'What torrid love life?'

'The bevies of randy birds.'

'I've only met one woman I liked since Christmas and she's not randy as far as I can see,' I said. 'She plays in the Chamber Consort.'

'Jesus,' Terry said, 'It sounds an exotic rendezvous. Who is the lovely lady then?'

'An oboist called Daisy Smuten.'

'Not Dirty Daisy! You're not getting off with her are you?' Terry was laughing his frock off.

'What do you mean Dirty Daisy?' I said, a bit aggravated.

'Only that she's being laid by every bigwig this side of the Pope – including,' and Terry prodded his finger on the table for emphasis, 'including Sir Ormerod Wilkie. If you're playing in that league, you must be more important than I thought you were, George.'

'For God's sake, Terry,' I said, 'I only met the woman last night.'

'Well give it time. Can I get you another pint then?'

'Yes you bloody well can.' He was always dirty-minded, was Terry – and with a good imagination. Sir Ormerod Wilkie was one of those pillar-of-society people, JP, Old Links golf club and all that, and the biggest textile man around Bolton.

'Where did you get all that stuff about Wilkie?' I asked Terry when he came back with the ale.

'Talk of the town, old boy.'

'Cheers. Not my bit of town, it isn't.'

'Well you must be in the wrong bit.'

'Obviously.' I had a bite of sausage.

'Anyway,' said Terry, 'Wilkie's not the only one. There's Alderman Shuttleworth, Councillor Croxdale, Cedric Warburton, the bank manager. There's supposed to be quite a few young blokes and all. I suppose she just fancies them for a change.'

'You what? She's only been here a month. You must think

she gets around some.'

'Well she's got the perfect job for it hasn't she? No questions asked. Last week she went to take a picture of Wilkie on his new cabin cruiser – photo in the paper. Nice little orgy afterwards – nothing in the paper. Now she's on the orchestra lark. You lucky sod.'

As Terry left I lit a cigarette and stared at the bits of sausage floating in the warm remains of my pint. I didn't know what to think. People might invent an affair between Daisy Smuten and some bloke or other – but not with half the bloody town. Terry was a bit of a lying hound, but he moved in the right sort of circles for picking up the dirt on Bolton's top brass.

Even so, you have to take people as you find them. All I knew about Daisy was that she looked marvellous, liked music and ate chips out of a bag. Hardly Terry Banister's raging nympho.

I left Ye Old Man and bought a lunchtime Evening News from the old dear at the corner of Bradshawgate to check the yarn prices. On page three there was a large picture of a group of blokes shaking hands. Underneath, it said: 'Sir Ormerod Wilkie (centre) and Mr Cedric Warburton (left), judges of the Bolton Businessman of the Year award, congratulate the winner, Mr Thomas Shone, at yesterday's luncheon in the Young Businessmen's Club, Bolton.' And in italics at the end, it added: *Picture by Daisy Smuten.*

It was like coming across a new word in a book. You find out what it means, and then it seems to turn up ten times a day for weeks afterwards. That's how it was with the Dirty Daisy stories.

A friend of mine in the lounge at the Swan swore blind that a senior police officer had had her in the back of a patrol car at Belmont. Another mate at Heaton cricket club described what had happened with the Vicar of St Cedric's after she'd taken pictures of the Rose Queen. In the billiard room of Top o' t' Bank Conservative Club, I overheard that she'd spent a weekend at Fleetwood with a Bury councillor on the pretext of doing a photofeature on trawlers.

She was getting to be as well known as Nat Lofthouse.

I didn't see much of her myself. After one rehearsal, we had a quick drink at the Lower Nag's Head where she told me how come a picture of a golden wedding couple appeared in the paper over the caption: 'Wreckage strewn over the road after today's fatal accident.'

I did drive her home twice – but only as far as what she called 'Cone Winders corner' because she said it sounded a lovely job.

After other rehearsals she wasn't going straight home, thanks very much all the same. So I didn't push my luck.

The rehearsals themselves went all right until the last Tuesday – a week before the concert – when we had a dry run of the whole programme. Disaster struck during the Brandenburg slow movement.

I sit that one out, so I was having a smoke at the back of the hall. It was Edward Grey-Smith who loused it up really. He's got such a wet and windy tone that when he goes wrong he keeps fluffing along until he picks it up again and people don't really notice.

The oboe always seems to stick out a mile at times like that, so when poor Daisy made a right pig's ear of things, thanks to Edward, she really copped for the sour looks from the catty old cellists. Funnily enough she romped through the fatal entry, but she was obviously upset. I drove her home.

I stopped the car at Cone Winders corner and gave her a cigarette. I was keeping my fingers crossed that she wasn't going to cry. I'm hopeless with that sort of thing.

She stared at her shoes a bit then said: 'I'm sorry George. It's just a bit unnerving, that's all. I've been killing myself to get that last movement right and now, Christ – I discover another Achilles heel at the last rehearsal.'

'It wasn't your fault, though,' I said. 'It was Edward, daft pillock.'

'I know. But I shouldn't have let him throw me. I suppose I'm more annoyed with myself than anything.'

She looked round for somewhere to put her ash. I leant across, ignoring the ashtray, and wound down her window. As I straightened up I kept my left arm round the back of her seat. According to Terry Banister, she must have been through that one a million times.

Anyhow, I gave her shoulder what I intended as a fatherly squeeze – though that's not what it felt like, I can tell you.

'Look,' I said, 'are you working on Saturday because I was just thinking, you know, that if you weren't – well, you might like to come over to Yorkshire with me. Make you forget the Consort and all that.' It was simple really, when I got round to it.

'No, I'm not working until the evening. Yes, I'd like to come,' Daisy said. 'Now can I wind the window up?' And we both had a laugh. 'Where are we going?'

'Well it sounds daft, but I was thinking of going to a monastery – the Community of the Resurrection, at Mirfield, it's called. It's the headquarters of some Anglican order and a mate of mine, Tim Stringer, is a novice.'

'And what are you, George?'

She got out of the Zephyr, walked away and then turned to wave goodbye. I opened her door to give it a proper slam. 'Don't forget your long woolly coms,' I shouted. 'It gets proper parky in Yorkshire in early October.'

Saturday turned out very nice. There was a thin mist hanging round the rhododendrons in the morning, but when I backed the Zephyr out into Harper's Lane after lunch the sky was clear and it was mad hot.

Daisy was waiting for me at Cone Winders corner – where else? She was dressed in trousers and blouse with a dark green cardigan round her shoulders and was hugging her photographic gear to her, the way that schoolgirls hold satchels.

She piled in and put her stuff on the back seat. 'Got your weekend gear on, have you?' I asked as I cut across the traffic and headed down towards town. I was a bit hurt she'd brought her cameras.

Daisy leant her head on the back of the seat. 'It's a lovely day. I adore these porcelain blue skies, don't you?'

'Very nice.'

'Mind you I like the early morning just as much at this time of the year. When I walk along that huge stretch of mill wall on the way to the bus, that great expanse of brick seems really beautiful in the chilly mist. I've taken quite a few pictures of it . . . but I've not got it yet. It's like being alone in a dream where nothing actually happens. Try getting *that* on a photographic print.'

We pulled up at some traffic lights. 'Musgrave's mill is supposed to be the biggest spinning set-up in the world, you know,' I said.

I concentrated on looking at road signs as we drove through Bury and Rochdale. As bad as Hampton Court maze they are, those places. Especially with all the lunatic Saturday shoppers cluttering the place up with prams and grousing husbands.

'Not a very thrilling drive,' I said to Daisy – who seemed to be enjoying it, to tell the truth. 'Do you know round here at all?'

'Only the places I've been to on jobs for the Evening News. Considering I'm a Lancastrian, I know precious little about Lancashire.'

'You weren't born in Lancashire, were you?' I said.

'Yes, in Liverpool.'

'Get away!' I said. She didn't sound it.

'I suppose it was a romantic thing I had about the grim but honest North. I felt I had to come back up here to start all over again.'

By this time I'd gone wrong somewhere along the route and we were going round the outskirts of Halifax. I saw a pub which looked fairly salubrious. We nipped in for a jar and to ask the best way to Mirfield.

'Now then,' I said, grasping my pint, 'you can't get away with it just like that. Why suddenly take up photography at your age?'

'Well thank you and good night, Prince Charming,' said Daisy. I hoped I was blushing a bit. 'Without going into the sordid details about my age, I've just been wandering around doing nothing ever since I was so high. I've been in all sorts of places, done all sorts of things, but. . . . Oh, I don't know, George. It would only bore you. . . .'

She put her hands over her ears and lowered her head till she was looking into her shandy. All of a sudden she seemed tired and fed up. I was sorry I'd spoken. Trust me.

'I just decided I'd get a job, work like hell at it and become somebody by doing it well.'

'I wouldn't think Bolton was much to write home about when it comes to learning photography.'

'That's just it. I'm not learning photography. I'm learning to be a photographer. It's not knowing all about exposures that counts, it's being able to take pictures to order in all sorts of rotten conditions.

'That's why I'm here – in Bolton, that is. I wanted somewhere where they believe in hard work and where I could learn the job from the bottom. As long as you know what you're doing and quit before you're brainwashed into thinking that the local dog show is what it's all about, you're all right. And I'll be all right. You wait and see.'

There didn't seem any answer to that, so I shut up. I'd never seen her look so determined and confident. Cocky, even.

'But don't get the wrong idea. In lots of ways these boring pictures of people having golden weddings, winning singing competitions, flower shows, well, they *are* what it's all about.'

'How d'you mean?'

'I take his picture and wish him all the best and he goes home to tell his wife what the girl from the paper said. The next day it's all over and they've nothing left to do but cut the picture out and put it in a drawer. That's about all I'd like in life, wouldn't you George? Just a little remembrance to prove you existed.'

I didn't know what she was talking about.

Tim must have been keeping a lookout for us because he came out as we crunched into Mirfield's gravel carpark. Daisy and I got out feeling hellish sticky.

I introduced her to Tim in the manner my mother would have approved of. 'Well, hello there, Daisy,' he said. 'I've heard a lot about you.'

'Aye, aye,' I thought, 'he didn't waste much time picking up the gossip during his holidays.'

'I expect you could down a cold drink, Daisy,' Tim said as he led her through an archway and down a sort of cloister. 'You too, George old man.'

'I should bloody well think so,' I thought to myself, and I

pottered along behind.

'Why aren't you in a cassock or whatever you call them?' I heard Daisy ask Tim.

'Aha! On Saturdays, we're allowed to be in mufti except for services. Most of the lads have visitors today, so we all dress as casually as we can, and smoke and swear a lot. You could say we're over-compensating, I suppose.' Tim was always good at the fancy chat.

We arrived at a sort of lounge. Tim pushed the double doors open for Daisy. One of them swung back as I followed forcing me to dodge it.

I fancied some ale, I must say, but Tim shoved iced orange into our hands. Still, it was better than a poke in the eye with a sharp stick. 'Get that inside you and then you're off to savour Mirfield's prize delight,' he said, looking pleased with himself.

'Oh aye?' I said.

'Yes indeed, my friends. Ten guesses at what it is. . . .'

'Vespers with Cliff Richard,' said Daisy jokingly. Which put Tim off his stroke for a second, I was glad to see.

'Sorry madam, nine more guesses. No can do? The answer is,' he cupped his hands to his mouth like a trumpet, 'tan ta-ta ta-ta-ta taaaa . . . croquet.'

He took Daisy by the arm and we went outside. 'Such a gay life you must lead,' she said, 'what with croquet and orange juice.'

She was taking the mickey out of Tim. He obviously fancied her as much as he fancied himself, but he wasn't sure what to do about it.

I wished I'd brought my sun specs as we strolled down to a huge great lawn surrounded by ye olde rhododendrons, lots of students and their friends and a scattering of monkish cassocks.

Thanks to Daisy's appearance, a lot of blokes round the lawn were sitting up and taking notice by this time. I bet a few girls were feeling the draught. Anyhow, there was a hefty crowd watching as I kicked off, with Tim telling us what to do. Daisy listened intently, almost fanatically, picking up the rules, determined to do it all properly. I made mistakes, to Daisy's annoyance, and felt very out of it. Her concentration was amazing. I felt exhausted afterwards, but she went off to take some pictures.

Tim and I were sitting sweating on a bench in the quadrangle when Daisy found us again. 'Gosh, it's hot,' she said, plonking herself down next to me and dabbing at her forehead with her wrist.

Tim leaned over: 'Did you find some good photos?' he said. As if he cared.

'Oh marvellous, terrific. I could stay here for years.'

'I'll see what I can do,' he said, never one to miss a trick.

'I spent a lot of time in the church itself, I hope that was all right. I love the silence and the feeling that you're part of something that isn't really there – it's like listening to your favourite poem.

'I could just see the monks of hundreds of years ago filing in there through the early morning frost and thinking to themselves that their feet were cold.'

'I thought that the church was built this century, Tim,' I said.

'What does that matter, George?' said Daisy tersely.

We had a few sandwiches with Tim who talked about what he was studying and was hell's boring. Then it was time to drive back. For a long time we motored along saying nothing. Then Daisy lit me a cigarette because she must have felt like one herself.

'You never did tell me where the ashtray is,' she said. I showed her. 'Look, George,' she said, pretending to rummage in her handbag, 'I'm sorry about losing my temper over that stupid croquet this afternoon.'

'Oh, it was my fault,' I said. 'I never take these things seriously enough. It's the same with cards. People are always telling me.'

'No, it's me. I shouldn't get so het up.' There was a pause, then for no apparent reason she said: 'You're sweet.'

'Aw, shucks,' I said grinning but not really knowing where to look.

I glanced out of the window into the night and saw we were just going into Bury. There was time for a drink.

'I tell you what,' I said, 'if we pass a pub that we fancy, we'll nip in for a quickie.'

But we didn't fancy any of them.

The next time I saw Daisy was just before the concert – and only just, at that.

We were all standing round in the long narrow room below the stage in what used to be the technical college.

I was feeling uncomfortable – for one thing we were in evening dress, and for another my dinner jacket was my father's – double-breasted and with giant lapels. It never seemed worth buying one of those roll collar jobs for just once or twice a year. Edward Grey-Smith had one, of course.

Daisy breezed in with about ten minutes to go – breezed isn't the word, really, because she looked like death warmed up and was out of breath.

'Hello, George,' she said, and held my arm for a second while she bobbed her head on to my shoulder to get her breath back. It was the first time she'd ever done anything like that.

I wondered if she'd been on the point of not coming, and had then had to get there in a hurry.

I hung her mac up while she got her oboe warmed up, playing a few of the little runs and nervous octaves that she always played. She had on a plain little black dress with her shoulders bare. She looked terrific.

I gave her a cigarette while Ronnie made his usual daft over-the-top speech before we went on. It always sounded as if it was the same one he gave his school orchestras, finishing with the same joke: 'Tonight, I want you to play as you've never played before – in tune.'

Daisy, who had been tapping non-existent ash off her cigarette all the way through, gave a quick little smile to herself, and sucked at her oboe reed. She stubbed out the cigarette inside a wastepaper bin and, acting the fool, I pointed dramatically to the steps leading up to the stage. 'Over the top,' I said.

There were about two hundred and fifty people in the audience according to FWT in the Evening News next day, and they enjoyed an excellently varied programme well up to the standard FWT had come to expect of Mr Ronald

Glasgow and his musicians. I've still got the cutting somewhere.

Whether it was because Daisy was on the paper or because he was just making allowances I don't know, but FWT made no mention of how Daisy fluffed her fatal entry after all. He must have noticed, because she left me playing on my own after coming in wrong, not daring to try and pick up her part in case she blundered in wrong again.

During my first bar's rest I glanced at her and saw that her eyes were full of tears. I don't know how she managed to keep going to the end. As we stood up to take our bow she said: 'Oh, God, I'm sorry George.' I wish now that I had said something back.

There was plenty of applause, just the same. We all got halfway down the stairs then stopped in the customary huddle, waiting for Ronnie to decide when to go on again for more rapturous applause.

He kept whispering: 'Well done, well done everybody,' as if someone might overhear. Then he suddenly hissed: 'I think it's time,' and jogged up onto the platform leaving the rest of us to catch up.

It wasn't until I was half way up the gangway between first and second violins that I realized Daisy wasn't behind us. But there was nothing I could do.

On stage again we played the National Anthem. Ronnie always took it at the speed of a dirge, but that night seemed the slowest we'd ever played it. I kept thinking of Daisy, probably crying her eyes out down below.

I followed in Ronnie's wake as he left the platform and was one of the first in the dressing room. But Daisy wasn't there. Her mac had gone.

I slammed my clarinet into its case without wiping it out and didn't wait for the post mortem on the Brandenburg which I could hear people already starting. 'Cheerio, all,' I shouted. 'See you at the Proms.'

'George is in a bit of a hurry, isn't he?' someone said as I closed the door. They were right, I was. But after I'd got outside and carved through the concert-goers to my car, I couldn't think why. I wasn't going to find Daisy now.

She could be anywhere. And if 'anywhere' was her flat, I

didn't know where that was either. In any case, I thought, as I sat at the wheel and shoved my instrument on to the parcel shelf, even if I saw her what could I say except something corny? And playing the bloody piece well seemed to mean so much to her.

Also she'd probably got people much closer than me she could talk with, and if the rumours were anything to go by, do all sorts of other things with as well.

I decided to go to Fanny's and get pissed.

It turned out Daisy Smuten had left town – that bit of news didn't take long to spread, I can tell you.

Everyone but everyone who had seen her leave the concert platform never to return decided at once that I was the nigger in the woodpile. Suddenly, it seemed that half Bolton had witnessed dramatic scenes at the technical college on Tuesday night.

But the sensational rumours about me and Daisy told me one thing – where those lurid Dirty Daisy stories had come from – obviously from people's steamy imaginations, all of them a load of codswallop based on one tiny fact.

Not that that helped me much, or all the others I'd heard about – Alderman Shuttleworth, Sir Ormerod Wilkie, the Vicar of St Cedric's. We were all lumbered with reputations that it was no use denying, just because people had decided what sort of girl Daisy was, and that was how she was going to stay.

After denying the story to a few mates, I gave up. It was a bit hard on Daisy, I suppose, but everyone started thinking what a great bloke I was because I'd had it away with their fantasy bird. I'd been away for the day with her, hadn't I. I got used to the idea. Most of the girls I'd ever known started bumping into me, accidental like.

It was about this time that the Evening News started a new series called Textile Town. By interviewing bosses of firms, they were supposed to show that textiles were still Bolton's bread and butter even though the traditional mills were closing.

The first interview was with me. They were obviously all sitting round the newspaper office thinking: 'Who the hell can we interview for this crappy series?' when some bright spark said: 'What about the famous George Darby the one who laid Daisy?' Guffaws all round. Anyway, I got my photo in the papers for the first time since I won a music competition in the Army.

They made me out to be some sort of whizz kid who was revolutionizing a little old family firm. Because I didn't really believe it would appear, I let myself go, boasting about the really high quality stuff I could produce, only nobody would let me. On the strength of it, I got three offers, one of them from London. I told Wolfe to go and get knotted.

I've never looked back since. Why, just a month after the interview and the beginning of my success, I was even invited to join the Masons. All thanks to Daisy Smuten.

I Knew Daisy Smuten

Doughty St, WC1
May, 1961

DEAREST REG,

This is where I came in and at the moment I feel like going out, for good. I've come to the conclusion that those six months in Bolton were a waste of time. Nobody cares in London. What matters is first of all who you know, and I know nobody, and secondly, what have you done, and I've done nothing. I mean, a folio full of Bolton golden weddings isn't exactly having the colour supplements wetting themselves. I ring up and they say don't bother to come in with your stuff, we'll ring you if we ever have a job up your street. But how do they know what my street is? I'd be willing to do anything, anything Reg, to show them my street. The thing is they don't give jobs to people they don't know. And if they don't give you jobs, they can never possibly know you. It's a vicious circle. But I know I'm good. Honestly. You know it's not boasting Reg. If only I could get in somewhere, see an assassination or something which no one else has got. Do you know how much agents take? At least thirty per cent! And even they won't take me. I'm giving it another month then my savings will have run out and I'll have to do some temporary work as a secretary, perish the thought. Reg, you don't know anything or anyone, do you? I mean, have you got any openings? It's funny to realize I don't even know what you look like, never mind what you do.

I'm going to quite a lot of parties, meeting people, but the only people I meet from magazines seem to be queer or have thirteen skinny models hanging on to them so you can't get near. Then all these Sunday newspapers closing doesn't help. I hadn't even heard of some of them, like the Sunday Graphic and Empire News, but they sold millions. Perhaps I should have gone into tele.

Guess what. I was on a bus going up Piccadilly yesterday and I saw Gerald coming out of the tube station. He looked about a hundred. Hmmm. I wonder how old I look. Wasn't it funny though. In a place of ten million I should see his lousy face. They say if you sit at Piccadilly Circus long enough you meet everyone you've ever known in your life.

Christ, what a thought. I'm now going to put the light off and go to sleep. The shilling's going to finish any minute anyway. Did you know Charles Dickens lived in this street? I chose it to be near Fleet Street. Oh, another amazing thing happened. I was going

Next day. Must rush to catch the post. See you.

DAISY

11

Philip's story

Whenever I see tigers I remember Daisy Smuten.

Unlikely then, you might suppose, that I should be reminded too often, or too poignantly of what was, I confess, a brief encounter. But to each his own absurdity. Tigers are part of my life. Elephants too; also wallabies, lemurs, skunks, and boa constrictors. A veterinary officer, as a colleague at my first zoo once remarked, sees nature red in tooth and claw.

Sir Giles Comstock, now deceased, was handsome, vain, arrogant, ambitious, abusive, and, in every imaginable way, my superior. His title was Zoo Director, an appellation on which he insisted. Conversations with Comstock were like rides on a shunting engine. 'Yes, Director', 'No, Director', 'Right away, Director'. There was no flow, no fruitful dialogue. We proceeded by a series of collisions. He made no effort to disguise the fact that he despised me. He was not alone in this. Comstock's minions were chameleon-like in adopting his opinions, his manner, even his cornflower buttonholes.

Life in a zoo, I think, is remarkably like show-business. It has its stars, its impresario, its managers, even its own permanent audience whose sole function is to applaud. A successful zoo is made electric by temperament. Comstock supplied this in abundance. His – admittedly high – reputation was based on papers written years ago on the homosexual pair-bonding of baboons. In its time it was revolutionary. But among his curators were droves of bright young men, all of them busy propounding their own theories, appearing on TV, writing books, stealing – as it were – the well-buttered bread from Comstock's greedy mouth.

The effect was curiously stimulating. Both Comstock and his curators were kept on their toes. But while they ran record-breaking laps around each other, my own progress was, to say the least of it, pedestrian. I had no theories to advance, no arguments to offer. Nominally, I was in charge of the zoo hospital. But most of the work – once one had become accustomed to the variety of patients – was drudgery.

I bred locusts (the scourge of ancient Egypt, a Keeper who was also a Jehovah's Witness informed me) to provide protein for the monkey's diet. I pared the toe-nails of elephants, a task which always reminded me of trying to fell giant redwoods with an emery board. I treated wolves suffering from constipation, and concocted meals to increase a panda's virility (a complete waste of time as the beast was undoubtedly queer). I supervised an out-patients clinic which served small boys bearing jars of goldfish, and old ladies clutching ulcerated cats. Understandably, Comstock saw me as a mechanic who offered nothing in the way of entertainment. As I was also unmarried there was not even a wife in the offing to excite his interest. He was, I should add, something of a sexual buccaneer.

My friends, those few that I have, call me Philip. But to Comstock I was always 'Mills'. Not 'Mr Mills', an elementary courtesy which might have cushioned the impact of our exchanges, but Comstock was graceless beyond belief, believing I suppose that manners unmade the man.

One morning in June he marched into my office unannounced, and tossed a buff folder on to my desk. 'How soon can we set it up?' he demanded. 'Sir Frank has agreed to perform the operation.'

I gaped at him. 'Set what up?' I had the feeling that I had been caught dozing in class.

'The tiger,' said Comstock. 'The tiger with the eye injury. Sir Frank Cargill has agreed to look him over.'

I knew then what he was talking about. One of our patients at the hospital was a twelve-months old tiger named Salim. Some days previously, while sparring with a cage-mate, he had taken a blow on his left eye which detached the lens and flipped it – like a tiddley-wink – back into the eye itself.

He was able, we thought, to distinguish light from dark, but little else, and unless the lens was removed quickly and completely there was a serious risk of total blindness. For a week he had lain dopily in his cage at the rear of the hospital, his food heavily laced with tranquillizers. I myself had recommended prompt action, but now I realized, with a quite uncharacteristic spurt of anger, Comstock had taken the matter into his own hands.

I glanced at the case history. 'How about next week,' I suggested. 'Tuesday morning perhaps.'

'Earlier than that.'

'Monday, then.'

Comstock slammed his open palm on to my desk. 'For God's sake, man, I mean *soon*. We have to catch Sir Frank while his interest lasts.'

We were back on the show-business circuit I realized. Sir Frank Cargill was an opthalmic surgeon, whose patients were not merely top drawer. They were social super-stars. Back in the dark ages he had been flown to Cairo, by private jet, when King Farouk had developed a stye. His fee for the round trip, it was rumoured, was ten thousand pounds. He had been summoned to Scorpio when Callas went down with conjunctivitis. He had been whisked to Balmoral when a salmon hook became lodged in the eye of a visiting princeling. His association with the zoo was a long-standing whim. It provided him with anecdotes to beguile his patients, consulting room chat to buff up his reputation as a brilliant eccentric. Often I had pictured the scene. A dowager clutching her lace hanky, while Cargill laundered her eyeball with Optone at twenty guineas a go. 'There was a very amusing incident last week, your grace . . . an orang-outang which needed glasses . . . as you say, your grace, almost human . . . science is marvellous . . . same time next week.' Ring up the till, and a great big hand for my favourite and yours.

Except that he was not a favourite of mine. Whenever Sir Frank Cargill descended on the zoo hospital I was instantly reduced to the status of errand boy. 'He has suggested that you act as anaesthetist,' said Comstock.

I nodded, thumbing through the diary to see how the week could be rearranged to suit the convenience of our star performer.

'It's a compliment,' said Comstock.

'Yes, Director.'

'Sir Frank is an exceedingly busy man.'

'We are all busy men, Director.'

'Of course, of course. But we must be adaptable.'

Today, I thought, was Tuesday. If I switched the armadillo to Wednesday, and the gibbon which had, apparently, sprained a wrist, to Thursday, we might, with luck, have the operating theatre clear for Friday. Provided, of course, that nothing went wrong in the humming bird house (visitors to the zoo were often tempted to swat them in mid-air), and that no animal fell seriously sick, or ate something toxic, or went into a mysterious decline within the next seventy-two hours. 'We should be able to manage Friday,' I said.

'If that's the soonest you can make it.'

'The very soonest, Director.'

Comstock sighed, signalling exasperation and acceptance in one breath. 'Very well.' He turned on his heel, and then paused, his hand on the door knob. 'There's one more thing. I've invited an observer. A Miss Daisy Smuten. She'll be photographing the operation.'

It was typical Comstock. No hint of a request, no pretence of consultation. I breathed deeply and counted to ten. 'Is she a journalist, Director?'

'Of course she's a journalist.'

'Does the Press office know about her?'

'I've no idea.'

'I'm supposed to clear any press visit with the Press Office, Director.' I could hear myself arranging the words like igloos of alphabetical bricks. I sounded, I thought, like a low-grade moron.

'Miss Smuten is my guest, Mills. There is no need to consult the Press Office.'

Very well, you bastard, I thought. I hope she's stung by a scorpion, or raped by a baboon. On your head be it.

'In fact,' continued Comstock. 'Miss Smuten is already in the building. I've told her that you will show her round the hospital.'

'It's rather a full day, Director.'

He glared briefly at the ceiling. 'Make time, Mills. Make time. Miss Smuten will be providing a valuable dossier. Sir Frank is most anxious to have the operation photographed.'

'Is she experienced, Director?'

The veins on his forehead swelled like leeches bloating themselves on a piece of steak. 'Experienced! Of course she's experienced. She's a most accomplished young woman.'

Message received and understood. Miss Smuten was on Comstock's short list. It hardly mattered to him whether she could use a box Brownie. He wanted her there to be dazzled, not to take pictures. 'Accomplished' was the give-away word. It featured frequently in Comstock's sound and fury, and what it signified was nothing more than sexual ambition. Privately, I had it filed away as one of those PR adjectives to be applied when no precise compliment would fit. 'Perhaps I could meet the lady,' I said.

He flung open the door and strode into the lobby. By the time I had caught up with him he was clutching the arm of a blonde who was gazing down at him (Comstock, I am delighted to recall, was a very short man) with an expression which combined worship, gratitude, and promise. An attractive package deal, I thought furiously.

'Mills,' he said, without bothering to turn his head, 'this is Miss Smuten. I've told her you'll show her round for an hour or so. I'm expecting a call from Basle, but I'll be back to collect her for lunch. That is,' he said, stroking her bicep, 'if those blessed continentals don't keep me waiting.' He gave her arm a parting squeeze and strode off in a blaze of glory.

The silence that he left behind was tangible, like water turning rapidly to ice. I felt it coagulate as she spoke. 'I'm sorry if I'm a nuisance.'

'The Director doesn't think you're a nuisance.'

'But you do.'

'That's not important.'

'Will you have a cigarette?'

I shook my head. 'There's no smoking in the hospital.'

'Why not?'

'Hygiene, danger to oxygen cylinders. There's a house rule.'

There wasn't, of course, and she knew it. 'Can I just follow you around?'

'If that's what the Director had in mind.'

'Damn the Director!'

'I beg your pardon.' I honestly thought, for one moment, that I misheard.

'It's your hospital. It's up to you to say what I *can* do, and what I can't.' Her face was very close to mine, and I found myself studying the bloom of her skin, and – in miniature – my own reflection in the pupils of her eyes. It was an extraordinary experience. At forty-five my knowledge of women was scant. I was attracted to the idea of marriage, rather as a traveller scourged by an east wind thinks of a hot bath. But the idea had never taken on flesh. My sexual tastes and appetites were – and remain – conventional. I would not describe myself as inhibited. But I lack confidence. The advertisement in which a bluff, sanguine individual offered to be one's father might have been designed with me in mind. Advice was what I needed; rejection was what I constantly got. Until, that is, the day I met Daisy.

What she made me aware of was my potential. I am no fool. Even in my most embattled moments my wits remain sharp, and I was perfectly aware of the tactics that were being used. Although Daisy was under the wing of the unspeakable Comstock she still needed my cooperation to obtain the best results, and to get it she was prepared to play the role of subversive sympathizer, warmly concerned with my self-esteem, ready to form alliances which would change, I had no doubt, when the necessity arose. At the same time it was impossible to ignore her physical presence. It was not blatant. She was not big-breasted; her appeal was, in no way, threatening. But as some male animals, wolves for example, can be stimulated by impregnating their cage with the musk of a female in season, I found myself responding to the intruder, desiring her even, while resenting her invasion of my territory.

I stepped back several paces, giving ground, as it were; but she remained where she was. 'Honestly,' she said, 'you can tell me to go to hell. I wouldn't mind.'

'The Director would mind.'

'I've told you. It's your hospital.' She dug her hands into the pockets of her reefer jacket, and cocked her head on one side. The next move, she implied, was mine. She was inviting me to take the initiative. It was just as though someone had thrown a switch, releasing reserves of power which, until then, had been sulking in some hidden turbine.

'Just follow me,' I said. 'You'll need to know the lay of the land if you're not going to get in the way.'

She suppressed a smile, and I had sudden doubts. 'What's funny?'

'Just something you said. About the lay of the land. It sounds like a title for someone.'

'I didn't mean it like that.'

'I didn't think you did.'

'I'm told that I have no sense of humour.'

'They say things like that to put you down. Don't believe them.'

I pushed open a door and stepped aside to let her through, and, with the back of my head jammed against the frosted glass and our stomachs grazing I was breathing her body scent, the odour of newly-washed hair, the mist of her breath. In the current idiom I was, I suppose, turned on. I was also alarmed. I felt my reserve dissolving. 'Just follow me,' I said.

I showed her everything. For an hour she inspected instruments, dissecting rooms, laboratories, the outside cages where animals in the last stage of their convalescence were kept, the operating theatre, the private wards.

These had been built to my own design, extensions, I sometimes thought, of a dream which any psychoanalyst would have loved to probe. There were six of them, all intended to house large mammals. There were no corners. Floors, walls, and ceilings curved gently like the inside of a large, compressed egg which had been coated with thick, black rubber. There were no sharp angles, no projections. There was a ceiling light, a sprinkler system which made cleaning easy, and a drain in the centre of the floor. Each ward was, in a sense, a padded cell in which the patient could lie comfortably, or rage impotently without inflicting any damage either to itself, or to the fittings. The door was flush with the wall, impossible to open, except from the outside corridor. The only window was a small porthole, protected by a thick wire mesh.

'This is where we'll bring the tiger after the operation,' I said.

She looked round, her arms folded across her chest. 'Very cosy.'

'I'm prepared to consider renting one. Reasonable terms.'

'I'll let you know,' she said. 'I like to be private sometimes.'

We heard doors swing open and shut, and then footsteps along the corridor. 'Where are you?' called Comstock. 'What on earth are you doing?'

Daisy squeezed my hand and smiled. 'See you on Friday.' She went to greet him, and I remained where I was feeling both elated and empty. It was ridiculous, I told myself (I remember actually speaking the words aloud). Daisy Smuten was in the Comstock league, therefore she was unattainable, and – if I could nerve myself to analyse the situation – undesirable too. Where Comstock sipped, I abstained. And yet, I found her not only exhilarating, but likeable. That's what I remember now. Before anything actually happened, I *liked* Daisy Smuten.

The rest of the week was a nightmare. Comstock, whatever else, was a dedicated artist, and Friday's operation was now his personal production. Book, lyrics, lighting, lead parts and supporting roles became his sole concern. We held rehearsals (I almost said auditions). The routine was checked and double-checked. We could have gone on at the Palladium, and sold every seat in the house.

'The problem,' I told him, 'will be space.'

'Space? Space?' It was as though I was addressing him in Swahili.

'There are six people in the operating team,' I pointed out. 'You will also be present; so will Miss Smuten. The operating theatre is a small room. To say the least of it we will be cramped. Photography will be difficult.'

He waved his hands irritably, as if erasing some graffiti I had left in the air. 'Nonsense, man. Be flexible. The photographs are part of the operation too. You must take them into account.'

Since the subject first arose I had done little else. 'Where will they be published?' I asked.

'Here and there. I believe Miss Smuten has an agent.'

And no actual job, I thought. The pictures were to be her calling card here, there (as Comstock had said) and everywhere that a new photographer needed to make her mark. 'We'll try to give her a good show,' I said.

'A good job, conscientiously done is all that I expect,' said Comstock. 'Nothing more, and certainly nothing less.' There were times when Comstock seemed to be reciting a prepared text, an inscription almost, piously chiselled on civic stone. He was so detestable that I was half-way proud of him.

'You anticipate no out-of-the-way difficulties?' he asked.

'I try to anticipate everything, Director.'

He raised one tawny eyebrow. 'I dislike levity, Mills.'

Get knotted, I should have said. 'I'm sorry, Director' is what I did say.

The week galloped by without plague or pestilence, and at nine o'clock on Friday morning I watched the tiger eat his breakfast. I've always liked the big cats. For one thing they answer back when you greet them. Not verbally, of course: you make a whiffling noise with your lips, and they whiffle back. It's a limited exchange, but genuine, for all that.

There are some tigers who permit far greater liberties. I believe that they enjoy company, and who wouldn't after boring hours spent padding round a cage, rubbing your nose bare on the bars. One keeper I knew used to pay visits after hours, and once I caught him squatting in a corner with the tiger (*his* tiger) sprawled across his lap, purring like a hive of bees while its belly was rubbed.

Salim, however, was not like that. He weighed fifteen stone, and every ounce was evil. As a professional man I'm aware that I should not use such an emotive word. But, looking at Salim, I was always reminded of the Blake poem: 'Tiger, tiger burning bright, In the forest of the night.' I can never remember how the rest of it goes. But Salim was Blake's kind of tiger. He burned with an unquenchable malevolence. He *knew* that he was designed to kill, and he resented the fact that he was denied his true function.

For several days we had been lacing his food with tranquillizers, and moments after he licked his platter clean I saw his eyes (the good one and the bad one) close, and his whole body assume the heaviness of sleep. I waited for another thirty minutes, then unlocked the door and went into the ward. Salim snored gently. I lifted his left fore-paw, shaved a small strip of fur and sealed his sleep with an intravenous injection.

Everything now had to go according to clockwork. Quite literally. It is difficult to calculate how long an animal will remain under sedation. The rate of metabolism, which burns the drug up, can be gauged, to some degree, by body weight. But, without falling into the trap of anthropomorphism, I would say that some animals are like some people. It is possible to make comparisons. Codeine, for example, which relieved my mother's headaches within minutes, does nothing to help me. At functions where rugger hearties drink tumblers of whisky with no apparent effect, I become tipsy on half a pint of lager. Salim, I thought, was a fairly hearty beast, and I was not prepared to take any chances.

The operation was timed to begin at ten o'clock. By nine-thirty Salim was loaded on to a trolley, wheeled to the theatre, and edged carefully on to the operating table. I tested his reflexes by jigging his paws, and pulling out his tongue, and, with some difficulty, wedged a wooden gag between his jaws through which I inserted the tracheal tube which would pump a mixture of fluothane and oxygen directly down his windpipe. As the anaesthetist it was my job to control the mixture and the flow. Too little, and we would be in trouble. Too much, and the zoo would lose a valuable item, i.e. one tiger, worth a thousand pounds give or take a few rupees.

At nine forty-five the stars assembled. Everyone wore an operating cap and gown and a surgical mask, but even with the disguise there was no mistaking who was who. Comstock's eyebrows toiled up and down his forehead, signalling authority, virility, and (was I mistaken?) anxiety. Sir Frank Cargill's gold-rimmed spectacles twinkled merrily (he was so damned Pickwickian that I had longed more than once to sentence him to ten years hard in Dingley Dell). And as for Daisy, cameras hung about her neck like fertility symbols, twentieth-century charms against professional barrenness. I checked the dials on my cylinders and nodded. 'Ready when you are.'

Cargill's glasses flashed in Daisy's direction. 'Are *you* ready,

Miss Smuten?'

'Perfectly.'

'Do you have a good view, Comstock?'

'I have indeed.'

'Very well then.' Cargill inclined his head, as solemn as a priest at his rites. 'Let battle commence.'

He even used a Lancashire accent. I was grateful for my mask. Behind it I could utter abuse, comment, criticism without being spotted. It was just as well. Within seconds the operation had been transformed into the Comstock v Cargill show, with Daisy as the object whose attention they mutually and competitively wished to attract.

One of the male nurses swathed Salim's head in a sterile cloth, with a central hole exposing the damaged eye.

'Scalpel,' said Cargill. 'You see Miss Smuten, I have to make my first incision here above the cornea.'

'In order to probe for the floating lens,' said Comstock.

Cargill's gold-rims glinted warningly. 'Precisely,' he said, edging slightly to the left. 'Just snap away,' he told Daisy.

'Can you see it?' asked Comstock.

'See what?'

'The lens, man. The lens.'

Cargill shook his head. 'It must be behind the eye.'

'We had already decided that.'

The camera clicked and whirred. 'What is important,' said Cargill in his best lecture-room manner, 'is to avoid causing any further damage. The surgeon must be bold, but not reckless.' He posed, scalpel in hand. 'How's that?' he enquired.

'That's fine,' said Daisy. 'Just carry on. Forget that I'm here.'

'Impossible,' said Comstock. 'How could we possibly forget that *you* were here.' His eyebrows flexed, buckled, and then subsided. The fluothane-oxygen mixture hissed down the tube, and I glanced at the dials. There was too much chat I decided.

'Probe,' said Cargill. 'Increase the anaesthetic.'

I did as I was told.

'You checked your calculations, I suppose,' said Comstock.

He was talking to me I realized. 'What calculations, Director?'

'The correct dosage.'

'Of course I did.'

'There's no of course about it. I'd like to be sure.'

'Excuse me,' said Daisy, changing cameras, and moving in for close-ups. Again Cargill struck a pose, shifting positions until the reel was exhausted.

'We want to be sure you have full coverage,' he said jovially.

'Absolutely,' said Comstock. 'Everything you need.'

The tip of Salim's tail twitched like a bell-rope touched by a draught. I cleared my throat, and tried to combine a note of urgency with professional calm. 'We haven't a great deal of time.'

The gold-rims gleamed. 'Rubbish, there's plenty of time.' He rummaged around in Salim's skull, and waved Daisy to come closer. 'You see,' he said, 'we're almost there. We're coming to the best part now.' He probed some more, and then paused. 'You *are* using colour, I suppose? Excellent, excellent. Black and white doesn't mean a thing. You lose the drama. You need colour to bring out the actuality.'

Salim belched quietly, and the tip of his tail switched from left to right, and back again. 'Sir Frank,' I said. 'I really think we should hurry.'

The eyes which peered over the gold-rims were bright blue and very cold. 'Are you always so apprehensive?'

'Not at all.'

'You're an old woman, Mills. Increase the anaesthetic.'

I shook my head. 'I can't do that, Director. In my view it would be too risky.'

Comstock snorted, and his mast billowed like washing on a line. He steered Daisy nearer to the table. 'Get it while you can,' he advised. 'Mr Mills' (he emphasised the 'Mister') 'is feeling the strain.'

We exchanged glances, and Daisy shrugged her shoulders. I sensed sympathy; amusement, perhaps; understanding, without a doubt. But she went on taking pictures. There was no let-up in her professionalism. Without heat, I hated her.

'I've got it,' said Cargill suddenly. He fished around with his forceps, and there, gleaming in the theatre lights like a sliver of melted glass, was the missing lens. 'The historic moment,' said Cargill. 'One more for the family album.'

The camera clicked and buzzed several times more. The lens was deposited in a kidney dish, and Cargill started on his repairs. First, he stitched the cornea. Next he sewed the eyelids together. Finally, he stood back and admired his handiwork. I had to admit, he was a dab hand with a needle and thread. 'Happy now, Mr Mills?' he enquired.

'Not especially. I think we should clear the theatre.'

'After *you*,' he said.

'Not bloody likely.'

'I beg your pardon,' said Comstock.

'This is *my* hospital. This is *my* operating theatre. And this is *my* responsibility.' That, at least, is what I am told I said. Mentally, I was pre-occupied with composing my letter of resignation. 'You are the one who will get out,' I said. 'If you don't get out I shall take the greatest pleasure in throwing you out.'

I can remember the moment still, a crystalline fragment of time, as perfect as a tear-drop which hung on the cheek of the morning before splashing thunderously to earth. I thought I had imagined the sound until I turned to see Salim sliding from the table, the tracheal tube still in the gag which bound his jaws, but growling through it, like a singer (I thought irrelevantly) projecting his song through some sort of internally-fitted microphone. He rolled drunkenly on to his side, then struggled to a sitting position, swiping meanwhile at those nearest to him.

'Everyone out,' shouted Comstock, leading the retreat.

Salim's paw hooked around Comstock's ankle and he crashed against the instrument trolley. Salim moved in, pinning him to the floor.

I looked for Daisy, and saw her crouched beneath the table photographing the chaos. I grabbed her arm, but she shook me off. 'For God's sake,' I shouted. 'Don't mess about. It's time to go.'

She shook her head, and dodged round to the other side of the theatre, her camera snapping as she ran. Salim lurched on to four paws, and followed her. There was no move from Comstock. Not dead, I surmized, but out cold.

'Daisy!'

'Wait a second.'

Salim reached out and the front of her theatre gown was ripped from top to bottom. I saw white, naked flesh, a thread of blood, and without pausing to think, I launched at the tiger with the instrument trolley, screaming (Daisy informed me later) like a samurai, and barging Salim into a white-tiled corner where his paws sent scalpels, probes, and spatulas whizzing through the air like metallic minnows.

I hung on to Daisy's wrist, while she hung on to her cameras, and together we bolted into the corridor, with Salim in drunken pursuit. I jerked open the door of one of the animal wards, and pushed Daisy inside. The metabolism of a tiger, I thought, still is a matter for conjecture. I pulled the door shut, and looked through the porthole. Salim's one eye looked back at me, and patiently he lay down and licked a paw.

'He can't get in,' I said.

'And we can't get out.'

'They'll let us out when he's back in his cage.'

'How long will that be?'

'God knows.'

'In that case,' said Daisy, 'let's be comfortable.'

Solemnly, ritualistically, she removed her cameras and stacked them in a line against one wall. She tested the floor, jumping up and down in one spot as if she was demonstrating to a keep-fit class. As she jumped, I could see her breasts jostling each other through the rent in the theatre gown. Following my gaze, she traced with one finger the deep double scratch that ran from her throat to her navel.

'Does it hurt?'

'Terribly,' she said.

'It ought to be disinfected.'

'It'll have to wait.

'Is it still bleeding?'

'Take a look. You're the doctor.' She peeled off the gown, and parted her shirt, still buttoned, but sliced by Salim's claws, so that it hung like bunting over her ribs and flat belly.

I hesitated. 'I'm not really a doctor.'

'You deal in medicine. You make things better.'

'Hardly. I'll need some first aid myself after today. You

heard me in there. I'm finished at the zoo.'

'That needn't be bad.' She placed a hand on either side of my face, and studied me as if she was looking into a mirror. 'Everyone has to make a move some time,' she said.

I nodded miserably. 'I know.'

'Then make it.'

I stared at her without understanding.

'Make it now,' said Daisy, and kissed me. After that, I find it difficult to remember anything in detail. The total impression is unforgettable, but the sequence of events is confused. I remember the taste of her mouth, the texture of her body, the amazing elasticity with which she contained and captained me. I recall the resilience of the floor, the harshness of her pelvic scrub, the smell of sweat, and the sensation of shipwreck as I fell back staring at the ceiling.

I stood up and peered through the porthole. Salim still lay outside the door like an enormous watchdog. Otherwise, the corridor was empty.

'How do you feel now?' asked Daisy.

'How do you mean, how do I feel?'

'Are you happy?'

I thought hard. 'Very happy.'

'You should be. You beat them all to it.'

'I can hardly publish the information.'

'You don't need to. They'll know.'

'You should get dressed.'

'Why, are they coming?'

'Not yet.'

'Then there's no need to get dressed.'

Male and female logic, I had long ago decided, are entirely different processes. She stretched out her hand, and pulled me down. 'Make the most of it,' said Daisy. 'Time is the worst thing you can waste.'

An hour later they came with nets, and Salim was bundled into the next apartment. There was an enquiry, of course, and Comstock insisted on my resignation. Not that I cared. I had passed some sort of milestone, and to stand still would have been to turn back. I joined an expedition to Saudi Arabia where one of the local sheikhs had been bribed to conserve at least one out of five oryx that came into his gun-sights, and it was in Abadan that I finally saw Daisy's photographs in an old copy of Paris-Match.

Nostalgia has rarely been so skilfully mixed with farce. There was Salim on the table. There was Cargill, scalpel in hand, with me scowling over his shoulder. There was Comstock diving for safety. And there was Daisy herself, brave and bloodied (a studio shot re-creating the scene, I decided) – the undoubted star of the occasion.

Of course, we never met again. But I did receive a card from her, posted in Germany, and showing the tigers' enclosure at the Berlin Zoo. The message was cryptic (to all others but me) and, I supose, typical. 'Waste not, want not' it said. And then, apparently as an afterthought: 'Another time?'

I would like to think so; indeed I would. But I can hardly imagine the occasion. Next week I join an expedition to the Himalayas where new tracks of the Yeti have been discovered. I learned today that a French woman photographer will be accompanying us. I anticipate nothing. Hope, I believe, is every man's enemy. But the unexpected does, occasionally happen.

I Knew Daisy Smuten

Blankers Hall
December, 1961

DEAREST REG,

You know I've always said I never fancied older men, well all I can say is I've heard about older men but this is RIDICULOUS – he looks exactly like C. Aubrey Smith and the other day I stubbed my Rothman out on his false teeth which I thought was an ashtray graciously placed on the bedside table, it was frightfully embarrassing, I felt just like a Peter Arno cartoon. The glamour of his having a title wore off pretty sharpish but his 'place' is rather smashing although he keeps on saying what a pity it is it faces the wrong way (I mean the *house,* dear!!) He's got a brood of children all years older than me who I expected to eye me with the deepest suspicion but to tell you the truth they don't seem to have taken me in at all which is rather galling. They go out shooting all day but I don't have to go too so I hang around the house (Wankers, I call it) and read old Country Lifes. Can't *think* why I got myself into this but I'm getting out soon and I'm sure when it's over I'll have a terrific reaction and become a ruthlessly predatory *cradle-snatcher!*

I'm supposed to be doing a series on the stately homers at home. It's too bloody easy for words. They're all cretins, except in bed when they're as perverted as hell. Thank God these days I only have to have it off with people I fancy. And boy, did I fancy that bloke in Mexico. (Did you get my card or did the customs object to the pic!! Thought you'd like it for your collection.) When I finish this lot off, they want me to go to the States again, but I rather fancy Vietnam. I've a feeling that war is on for a few more months yet. I haven't done much reportage. What am I drivelling on about. In six months I feel I've done everything and been everywhere and feel absolutely shagged! No comments.

I just can't keep up with the foreign rights. My stuff is being syndicated everywhere, but it's such a drag keeping an eye on it. I've changed agents once and I'll probably have to do it myself in the end. None of them are clued up. Honestly, you'd think these experts knew what they're doing but they're all idiots. You don't know a good accountant do you? Mine is so dopey. I keep getting offered staff jobs, but this PAYE lark is obviously a big con. I might try it though. I'll ask something really ridiculous, just to see what they say. It's quite prestige to work on good mag. I've got money now so I might as well see what prestige is like.

Lots of love from your v. successful friend,

DAISY

PS And v. much nicer.

London, NW1
May, 1962

DEAREST REG,

A boy who works on the same magazine told me about a fabulous fortune-teller, not a crank at all apparently, big business men and politicians and people like that absolutely swear by him. He lives in Torquay and you have to send him some object that you always have on you, like a ring or a handkerchief or something, and then he holds it and goes into a trance and knows everything about you. I couldn't think what on earth to send him as I was afraid a ring might get lost in the post and a hanky seems rather disgusting somehow – I mean if it's been used, and if it's clean then it's not really personal, is it? – so I finally took the risk and sent the little nutmeg charm that Kenneth gave me. I've always thought it brought me luck – but when you come to think it can't have as I'm always so frustrated and miz. Well, he sent it back again all right with this absolutely fascinating letter, honestly it's quite uncanny the way he's got me right, and it's not as if anybody could have told him about me because he doesn't know me and I *absolutely* trust this boy I mentioned. Weird. He says I'm very sensitive and artistic and that my work is connected with the arts and that I have a lot of friends but none of them really appreciate or understand me. I can be led but not driven, he says. He says I'm a perfectionist and have yet to meet the man who measures up to my very high standards. I know all this sounds very corny and perhaps he tells it to everyone – but you must admit Reg that it does fit me like a glove! He says there's going to be a *tremendous* crisis in my life when I'm thirty-five, he doesn't know what it is exactly but it will affect all sorts of people, not only myself, and yet I will be the central figure in it and everything will depend on what I do. He seems great pleasure and great pain, all kind of jumbled up. Well darling, what on earth do you make of *that*?

Loads of love,
DAISY

12

Lucia's story

I must be one of the few people who really hate Daisy Smuten. I ended by hating her with that sort of twisted, blind hatred that finally damages the hater more than it ever can the hated. It was for this that I will never be able to forgive her. She destroyed not only Tom, and Tom and me, but a part of me changed after Daisy came into our lives and will never be quite the same again. In some profound way I feel uglier, diminished, crippled because of what she did.

It is difficult now for me to remember exactly what I thought of her that first evening when Tom brought her home to dinner. I remember that I was pleased because usually when he brought home unexpected guests they were unbelievably old, renowned in some obscure field like sun-worship in Outer Mongolia. They were usually grubby so that even if there wasn't egg down their fronts you found yourself looking nervously to check. I see them in my mind's eye as a long line of bespectacled, dingy people cluttering up whole evenings of my life. Years of being courted and attended to had totally extinguished in them the will to contribute anything other than their presence. Life they seemed to say has been enriched simply by having us around. Like hell it had. Daisy sounded a much better proposition.

'Is she nice and is she pretty?' I asked Tom over the phone.

'Well . . . mmm . . .' he started. 'She's not exactly pretty but she's rather good value all the same.' I didn't notice it at the time but that kind of 'well . . . mmm . . .' nearly always means that they're *much, much* more than pretty. 'She's taken some rather good photographs actually,' he went on, 'and I have a hunch she's going to become much better, so it might be very useful to get to know her.'

Even that didn't really send the alarm bells ringing. I was busy wondering if I could put her next to that lecherous Professor Goodrich (that would at least keep his clammy hand off *my* knee for one evening) and if the fillet of beef would stretch round one more person. If I'd stopped to think I'd have realized that actually it was of far more use to Daisy to get to know Tom than the other way round. A director of a very reputable publishing firm could do a lot for a photographer who had ambition and still a long way to go. A collection of glossy photographs with their imposing imprint would just about set her up.

Well, anyway Daisy came to dinner that night. She came late and breathless and somehow just the way she said, 'Oh, I'm so sorry and I haven't made the soufflé burn, have I?' made one forgive her immediately. To a greater degree than anybody else I've ever known she had that gift for making the banal remark sound somehow original and witty.

I took in what she was wearing. It was like nothing I have seen before or since. (I would have been less astonished if I'd known then what I was told later, that she had just come back from a short flirtation with the East.) She was wearing what seemed like a collection of so many garments, all of them glittering and shining, that it was difficult to tell where one started and the other began. There was a sort of jewelled cap on her head beneath which her glorious blonde hair (dyed I'm sure) came tumbling out and on her arms were great diaphanous glittery sleeves and then there were waistcoats (although I suppose there can only really have been one) and a cummerbund and a great wide skirt below. But the truly remarkable thing was her bosom which with all this clothing billowing about was neither obscured nor diminished. She wore, it was quite clear, no bra of any kind and this in itself was startling enough (this was long before it became the fashion) but the diaphanous top parted in time to reveal a delicately pink cleavage whilst beneath the blouse her breasts bounced and bobbed and occasionally a nipple could be seen outlined against the flimsy material.

Old Professor Goodrich's eyeballs hadn't had such exercise

in years. As for the rest of them they were spell-bound. I, too, was entranced. I felt the evening was made. Somehow I couldn't get over Tom bringing home this exotic creature, this genuine eccentric, she was so unlike anybody he'd ever brought home before.

All through that evening Daisy sparkled and shone. She sat at Tom's right hand, glittering like some multi-coloured, multi-faceted jewel, whilst the rest of us listened and looked.

She had a large, soft mobile face which moved from happiness through to excitement, wonder and an almost childish glee. When somebody put a faintly questioning point it could register doubt and disagreement in such a delicate and charming way that you felt you were indeed lucky to be doubted. There was no doubt about it, I now realize, Daisy was trying very hard indeed that night, so hard that I should have guessed that she wanted something more than she can ever have wanted anything until then. Or perhaps that was her secret – she always did want everything with that same kind of intensity.

'It's an actress she should have been, not a photographer,' I said, somewhat sceptically to my neighbour, one of those perennial bachelors that London dinner parties always have. Even I could hear the slight ugly tinge of envy in my voice.

'You're right,' my neighbour said. 'Have you noticed how she's perfected every movement? She can start like a fawn, she can look dreamy as a cumulus cloud and I bet you anything she sleeps all sweetly curled, just like a little kitten.'

She'd undoubtedly got it taped. No ugly expression ever crossed her face, no sulky pout, no genuine frown of anger, no little line of boredom.

But Daisy's crowning natural gift, the thing that really made her stand apart, was a kind of yearning quality that she had more than anybody else I've ever met. There was about her an air of searching for something as yet unattained, perhaps even unattainable. Those tilted eyes of hers would search about her and you felt great reserves of longing welling up within her.

From that first night at dinner Daisy made me feel homespun and ordinary. Where Daisy yearned, I felt contented and at peace. I had exactly what I'd always wanted and that seemed, beside her, a prosaic and almost fatuous way to be: to want and be contented with what was after all, such an ordinary, limited life. A husband, usually kind, occasionally not, successful in his way. Two children, one a boy and one a girl, neither pretty nor plain, neither clever nor dull. I wasn't plain, I knew that. I didn't have Daisy's darting, questing vitality, her vivid colouring, her mesmerizing personality but in the way that many English women are I was blonde and clear-skinned with good legs and a passable kind of figure. Sometimes in the days before Daisy came along I would look about me and wonder what I'd done to deserve it all. But Daisy made me stop and think, perhaps there were marvellous worlds unknown, waiting just beyond the horizon within one's reach, if only, like Daisy, one wanted and yearned enough.

I suppose I was the ultimate suburban wife (that we didn't happen to live in suburbia but in the heart of London was a geographical detail). I was trusting to the point of foolishness. Guilelessness itself, quite unable to cope with a rival like Daisy. I was the sort of person who friends automatically trusted and came and wept and told me of their lovers and their husbands' lovers. And if they were going away they would say, 'Oh darling, you will ask John to dinner, won't you? I know he'll be safe with you.' That just about sums up the differences between Daisy and me.

That winter Daisy became part of our lives. It took me a long time to realize just how much she had wound her way into Tom's consciousness. There were, of course, perfectly rational reasons why he should see quite a lot of her, why she should be asked to those frequent dinner parties that seemed to be part of a publisher's way of life.

Tom himself told me about it. 'Daisy has this collection of photographs and she would like us to publish them in a glossy, full-colour prestige edition. Jasper and Humphrey (they were his co-directors) feel that the quality of the photographs and the likely sales only justify a smallish black and white collection. Anyway all her best ones are those black and white ones she brought back from India and the Middle East. Sell it for twenty-five shillings and we'll do quite well out of it. She's not ready for a glossy full-colour job yet. She's not enough of a name. I can't help feeling they're right, really, but it's difficult to persuade Daisy. She's set her heart on the full treatment.'

In a simple, trusting way, I accepted that this was why Daisy was around. All my married life there had been authors in our lives. They came to dinner, they drank our drink, they took Tom's time and if I was lucky I got a bunch of roses the next day. There never had been much in it for me. The occasional flash of empathy across the dying embers of a dinner table conversation, the illuminating glimpses into some other lives, the gossamer glimmer of an awakening interest, that was the most that I had come to expect. It was Tom's world to which I myself had no entrance pass. I was there because he was there. Daisy belonged. It had become Daisy's world far more than it had ever been mine. And for that I have nobody, not even Daisy, to blame.

So all through the winter of that year there was Daisy, either at our dinner table, casting a special kind of glow, or in Tom's conversations. In the way that lovers have, Tom was unable to prevent himself talking about her. Then, finally, and most momentously of all, she came to Whitefriars.

Rain, rain . . . the sky melting into rain. Grey, nothing but grey above and around. And me, leaning out of the top floor window at Whitefriars, waving to Daisy and Tom as they came round the corner of the drive. Why does one just go rushing headlong on, mouthing useless sounds, repeating old, stale gestures? Why does the heart make no sound as it breaks? Perhaps it just disintegrates.

They came tumbling out of the car. He and she together. They both looked flushed. They were laughing and Daisy was looking up at Tom and there was something in her look that made me feel unease. It had simply never occurred to me before. Tom had had a dinner engagement in London the night before so it seemed natural to me that the children and I should come down to Whitefriars on the Friday afternoon, leaving Tom to bring Daisy the following day. I realize now that no-one should ever be that sure of anybody. It is in its own way a form of insult.

I somehow welcomed them in and produced plenty of wine

at lunch and with the chattering of the children in the background I could pretend to myself that all was as it always had been. My little world was safe.

Later I tried to make light of my feelings. I tried to talk to Tom about it. When we were going to bed that night I said casually: 'I understand now why people are a bit afraid of divorcées. They somehow do seem much more of a threat than any other sort of woman, don't you think? Sometimes when Daisy looks at you I think "now I wonder what Tom makes of her".' Tom wouldn't be drawn, though I knew he didn't like me referring to her as a divorcée. He gave a sort of laugh. 'Well, I don't think a bit of competition does anybody any harm. After all, you have been looking a lot smarter these days.'

I wasn't hurt. I wasn't even sad. In fact, his remark made me feel better. Somehow the tacit admission that she was a bit of competition made us feel like accomplices, in on the same conspiracy. For some completely stupid reason I even felt *reassured.* I must have been crazy.

It was the next day just before lunch that it happened. Daisy and Tom were in the sitting-room reading the Sunday papers and I was with the children down at the bottom of the garden, mucking about with a new rope-ladder. I suddenly remembered there was a bottle of champagne in the fridge, put there in honour of Daisy coming down. I went back into the house, got the champagne and took it into the sittingroom.

Tom had Daisy in his arms. He was kissing her. It doesn't sound very much for nowadays but I knew that if Tom kissed somebody it meant everything. He wasn't the flirtatious sort. He didn't smack bottoms or caress bosoms unless it meant something. Everything about his attitude now told me how he felt – that he wanted to be alone with Daisy more than anything else in the world.

Of course they sprang apart at once. I felt as awkward as if I'd been caught misbehaving. I stood there looking ridiculous with an apron on, a tray full of champagne glasses in my hand. Nobody said anything. We just looked at each other, all of us now burdened with too much knowledge about each other. We stayed there the three of us as if caught in some ludicrous kind of miming show. And then there was nothing to do but drink the champagne. I could almost have laughed – it seemed such a terribly British kind of thing to do. If only I could have rushed screaming from the room and fetched the carving knife. But I could no more have done that than I could have brought myself to talk about it all with Daisy sitting there.

Somehow we got through lunch, another lunch like the day before, with the children's chattering providing the backdrop, making enough noise to cover up the awkwardness of ours. I wondered how people without children ever got through times like this.

I made some sort of excuse to get back to London earlier but nobody was fooled. I didn't suggest that Daisy came with me. I just left. I knew that Tom had to drive his own car back and would take her. The children and I came back alone.

They chattered and quarrelled and finally subsided into a drowsy, undemanding duologue. I drove on and on, the miles reeled away and I could think of nothing but how foolish I felt. I couldn't get over the fact that I had been so totally taken in. I must subconsciously have acquiesced, I suppose. If I had cared enough I should have realized. I should have fought. For once in my life I should have taken a stand, I should have said, 'Tom, we have seen enough of Daisy. Hurry up and decide about the bloody photographs and let her leave us in peace.' And perhaps if I had said it early enough it would have worked. For there was a bit of me in Tom. He, too, acquiesced too easily, he, too, hated to take a stand.

Tom came in late that night. I was surprised he came in at all. He crept into bed beside me without a word. I just lay there weeping silently (Tom had never liked women who cried). Then I became cross. Who did people like Daisy think they were, just reaching out and taking what they happened to want at the time?

I realized I didn't even know where she lived. It was Tom who had always asked her round. Tom had always done the telephoning, the arranging. It struck me then how strange it was that never during all those months that we'd known her, when she'd eaten at our table, drunk our wine, shared our friends, had Daisy offered us so much as a glass of sherry in a pub. Daisy didn't give. She expected others to provide.

I rang Tom's secretary. I asked after her mother, her migraines and said how Tom had said how nice she looked now that she was growing her hair long. And then I said I was planning a party . . . a surprise for Tom . . . don't breathe a word . . . but did she happen to have Daisy's address?

I dressed myself up. I decided that at least I wouldn't feel at too much of a disadvantage.

Daisy lived at the top of a discreet but very luxurious block of flats. Suddenly another bit of her life fell into place. The lift had ankle deep carpets and a chandelier and golden gates. I had never thought of Daisy as being either poor or rich, but now I realized she must be rich. Now I knew why when she came to us she always seemed lent by some other more glamorous, more exciting world. We felt we were privileged to have her, that she could have been doing so many more exciting things.

We lived well, but with two homes and school fees and entertaining, life always seemed a struggle. I tried not to think of what it must mean to be rich. It was Tom and I and the children that concerned me now. I was ashamed to admit it but I realized I wanted him more than ever now that I knew Daisy wanted him, too. I tried to look at him with Daisy's eyes, to discover in him something that I'd missed before. I must subconsciously have been undervaluing him all these years.

I got to her flat and then I pressed the bell. Daisy herself came to the door. She didn't look quite as she'd looked the day before. Her hair was beginning to look as if it needed washing, her clothes were expensive but not put together with her usual compelling flair. Those tilted blue eyes widened as she saw me on the doorstep. She drew back a bit and made as if to shut the door but I said quickly, in a conciliatory tone (I, too, was learning how to deceive) 'It's only me, let me in Daisy, I want to talk to you.'

Reluctantly, looking more embarrassed than I had ever imagined Daisy could look, she let me in. I was so busy wondering what I was going to say that I hardly took in the flat at all, but I remembered the smell. It stayed in my nostrils for weeks afterwards and it was unmistakable. It was the smell of staleness. Despite the obvious luxury, it was stale and flat.

It brought to mind old coffee cups and unemptied ashtrays. I wondered if it was this smell which had made Tom come home last night. He hated anything at all musty or scruffy.

Daisy flopped onto a sofa and lit a cigarette. I stood in the middle of the room, going through in my head what I was going to say, what I was going to ask, to demand, but I'd gone through it so often already it seemed as stale as everything else. As if it had been used up already then left behind, ignored, forgotten.

'Excuse the mess,' said Daisy, offhand, not caring if I did or not, but at least she must have been aware of it.

'It's a nice flat,' I said, looking round, desperately, despising myself for not having said what I'd rehearsed. And lying as well. It was a nasty flat. It was Daisy's. Everything about her was nasty. Yet my background, my upbringing, was forcing me into polite platitudes.

'It's horrible, actually,' said Daisy. 'I'm surprised you like it. It's nasty. And it smells. I hate it. You can have it if you like. It was given to me by some French count, or cunt, I should say.'

She looked at me, testing me with her language. She'd sworn before, but I'd never heard her be obscene.

'What are you thinking? Would you like the flat, then?'

'What do you want with Tom? Have you thought what you're doing to me and the children?' It all came tumbling out, the time-honoured weapons, the children. I couldn't really think of anything better, but after all, it was a time-honoured weapon because it was a good and a true one.

Daisy looked shifty. Even then I remember noticing that it was the first time she had ever, in my presence, allowed an expression that was less than beautiful to cross her face.

'I don't know what you mean,' she said.

'Oh, yes, you do,' I said. 'You know perfectly well what I mean. I've got eyes, I can tell that Tom has been drooling over you for weeks and maybe months. I admit I was slow on the uptake but you must have done some of the running. A man like Tom doesn't go on like that with no encouragement.'

'I've done nothing,' she said, 'It's not my fault if Tom always wants to be with me. He must get little enough satisfaction at home.' I got angry then.

'Well, what do you want with him now? What do you intend to do? Any other woman would at least stop and think of me and the children.' I kept coming back to them. I couldn't think of a single other thing.

'What the hell do you think I could possibly want from him? I've got everything I want now. You can do what you like with him.' I could hardly take in what she was saying. There were these hard, pointed words falling into my eardrums, coming from a Daisy I had never seen before. Something had happened, something had changed. She was going on.

'How could you think I would ever want that husband of yours? What's he got that's special? A tubby, middle-aged man already going bald. If you really want to know he bores me until I could scream. I smile and smile and smile and inside all I want to say is, "Shut up, if you don't shut up I think I shall have to hit you." He wanted to sleep with me last night but I couldn't face the thought of it, his white hands touching me, that flabby stomach next to me. Why do you think he went home last night? For your sake, for the children's? It was because I wouldn't have him and he had nowhere else to go.'

I started to cry. I couldn't bear it. She had never wanted him. She had despised him and me and everything we stood for. She had destroyed Tom in my eyes. She'd made him seem ridiculous and pathetic; a middle-aged man out for his bit of fun. Now she'd finished I could have him back. It was the one really, unforgivable thing she did. If she'd really wanted Tom, loved Tom, I'd have forgiven her.

I didn't see Daisy again for a couple of years and then I bumped into her at a party. I was with my new husband and I could see she didn't recognize me. I hardly recognized her. It was only her distinctive tilted blue eyes that hadn't changed. Whatever it was that she had hoped for, yearned for, when I knew her, she had it now. There could be no mistake. She had that indefinable air of achievement about her, she was a woman who had everything she'd ever wanted. But the funny thing is it wasn't the same Daisy. She'd lost something irreplaceable on the way.

Hotel France et Choisene
Paris, August, 1963

DEAR REG,

John and I bumped straight into – GUESS WHO! Barry at New Jimmy's – which had its funny side. I had an awful time with B, did I tell you, and that is completely finished too – he kept *on* saying things like what's the point of all this and being *so* perverse and anyway *au fond* he is, at least to me, a B-O-R-E. I'm again in a *hopeless* muddle with life and can't bear anybody and am seriously thinking of taking an overdose of something but what I'm not sure. The only person I'm not bored stiff or irritated beyond endurance by is you which is too absurd really. Somehow so typical of me, darling, I mean not being able to have a proper relationship. Nothing *new* ever works as the pattern of one's life becomes more unbreakable as time goes on. I'm getting so *bored* with being unhappy and feeling there's no solution – oh well, we'll see something has to be decided soon. Tomorrow we're going to Deauville to gamble, John feels he has worked out an unbeatable system for roulette and is bound to win at least a million. He's very nice and *of course* I'm in love with him. Isn't it (me) ridiculous? Jenny says all women are raving mad so perhaps that's the simple explanation. I hope this letter isn't too gloomy and silly darling but I do feel very black and despairing and you do know don't you that you're the only person I can be myself with. What would I do without you?

Absolutely masses of love from
DAISY

PS Perhaps we'll bump into Barry at Deauville! I hope not.

Daisy Smuten Studios
Beauchamp Place
London
December, 1965

DEAREST REG,

Thank you for your sweet letter. I hated the Bailey picture in *Vogue* and didn't think it was a bit like me, but I'm glad in a way you saw it and didn't think I looked too much of a spook. Actually darling I think it's frightfully silly for photographers to *be* photographed and to have any publicity at all. The whole point of being a photographer is that one ought to be as anonymous as possible – you know, 'I Am a Camera' and all that – but for some reason everyone seems so *interested* in photographers now, rather like we used to feel about film stars. I'm *much* more pleased when you write and say you saw photographs I took myself, and didn't think they were too bad. To tell you the truth I'm beginning to think there's something basically silly about being a photographer, the whole world of magazines and art editors and models and so on is so *brainless* somehow. I know people think it's glamorous but it isn't if you're in it. Perhaps nothing *is* glamorous if you're in it – Christ, what an awful thought! I feel my *mind* has been so neglected all these years, somebody I met recently said I really had a very original mind, and ought to read more, and he gave me such an interesting book by Albert Camus. It was quite uncanny when I read it, there were moments when I thought it must be *me* writing, everything one had ever felt suddenly made sort of clear. So I bought another one which I didn't like *quite* so much, and now I've definitely made up my mind I'm going to read everything that's any good and really try to understand and then perhaps I'll understand myself more, which as you know darling I've never really done.

Tons of love from
DAISY

PS That book I mentioned was called *The Outsider*. I wonder if you'd like it?

13

Lesley's story

The previous resident artist at Sussex University had been a chalk-coloured man with plenty of artistic integrity, which he proved by wearing permanently paint-stained jeans and accepting Woodies and Newcastle Brown off anyone who'd just been to the bank. He did lovely abstracts, thick with tracks of paint and bits of tin and wood which he strained from the heavy tide line of washed up debris on Brighton beach and he sold his less successful canvases cheaply to capitalistic students who thought they were investing cleverly in the future. He was all right. He was unobtrusive. He worked quite hard. Daisy Smuten was quite different.

I shared a huge flat, right on the seafront, with a balcony splitting its view drunkenly between the two piers. We thought we'd found paradise – Liz and Albie, Janie, Lin and me.

One day Lin and I met somcone coming up the stairs. She had rumpled blonde hair, slightly shaded at the roots, and an attractive, lived-in sort of face. She was carrying a large case and a bundle of rugs and we all muttered polite things at each other as we passed. Then she saw our library books.

'Are you from the university?' she said. Yes we said.

'Well, I'm going to be working up there this term. My name's Daisy Smuten. I'm just moving into the flat upstairs. I have room in the car for passengers, so if you ever need a lift, let me know.'

Thank you, we said, and how kind. She vanished upstairs with the case. At nineteen, scruffy, impoverished and clothes-greedy, the main thing I noticed was how great she looked.

She was wearing a long purple sweater, belted with snakeskin over a pair of black velvet trousers and purple boots. Lin and I felt shabby immediately. On our way back from Falmer that afternoon, we went shopping in West Street and bought a purple sweater each. Daisy was going to cost us a lot.

We hadn't liked to ask her for lifts because we were slightly intimidated by her glamour and self-confidence. The next time we saw her was in the University bar.

A group of Trots monopolized a mushroom ring of stools and a scrum of rugger players at the bar, downing pint after pint, were cheerfully recalling the summer's endless piss-ups. Two philosophy lecturers crouched over their halves of bitter and lone individuals in corners were frantically scrawling the last pages of an essay and submerging their guilt and pre-tutorial nerves in Newcastle Brown. One of them was Pete.

'Hello, Pete,' we shouted, throwing our bags and books on the table and crowding his foolscap into a standing pool of beer.

'It's me vac essay, innit? Should have been in on Wednesday, but I couldn't get any of the books. Luckily Ina had the same essay last year so I borrowed his. But the bastard didn't tell me he hadn't finished his either. So I'm stuck now.'

We sat down and drank with the fish-eyed expression you get from watching doors to see if your friends will walk in. The door was opening and shutting as fast as a cup final turnstile. Then Daisy came in. Behind her, twitching with social success and gratification, oozed one of the tutors.

'Look, that's Daisy Smuten, the photographer,' I nudged Pete. 'Fancy that, do you?'

Daisy looked smashing again. She was wearing brown suede trousers and waistcoat and a chocolate silk shirt. A dart made the jarring snap that comes from hitting concrete and missing wood. Someone's concentration had slipped.

The tutor clicked an academic finger at the barmaid and smarmed attentively at Daisy.

'Double scotch, please, with ice,' she said.

The tutor twitched again. No girl had asked him for more than a cider in years.

Pete loathed this particular tutor. 'Fucking hell, he's out of his class.'

'I bet she'll be at that creep's sherry party this week,' said Janie. 'She ought to take her camera along and get a few pictures of sycophants at play. I wonder if you ever get asked just for yourself alone and not because your dad is a famous something.'

'Ooh, I wouldn't half fancy that if I could afford it,' said Pete. 'I've always wanted some lovely older woman to initiate me into whatever I've missed out on. I wonder if there's a husband in the background.'

'Go on then, Pete, why don't you chat her?'

'Oh, I wouldn't know where to begin.' He flicked his eyelashes mournfully at the bar.

Daisy leaned back on the bar, scotch in hand, surveying the room like John Wayne sizing up a bar full of toughies.

For a moment her face showed the slightly calculating expression you see on attractive people weighing up the talent at a party.

The door opened again and Ronnie walked in with an endearing air of flash self-confidence. One or two of his beach-boy mates were sauntering in behind him, but the inbred self-effacement of their middle class upbringing undid the effect of the hopefully Californian tans and the skin tight T-shirts. They might just as well have been wearing school uniform. Ronnie swaggered across the room in a red suede jacket, plum coloured trousers and pink suede boots.

' 'Ullo then darlings, you all look lovely – I don't know how I managed without you all summer – 'Ullo, Peter, still working as hard as ever?' He guffawed meanly, his phoney cockney accent sticking out a mile. 'Can I get anyone a drink – don't all shout at once. I thought not. Excuse me.' He vanished to the bar and came back with a pint.

'Fucking hell, what's that?' he said, jerking his head at Daisy. 'Just tell me what she's teaching and I'll be in there.' He rose, half joking from his seat.

'That's Daisy Smuten,' we said, glad that we knew her.

'D*ai*sy S*mu*ten . . . ?' said Ronnie, stressing every syllable and pretending to be impressed. 'Not *the* Daisy Smuten . . . ?' He raised his mug to Daisy at the bar and she grinned.

'Christ,' said Janie. 'Look at the time, I've got a tutorial in five minutes.' She picked up her books and began to move.

'Wait for me,' I said. We all left for the arts block and the library, except for Ronnie.

I was sitting falling gently asleep behind a pile of philosophy books when Ronnie found me. 'Your friend Daisy Smuten,' he whispered, 'She asked to take my picture. I tell you, she fancies me. Fucking fancies me!' He winked and disappeared behind the bookshelves.

A week later, I went down with 'flu.

I lay in bed with a tatty old shawl round my shoulders, trying to read *Women in Love* although my head ached. I dredged a cold hotwater bottle from the bottom of the bed and padded into the kitchen to make a fresh one and a cup of coffee. As I was pouring them, I heard Daisy's front door click open and two pairs of footsteps go down her corridor.

Back in my bedroom the windows were rattling with the sea-wind. I jammed newspaper into the cracks and turned the fire up. The sea was boiling up the beach, dragging stones down the drenched pebble slopes and churning the dark water under the piers. I felt quite glad I'd got 'flu and climbed back into bed, throwing down Lawrence and picking up *Return of the Native*.

I could hear small bursts of conversation from the next room, then someone got up and flung themselves on the bed. It must have been right against the wall because I could almost feel the thud of their back against it.

'Nice place you got here, Daisy.'

It was Ronnie. I knew his loud voice anywhere. I heard the faint murmur of Daisy's voice answering.

'Nice taste you got. Anyone can see that you're a sensitive, artistic person.'

'Oh, Ronnie, don't be so corny,' I thought, turning over a few pages of Hardy. I tried to ignore the low conversation, then it grew quieter. They must have been working, I suppose. I heard Ronnie ask 'More smoke?' I think. And I heard the faint click of a camera. 'Like this?' he said and the bed shifted again.

I turned over, sneezed, grovelled for a Kleenex and then, in a fit of bad temper and self-pity, I settled under the bedclothes and tried to go to sleep.

I was woken up by a blocked nose and a low moan from the next room. Not just a low moan either – a sharp cry, a touching of heavy breathing and the pinging of bedsprings.

'Oh God,' I thought, and I stuck my stuffy head under the pillow. 'Can't I even sleep when I'm ill?'

The noises changed. I could almost follow the pattern of their love-making, and then I lost the thread. They started a strange drumming on the wall – feet – or a foot maybe? or three feet? Possibly. Could be elbows – unlikely to be knees. Could it even be a head? Then there was a tremendous thud, as something, someone fell somewhere. And a clatter. And someone said, 'Oh Christ,' then 'Please don't stop. . . .' Then more heavy breathing and a strange squeaking noise.

The pounding and pinging and breathing was thundering through the wall at me like a rodeo. It was too much.

I got out of bed and went into the kitchen to make a cup of tea. I lurked a bit and warmed my hands at the gas ring and I washed my face and I ate a sandwich. I felt driven out of my own bedroom, but after I'd lurked about for half an hour, I went back.

Christ, they were still at it.

Thud, thud, thud. If it weren't for the little cries of pleasure, I'd have said they were re-constructing the Old Bailey in their sitting-room, anything but sex.

Ten minutes later, chugging and puffing and hooting like the Flying Scotsman pulling into Euston, they came to an end.

'Hold it,' said Daisy, and the camera clicked again. 'Beautiful, beautiful,' she said.

Ronnie was the first. I don't know if she had him again. I don't think she had the time.

Daisy carried her functions as visiting Fellow of the Arts Centre with sympathy and professionalism. At certain times, she was available for advice on photography and according to the students who went, she gave it lucidly and helpfully.

She picked up students at the bus stop for lifts into Brighton and never charged a fare. She was kind to people she liked, and funny and sharp with the inevitable students who knocked her, who said she was a sell-out and resented her presence in the university.

When she wasn't dealing with all these things, Daisy went hunting. I know, because as the term went on, I began to feel that I lived in an extension of her lair.

Her methods seemed to be consistent. As far as I could tell, and I liked watching to see how she did it, she would eye a bloke with detached, professional interest and make sure he knew she was watching. By the time he was feeling flattered, unnerved or simply expectant, she came up and introduced herself as she had with Ronnie – what an interesting face, how photogenic, if you had the time – the corniest lines in the world and it worked. My ragged sleep was a testament to the success rate. She was a self-confident, seductive woman, and they, for all their polish and assumed cynicism, were pushovers.

I watched her at a lecture once – one of the few I ever went to, but Daisy went to lots. She sat in a prominent place, flattering an academic vanity by her attentive presence. With the confidence of an equal she'd approach them afterwards – and hand them the same awful lines. Flamboyant lecturers, or pedantic lecturers, eminent or young and aggressive, they all wanted to believe Daisy. So outwardly sophisticated and so tough, yet with such a guileless approach – the girl just had to be sincere.

I began to think Daisy was just sending herself and the whole place up.

From the pick-up, they always ended up at the balcony flat on the seafront where Daisy could be artistic about the view. Then the next thing, there they would be, drumming away at the wall, moaning into the mattresses, ruining my sleep and destroying my concentration on Kafka with the pounding of the bedsprings. And always the insidious click of the camera, and Daisy's breathy, après-bed 'Beautiful, beautiful.'

I began to think she meant the pictures she was taking and not the endless orgasms.

Halfway through the term, I only knew one thing for certain. I was mouldy from lack of sleep and my work was always late and bad. Whenever I tried to sleep, it seemed to me the peace was broken by the pantings and strainings through the thin wall. If I was tired, Christ knows how Daisy managed. Eventually, I decided to go up to the Health Centre and see the doctor.

I trudged up the valley and picked my way through the builders' mud and then I had to wait half an hour in the surgery, surrounded by gloomy posters about cancer. I almost fell asleep, but the nurse dragged me awake and I followed her into the doctor's room.

'Now then, what's the trouble?' he said cheerfully, looking at my file. 'One bout of 'flu already this term, I see – starting early this year.'

'I'd just like some sleeping pills,' I said. 'I've been sleeping terribly badly lately and my work is suffering.'

He looked up sharply. 'Sleeping badly? Now why is that?'

'Well, I suppose it could be because the room is terribly noisy.'

'Oh come, my dear, that may help sleeplessness, but it's hardly a root cause. Are you sure that there is nothing that's really bothering you? Any trouble or disturbance?'

'No really, doctor. There's absolutely nothing the matter with me. I'm just not sleeping. If I had some sleeping pills I'd be perfectly alright.'

'Now sleeping pills merely cure the symptom. What we are after is the cause. I suggest you go and lie down in the next room and I'll come and talk to you in a minute. We'll soon find out what the matter is, maybe a little psycho-analysis would help. I know what worries you students have to go through, especially in finals year. Just lie down in here and I'll be through in a minute.'

I went through into the next room, and as soon as he disappeared I ran.

'I'm not a nut, I'm not a nut,' I chanted hysterically to myself as I disappeared towards the tunnel which led to the arts block.

'Hullo,' somebody called from the car park. 'Would you like a lift into Brighton?' It was Daisy Smuten.

I hesitated, then 'OK,' I shouted.

'I haven't seen much of you since we met on the stairs,' she said as we pulled out into the Brighton bound traffic.

'No, well, we always go up to Falmer at such funny times. I suppose we don't like to bother you for a lift.'

'You should all come and have a drink sometime.' One of those vague social politenesses. 'Have you been up to the Appointments centre? You'll be thinking about a job soon, I suppose.'

'No, I went to the Health Centre, it's in the same block.'

'What's the matter, aren't you well?'

I swallowed and shuffled my feet.

'Well, actually I haven't been sleeping at all well lately. My room is rather noisy.'

Daisy changed gear, then glanced across at me. 'Noisy? I didn't think those flats were too bad. . . .'

'It depends on which room you have.'

Daisy suddenly began to laugh. 'You mean me? Oh, my God, am I that loud . . . why on earth did you never bang on the wall or scream or shove a rude note under the door or something?'

'Well, I didn't like to somehow . . .'

'But if the wall's that thin, you must be so quiet, you never make a sound.'

'I try not to, I suppose. I thought you'd got a home building kit at first – all that banging and things.'

Daisy roared with laughter – 'I think I'll have it in the kitchen in the future, then no-one can hear but the mice. I am sorry, love. I'll make sure you sleep more soundly in future.'

'Oh, that's alright. I wouldn't have mentioned it. . . .'

I felt even more stupid.

'I think I owe you a drink,' Daisy said. 'Have you got time?'

She found a parking meter on the front, and collars up against the wind, we crossed into the warm, mock-Tudor comfort of Henekeys up the stairs and into the gallery.

'What would you like?'

'Oh,' I said, conditioned by three years of student grant. 'I'll have cider.'

'Wouldn't you rather have wine?'

'Oh, yes please.'

'Well, grab a table then and I'll get it.'

She came back with a whole bottle. I was tremendously impressed with such prodigality.

'Daisy, you can't pay for that all by yourself.'

'Don't be silly, of course I can. There's no need to feel guilty. I like giving underprivileged people things as long as I'm not conned. It makes me feel generous and altogether admirable.' She grinned.

I felt awkward. Despite her friendliness, Daisy still seemed to me to be glossier, more self-assured than I could ever be. It seemed silly to be intimidated by someone you heard gasping through the wall every night.

'That's a beautiful coat,' I said enviously, looking at her red fox. 'Where did you get it?'

'I had it made, with the proceeds of the Aberfan job I did for Life magazine.'

I must have looked visibly impressed because she laughed at me. . . . 'If I said that to half the students here, they'd start saying what crap Life was, or how it was immoral to make money out of photographing dead and injured people or how I was a capitalistic sell-out and had no right to be the resident artist at a new university. They're quite right. What about you? Are you ambitious? What are you going to do next year?'

'I don't know,' I said. 'It depends on my finals. . . .'

'No, it doesn't. Exam results don't matter at all. The good ones here will get somewhere because that's what they are, not because of bits of paper.'

'But it's easy if you've got a talent.'

'Talent nothing. I never had a life-long urge to be a photographer. I only took it up a few years ago. My ambition was to be a success, that was all. Lots of pompous academics and arrogant little students think that success is the kiss of death. It can be. But you've got to have it first.'

I munched a crisp and thought.

'But you seem to like them,' I said, 'At least. . . .'

'You mean I lay them?' Daisy propped her face on her knuckles, stretching the skin round the eyes slightly.

'That's not the same, is it? It's more like lust, really.'

She laughed, and leant forward. 'I suppose it's a masculine thing. I feel very masculine here. When I first went into the bar, or into a dance at Falmer House, do you know what I thought when I looked round? It's absurd, really. I thought, in those very words – "Christ, crumpet." That's what I thought.'

I giggled.

'No, I did, honestly. All those unlined, attractive faces. I knew perfectly well it would be tiresome if I just laid one, so I thought I'd have the lot and not get involved at all. I just couldn't hold back. "Can I take your lovely snapshot?" The corniest line in the world. But it works. That's why I chose that Ronnie bloke first. I thought, if he thinks I'm being corny, he'll throw it back at me and it'll be a joke. But no, he took it all. I bet he still thinks he did the real chatting.

'I'm a bit tired of it now, actually. I'm beginning to feel like some haggard old vulture swooping on harmless little boys. And they are getting a bit boring. It's probably a good thing I'm only here for one term.'

'But what about the older ones?' I said. 'All those awful faculty people. At least, sorry – I shouldn't have said awful.'

'Of course you should – they all are. Except a few really interesting ones and I wouldn't insult them with a Daisy Smuten pick-up. I'm only here a short time, I can't get everyone in.

'But the rest – you know some of them try to educate me. They talk about logical positivism and all the time they're sliding their hand up my leg. I really find it very hard not to laugh. But I like young boys, the older I get.

'It's a bring-down, a power complex. I like to see them all pompous and then just begging for it. I suppose it's only because there are so many men here all crowded into one space. It's sort of irresistible, like free-loading. And it's good for work too. One day, love, I'll show you my rogue's gallery.'

'Actually, I ought to be going,' I said. 'I've got to go and see this bloke and cook him some food.'

'Why doesn't he cook you some – or take you out?'

'Well, he says he can't cook, except coffee and toast, and he hasn't got any money. Besides, I like cooking him things.'

Daisy looked disbelieving.

'I suppose you've bought the food too,' she said. 'One day the girls here will get over the slave and martyr bit and then the blokes might be a bit more likeable.' She stood up and pushed her skirt down over half an inch of greying petticoat. 'Come on, I'll give you a lift.'

The term went uneventfully on towards Christmas. Daisy kept her promise to be quiet or chaste or something. Anyway, I slept better, and I hardly ever saw her.

Then we had a suicide. The funny thing was that I almost saw it. Lin and I were sitting by the window on a late November evening looking out at the black sea. It was nearly dark and the piers had closed for the night. The strings of lights along the promenade were swinging unlit in the wind and we were watching the pattern of the pier structure being swallowed and regurgitated by the sea.

'Imagine being on the pier after dark,' said Lin, pressing her nose whitely against the window-pane. 'Like being locked up in a church, with everything switched off and looming at you.' I shuddered, then Lin said flatly. 'I think something just fell into the sea.'

'Where?'

'There, halfway along the West Pier . . . I'm sure it did.'

We opened the balcony window and rushed out to look, but through the darkness, the surface of the sea looked unbroken, except by small heaving heads of foam.

'You must have imagined it, frightening yourself.'

We stared until our eyes went screwy. It was cold outside. We shut the window behind us and forgot about it.

Next morning, the body of a middle-aged woman was washed up on the beach under the barnacled pillars of the West Pier. It was Mrs Ellison, the wife of one of our more grey professors. It was a smashing bit of scandal for the coffee bar and the refectory. Mrs Ellison was a notorious nut, neurotic and extremely boring. She used to go over her husband's lectures and correct them. She believed in the loco parentis bit too and unsuspecting students would find themselves stabbed with a pin on some list and invited to an uncomfortable dinner at the Ellison's Hove flat to have their every word analysed.

Everyone thought it was a bit of a joke, her throwing herself off the pier. Some people muttered about the menopause.

Others said Professor Ellison had some guilty secret that would yet come to light.

I got back from the University that day and found Daisy's door half open. I could see Daisy hauling a box down the corridor.

'Hullo,' I shouted, as I pushed my key into our lock.

Daisy came down the corridor to see who it was. Her face was dusty and she wasn't wearing any make-up, but she looked surprisingly good. Her face was a strong shape, although her eyes could look a big baggy and shadowed. You could tell she must be thirty. She pushed back a strand of hair.

'Oh hullo love, how's things? I haven't seen you for a while.'

'Oh, things are OK thanks. Lovely bit of scandal. Mrs Ellison jumped off the West Pier last night and the funny thing is, Lin and I saw her. I suppose it isn't funny at all really, but we couldn't possibly have done anything in time.'

'Yes, I heard,' said Daisy. 'Are you doing anything, or would you like to come in and help me pack some things and have a glass of champagne?'

'Champagne? Gosh, are you celebrating something? I'll be right in – just hang on while I put my things inside.'

She disappeared up the corridor, wiping a grimy hand on the back of her blue velvet trousers. I made a mental note to look for some blue velvet trousers when my next cheque came through.

I shut my door and followed Daisy up the corridor. I'd never been in the flat next door before. What there had been of Daisy in it seemed to be lying in confusion on the floor; glossy photographs, a few pictures and a case of books sitting on the carpet.

'Gosh, are you going?'

'Not entirely. I'm just moving out of here and going back to London.'

'Don't you like it here then?'

'Hang on, I offered you some champagne, didn't I.'

She scrambled up and disappeared, coming back with a bottle of champagne already half empty and an extra glass.

'Don't worry, there's more in the fridge.'

'Are you celebrating leaving?'

'Sort of. I often drink champagne just to cheer myself up or to keep myself cheered.'

There I was, being impressed again. Actually, I didn't like champagne all that much, but I took it. Daisy made me feel like a little girl on the fringe of a big party. You weren't sure whether all this largesse and kindness was really for you, or how much you were meant to join in.

'Don't you like it here, then?' I said again.

'Do you?'

'Well, yes, I suppose. Well, I know one's supposed to knock it, but yes, I do like it.'

'Supposed? Who supposes? Why don't you just say what you think?'

'Then I like it.'

'You wait love, you wait until you've been working a while outside, then see if you can stick your ivory tower by the sea.'

She poured the rest of the champagne into her glass, and pushed her shirt back into the belt of her trousers.

'Pass me those books over there, will you?'

'What's wrong with it here, then?' I said.

Daisy sat back on her heels, books in hand, and screwed her face up into a thin look. 'It's not as good as it might be, that's what.

'When I was asked to come here, I was knocked out really. I'm a good photographer, but in everyday work you tend to get bogged down with material and practical considerations. I thought, well, it's very flattering to be asked.

'I could help other young photographers. I would have lots of time to myself to do pictures. I felt like doing lots of faces. I thought I'd like to do something lovely and artistic, you know, and then, I fancied myself here. I thought I'd be, you know, impressive somehow, glamorous. Like I said, I was knocked out by all those available blokes. Now I've had this place, right up to here. It's just not real.'

She started packing the books carefully into the crate.

'You've all been protected and nurtured and sheltered into this middle class haven. I could forgive you that, I could forgive anything but the awful arrogance that results. I don't know, maybe it's jealousy, an excess of freedom, of privilege, that makes you unbearable to people like me.

'And the extraordinary affected way some of you pretend to despise the world. Just let these kids wait until they're still being professionally unworldly at thirty, with a wife and two kids and a mortgage and a mindful of great unwritten books . . . the pre*tens*ion. . . .' She paused for a breath, I think.

'I thought the champagne was supposed to cheer you up,' I said.

Daisy looked at me and laughed suddenly. 'I'm sorry,' she said, 'After all you like it here. I would at your age too.'

I stood up. 'Can I look at your clothes? I mean, if you're packing them anyway. You always wear such smashing things.'

A good move, because she insisted on me taking several shirts, jackets and a skirt she said she never wore. The skirt needed shortening because her legs were longer than mine. It was only later I saw how stained and dirty and uncared for so many of them were. But my friends were very envious when they saw.

'What else did she have?' Liz asked.

'Oh, smashing things, couple of suede coats I've never seen her wear and incredible underwear, all printed and gorgeous, a bit grubby but you can't have everything.'

At the back of her wardrobe were folders and folders of pictures.

'Are these yours Daisy? Can I look?'

Daisy turned round from the chest of drawers. 'Oh yes, I promised to show you my gallery once didn't I? OK, take them through there.'

She started piling clothes untidily into a case, while I carried the pile through and spread them on the carpet.

There were pictures taken by the sea and in Brighton; grainy, impressionist black and white landscapes, seascapes and studies of old people.

'They're very good, Daisy,' I called.

I opened the second folder. Full of faces and people blowing smoke at the camera, or simply blank and beautiful, or smug and self-confident.

Daisy was standing behind me, thumbs in her belt. 'Aren't

they a lovely lot,' she said, giving them a stir with the toe of her boot.

'Hey, look, there's Dave and that's Chris . . . and . . . gosh,' I said pulling out a full-length of Ronnie, lying in bed, blowing self-confident kisses at the camera.

The third folder was full of older men, some attractive, some uncertain, some with the conceit of a thousand tutorials in their faces. Then I found a picture of Professor Ellison.

'Oh Daisy, it's awful,' I said, shocked. 'How could you?'

Professor Ellison was sitting on the edge of Daisy's bed, squinting at her in an exhausted way, hair in one eye. He was wearing his jacket, and woolly waistcoat and tie, and one sock. He had no trousers or pants on at all. He looked ludicrous, and old and sad.

'Really, Daisy, that's horrible. Why did he let you take it? Did Mrs Ellison know then . . . ?'

'He was a bit shell-shocked,' said Daisy, taking the picture out of my hand and tearing it up. 'Yes, his wife must have known, but only because he felt the need to confess, and OK, yes, I wish I hadn't done it in a way. More because of what it tells me about me, than because of her.

'Don't look so taken aback, love. I wasn't going to sell it to the News of the World. I suppose I took it for my own satisfaction because he was pompous and boring and I thought it would be funny.

'There are worse pictures than that. You'll see the kindest pictures hanging in my exhibition in the JCR next week. All those men will think it's terribly smart to be in it, you wait and see.

'Here, I found this half bottle of *Ma Griffe* in a drawer – would you like it? Someone gave it to me once and it's not my favourite smell.'

We started the second bottle of champagne and Liz and Albie came home and joined us. When we said goodbye we were all pretty drunk and Daisy was muttering about how Sussex was like going to a posh party you were looking forward to and getting too drunk to enjoy it and deciding it wasn't any good in any case. She thrust an extra bottle of champagne at us and kissed us all goodbye, especially Albie, who she'd never got round to photographing.

She semi-disappeared from the university that week, but she came back for the exhibition. It was a huge success, and there was a drunken private view where Daisy turned up in a gorgeous gold kaftan and downed lots of free drink.

Everyone said how exciting it had been to have her around and we'd all look for her name in the paper. She kissed a lot of people in a very cheerful, extravagant way. Unless you'd known, you wouldn't have realized she thought they were mostly a load of old shits.

I did keep my eyes open for her name and then in March I found it, in Nova.

A well-known feminist lady was writing an essay on the natural arrogance of men and there were two pages of Daisy's pictures of awful men.

I thought it was a bit mean of Daisy. After all, she'd told me it was for her own satisfaction and was even a bit ashamed of herself. I can only suppose someone had seen them, like I had, and offered her a lot of money.

I tucked her cast-off silk shirt into her cast-off skirt.

'Sell-out,' I thought.

Daisy Smuten Studios
August, 1966

DEAREST REG,

I've been having some very funny dreams lately. I read somewhere that if you take sleeping pills they stop you from dreaming, well darling I'm here to tell you that that is *balls* because I'm on to two Mandies every night now, sometimes three. (Not to mention three Drinnies a day – I hope I'm not turning into a junkie!) Last night I had such a haunting dream, I can't get it out of my head. I don't remember it very clearly in detail, but the *feel* of it sort of follows me around. It was the war, I think, which is funny because I scarcely remember it now – anyway there was a black-out, and an air-raid going on, and I was walking down this long dark street looking for somebody I think it was my mother I was looking for (although I've quite forgotten her really). I knew she was in one of the little houses but didn't know which. Then a man came walking down the street to meet me, I couldn't see his face because of the black-out and so darling I had this idea that he must be *you*, anyway he didn't speak but just pointed in the direction of a door and walked away. I opened the door and then I seemed to be in the most beautiful room you can imagine, with a painted ceiling, like one of those old *palazzos* in Rome, full of baroque sculpture, and super portraits by Titian and Velasquez and Van Dyck. I was alone in the room and I knew if I just waited somebody would come down this immense double staircase and that when this person came everything would be all right. I was a bit frightened in case it would turn out to be my mother and I wouldn't recognize her. There was an old grandfather clock ticking away (most inappropriate for the room!) and I stared at the clock and stared at the stairs and nothing happened and then I woke up. Do you think I ought to see an analyst?

My love as always,
DAISY

14

Godfrey's story

'Southern Airways' flight number two-five-nine is about to depart from Gate Thirty-nine for Montgomery, Jackson and New Orleans.' The southern country voice, as smooth as buttermilk, was calling the flight already as I got to the airport lobby. I picked up my holdall in one hand and my Olivetti in the other and ran. When I got to the gate the plane was full. The airline agent explained that they always kept two seats on that flight for military priority passengers, so that if I cared to wait I was almost sure of getting on.

So I pulled out the Washington Evening Star and re-read for the dozenth time the ill-written story from a wire-service stringer which had made me catch the first plane south without waiting for the office in London to send me.

> 'Selma, Ala., March 6' – it began – 'Alabama Governor George C. Wallace, Jr., predicts major racial violence in this central Alabama Black Belt community here tomorrow (Sunday) if Negro protesters hold a scheduled rights march. In another development, aides of Dr Martin Luther King, Jr, today said the Negro pastor, head of the Southern Christian Leadership Council, intended to keep a long-standing promise to lead the march in spite of death threats they alleged he had received.
>
> Crosses were burned in three central Alabama communities last night, indicating some residents may oppose the marchers' goals....'

It might pass off quietly, of course. In which case, I would have a couple of hundred dollars in expenses to explain to the office. But then again there was every indication that it would not pass off quietly at all. Two people had already been killed in Selma that week. I rolled the newspaper up and stuck it in my pocket. The agent was just letting me past the barrier, when two heavily built colonels in uniform with iron-grey faces bustled importantly up and claimed the two last seats. The agent shrugged helplessly. I swore, and turned away, and there she was.

She was blonde and about five foot seven or eight, and she was wearing a light brown trench coat over flared slacks. I couldn't see her eyes, because she was wearing those big round goggle-eyed shades that they were just beginning to wear that year, though not in Atlanta. What I noticed first was her mouth. It was full without being loose, and even then when she was frowning it didn't turn down at the corners. When she opened it I realized she was English.

'What chance do I have of getting on, then?' she said, rather crudely I thought.

The agent and I both laughed. Perhaps it wasn't such a crude approach.

'I'm real sorry lady, but there isn't a darned thing I can do about it. Not even for you.'

It was her turn to laugh then.

And only then she turned to me.

Five minutes later, we were sitting in the airport bar, each gripping a cautious bourbon and looking each other and the situation over.

She was a photographer, and she had been sent out by a paper in London. Not my direct competitor, as though that mattered. Her entire luggage was in a black leather bucket bag, of the kind they sell to the tourists in Morocco. Once you had put two Nikon F cameras, an exposure meter, a long lens, and a couple of dozen rolls of film in it, you couldn't have room for a very elaborate wardrobe. That struck me as a professional touch.

We both had to be in Selma, seventy miles the other side of Montgomery, and a good two hundred and fifty miles from where we sat, by noon the next day, which was when the march was supposed to move off, at the latest.

The plane we had just missed was the last that night, and there was nothing early enough in the morning to get us to Selma on time.

I wouldn't say she was beautiful. What you could say was that she corresponded uncannily with the fantasies you have when you are stranded in godforsaken airports about the sort of girl you would want to be stranded with.

'We could always drive,' she said. 'It's only about five hours by car. Have you got a credit card and a driving licence?'

It was only after I had thrown the holdall, the Moroccan bag and the Olivetti into the trunk of a cream Mustang that I asked her name. I'd never heard of Daisy Smuten. I think she thought I should have done, but then I've always found photographers, especially young and pretty ones, rather conceited.

The Hotel Albert, in Selma, is beyond question the finest replica of the Doge's Palace in Venice to be found in the Alabama Black Belt. The period which is regarded locally as setting the standard of normality is the 'flush time' of the 1850s, when cotton sold for ten cents a pound, sir, and good strong fieldhands to pick it cost five hundred dollars from Virginia. The big sternwheel paddlesteamers came two hundred miles up the Alabama and the Tombigbee and the Big Black rivers to take the cotton out to Liverpool, and they brought Ruskin Gothic back with them.

I had done all the talking in the car. I tried to explain why I found the South not merely horrifying, but fascinating as well. I tried to get her to understand that in a society where negroes were brought up always to go to the back door of a white person's house and hold their hat in their hand while they talked to them, even a modest gesture of sympathy across the wall was worth all the liberal words that had ever been spoken by liberal persons in London North West One. And I told her about some of the horrors; not only the lynchings and burnings and murder, but the smaller things that had happened to people I knew, like the lawyer who lost his clients and had a bomb thrown through his children's bedroom when he took a case for a black client.

Daisy was a good listener. Every now and then she would ask a question that proved at least that she had been listening. But she said very little, and I wasn't sure that she was really interested, either in Alabama or in me. After we had been driving and talking for about a couple of hours she said dismissively that it all sounded bloody barmy to her, like the Everton and Liverpool fans fighting outside the pubs when she was growing up on Merseyside.

It struck me as a rather stupid thing to say, and I remember looking at her rather sharply. And then it struck me that that was the way smart, cynical kids talked. Daisy was not quite young enough to say things like that. I looked at her more closely. She must be thirty. Daisy must be talking the way the people she met talked. And a lot of those people were younger than her. It struck me as a perfectly forgivable affectation, a first hint of vulnerability under the exterior varnish of toughness and competence.

I asked her why she wanted to do a job like this. I didn't say so out loud, but what I meant was, 'when you obviously have only a very limited interest in politics'. And she explained that for a girl, especially, reportage is something you have to do now and again if you are going to keep your name big. By being able to do everything, from fashion to foreign wars, it means you can *choose* your job and do it on your own, in your own studio, on *your* terms. Oh, I said. I see.

And then we stopped talking. I knew too little about dark-room equipment and running a studio to have much to contribute, and she seemed to have very little to say about Alabama. For a while she stared moodily at the dismal pine-woods scudding past the car windows.

'Where are the bloody magnolias?' she said. And then to my surprise she put her hand over mine on the steering-wheel. 'Never mind,' she said, '*you're* smashing.' And she yawned and with great poise and without apology went off to sleep.

As soon as the sleepy room clerk had finally finished his ritual with the guest register, overcoming an insolent incredulity that we were registering separately, she smiled groggily and disappeared without a word to her room. 'You're smashing,' I repeated over and over to myself as I undressed and got into bed, and I fell asleep with a grin on my face.

'1402', I scribbled in my notebook, with a slightly compulsive precision which I knew from experience would be abandoned as soon as something happened, 'mrch crssg brdge'. Predictably, the great man who was known, ambivalently, to his devoted followers as 'De Lawd', had arrived one hour late, and it had taken another hour to marshal the Lord's host into line of march.

It is a long bridge of steel girders, and the footsteps of the marchers echoed mournfully as we crossed it. The leaders and the ministers, black and white together, marched with linked arms, liturgically intoning the anthem of their Movement: 'We Shall Overcome.' The rank and file shuffled behind them so slowly that they seemed scarcely to be moving. And the reporters hovered uneasily on the flanks, half-consciously seeming to underline their neutral status. Comment, most of them seemed anxious to say by their attitude, was going to be rigorously separated from Fact.

For a mile or more beyond the end of the bridge the highway ran on an embankment above the inevitable outskirts of a southern town: drive-in movies, their white screens towering above the empty passion pits, trailer camps and used car lots hung with plastic bunting. Bill boards advertising soft drinks, which came towards you at a rational clip when you were driving, seemed now as we plodded endlessly towards them like grotesque slow-motion caricatures. BEAUTIFY AMERICA one of them went on ponderously for twenty minutes as we marched, long-haired and many of us bearded, towards it, till at last we came to the pay-off GET A HAIR CUT!

In the back of my mind I heard a car coming up fast from behind. I stepped involuntarily on to the verge. Well before it reached me, people were jumping to safety.

It was a big white sedan, going like the clappers. Behind it there was a second, then a third, and then a stream. I counted twenty, each with a red rotating lantern on the roof and an outline map of the state on the door. Then I gave up counting. The Highway Patrol. The Governor's private army. Reckoning six men to a car, a good hundred and fifty of them. I could see their beefy faces as they streaked past, ominously emotionless under their blue riot helmets and rimless sunglasses.

At the same instant, the line in front began to crumple back on us. I heard a noise which you never mistake once you have first heard it. It is an angry noise, and yet remote, like a big surf breaking a long way away. I recognized it with a retching feeling as the noise of a crowd beginning to panic.

Next to me half a dozen white students linked arms and began to sing feebly. A tall negro in a shabby overcoat began to shout. 'Stan' your groun'! Don't panic!' Then I saw the wavering white tail of a tear gas shell in the air. It landed twenty feet in front of us, and we all ran for a few yards. Some kept on running. Some slithered down the grass embankment. And some stood and gaped, like me.

Towards the head of the column, I could see the blue helmets moving steadily towards me, their billy-clubs rising and falling rhythmically. The tear gas was thicker now, and people were stumbling blindly past, choking and coughing. One elderly black minister dashed past me with blood pouring down his cheek from shattered glasses and the staring, surprised look of physical shock.

I managed to swim through the crowd to the side of the road, and found the grass bank more dangerous still. Blueshirts were chasing individual demonstrators, the blacks were running ziz-zagging like wounded partridges, arms up to protect their heads, and the troopers beat them across the shoulders with flat, heavy thwacks like a woman beating carpets.

Mounted troopers galloped past, the horses slithering down the muddy embankment. One of them turned and charged at a black boy with what looked like a short lowered lance. He screamed and jumped in the air as it touched him. Electric cattle-prods. I thought: they're out of control, they'll start to shoot any moment now. And I ran.

I ran until I was out of breath. Then I walked, not along the road, but along the bottom of the embankment, back to the bridge. I went back to the church and checked that there had been no fatal casualties so far as anyone knew. Professional reflexes were beginning to take over. I telephoned the city jail, and then the county jail, to ask how many prisoners had been arrested. 'We're stacking them like sardines,' I was told laconically by a sheriff's deputy.

Word had just come in that a white girl had been shot on the highway. No one knew her name, and it was not thought that the police had done it. Just some of those good ol' country boys who ride out in their Ford pickups with rifle racks in the back window when there is reason to believe that it is open season for Negroes. I waited until seven-thirty, when the civil rights workers who had been checking came up with a name and the bare details of the murder. And then I went back to the Hotel Albert to file.

The first person I saw as I rushed into the lobby was the sheriff, in his hat and guns, his belly bulging over his belt, and his neck bulging over his collar. He was just leaving.

And the second person was Daisy. She was wearing a brown leather dress, very short, and a pink silk shirt, and she had a big black leather donkey bag. She looked marvellous. But there was something else: a quality I had not noticed the night before. She looked pink, ruffled, excited, almost triumphant.

I was rushing past her to the stairfoot. But I checked, put the brakes on, and I dare say my jaw dropped.

'Hi.' I said involuntarily. 'D'you want a drink?'

She said, 'I'd love a drink.'

I told her my room number. 209. I've still got the key – not for sentimental reasons, just because I forgot to drop it in a mail box. And she said she would be along in ten minutes.

There is an old saying that there are only two kinds of reporters: those who have filed, and those who haven't.

The idea is that the men who have their story still to write are dedicated, single-minded, able to think of nothing except the flawless opening paragraph they will dictate down the phone when deadline comes. In my observation, there are exceptions. There are reporters, and some of the best of them, who are able to spend the whole day, before and after filing, in the same undifferentiated state of boozy bonhomie, from which they emerge only for long enough to dash up to their hotel room and write and dictate a thousand words.

But I am not one of them. As long as I have still got my piece to write, I find it hard to think of anything else. I make it a rule not to have a drink, and – well, I cursed myself for my foolishness in asking Daisy up.

For a couple of minutes I paced neurotically up and down that threadbare little room with the awful furniture. Why the hell had I asked that girl for a drink *now?* I looked at my watch. I had a story to write, a great story. I had been there at what I could recognize as a turning-point in the long history of the negro revolution. Declared non-violence had been met, for the first time, with open, unashamed official violence. Blood had been shed. A bridge had been crossed. I understood what that meant, and I had – I looked at my watch again – at the most ninety minutes to write it with any chance of getting it into the paper.

As for this bloody girl, she obviously hadn't the faintest idea of what the story was about . . . where had she been, anyway? It was one thing to fool a passing stab of sexual curiosity, the first night out on a story. But with a great story to write, what could I be thinking of, to ask a bird like that, who didn't know a story when she saw one, to come and drink with me when I had work to do.

That's probably unfair, I thought, and anyway she looked marvellous, I fancy her, I wish I could have a drink with her, but it's ridiculous, I have to get started. I made up my mind to tell her I couldn't manage it. I was on deadline, anything. I unzipped my Olivetti and started to type, rocking slowly backwards and forwards on the rickety bedroom chair in the effort of concentration as I worked.

Seven tops and seven carbons, each with the date, my name, my paper, its cable address, and 'Selma, Alabama', neatly typed on them, followed by a discarded paragraph, had all gone into the waste paper basket. But at last I had a lead which worked, which summed up the essential gist of what had happened, and at the same time set out the themes of what I wanted to say about it in such a way that it would be hard for the cunningest subeditor to cut more than a few dependent clauses, when there was a tap at the door.

'Look – ' I began. The room behind me was full of smoke, and there were drifts of paper all over the bed. Suddenly I knew that I really wanted her, not urgently, not physically, but badly.

'I know, I know,' she said. 'You're on deadline. Do you want me to go?'

'No, of course I don't – '

'Good,' she said.

'Listen, I'll tell you what, I'll meet you later, we'll go out and eat,' – I was improvising – 'I'll buy you the best dinner in Selma. . . .'

'You won't, love. There's practically a bloody curfew. They told me downstairs all the restaurants in town are shut. And I'm off tomorrow. No, I know an idea worth two of that. You give me your toothmug and the whisky and a book, and I sit down with them over this side of the room, and you sit down like a good boy over your side and finish your story, and then when you've finished, not hurrying, we'll have a drink together. In fact, I think we might get ever so slightly drunk together, as a kind of private celebration.' And again she had the mysterious, faintly triumphant look she had had in the lobby.

'Are you sure?' I said. 'It might take ages – '

'It had better not take ages,' she said firmly, 'or it won't get in the paper.'

'That's true,' I said. As I passed her to go to my side of the room I gave her a small hug and laid my cheek momentarily on hers. Then I handed her the whisky, the mug, and a paperback.

Forty-five minutes later, I straightened up. It was written. It wasn't Ernest Hemingway, but it was an important story, clearly told, and it was what the elderly Yorkshiremen on the back table call clean copy.

I stretched and made a roaring noise of the kind that helps first thing in the morning. Daisy looked up from her book, grinned, and tossed it on the bed. She held out a mug of whisky. She stretched, too. She looked pink and pleased and surprisingly restful. I gave her another non-committal little buss near the ear and my arm felt her shoulders through the pink shirt. I explained that I would have to take my story to the cable office.

'Would you terribly mind sending a cable for me?' she said, and fished the message and a credit card out of the donkey bag. 'I'm too lazy to come with you. Hurry back.'

The Western Union office was only three blocks down the street, and it should only have taken a couple of minutes to file. But there was only one clerk on duty, a southern lady of the old school, with blue-rinsed hair and a little chain to keep her spectacles from straying, and she was involved in an altercation with one of the other reporters. Something in the copy he was sending to New York offended her, and no amount of pompous little speeches about the freedom of the press would induce her to send it. In the end she took my story ahead of the other man's just to spite him.

Just as I was leaving I remembered Daisy's cable.

It was to someone called Steven, and it said:

> PIX ARRIVING LAP 0930 TWA FLIGHT EXATLANTA MARCH EIGHT WAYBILL NUMBER 778/TW/58933 STEVE WE MADE IT EYE REALLY MEAN IT GIVE MY LOVE TO THE TWO MIKES AND TELL THEM KODAK D 76 AND MAKE THEM PUSH IT ALL THEY CAN STEVE SERIOUSLY TRY LIFE LOOK MATCH EVERYBODY STOP GOOD LUCK STOP ALSO AM SMITTEN STOP DAISY

I ran the three blocks to the hotel. And I didn't bother to wait for the lift, I took the stairs three at a time.

'Hello,' said Daisy as I opened the door. 'I had an idea while you were gone.'

She was already in bed.

'Mmmm!' she said several asterisks later. 'That was good, to break the ice. Now let's do that again, slower.'

So we did that again, slower.

Much later she got up and crossed the room to get some cigarettes. It seemed an impossibly long journey from where we had been. It was the first time I had seen her naked. When she turned and saw me watching her she smiled. She came and sat facing me on the bed, with her knee just touching my side, and lit a cigarette for me. I had given up smoking but it never crossed my mind to refuse it. Brief and potentially dangerous, I thought, the appropriate sacrament for twentieth century love.

I said so out loud.

'Christ, that's what you get for going to bed with literary

gents,' said Daisy. She put the cigarettes and her flat metal lighter on my belly. The lighter was cold. I shivered and laughed and put my hand up to pull her down by the angle of her neck and shoulder, and the lighter slid off and landed with a little bump on the floor. And I remember telling her at that moment that I was happy, and I meant it. And she kissed me again, and said why did I talk so much.

And later still I asked her, 'Who's Steven?' and she laughed and said 'My agent, and you really shouldn't be jealous of anyone right now, and the two Mikes are the boys in the darkroom.'

And for some reason I still didn't ask her about the pictures. I got side-tracked on to my theory about the stages of a love-affair. The first stage is the stage of imagination, when you know practically nothing about a woman except that you fancy her, and you make her fit what you want her to be like. But the second stage is the stage of curiosity, when you want to know everything about what the person is really like. And then if things go badly the stage of jealousy comes later, when you imagine things again, bad things. And Daisy asked what stages we had got to, and I laughed and said things seemed to be moving rather fast, but if she really wanted to know, I was at the curiosity stage.

It had never reached the curiosity stage for years. It wasn't that I hadn't allowed it to. I frequently had the opportunity, travelling round the world on assignments. Perhaps as I get older my tastes have become finer. Perhaps it is simply that life is complicated enough without messy, hole in the corner, unsatisfactory, rather nasty affairs. Perhaps it is because I happen to love my wife.

We made love again and afterwards I lay wondering if she was wondering about me. Since the car ride, she hadn't asked me one question about myself, my life or my views. Did she realize I was married and didn't want me either to admit it or to be pushed into some pointless lies about not having a wife or a family. I have a family. Seven to be precise. I love each of them. I would do nothing to harm them.

I'd had one-night stands in the past, in and out with no feeling, no connections, no emotions, nothing. I've had passing erotic fancies, like all husbands, but I'd never let them get to this stage. Yet here I was with Daisy, feeling everything, not just curious. But I didn't feel guilty. It was as if it wasn't me. It was some other very happily very much married father of seven. Because it wasn't me I decided to let it ride, to go with it and see what happened.

'Tell me, Miss Smuten, can you remember what you were like before you were famous?'

And she lay back with her hands behind her head, and talked about herself. She told me about her parents, and her childhood, and her work, but she told me very little about the men in her life. Perhaps she was afraid I would move on to the jealousy stage. But I understood from the way she talked that while she had been very happy physically with men since she was very young, it had taken a long, long time to find out for herself how she wanted to live. Now she was about the best female photographer there was, that was what she'd wanted most.

She said this in a completely matter of fact way. She wasn't bragging, and she wasn't even trying to persuade herself. I had asked her to tell me about herself, and she was telling me. So at this point, I remembered the march and the cable, and I said: 'But what the hell did you take pictures of this afternoon then? You weren't at the march.'

'Oh yes I was, lovely.' She frowned.

'Where were you then? I never saw you.'

'I saw you, my love. I was in the Sheriff's car, and you jumped about a mile when we went by!'

'How on earth – '

'It was the obvious thing to do. The thing was that I had worked out that everybody would come looking for pictures which would prove how amazingly right-minded and tender-hearted they were themselves. Right? And so they would all traipse along with the marchers, OK? And because there would be such a mob of them, they'd all get in each other's way, and because they are all such brilliant and determined photographers, they would get some pictures, all right, but they'd all be the same.'

She took a cigarette out of the pack and sprawled unself-consciously across the bed with her beautiful bottom in the air to retrieve the lighter from where it had fallen.

'I expect you thought I wasn't listening at all in the car last night. You did look a bit hurt. But you were a fantastic help, really, darling, you really were!'

'How the hell was *I* a help?' I asked, amused.

'You remember you told me how the good ol' sheriff, while a pillar of respectability down here, once got caught out being rather a naughty boy in Washington.'

It was quite true. The whole of Washington laughed for a week after the virtuous sheriff from Alabama got involved in a row in a night-club over a hundred dollars which he had given to a black gentleman to give to a black lady. The black gentleman took it and ran away and told the whole town about it.

'Well, that suggested that he might not be entirely indifferent to a little lady-like charm.'

And Daisy waggled her hips on the bed in a way which would have been impeccably lady-like if they had not been naked.

'And it worked,' I said.

'It worked. He took me along in his car, after I said it was important that the world should see the fabulous work he was doing to preserve law and order. It was rather like Z-cars really until it all started happening. He was rather sweet, in fact, in a fascist sort of way. That's one reason why I have to go tomorrow. Because I said I'd have dinner with him. And I'd much rather have dinner with you, say in New York.'

'But what pictures did you take, for God's sake?'

She looked out of the window. And then she looked at me for a moment.

'They are the best pictures I have ever taken in my life. And they are going to make me a mint of money.'

She was awake before I was, and I would have known she was nervous even if she hadn't smoked constantly. At eight o'clock she jumped when there was a knock at the door. But it was only the chambermaid, following the mysterious, unvarying ritual of American hotels. She opened the door with a passkey on a huge brass circle, advanced impassively into the middle of the room peering about her, though the most casual of peeps round the door would have told her that the room was occupied by two naked adults, as follows: one white male, one white female, and announced solemnly that she was 'Just checkin'!'

Finally, just as we were ready to go down the red light flickered on the bedside phone. I picked it up, and a voice said that there were two cables for Miss Smuten. The maid's reconnaissance had not been in vain. I said to send them both up.

> CONGRATULATIONS, said the first one. DELIGHTED INFORM YOU YOUR BRILLIANT PIX BOUGHT FOR $7,500 STOP POSSIBILITY ONE MAY BE COVER STOP WELL DONE STOP PLEASE CALL WHEN YOU ARRIVE NEW YORK

It was signed by the editor of Life magazine. The second cable was from Steven. It was more poetic.

> LIFE DEFINITELY STOP MATCH DEFINITELY STOP STERN ALSO FALLS FOR ALABAMA STOP AND TOMORROW OGGI STOP WILL YOU STILL NEED ME COMMA WILL YOU STILL FEED ME STOP ANYWAY WELL DONE LUV STEVEN

I was glad he spelled love the coyly comical way.

We did have dinner in New York. We stayed in all three days, at the Plaza. Daisy arranged it. She always stayed there. On my allowance I'd never afford more than the Algonquin. I couldn't leave the States until my office called me back. Daisy was getting continuous cables to come back, everyone was trying to get her, there were contracts to sign and new commissions to agree to. She said to hell with them. She'd go back when she felt like it, or till I had to go.

'You really mean that?' I asked. We'd just awoken one afternoon at three, having been in bed since three the previous afternoon.

'Well what the hell do you expect me to do? Stay in this goddamn old fashioned city and play with myself?'

I wanted her to say that whatever I had to do, she would do as well. Or did I. Didn't I really want just to wake up and she'd be gone, a beautiful dream, all made up by me, lovesick and a long way from home?

'It's your oldness I like about you,' she said, coming back from the bidet.

'Thanks,' I said, putting on a hurt look.

'I mean apart from being a smashing feller.' She leaned over the bed, her breasts caressing my lips, and kissed me where my wife had never kissed me. I nearly told her that, then stopped myself just in time. I decided now I would tell her I was single, though I didn't want to bring up the subject of a wife and family.

'Perhaps mature, that's what you are, not old. Funny, really. I've always had a thing about young lads. Did I tell you about the time I was at Sussex? Remind me to some time. Where's the ciggies, love?'

'Kiss me again and I'll tell you.'

She did. Asking my wife to do anything in that region always had the opposite effect. Daisy did more than kiss me.

At six o'clock we woke up and Daisy rang for champagne. I was exhausted. I wanted to go away, then come back. I couldn't perform again at the moment, despite the years of boasting to myself, and to my wife. Those carnal thoughts I'd enjoyed had come true but I'd been left at the post, well, perhaps just a bit past the post.

'Don't worry,' she said. 'I understand. Have a rest. I don't want you to end up in a truss. I'll be needing you again.'

'*I'm* not tired.'

'Don't lie. Your eyes are bigger than anything else. It happens, at your age. I think it's great. Such a solid, mature, sensible, rather pompous, terribly knowledgeable man of the world and he's lying there all curled and soft and squelchy. It couldn't hurt a flea, let alone me. I love it. Hmm.'

She kissed me again then opened the champagne, making the most of the cork flying across the room and the wine spurting everywhere, then she had to sit down to stop herself giggling.

'About your wife,' she said. I had one leg through my Y-front pants. I stopped suddenly for a second, then went on, hoping she hadn't noticed, hadn't sensed a lie forming up at the back of my tongue. Instead, I heard myself grunt. She started laughing at my grunt then came to help me on with my pants, deliberately pouring most of the champagne over me in the process. She rang for another bottle.

'Lord Baden Powell always said a cold champagne shower would do the trick,' she said.

'Well it hasn't,' I said, going over and embracing her. She was still naked. Slowly, she took off my pants. We didn't waken this time till midnight. I awoke first. She was the most marvellous lay I'd ever had. Not lay. That somehow makes it crude. Woman, female, girl, lady, human being. If she woke up now and said leave your rotten wife and seven rotten kids I'd say yes. I wouldn't be able to say no.

'Thinking about your wife, hmm?' she said, waking up. She put her hand on my brow and said soothing things. I almost said no, but stopped myself. Daisy didn't lie. She was honest, like an animal, giving herself all the time, concealing nothing, with no evasions and no petty lies or hypocrisies. If anyone, she was mature, not me. This was something else I'd never met in a woman before, her sort of sexual maturity, taking it as it came, not grasping or not as part of a marriage bargain.

'I won't tell her, don't worry. I've found you too late, that's all. It's my hard luck. But we can still have a lovely time, can't we?'

'Any time,' I said, leaning over her.

'But not now, love. Let's go. I feel London coming on.'

About a month later in London she rang me. She'd said she would, but I'd never believed it. She rang me twice in fact, suggesting first of all Brighton and then the Ritz where she had a suite and some champagne waiting. It's hard to say why I stood her up. If she had asked me at that minute in New York to leave my wife, I swear I would have done. I think it was the way she smiled, almost smugly, almost satisfied, when she said don't worry, she wouldn't tell my wife. She was pleased I was married, pleased I really didn't want to leave my family. She could give, freely and honestly, but Daisy was Daisy. Anything intense or permanent or deeply emotional wasn't Daisy. She knew it. I knew it. In self-defence it had to be me that said no in the end.

Ritz Hotel,
Lisbon
November, 1967

DEAR REG,

Did I ever tell you that I picked up a dose from one of them goddam students? You remember, a hundred years ago when I went to Sussex for the term. I can only tell these personal things to you. Who else have I. Anyway, my IUD is playing up, the coil, you know, and it's as bad as when I had a touch of the old clap. The mess is awful and I'm in agony. It's been so great up to now, though Godfrey would go on that he could feel it. (Did I tell you about Godfrey?) I can't go back on the diaphragm after all these years, that would be like going back to the ark (Are you a virgin Reg?). Which leaves the pill and that scares the shit out of me. I'm so forgetful and untidy that I'd lose them. It was bad enough on the diaphragm. I once sent Gerald to work with it in his briefcase. I went to my gynaecologist before I left but he's so randy I can hardly bear him to touch me. I'd rather go to bed with Peter my boring accountant. With the light off at least I wouldn't see his popping eyes. (I wonder if he's had VD?) He says he can recommend Adalen 31, my gynaecologist I mean not Peter, as it has no oestrogen in it, whatever that is – or have I got it mixed up with that super film? If I drop down dead with a thrombosis, Reg, you will turn up at the funeral, won't you. You should find my will pretty amusing anyway. You didn't know I was loaded, did you? Did I tell you I'm leaving it all to you – whoever you are.

Lots of funny love,
DAISY

15

Peter's story

I first met Daisy Smuten in 1960, during the high summer of Mr Harold Macmillan, the premier who had assured the nation that we had never had it so good. Such was the effect of her irruption into the somewhat grey and arid tenor of my life that I was prepared for a long period to believe every word he had said. She walked out of my office, for the last time, on November 17 1967 – two days before Mr Harold Wilson informed me, and my sceptical fellow citizens, that the pound in our pockets had not been devalued. For seven years she had been the currency in my life – the gold and silver of my emotional economy – and I no longer believed a single syllable.

I am an accountant by profession, specializing in company and, to a lesser extent, in those days, personal taxation. We were small, but reasonably well-known in those circles where knowledge of the fiscal minefield is appreciated and rewarded. My two partners and I practised from one of those quiet Bloomsbury streets which appear, quite falsely, to be insulated from the atavistic rat-racing of the City and the West End. At week-ends I normally depart for Wiltshire, where my wife and three children are engaged, graciously and with considerable energy, in spending the quite substantial income I extract from a detailed acquaintance with Betterment Levy and the more esoteric rules of the manipulation of offshore investment portfolios. The rest of the time, it has been decided, I am much happier in a convenient service flat in Maida Vale, where I can read my old books, play my old piano, and amuse myself with my own, old thoughts.

On the whole, I am not discontented with the arrangement. It has lasted for a long time.

Daisy Smuten arrived by appointment, late one afternoon. I had spent the earlier part of the day with a group of my more normal clients – large, confident characters, with a taste for gin, and a deep interest in the twin subjects of bond-washing and the Kuwait Gap, through the second of which, at that time, it was possible and highly profitable to funnel the quasi-illicit proceeds of the first. She stood in the doorway, picked out by the sunshine, as it shone theatrically through the dust and the cigar smoke, smiling rather nervously. I realized, with a thump, that whatever this beautiful vision might want from me, I would be deeply unhappy if our relationship ended with the mere interpretation of the Inland Revenue Code as applied to self-employed females (aged twenty-one to sixty).

That was, of course, the object of the visit. She had just started to make a reputation, and a reasonably substantial amount of money, out of her freelance photography. One of her Fleet Street friends for whom I did the occasional tax job had kindly suggested that there were few men in London who could bend the allowable limits of a Schedule D expense allowance further than I. And it is true: I am not larcenous by nature; but I extract considerable intellectual pleasure from the chess game which the good accountant plays with those devious characters who draft the Treasury's more convoluted legislative paragraphs. And although, I am not, perhaps, quite an Alekhine or a Tarrasch, I can claim, I think, without undue immodesty, to be at least in the Bobby Fischer class.

Daisy, however, was not, then or later, interested in the finer subtleties of the fiscal end-game; like many people who start life without much money and then discover a talent which allows them to strike it reasonably rich, she was appalled at the steeply progressive greediness of the tax authorities; and she was determined, with womanly obstinacy, to preserve as much as possible from their clutches.

Her obstinacy turned to pop-eyed indignation and then to pink-faced fury as I explained, carefully and in detail, just how greedy they were likely to be. I don't think I have ever seen anything so heart-stoppingly lovely, as she sat there, knees tensed together, small perfect breasts jutting with anger, and a succession of astonished emotions crossing that extraordinarily expressive face, as I listed – with malicious pleasure, for I was enjoying my audience thoroughly – the cruel enormities with which Her Majesty's Commissioners of Inland Revenue are wont to visit the successful working woman.

She was certainly far too indignant to register my existence as a human being, with feelings and emotions of my own. And indeed why should she – she was twenty-five, talented, attractive, experienced, with an adequate portion of the world already at her feet; while I was fifteen years older, grey, dry, probably rather pompous, and in the traditionally invidious role of bearer of bad tidings. But there are strengths as well as weaknesses in the professional adviser relationship – psychiatrists are not the only people to observe a transference effect when they are able to relieve some of life's stresses. And it was with this firmly in mind that I set out, after outlining the bristling horrors of her tax situation, to sketch some of the more elementary ways in which a suitable Sir Galahad – such as myself – might possibly gallop to her rescue.

Her problems at that time were in fact pretty routine – the kind of thing my articled clerks advise on for ten shillings an hour when they think I am not looking – but I was not about to reveal this to my newest, and by a long way most delectable client. I am not one of those accountants whose everyday business takes them among pop stars and dress designers – overweight males, of indeterminate age and nationality, and a strong aura of cupidity, are more in my normal line. My one determination now was to make sure that this exotic, intoxicating creature should become a regular, and hopefully frequent visitor to my otherwise somewhat humdrum aviary.

I succeeded better – and at the same time much, much worse – than I knew. That afternoon, as I flaunted (for almost purely sexual and peacockian purposes) my easy skill among the tax statutes, I kindled a new spark in the Smuten powder-keg. For Daisy, as it turned out, was one of those people with a hidden, but late-developing talent: in her case, a powerful, intuitive instinct for negotiating that frontier where tax avoidance (which is legal if socially disreputable) joins hands with tax evasion (which lands people with large fines, if not a spell in gaol). And it was on that afternoon that I quite unwittingly fanned it into flame.

Naturally, I failed to notice any such development at the time. In the normal way of human vanity, I took the intensity of her attention merely as a rather flattering tribute to my own easy professional exposition. And when she slipped in a couple of extremely acute questions about the extent to which it was possible to feed, house and clothe oneself under the protection of a relatable expense allowance, I dismissed this, with gross lack of perception, as just a random reflection of my own intelligence. In any case I was not in the least interested whether she understood what I was talking about – I only wanted to make sure that I should see her again. And when she stood up, a few minutes later, and murmured that, yes, she would be happy to put her affairs in my hands, even the uncompromisingly ugly appointments of my office took on a mellow, late-romantic glow. As we fixed up a further appointment, to go through her financial arrangements in more detail, my whole personal world, which had been a pretty grey, pencil-and-wash affair since my wife and I made the tacit decision to put three-quarters of our lives in separate boxes, suddenly acquired a touch of colour again. And in the days that passed before our second meeting, I felt the colours deepening, and enriching themselves, until, in the last hours before our second appointment, the view from my window – the streetscape through which her taxi would arrive – started to look like one of those golden Samuel Palmer avenues, where the trees appear almost pregnant with autumnal fulfilment. No woman's magazine, in other words, could have failed to diagnose my condition for one moment; and even I was beginning to get some faint notion that Daisy was destined to be more than just another client. So the actual event had all the elements of a classic let-down.

A rather battered red MG roared down my Samuel Palmer streetscape, threw up a cloud of dust and dead leaves, just missed one of my partner's Humber, and pulled up at the door. Out of it stepped, not Daisy, but a somewhat epicenelooking youth with an envelope. And when, a few minutes later, my secretary showed him in, it was merely to toss the papers on my desk, with the message, 'Daisy's off to Antigua on a fashion jaunt; she says you're to sort these out and let her know what you've fixed.' As he had no idea when she should be back, or where I could get in touch with her in the meantime, that seemed to be that; and my new rainbow world collapsed comprehensively back into its normal, drab black-and-white.

Not that there was anything drab about Daisy's accounts, when I finally got around to opening them. She hadn't missed a word I had said about the nature of allowable expenditure for those whose vocation requires them to make friends, and impress and influence people. As far as I could see from the bills, she had stripped every dress, hand-bag, and junk jewellery shop from Wigmore Street to Sloane Square, entertained every picture magazine editor in Europe, either to lunch at the Ecu or to dinner at the Etoile, and acquired a rather dinky little sports car, with a petrol consumption of about fifteen miles per gallon as a necessary means of 'professional transportation'. And all these, she somewhat peremptorily assumed, I would persuade the Inland Revenue to allow for full tax rebate.

My first reaction was to return the lot, with a suitably frosty note. But then I remembered, with deepening guilt, the self-congratulatory monologue which I had performed at that first interview; and the beautiful, sweet, trusting expression on Daisy Smuten's face as she drank it all in. Whose fault was it, if she thought that she could buy up half London at the tax collector's expense? Mine, all mine! And more practically, if I ever expected to see this fascinating creature again – let alone improve the acquaintance – I had better buck up and do something about fulfilling her instructions.

It was a considerable struggle. Accountants' accounts of their clients' affairs are rarely pure fiction – any more than they are usually pure documentary – but this came as close to the borders of fairy-tale-land as members of the Chartered Institute would normally recognize as feasible, let alone prudent. But it is of the nature of the relationship between tax inspectors and tax advisers that, up to a point, they must accept each other's point of view. And by drawing heavily on my fund of past probity and good-will I finally rammed Daisy's quite exorbitant relief claim through, with the result that she paid virtually no tax at all for that first, highly successful year when you could hardly open a magazine without seeing her work.

By this time, of course, I had seen her again a couple of times, though only briefly – just enough to get her signature on the tissue of imagination which I was selling on her behalf to Somerset House. But even those two occasions were sufficient to rekindle the first sunshine. And when the assessment was finally agreed, in early 1961, I decided that I could now reasonably attempt to advance matters a little, by asking her out to a celebratory lunch. When she accepted, my happiness knew no bounds; and my professional self-confidence didn't suffer either – there were two discretionary trusts I devised for other clients that week which for sheer obfuscatory brilliance have probably never been matched.

When the day came – it was one of those superb, slightly sharp spring days when every daffodil looks as though it has been crisply stamped out of enamelled aluminium – I collected her from the Vogue offices in Hanover Square, and drove her through the park to one of those quiet but expensive places on the river, where the City tends to entertain its more attractive lady acquaintances. I caught a glimpse of the pair of us, reflected in the big picture mirror over the bar, as we walked into the room – Daisy tremendously elegant in plain oyster silk, with a single splash of emerald at the throat; and myself looking as close to the middle-aged Man of Distinction advertisements as my tailor and barber could be reasonably asked to achieve. My heart did one of those unheralded cartwheels which, even at the age of forty-one, indicate that you are really quite immoderately well pleased with yourself, and with the ridiculously well-appointed world around you.

Alas, the mood did not last. I wanted to talk about spring, white wine, South Sea islands, lobster quadrilles and the delights of being with the most diverting client in the history of British accountancy; she, it became only too clear, was only really interested in discussing her own financial affairs. She laughed in all the right places, and even added some appropriately sparkling touches of her own; but there was always the tinkle of ice behind the laughter. And suddenly I felt an overwhelming affinity with the boy in 'The Snow Queen', whose mis-directed love turns the whole world into a beautiful frozen waste (not to say, waste of time).

It was a feeling which occurred with considerable frequency in our relationship. But as I was no more capable than the youth in the fairy-tale of getting up, breaking the spell and generally cutting my losses, I just sat there and listened. And as I listened my role gradually became clear. It was to spread a cloak of ingenious near-legality over the increasingly muddy puddle of Daisy's monetary arrangements; and if I wished to stick around Queen Daisy's particular court, I had better get on with it, and forget any romantic notions about recompense or reward, at least in those forms of personal currency I was interested in. Politely, off-handedly, and probably unconsciously, she indicated that to be with her and to serve her was reward enough for anyone. And if the art of bargaining is to know the minimum outlay for which you can obtain the desired commodity, then she was right. I found, on inspecting my resources, that I was unable to reject her terms.

Daisy, it appeared, had been talking to people. And the people, who resided in the more opulent recesses of publishing and the fashion business, had been telling her about the fascinating possibilities which at that time were available to a person of talent who first turned herself into a limited company or preferably a whole series of such companies; and secondly had the forethought to register some of these companies in selected havens abroad. And thus, in the fullness of time, were born such shadowy corporate entities as The Smuten Corp. (Nassau), Smutco (Dutch Antilles) and Les Entreprises Ensmut (Liechtenstein), which had lately caused so much head-scratching among the higher echelons of the surtax unit at Thames Ditton.

The trouble was that, by this time, Daisy's various activities were bringing in quite substantial sums of money, one way and another; and although, being a highly intelligent creature, she was capable of reading the financial headlines, she was quite incapable of adapting her own economic pattern to accord with whatever the current Chancellor of the Exchequer was advocating at the time.

That year, for instance, the Chancellor was worried at the rate of growth of public and private spending; but when I made the same suggestion to Daisy, she merely laughed and told me to investigate the tax advantages which her 'friends' said could be extracted from the ownership of young, uncut woodland. (They could, too; which is why the Smuten executors, heaven help them, will one day find the deeds to ten acres of Kentish silver birch coppice among her somewhat complex papers.)

Naturally her reaction to Mr Selwyn Lloyd was to say 'Go' every time that he said 'Stop'. Britain borrowed extensively and expensively from the international bankers; Daisy more modestly, but a good deal more cheaply, from a growing group of international admirers (none of whom, I was glad to see, made any more of an emotional dent in her life than I did). And it became clear that Daisy's efforts to join the Common Market were substantially more successful than anything achieved in Whitehall.

Where Alec Douglas-Home used match-sticks to perform the more intricate type of financial calculation, Daisy, I discovered, tended to use hair-pins; but her results – reinforced by my own efforts – turned out to be rather more impressive. And by now, in a quiet way, she was becoming quite a rich woman. When Reginald Maudling made his break for prosperity in 1964, Daisy was already some considerable way ahead of him.

During these years, my own personal and professional life had slipped, by imperceptible stages, into a state of untidy but none-the-less far-reaching dependence upon Daisy and her affairs. Not that the affairs, by the standards of my City clients, were anything very enormous – quite the contrary. But they did seem to take up a great deal of time. And somehow they always involved my having to go round to her current flat, to see her for lunch, or meet for a conspiratorial drink.

The truth is, of course,that I made sure they involved this kind of frequent contact – it was virtually all that I had to show for the years I was investing in the distant prospect of Daisy. I once saw that blowsy old Dietrich film 'The Blue Angel', where the headmaster goes totally to pot in pursuit of the girl in the local strip club; but at least he got to share her dressing-room. I rarely got further than sitting around in whatever apartment we were renting for good tax-minimization reasons at the time – Hampstead, Chelsea, Beauchamp Place, Islington, all according to the state of Wall Street and the Smuten off-shore investment programme – and watching her queen it over a gaggle of other hangers-on. If she ever noticed that there was anything out of the ordinary about my devoted attendance on her interests, she kept the observation strictly to herself.

However, devotion it was. And it was also going to pot, though more gradually and a good deal less dramatically than Mr Emil Jannings'. One of my partners had died in a nasty car smash, and we had not replaced him. The other one was ten years older than me, and already more concerned with his golf and the orchid house he had built to occupy his retirement than he was in extending the practice. And I myself knew, in those few moments when I faced up to the situation, that my interest, my ethical sensibility and my technical brilliance, had all lost that last, fractional degree of edge which is the mark of the outstanding performer which I had once been. In fact, I had to admit, that on some of those days when I was itching to get away, my concentration on non-Smuten matters tended to drift from the perfunctory to the downright sloppy. I was hooked, as badly as any narcotics addict; without my regular fix, I became twitchy, irritable, headache-prone and snappy with my staff. And although I kept sufficient control to satisfy the clients I had got, few new ones nowadays ever came to call. The practice had dry-rot in the floor-boards and death-watch beetle in the roof; and I could somehow never summon up the time or the energy to call in the fumigation squad.

Unfortunately, it was at this time that the first signs of woodworm started to appear also in the ingenious structure we had erected to contain Daisy's financial activities. The tax-loss hobby farm in darkest Somerset had already had the foundations kicked from under it by an over-zealous

Chancellor; a chain of Smuten boutiques which some enterprising operator had proposed, collapsed under the premature scrutiny of one of the Sunday financial columns; and now it became clear that Harold Wilson's hundred-day onslaught on Britain's balance-of-payments deficit could do substantial harm to Daisy's carefully built-up overseas surplus.

We received a particularly nasty blow when James Callaghan stood up in the course of his second, or third, Budget speech, and announced darkly that he proposed to end what he chose to call 'Siamese Twin' operations. To most of his listeners, and indeed even to the great majority of people in the City, this remark appeared totally obscure. But to Daisy and me, who were listening to the radio on the balcony of her rather pleasant Cheyne Walk maisonette, which had been largely financed by just such a piece of advanced fiscal finesse, it was only too blindingly clear. And not all the Swiss numbered accounts in the world would protect our arrangements from a really thoroughgoing assault in this vulnerable area.

It was from that afternoon that my relations with Daisy, as well as the rest of my life, started to go down hill. Suddenly, every arrangement we had made seemed to spring a leak, or develop an incurable fault. The Revenue people challenged a couple of particularly subtle ploys which I had devised; we lost the appeals; and there, stark and inescapable, lay a demand for fifteen thousand pounds in back taxes, which came close to putting Daisy in the bankruptcy court. We scraped the cash together somehow, selling several promising-looking shares at a thumping loss, and liquidating the Bahamas company. But the gilt was off the ginger-bread with a vengeance. For weeks we barely spoke, beyond the odd word needed to get cheques signed and transfer forms completed. And even when the episode blew over, and funds started to flow in again, things were never the same.

We argued, angrily and frequently. And although to Daisy, naturally, they were just arguments about money, to me they were as wrenching and wretched as lovers' quarrels – which to me, of course, was exactly what they were. And to my anguish, Daisy started to talk – at first lazily, and then increasingly more pointedly – about the advantages of going to live permanently abroad.

As a tax adviser, I could hardly take exception to this. At Daisy's income level – especially when the money tends to come not regularly, but in intermittent spurts – the attractions of Switzerland, Jersey, Nassau and the rest are almost overwhelming. But from my personal, selfish point of view the notion was unthinkable. Even if I had been in a position to throw up everything and follow her – and my weekend family life in Wiltshire, though frequently strained during the Daisy years, had never formally broken down – on what conceivable basis could I propose such a step after remaining silent for so long? Yet the alternative was that I should never see her again.

For the moment, I succeeded in arguing her out of the idea. But even Daisy noticed the extreme emotional effort I had put into the attempt – not at all the calm, rational, reliable advisory figure which was the only role in which I had been allowed access to her circle. And from then on, I realize in my more rational moments, my ultimate banishment was only a matter of time.

The blow was delayed, for one reason and another, for another two years. But when it came, in late 1967, it was with brutal and shattering suddenness.

Daisy, who was in Europe on some affair of her own, as far as I knew, rang my secretary from London Airport in the morning, and asked for an urgent appointment. This in itself was a pretty extraordinary departure – she had hardly set foot in my office since our first real meeting seven years before: I had always gone to her – and by the time the appointment came round, in the late afternoon, I was pretty certain that nothing good would come of it. I sat at my desk, watching the last of the chestnut leaves blowing untidily in the gutter, and promptly at four o'clock a large, black, ostentatiously shiny Aston Martin pulled up outside. A tall, mid-Atlantic character, with a black silk suit and one of those briefcases that look as though they contain two gold bars and a collapsible machine gun, slid out of the driving seat and went smartly round to open the passenger door. Daisy descended, with her usual grace, and an air of controlled determination which put the final seal on my forebodings.

Freezing internally, I waited for Miss Carruthers to show them up. There was dust on the top of the desk, picked up in the late November sunshine, and a couple of files which should have been sent to counsel a fortnight before. Nothing seemed to matter much any more.

Daisy stalked in, with an expression which said, as clearly as if it was written in the sort of letters the Daily Mirror puts on its more portentous front pages, that she was furious with life, furious with herself, and completely decided to carry through the course she had set. She introduced the black silk suit, who came from one of those high-powered international operations, with offices in New York, Zurich, Beirut and Vaduz, and announced that she intended, forthwith, to transfer her affairs into their care, and remove herself, bag, baggage and statutory domicile, to the edges of Lake Geneva, where the Inland Revenue would no longer interpose its greedy hand between her talent and its rewards. That was that, and would I kindly deliver all papers, documents, agreements, memoranda, certificates, deeds and assorted securities into the hands of her new advisers' Zurich branch by January 1, or as soon as could conveniently be managed.

I didn't say a word – just sat there playing with a broken pencil. Short of a declaration of passionate love, there didn't really seem much that was worth saying, and at forty-seven I was still clear-eyed enough to realize that the time was some years too late for it. So I finally managed to summon up enough manners to wish her the best of luck and promise to put everything else in hand. And she, now that the worst was over, managed to squeeze out something about how sorry she was, but she couldn't see any other way, the way things were, and all that. . . .

I stood up. We all shook hands, in that ridiculous way people do, and Miss Carruthers showed them carefully down the stairs with the increasingly worn carpet, to the waiting car. As they pulled away, I thought I saw Daisy give a little wave, but I was probably mistaken. She wasn't really the kind of woman who waved.

As the early dusk gathered in the street, I sat. And sat. Like the pound in my pocket, my life was worth just the same, no more, no less than it had been half an hour before. But somehow it didn't feel that way.

Daisy Smuten Studios
March, 1969

DEAREST REG,

Well, your little Daisy has finally made it – the Big Time! What should I get this morning but an enormous invitation to luncheon at Buck House, no less – one of those 'informal little gatherings' one reads about which are supposed to give Her Majesty the opportunity to keep in touch with the worlds of Art and Sport and Journalism and the Theatre and all that crap. All my Republican instincts prompted me to throw it in the dustbin, but needless to say sheer vulgar curiosity triumphed almost at once and Miss Daisy Smuten has great pleasure in obeying the Royal Command, etc. Now of course I'm terrified that I'll get in a muddle about saying Ma'am and that my curtsy will turn into a pratfall and that I'll completely forget where I am and say something too awful about Princess Anne's hats or something. I suppose this is fame at last in a way, but honestly Reg who gives a shit anyhow? Still, it *would* be silly not to go, don't you agree? Details to follow. . . .

Lots of love,
DAISY

Daisy Smuten Studios
April, 1969

DEAREST REG,

It all went off much better than I ever dreamed, in fact it wasn't really a strain at all, after the first frightful few minutes, and the agony of getting there neither too early (which would be humiliating) or too late (which would be *lèse-majesté*), it turned out to be quite easy, almost cosy, anyway oddly *ordinary*. I suppose it's silly to be surprised at this, I mean they're just human beings like you and me aren't they? He was really awfully sweet and had a long chat with me before lunch about photography, asking quite intelligent questions about Leicas and Nikons etc., and even making a few funny remarks – they wouldn't seem funny if

I wrote them down because it wasn't *what* he said so much as the way he said it, anyway he made *me* laugh and feel quite at home. She's a bit sticky, but I think she's probably more frightened of *one* than one is of her and she said she liked my dress which was awfully sweet of her (so she bloody well should, it was Yves Saint Laurent). Dame Margot Fonteyn was there looking too lovely, and a tiny little man who I believe is a famous jockey who got rather saucy I thought after a dry Martini, and another Dame who does social work in the East End. At lunch I sat between Cliff Richard and a rather attractive youngish man who turned out to be the editor of the Listener who I think fancied me but perhaps he didn't. Oh, there was a fag there too, who does set design at Covent Garden and places. The food was pretty foul, Lyons written all over it, but one hadn't gone there to *eat* had one? I felt quite sorry when it was over though relieved to have got through it all right – but everything's going to be a bit of an anti-climax now I suppose. Prince Charles was there, but he didn't sit anywhere near me.

Love from your no-longer-Republican,

DAME DAISY

Daisy Smuten Studios
May, 1969

DEAREST REG,

Something very mysterious and dramatic and romantic has happened – I'm all of a sudden living in the middle of a Georgette Heyer! There's a woman called Caroline who I photographed once for *Queen,* married to a stockbroker, about thirty and very social and quite sweet, anyway suddenly she rang me up and asked me to dinner in Ladbroke Grove the following week so I said yes before I'd thought and then she said, 'Eight for eight-thirty, Prince Charles will be there so don't be late.' Well I immediately thought he must have taken a fancy to me the other day (though I hardly noticed *him,* to be honest) and sure enough I was quite right because when I got there there was only Prince Charles and Caroline and Rupert (husband) and I hung around waiting for the other guests to arrive and then Caroline said, 'Let's go in and eat' and it dawned on me there *weren't* any other guests and I'd been sort of procured for him (though in a frightfully nice way, of course). It was a bit sticky at dinner because I suddenly felt agonizingly self-conscious, I don't know why, but then we went to Annabelle's to dance and I'd had a drink or two by then and my dear we were still there at four o'clock in the morning! We found *lots* of things to talk about, he's really frightfully bright and not a bit unnatural or anything and I *know* he liked me because when they dropped me off he said, 'You must come and stay in Scotland this summer'! ! Oh dear, do you think I'm going to be the *older woman* in his life? Perhaps he's sick of all those debs in twin-sets and pearls . . . I can just see myself as a sort of Madame de Maintenon wielding tremendous power behind the scenes and intriguing for my favourites and ending up in a tumbril – or was that Madame Dubarry? I was never very good at history.

Masses of love from
NELL SMUTEN

Station Hotel, Inverness
August, 1969

DEAREST REG,

I'm sitting here in my tweeds with nothing to do for hours wondering how the hell I ever got myself into this. When the invitation to stay at Balmoral finally came I was tactfully given to understand that I should time my arrival *exactly* between five and six – apparently they're all still out shooting then so one is smuggled up to one's room to change etc. and then the Queen can greet one formally before dinner. If one turns up at any other time it's all frightfully inconvenient for some reason. Well all I can say is some equerry has goofed, because the only way of getting anywhere near the place is to travel by sleeper which arrives after breakfast in the *morning!* (The plane gets in too late, and to drive all the way from London would be too exhausting, and anyway the Rolls is having a paint job – I thought silver would be nice – and I doubt if the mini-moke could make it.) So one's stuck here in the Highlands for practically a whole day, quite alone, and if one was nervous to start with one's gradually going bonkers with terror by now. Thank God I've got you to write to, Reg. I *can't* make up my mind if I've brought the right drag or not, I do want so terribly not to seem over-dressed, on the other hand I don't want to be too dreary, and I'm sure everybody changes their clothes every five minutes at the Castle, and I do feel I owe it to myself to make a good impression though of course I couldn't care less what they think of me *really*. And what if I'm expected to go out shooting or stalking or whatever it is they do? You know I signed that anti-blood sports letter to the papers and I do feel frightfully strongly about it but I'm sure if I say I disapprove of killing living things they'll all laugh their bums off and think I'm incredibly *wet*. Oh hell, how can I get *out* of this, what if I took the next train back to London and sent a telegram saying I'm dead or something? Sorry Reg to be so hysterical – I know this is just a silly panic which will soon pass, after all I wasn't scared when I did that *Life* story in Vietnam and none of them can *do* anything to me and I must remember that *I am Daisy Smuten* and I don't give a damn for anybody in the whole wide world but me. There, I feel better already – extraordinary how you always cheer me up.

Best love,
DAISY

(*undated*)

Don't think me mad, Reg, but I'm in love again, and this time it really is the real thing. I feel I understand all sorts of things for the very first time – feelings like tenderness, and respect, and a deep sort of totally *not* egotistical sympathy and protective affection. Did you ever read *Chéri* by Colette? Well, I feel just like the old tart in that who meets this beautiful boy years younger than herself and sets out to teach him all about women and sex and then finds she loves him better than anything else in the world and knows she'll have to lose him in the end. He's like a son to me because he's so dependent, and also like a father because he's so much stronger than I am – I never had either as you know, Reg. It's a frightening feeling but it's also wonderful and I'm madly happy and scared stiff at the same time.

D

16

Kenneth's story

The cloud of dust may just have been one of those small whirlwinds that spiral along the horizon on hot afternoons, but instead of exhausting its energy and disappearing into the upper air, it had persisted. Now it was moving closer. It must be a car.

I dig each year in Northern Turkey, just outside the old Seljuk capital of Bursa, near the shores of Lake Apollyont. My period's the Neolithic, and I spend my summers squatting on dirt humps, sites of ancient cities, with my nose in a trench or pointing out over the grey-green hills looking for answers to the puzzles in my hands. And I hate company. Oh, I enjoy my share of it on the Bosphorus when the season of excavations is over. I recharge myself with gossip then, but strangers are not welcome when I dig. They disturb my concentration. No-one walks into a company secretary's office when he's balancing his accounts. Why should people believe I'm more freely available to satisfy their curiosity? It takes me days to build between me and the site that special relationship which I have heard others have envied. And I cherish it and nurse it as our dialogue grows more profound. Damn that car.

It had stopped now, and I shifted on my haunches to keep my back to it, and I stared at the contents of the straw basket between my feet. It held the day's finds. I could hear someone climbing up the hill in my direction: the fast breathing, the swish of feet swinging through the long brown grass. And then the sounds stopped. I stared more intently into the basket. There was complete silence for what seemed several minutes.

'You stuffy old bastard. Hello.'

My colleagues at the university have often remarked on my composure in critical situations; then what was this sudden surge in my guts? I tried to swallow but my mouth was dry. I knew the voice. Knew it over the span of over ten years. Knew who it was who stood behind me. And I was afraid to look. My tongue moved over my lips and slowly I turned my head.

She had changed little. Her blonde hair was now pulled back behind her ears. Her wide mouth was slightly less sure of its lines, and two furrows ran from the edges of her nose towards it. Her eyebrows still arched proudly, but the lids beneath them were sagging with the years. The first signs of crowsfeet pointed to the corners of her eyes like arrows, and her narrow nose – I'd thought it was long – seemed shorter. But my perspective was distorted, and her face was heavily shaded under a large straw hat which she wore characteristically tipped over her high forehead. I saw all this of course in reverse for I had lifted my head from her feet to her hair out of fear and some sort of shyness. A vivid pink shirt was tucked into jeans, and she wore sandals.

'Jesus,' I said.

'Wrong,' she said. 'It's only Daisy.'

And I burst out laughing, unwillingly let me say. I stretched out a hand and held her ankle. She knelt down beside me and kissed me on the cheek. And that had not changed. Like her voice, I remembered her lips from our days in London; and I remembered as well how we had split.

She had arrived late at a party I was giving for some of my students and others. I was a lecturer then in the university's department of archaeology. She'd been drinking heavily and had started to goad me.

We'd known each other for only about eight weeks. I'd met her at a student's party after she had just returned from New York, I think. She had no job and no visible means of support and I let her move in for a while. I knew that what she saw in me was a convenient meal ticket, yet I believed I was falling in love with her. But I had a habit of thinking things through that did not always produce the spontaneous gesture she most admired.

Jammed into the corner of my study between the bookcase and the fire, a fiercely whispered row blew up under cover of some early rock music from the record player. I'd been drinking too to hide my nervousness at her absence, and I went too far. She'd stopped talking, lit a cigarette, and then said, 'I'm sorry I'm late for the fourteenth time, but I've been fucking all afternoon.'

'You've been what?'

'You heard.'

'Er . . . who with?'

'Oh, some student you wouldn't know. And Christ it was good.'

Some idiot across the room shouted, 'For God's sake, Kenneth, stop nattering and pour out more drinks.'

'But *why?*' I was trembling. The ice in my drink was clinking against the side of the glass.

She blew smoke across the room and just before she turned to walk over to the bar, she said, 'If you like spaghetti, you can get it in all sorts of restaurants.'

'Come *on*, Kenneth,' shouted the idiot. 'Bloody fine host you make.'

And I walked straight out of the door, down into the street, climbed into my car and drove to a weekend flat I kept in Brighton. I sat there in the dark until I fell asleep as the sun was coming up.

'Kenneth?'

'You mustn't kiss me like that again. I've got a long memory.'

Daisy smiled, pushed the straw brim back off her forehead, and sat down beside me. I edged an inch or two away.

'What are you doing here? And how in hell's name did you find me?'

'Well, you're pretty famous now,' she said, 'and a phone call to Sussex told me where you were.'

'Yes, but. . . .'

'. . . and I needed a break. London's become too much. You'll never know how I needed a break. Anyway, after the charming way you left me. . . .'

'After *I* left *you* . . .'

'. . . after the charming way you left me, I followed what you were doing, becoming a Professor and all that stuff. I felt a bit guilty. Does that surprise you?'

'It may come as a bit of a shock to you,' I said, 'but I've kept tabs on you, too. Famous photographer . . . the giddy whirl of the world's capitals . . . escorted by millionaires. . . . In all the best magazines . . . the Sundays . . . the Mondays, the Tuesdays and the Wednesdays. Photographer and photographed. You name it, she's taken the pictures. . . .'

'Shut up.'

'So, what can I do for you?'

Daisy stared out across the hills and swung the camera hanging from her wrist gently backwards and forwards between her knees. The dust clouds now were no whirlwinds. The peasants were leaving their fields for the villages and each small convoy of carts, crowded with men and women, kicked up the surface of the roads.

'Tell me about your job?'

'You're joking. You didn't come a thousand miles to ask me that, did you? You could have asked me that question ten years ago when you lived with me. You must be joking.'

'I'm not,' said Daisy. 'I'm not. I want to know *now*.'

'Why?'

'Never mind.'

I looked hard at her. She wasn't smiling. Perhaps she did want to know.

'Why?'

'Kenneth, stop asking why. You always ask "why?" I want to know so tell me. Please.' She put her hand on my arm. 'And there might be some more intimate questions later. . . .'

'Nah, you 'ave under yer bottom one of the oldest known towns in the world what I 'ave discovered. It's about seven thousand years old give or take a 'undred years or more. Note the little (sic) rivulet what runs over there on the right. It's one of the reasons why they built this 'ere town. The sunflahers are new. To your left you will observe a cuttin' in the 'ill. It is where I 'ave fahnd painted plaster, a hodd skeleton or two, and this.'

'Don't be self-conscious, Kenneth,' said Daisy. 'You could never do a Cockney accent. What's this?'

She took the black stone, shaped like half an orange, from my hand.

'It's the world's first mirror.'

Daisy looked up as if startled.

I took it back and held the flat polished surface up to her face. She smiled into it. 'I can't see myself in it very well. Are you sure?'

'Pretty certain. It doesn't fit into any other pattern of use.'

'But look,' she said suddenly. 'I can see the sun in it.' And she whipped round towards the west where the hills were turning dark blue and the sky was silver green and orange. She then flipped back the case of her camera and started to lift the view-finder to her eye. I reached out and stopped her.

'What's the matter?'

'Nothing. But you don't want to do that now.'

She frowned. 'How do you mean?'

'If you stick your eye to that you won't see further than the lens. What do you want to use a view-finder for? You've found the view. There it is.'

Daisy began to raise the camera to her eye. I know I wasn't behaving reasonably, but I tightened my grip on her wrist. She strained against the pressure. 'You're hurting me.'

I'd never known till this moment how deep a wound her parting shot in London had carved out of me. I was filled with two sensations. The physical contact with her hand stirred me in a way I would not have thought possible. And my vanity had been breeched. God forgive me my vanity. In my right hand I still held the black stone mirror. In it for the first time Man had seen his unrippled reflection and vanity was born. Here, now seven thousand years later it came bubbling up from depths I dimly perceived. Then Daisy bit me.

I snatched my hand away. 'Look at the sunset. *Look* at the sunset.' I was punishing her for London. 'Don't glue your eye to that bloody thing all the time.' I spelt out the message slowly. 'Take . . . in . . . what . . . you . . . can . . . see. Remember it. Do you have to fill your mantelpiece with snapshots? Is your memory that bad? Can't you enjoy a moment without sticking it down on a bit of celluloid to show your friends, as if... as if you had to prove the moment had existed and therefore you existed. Can't you live without it?'

'Snapshots!' Daisy exploded. 'By Christ, you haven't changed. Why shouldn't I take it if I want to. You don't bloody own the sunset.'

I jumped up and stood between her and the hills, and pointed to a village in the distance.

'Those peasants have a superstition down there which might interest you. I found it out the other day when I was trying to trace the origins of some pots I'd heard they had hidden away. I bargained for an hour before they would even get them out of their houses. They were beautiful and all I wanted to do was to photograph them for reference, and they wouldn't let me. You know why? They said if I took pictures of the pots their magic would disappear. A little man in a tatty jacket and a flat peaked cap held one small pot in his hand as though it was the most precious thing in the world and he said if I photographed it its value would be gone.'

'Stupid peasants,' shouted Daisy. 'Just the kind of bloody ignorant thing they would say.' She grew more scornful. 'They're so backward. I saw them coming through. Women still with veils. Houses built of mud. Kids and goats everywhere. And you listen to *them*? Got nothing better to do, I suppose. Sitting here all day on this dump must be boring.'

I fell for that one. I started to justify myself. 'I don't need a camera.' I pointed to the objects in the basket. 'They're my pictures of the past... and they'll last a million times longer than your negatives. They'll tell me how these people lived. How they organized themselves to work. How art was born. What *you* do, Daisy, is copy things. You copy people. You've spent your life in a second-hand job, feeding off other people's actions. They're the ones that *do*. You were around to take notes.'

Daisy had wrapped her arms round her knees and was curled into a ball like an animal whose hard back was its only defence. 'And there was no art in it?' she asked quietly.

'Some.' I said reluctantly. 'But who were the people you took? I just adored those models in their cute clothes in those working class streets. The dustbins showed them off to perfection. And then there were those kids in Vietnam... the lovely way the deep red blood contrasted with the jungle green. Art editors, as I recall, went mad about *them.*'

'Forget about those models,' said Daisy, leaping up as though she were going to hit me. 'Who would have *known* about the real Vietnam without the photographers and cameramen? Those pictures went round the world and I'd like to think they counted. For Chrissake stop being so smug.'

'OK, I'm being smug, but I've never knowingly exploited anything or anyone.'

'I couldn't paint. I couldn't write. I couldn't even be a good secretary. But I knew about people. I learnt the hard way. And when I had a camera in my hands perhaps I have exploited them – but only to find out even more about them. You know about nations, whole races of people who lived thousands of years ago. But do you know about one single person living today? You ask why, why, why? You asked why in London. Why don't you once in your life do something impulsively? I've spent my whole life doing nothing else, and you and me are standing here in the middle of nowhere and who can say who was right? I came here because once in my life I wanted to stop and think. I came to you to do it.'

Daisy and I were standing within reach of each other and I dare not touch her.

'All right,' she said at last. 'Let's sit down and watch the bloody sunset.'

'We can't,' I said. 'It's pitch dark.' And we both burst out laughing.

In the car back to Bursa I said to Daisy, 'Tomorrow's the last day of my dig. Bring your cameras and see what you can make of it.'

'Really?' she said.

'I suppose I've used dozens of photographers on my digs over the years, but none of them have ever caught what I feel. You know me. You can try.'

I was called the next morning at six, took a shower, drank my thick Turkish coffee, ate a bowl of yoghurt, and crossed the foyer of the hotel just before seven. I was due at the site at eight. At the reception desk I said to the porter, 'Would you tell Miss Smuten in 48 that I'm downstairs.'

'She's gone, sir. She told me to tell you . . . how did she say . . . the early bird catches the sunrise.'

My driver Ridvan always likes to take the last stretch at speed. He would come out of the village and jam his foot down and race the last half mile to the tell. This morning he stood on his brakes and the car slithered sideways to a halt. He was showing off. Daisy's car was already parked on the grass.

That morning, and every morning for two glorious weeks, we roamed the site. Question after question. What had the people looked like? What did they eat? How did they dress? How did they govern themselves? Why did it start here? Unless she was a better actress than I suspected, Daisy had caught the mood. Changes of lenses. Switches of filters. Long pauses for examination and reflection; then swift action firing like a sniper. I watched her as I wound up my work and I hoped that her art and my profession would hit a perfect marriage. I felt exhilarated.

Then one day, without thinking it seems, she said, 'He'll be pleased.'

I turned over a fragment of pottery with my foot. 'He?'

'Oh, yes, someone I know. . . . He . . . er . . . thinks a bit like you. The same long view, you know.'

It had been a struggle, but I managed resolutely not to ask who he was, this person she was so obviously fleeing from. I'd almost asked, many times. But it was up to her.

'He sounds very sensible,' I muttered.

'He is and he isn't. He wouldn't love me if he was too sensible, would he. But he's so young. That's the trouble. He doesn't think so. I don't think so. But his family docs. And of course there's me. You can't get a bigger problem than me, can you? I'm so *old*. I feel a hundred.'

She was forcing me into a reaction, into questions, but I knew it was all rhetorical.

'I never thought it would get to this. Even worse, I'd never thought I'd get to this – *agreeing* not to see each other for a month. Just to see how we *really* feel. Me, impetuous me, the great believer in instinct and doing it now. Kenneth, why didn't you get married?'

'I am. Just six months ago. I thought you must know. She's

called Julie. I phoned her last night.'

'Julie?'

'Julie, my wife. I phoned her at the villa. We have a place on the Bosphorus, just up the shore from Istanbul. We've rented it for the summer and she went on ahead.'

'Julie. . . . Oh, yes. . . .'

'I always throw a big party each year when I get back to Istanbul. We'd like you to come and stay a few days. I'd like you to come.'

Daisy was reloading her camera. She took her time answering. 'That would be nice.'

At the hotel that night, just as we finished dinner on the terrace overlooking the mosque in the valley, I said to Daisy, 'I have a surprise for you. It's a ritual with me. I've ordered a Turkish bath for the morning.'

'You've what?'

'A Turkish bath. Don't say no. This is your genuine, gilt-edge, Turkish bath. You see that mountain behind us. It's Mount Olympus. It's been gushing hot water for a million years. When you've finished you feel two stone lighter and your feet won't touch the pavement. Honest. And you'll feel ten years younger.'

'You bastard.' Daisy laughed.

At eight the next morning there was a knock at my door. An attendant was waiting with a towel bathrobe. I slipped it on and stepped into the corridor just as Daisy appeared at the door of her room.

We followed the attendant down the hall to the lift which took us to the baths in the basement. As the gates opened a second attendant met us and led us across a deserted foyer to a door. Together we entered and the door closed behind us and the latch clicked into place. The back of my ears prickled. We were in a small room furnished only with two hard single beds, two pillows and a pile of towels.

Daisy spoke. 'He must have thought we were married.' I didn't trust my voice. Steam drifted from the room beyond. Daisy moved first. She took several paces towards an arched entrance, untied her wrap without looking round and dropped it off her shoulders to the floor. Her shoulder blades were visible beneath her tanned back, her waist was narrow enough for a man to clutch with two hands and almost encircle, her hips swelled gently and then curved into narrow thighs. The skin there was lightly dimpled. And then she was gone.

I threw my bathrobe onto one of the beds and slowly walked after her. The bathroom itself was made of white marble. It was a square room with walls twelve feet long. The bath about four feet deep was sunk into the floor towards one end. Three steps led into it. A cold water tap stuck out of the platform end and under it stood two small metal bowls. At the opposite side of the room a pipe jutted from the wall and out of it poured hot water from the mountain. The ceiling was domed like a miniature mosque. Daisy was sitting on the steps, the water level with the middle of her back. I crouched on the marble floor behind her.

'Soap me,' she said.

I took a tablet of white soap and gently rubbed it across her shoulders until a lather formed. Then pressing my thumbs into the spot where her neck began. I massaged her. She sighed and bent her head back. Then she stood up without looking at me and said, 'Front as well.'

I stood behind her, placed my hands under her arms and across her breasts and repeated the massage as her nipples rose. She gave a little gasp. My hands slid down over her waist and my fingers reached between her thighs. She pulled away, turned, smiled, trembling. 'My turn now.' I gave her the soap, and taking it, she moved her fingers across the length of my body until I was covered with white bubbles. I slipped my arms around her waist, pulled her tightly to me and kissed her on the lips. Her mouth opened wide. Her tongue flickered. Then she lifted her arms straight above her head and slipped like greased lightning through my grip into the water.

I plunged after her and we held on to each other and rolled over and over like dolphins sporting in the sea. The steam rose thicker from the surface of the thrashing water. It grew hotter and hotter and I went as limp as the day I was born.

Daisy dived for the steps. I lunged after her, caught her by the leg, but she slipped away like an eel. She half fell against the wall, turned on the cold taps into one of the bowls, and as I stumbled despairingly towards her, she flung the contents of the bowl across my stomach. I screamed, fell on her, and as she turned I whacked her across the arse. We were both laughing. Tears, sweat, water covered our faces, and I was as hard as iron. I bent down and picked Daisy up and she clung to my neck. I carried her into the ante-room and laid her on a bed.

'Slowly and gently,' she whispered.

Her legs dropped either side of the bed and we made love.

'Have you got a cigarette?' asked Daisy from the other side of the room. We were drying off apart.

I groped into the pocket of my bathrobe. A sodden packet squelched in my fingers. 'Not unless you like to bubble through water,' I said.

'Quite the little Turk aren't you,' said Daisy. 'In every way.' She reached across the gap between our beds and we held hands.

'Daisy. . . .'

'Yes.'

'Tell me more about who is "he"?'

'Don't press me. I don't want to – yet. One day you might know.'

She tugged at my hand and pulled me off the bed to my knees. She, too, knelt, in front of me. And we kissed very softly on bruised lips.

'Mehmet,' Julie called to a servant, 'I think we'll need some more iced water on the terrace.' She stood for a second or two at the top of the stairs, checking the great marble foyer of our villa below her.

The house stood on the edge of the Bosphorus, on the European side, seven miles out from Istanbul. In many ways it looked like a stranded ship, with its great wooden bow windows curving out over the brief lawn which separated them from the stone quay.

Julie, tall and dark, came carefully down the stairs, holding a rail tightly as pregnant women do. She held out a hand to Daisy.

'I'm sorry I wasn't here to greet you when you arrived.

Such a lot of new people have just reached town. I think we are going to be crowded.' Julie took my arm. 'Kenneth, take Daisy to see the garden before it gets too dark. I just want to see the chaos in the kitchen.'

As Daisy and I stepped through the French windows on to the terrace, Daisy whistled.

'Where on earth did she get that poise from? I could kill her, she looks so good. She's so young.'

'I found her in the bullrushes, just up the river there.' Daisy dug her elbow in my stomach.

'You're about the most facetious professor I ever took a bath with.'

'Daisy you promised not to. . . .'

I took Daisy round the traditional route, past the lemon trees, down between the beds of dahlias, and round to the side of the house where a tall hedge cut off from view the most secluded corner of the garden. It looked across to Asia. At our feet the water lapped against the quay. There was a whirring of wings and a vast grey shadow swept past us just above the surface of the Bosphorus. Daisy jumped.

'What are they?' she asked.

'They're sheerwaters. They feed on the wing between the Marmora and the Black Sea. There'll be another lot flying by in a minute. They do it every evening as the sun goes down.'

Daisy half-turned. 'I'd love to get my cam . . . No I wouldn't. Let's watch them.'

Julie with some friends was walking along the quayside towards us. There were loud voices in the house.

'Come on,' I said. 'The ball is over. Let party commence.'

'Who'll we meet?' whispered Daisy; nervously, I thought.

'This lot's from the consulate. There'll be the usual lecturers from the university, a few friends from London, Turkish businessmen and their gorgeous wives. And there's a young archaeologist I knew back in London, he's due out tonight.'

Daisy sighed. 'A regular little Buckingham Palace by the sea.'

By ten o'clock the house and gardens were crowded. It was a hot night, but the company was engaging and I could take a week or two of this before I would long again for the silence of the plateau. Twice I rescued a desperate-looking Daisy from admiring crowds. And once she said, 'Your dig out there has spoiled me. It's the noise. I've never really heard it before.'

I was crossing the hall with two bottles of scotch under my arm around midnight when a hand hit me hard across the back.

'Kenneth, you old bastard, you don't change. Sneaking off with the booze? Gimme a drink. I'm bone dry.'

'Paul,' I cried. 'Where've you been? I'd given you up.'

'I had to have dinner with Turhan at the Ministry before I could make it. By Christ, you look well. Julie tells me you've had a good season.'

Paul rocked slightly on his feet. He was a thick-set figure and had played rugger at Cambridge. As an archaeologist he was a good digger, not always inspired, but good enough. He'd been a plodder as one of my students, but I always rather envied his energy and his drive.

I grabbed his arm. 'Come on over here,' I said. 'I want you to meet a friend.' We weaved through the guests towards the windows of the drawing room, where I had spotted Daisy talking to Julie.

'Daisy,' I said, with an exaggerated bow, 'say hello to Paul Cooper. He's the man I was telling you about.'

'Well, I *know* Daisy,' said Paul, catching her by the wrist. 'Fancy, after all this time.'

I could see Daisy knew Paul. And I felt sick. Cold. Numb.

'Julie,' I said. 'Julie, let's get some air.' And we walked through to the garden, where I told her rather hurriedly I loved her.

The sky was getting greyer in the east as we waved goodbye to our last guests and, exhausted, Julie and I, our arms round each other's waist, strolled back to the house and the debris.

'Don't worry about this,' said Julie. 'Mehmet'll take care of it in the morning. I'm going up. Coming?'

I looked around for Daisy. The rooms were empty. 'Er . . . no, love. In a minute. I'll have a cigarette first.'

I waited for Julie to disappear at the top of the stairs and then I crossed the hall to the room we had set aside for Daisy. I tapped on the door.

'Daisy? Daisy?' There was no answer. I pushed the door ajar. The room was deserted. No luggage even.

The thought carried more pain than I could bear. Daisy and Paul. That bloody Paul. Daisy, not again after ten years. Please, not again. Then I noticed a scrap of paper. 'Dearest Kenneth. I'm not with Paul, you idiot. I've decided. I'm going home. Thanks for everything. Just what I needed. It was great. Especially the spaghetti. Have a lovely life. See you. Daisy.'

Buck House
September, 1970

Dear Reg,

Who'd have thunk it, as she said in that movie, whatever it was called. I haven't been out to the movies for ages and ages but of course these days, duckie, they come to us. We all get lined up and watch them as a family in our plush seats and all very intimate and I keep on thinking it's going to be some super blue movie, and hoping it's one I haven't seen, but it always turns out to be Doris Day or the latest boring Bond.

Everything's fantastic, as you've probably guessed. I don't know what happened while I was away, but they've all come round to it. I suppose they realized he'd set his heart on it so they'd better give in, even though the scarlet woman is thirty-five, divorced and all that jazz. (It's super having a maid to myself. I should have had one centuries ago. You know what a slut I can be. Now he'll never know.) The Archbishop of C. has been, I never knew he had such sexy eyebrows, and the PM, I never knew he had such lovely eyes. (We talked about Liverpool, natch.)

There's been a lot of talk about Mrs Simpson and Tony all rolled into one (if you can imagine that!). They've been asking me lots of questions and checking on my background. You'd think I was joining MI5. I feel a bit of a prisoner already, that's the only thing. But they're getting ready to announce something soon so I've got to keep out of the way in case some nasty press person finds out and darling, there are some nasty press persons in this world, so my maid tells me.

I'm the happiest person there is. Nothing can go wrong now. Least I don't think so, do you Reg. It's so great having you as my confessor. You'd never be a Crawfie, would you Reg. I feel even more alone at the moment with all the big decisions of State being taken behind my back. Look for me on the Tele! I'll be the one in white.

Love,

Daisy

Windsor
October, 1970

DEAREST REG,

Listen Reg, you've just got to help me. Something too difficult for words has cropped up, a real emergency, I can't even write and ask you. Oh God I've just got to *see* you. I know you've always said it's better for us never to meet and darling I do know what you mean but this is different. You are my friend and you're the only one I have, you always have been, I've got to *talk* to you. I mean it's not even a matter of life and death, it's *more* than that. No one knows where I'm staying at the moment but I'll be in London next week so please please *please* meet me at six o'clock on Thursday at the Ritz in the downstairs bar (not the Rivoli bar, that's the upstairs one) if you don't know the Ritz just ask for the downstairs bar and they'll tell you. I'll be wearing a long brown maxi-skirt and Russian boots and I don't know what yet on top, but look darling just to make certain I'll be carrying that old copy of Picturegoer with your ad in it which I've kept and never lost for twenty years! It's so tattered it's practically fallen to pieces – like me! Oh but I won't fall to pieces if you come, say you will, write and tell me you will – no you can't can you as I daren't put my address – but *come, come*. This is a cry for help.

DAISY

Ritz Hotel
London
Midnight, Thursday

REG,

What happened? I got here on the stroke of six, I went downstairs, I ordered a Negroni, I blatantly paraded the Picturegoer, I told the waiter I was expecting a friend (I think he thought I was a tart), I sat there like an idiot eating salted peanuts and stared at the clock and stared at the stairs. Nothing but couples came in until about seven when a man came in alone, Oh darling I thought he was you because funnily enough he looked a little bit like Farley Granger, only like he would be now, and I sort of smiled at him and he looked straight through me and I thought Oh God, he doesn't believe this is me, I'm a disappointment to him, what shall I do, then a woman came in and he kissed her and I knew it couldn't be you. All the time there was this *frightfully* creepy creature sitting there and eyeing me in such a spooky way, darling I know *he* thought I was a tart and I knew if he tried to speak to me I'd *die* because he was at least a hundred without a hair on his head and sort of pallid and flaccid all over and such a funny expression in his eyes. I think he must have been a mac-flasher at least or possibly a pedophile or something too sinister, anyway after about two hours he slunk (slank?) away and then I suddenly realized you were never, never coming so I just got smashed on Negronis and then I did my usual thing of bursting into tears and everyone was very sweet to me and then they began putting steel shutters up over the bar so I came upstairs and I've just been sitting here ever since feeling utterly hysterical. In an hour I'll have to go back to B.P. and face them. Oh Reg, Reg, why did you let me down, just when I needed you most?

D

The End . . .

The black Daimler with no number plates came out of Buckingham Palace, rounded the statue of Queen Victoria and glided up the Mall into the early evening winter mists and soon was lost in the swirling mass of cars in Trafalgar Square. In the back, Miss Daisy Smuten was studying a list of names.

It was now three days since that first brief staccato message, announcing her engagement to HRH, had been given out by PA. Daisy had thought the engagement was never going to be given out. She'd been completely stupid and unlike herself when in the midst of those endless questions from those faceless men she'd mentioned Reg. They couldn't believe that someone like her should have told such terrible things about herself to someone she didn't know. She'd said don't be silly, Reg is my friend, my oldest friend, my only friend, I just have to ask Reg and he'll give me back my letters.

She'd lied. It had been the only way. After the Ritz there had been three months of absolute silence. She knew the faceless men were waiting. She herself had done everything to contact Reg, but at his address, the one she'd written to for twenty years, no one had heard of him. At last, they must have been convinced she really had Reg's letters, and the announcement was given out.

But then there came that list of seventeen names. That hadn't been her fault. Christ, she wasn't that mad. She'd told the Special Branch to clear up every scrap from all her old flats and studios. How they'd missed that she'd never know. OK, she admitted it was silly ever having scribbled a list of old friends, but they should have found it.

She'd started immediately to contact them the minute their names appeared in the papers. At the same time she warned her art editor friends to say nothing. Even at this late stage, a few damaging letters or some highly coloured experiences could ruin everything.

In the three days someone else might now have found out something about those seventeen boring old friends from the past, most of whom she could hardly remember anyway. But she remembered enough to know that one or two could have a very dangerous story to tell. There were certain aspects of her life she didn't want splashed across the News of the World. God knows what they'd pay for five thousand words, however boring.

That cub photographer in Liverpool. He was probably dead by now. He was a nothing anyway. He was safe because he had nothing to tell, but some paper might be hard up enough to want to paint whatever boring sentimental rubbish he could turn up. But it couldn't harm her. The same with that drippy sailor from the South Coast. Why she'd doodled his name she didn't know. But he had nothing to tell. Or had he? Perhaps he'd touched her up without her realizing? She certainly hadn't touched him or done anything that could rebound. No, he was safe. But that Oxford undergraduate phoney. She had to silence him.

In the back of the car she read his story for the third time. It had taken her twice to even understand it. All that Nabokov shit was too clever for words. But she had been even cleverer. It was she who had written the letter to him, getting in first, pretending to be a newspaper after his memoirs. She knew that if a newspaper read it they'd soon make him spell out in simple, four letter words what exactly had taken place between them. She must have been mad to have touched him. All she could remember was his pock marked grey masturbatory face. But she had played with him. As a laugh. A joke. Because that lesbian type girl of his, Lucy, had egged her on, got her drunk, encouraged her.

She had his letter containing the article, but she needed something else. Luckily, he'd made it clear in the letter what he needed. He must be a teacher or something like that.

They were now in North London, somewhere in the wilds of Kentish Town. She took a brief case from the floor, checking that the five thousand pounds in one pound notes were in order. There were half-wits in Buckingham Palace as everywhere else.

Half an hour later, Daisy came out of the house. Her briefcase was empty. In her hand she had the affidavit, signed and legally sealed. The article was now hers. Nobody else could publish it. Should she tear it up now and scatter it over Hampstead Heath or keep it for her own memoirs?

Her lesbian interlude had been worrying for a while, but Daisy had seen to that already. 'Boy' was to be knighted in the New Year's Honours' list. And her Indian frolic had been relatively easy. It had only cost her ten thousand pounds, already on its way in the diplomatic bag. After all, that bloke had paid her fare back, for a consideration.

The vet, the one who'd helped at the Zoo over the tiger operation, had been a little more difficult. He was above materialistic considerations, though as a country vet in the wilds of Cumberland he could obviously have done with the money. Daisy took longest of all on this journey, not just getting up to see him, but in the reunion meeting at his house. The bedroom curtains were closed and Daisy was inside for well over two hours. She did manage to press some money upon him, but there was another favour she knew he would like. One which he had waited many years to have repeated.

The University of Sussex was rather complicated. There were twenty-seven people in all to contact. She'd retained the names, not in her memory but on the back of the photographs. Most of them were out of work, struggling anarchists and it took only a thousand pounds or so to silence each. The girl took nothing. She was insulted that Daisy should ask. She could have her story for nothing. No capitalistic photographer, even a Queen-to-be, would compromise her.

There were a few others amongst the seventeen with a dangerous story and they had been silenced in similar ways. Equerries had already been round the country with heavy briefcases and she'd had a final session with the PM's appointments secretary only that morning. Gerald, her very brief husband, never came into her head. He was too wet to even consider. But she'd set up a trust fund for her daughter, now a teenager, though they'd never met, nor did she want them to meet.

The Daimler was purring through the gates when her thoughts came back again to Reg. Because they'd never met, there was no face in her head. She'd told him things she even regretted at the time. Only he knew about that silly shop lifting. Only he knew her real thoughts, her real worries. How could she ever get the letters back? But perhaps there was no need. She'd trusted Reg. Never once in twenty years had he betrayed a confidence. Never once had he reprimanded her, or criticized her, or attacked her. He must love her.

At that moment in Westminster Abbey, when the Archbishop put the ring on Daisy Smuten's finger before a TV audience throughout the world of two hundred and fifty millions, the terrible thought suddenly struck her that it had been Reg after all sitting there in the Ritz bar. She smiled. She hoped he was watching his own little Daisy now. But he wouldn't be. He didn't care for TV. He was a picturegoer after all.

Notes on Contributors

ALAN BRIEN

Born in Sunderland, 1925. Educated at Bede Grammar School, Sunderland, and Jesus College, Oxford. War time air-gunner RAF. Critic and columnist Evening Standard, Observer, Daily Mail, Spectator, Sunday Dispatch, Sunday Pictorial, Sunday Telegraph. Writes weekly essay in New Statesman, monthly article in Punch and New York Times and a weekly diary in Sunday Times.

JILLY COOPER

Born in Hornchurch, Essex, 1937. Educated at Godolphin School, Salisbury. Has had twenty-seven jobs, most of them in journalism or publishing. Frequent contributor to a variety of journals and newspapers. Author of *How To Stay Married* (Methuen, 1969). Sunday Times columnist since 1969.

GEORGE DARBY

Born in Bolton 1942. Educated at Bolton School and Nottingham University. Joined Keighley News as a reporter in 1964, then Bradford Telegraph and Argus, Northern Echo and Daily Mirror. Joined the staff of Sunday Times in 1968 as a sub-editor. Editor "Look" pages 1970.

LESLEY GARNER

Daughter of novelist William Garner. Born in South Wales, 1945. Educated at Dorking Grammar School and Sussex

University. On graduation joined teenybopper magazine, then moved to the Observer and the Sun. Film and book critic of 19 Magazine since 1967. Feature writer on women's pages of Sunday Times since 1969.

GODFREY HODGSON

Born in Horsham, Sussex, in 1934. Educated at Winchester College (scholar), Magdalen College, Oxford (open scholar and 1st class hons) and University of Pennsylvania. Worked for the Times, the Observer and ITV's 'This Week'. With Sunday Times as editor of Insight since 1968. Has published: (in French) *Carpetbaggers et Ku-Klux-Klan* (Juliard 1965); co-author of *The Age of Austerity* (Penguin 1961); *An American Melodrama* (Deutsch 1969).

PHILLIP KNIGHTLEY

Born in Sydney, Australia, 1929. Copyboy; footloose in Pacific Islands; bubble-gum machine magnate; magazine editor, India; freelance journalist, London. Co-author *Philby, The Secret Lives of Lawrence of Arabia,* etc. Special correspondent of the Sunday Times.

IRMA KURTZ

Born in New Jersey, 1935. Educated at Barnard College and Columbia University. First job as waitress in New York. Saved up to come to Europe where she became cook on a Mediterranean yacht and an English teacher in Paris. Journalist for the last eleven years, firstly from Paris and now from London. Associate editor on Nova. Frequent contributor to Sunday Times.

MAGNUS LINKLATER

Born Orkney, 1942, son of Eric Linklater. Educated Eton and Cambridge, Freiburg and Paris. First job as reporter on Daily Express, Manchester. Editor of Londoner's Diary on Evening Standard. On staff of Sunday Times as editor of Spectrum since 1969.

DONALD MCCORMICK

Born in Rhyl, Flintshire, 1911. Educated at Oswestry School, Royal Navy and Kasbah of Algiers. Journalist since 1931. Has been editor of Gibraltar Chronicle and foreign correspondent of Kemsley Newspapers. Foreign manager of Sunday Times since 1966. Author of twenty-four books – seventeen under own name. Books range from biography of Lloyd George to *The Identity of Jack the Ripper* and *Murder by Witchcraft.*

MICHAEL MOYNIHAN

Born in Birkenhead, Cheshire, 1919. Educated Birkenhead School. Cub reporter on Birkenhead News and Daily Despatch during first two years of war. With News Chronicle for eighteen years – youngest British war correspondent, covering Normandy, Ardennes, the Japanese war in the Pacific (second British war correspondent into Hiroshima). Sunday Times staff reporter since 1962.

PHILIP NORMAN

Born in Wandsworth 1943. Jobs – Hunts Post, Cambridge Daily News, Northern Dispatch, Northern Echo. Novels – *Slip on a Fat Lady, Plumridge,* short stories (uncollected). Writer on Sunday Times Magazine, London editor Show magazine New York.

PHILIP OAKES

Born in the Potteries 1928. Educated intermittently between public school and orphanage. Entered journalism by way of Eric R. Sly's Court Reporting Service Ltd. Served time as film critic, scriptwriter, columnist. Published two books of poems, two novels – most recently *The God Botherers* (Andre Deutsch). Five years with Sunday Times, currently writing an arts interview column for the Review Section.

KENNETH PEARSON

Born in London, 1920. Educated Ivydale Road Primary School, Alleyn's Dulwich, Stalag Luft 3 and University College, London: B.Sc. (Econ) Honours. Has been insurance clerk, Fleet Air Arm fighter pilot. Co-authored archaeological mystery, *The Dorak Affair*. Helped design Fishbourne Roman Palace museum. Joined Sunday Times seventeen years ago; now its arts columnist and deputy director of Special Projects.

PAULINE PETERS

Born in Bradford, 1938. Educated at Keighley Grammar School. First job as office girl at the Halifax Daily and Weekly Courier and Guardian. Spent ten years on various provincial papers. Joined Sunday Times as a feature writer in 1965. Currently under contract to Sunday Times Magazine.

LUCIA VAN DER POST

Born in South Africa 1936, daughter of Laurens van der Post. Educated at Durban Girls' College and Cape Town University (1st class hons). Started in journalism in London on Woman's Own, 1958, then on Sunday Telegraph. Contributed to specialist magazines on design subjects. Home editor of Sunday Times since 1968.

PETER WILSHER

Born in Wakefield, Yorks, 1928. Educated Wakefield Grammar School, Gateshead Secondary School and Trinity College, Cambridge. Started in journalism as reporter on Hexham Courant, Northumberland; then Newcastle Journal, Sunday Chronicle (film critic), Sunday Graphic (gossip columnist), and Sunday Times since 1960. Editor of Sunday Times Business News since 1967.

FRANCIS WYNDHAM

Born in London, 1924. Educated Eton and Oxford. Started reviewing for New Statesman in 1946. Has contributed criticism of books, plays and films to numerous periodicals. Assistant Editor of Queen magazine 1959–63. Assistant Editor of Sunday Times Magazine since 1964.